New England

Seaside, Roadside, Graveside, Darkside

20 Wicked Weird Stories

By Steve Burt

Illustrations by Hanah Cincotta

New England

Seaside, Roadside, Graveside, Darkside

20 Wicked Weird Stories

By Steve Burt
Illustrations by Hanah Cincotta
Cover artist: Saphira

Stories collected from four of Bram Stoker Award-winning author Steve Burt's previously published books:
-***Odd Lot*** (2001)
-***Even Odder*** (2003)
2003 Bram Stoker Award Nominee/Finalist for Young Readers
-***Oddest Yet*** (2004)
2004 Bram Stoker Award Winner for Young Readers
-***Wicked Odd*** (2005)

ISBN 978-0-9856188-7-2

Cover by SelfPubBookCovers.com/Saphira

Contact information:
Steve Burt
17101 SE 94th Berrien Court
The Villages, FL 32162
www.SteveBurtBooks.com

CONTENTS

Awards

Grand Prize, 2019 New York Book Festival

Grand Prize, 2015 Florida Book Festival

5 Mom's Choice Awards golds

2004 Bram Stoker Award

2003 Bram Stoker Nominee/Finalist

Moonbeam Children's Book Award

12 New England Book Festival Awards

Halloween Book Festival Award

4 Hollywood Book Festival Awards

Paris Book Festival Award

London Book Festival Award

San Francisco Book Festival Award

Beach Book Festival Award

The Mason's Leech

It started when the demolition crew began knocking down the old nail factory around the corner. The factory's been empty for years—decades maybe—and except for being a spooky place for the kids to play in, it's just an eyesore. It quit operating as a nail factory back before Rick and me got into high school, and we been out of school for two years now.

We were down there, me and Rick, sitting on a rock wall that runs the back boundary of the nail factory property. We were like little kids watching the backhoe and the bulldozer and the wrecking ball that swings from the boom of the crane.

All of a sudden things stopped and the demolition crew crowded around this hole in a section of wall that'd been giving them trouble. The concrete was like iron, super hard, much harder than any other part of the building walls. From a distance we guessed it was three or four feet thick. But one of the workers yelled out, "I think it's hollow."

A half-dozen hardhats closed in and huddled in front of the hole the wrecking ball had pounded. Two of them whacked at it with sledgehammers and two others started in with six-foot pry bars.

Me and Rick walked over for a closer look.

"Hook onto it with that dump truck," one of the hardhats yelled, so the driver backed in close and ran a cable from the trailer hitch around the wall and back onto the hitch. Easy as pie the truck pulled the wall section—must've been 10 foot by 20 foot—whump—right over onto the ground in front of us. Everybody stood there dead quiet staring into the wall.

"What the devil is that?" Rick asked.

"Looks like a dead fox," I answered.

"Or a dog," one of the hardhats said.

"It's a pup," Rick said. "A German shepherd." He stepped closer in for a better look. "About six months, I'd guess."

Rick had owned a German shepherd when we were growing up. It had been killed by a car one day when Rick was supposed to be watching it and it got away from him.

"How come it's not rotten?" another hard hat asked. "It's been in that wall a lot of years."

"No air," somebody said. "Like a mummy in a pyramid."

"Looks better'n any mummy I ever seen," Rick said.

To me it just looked like it was asleep, except that it'd been sealed in that wall for 50 or so years.

"So how'd it get in the wall?" somebody asked.

"Accident," the truck driver said.

As the man said those words Rick reached toward the pup.

"Don't!" someone yelled. Rick pulled back like he'd leaned on a hot stove. It was the foreman who'd yelled. "It's not an accident. Look at its tongue."

Everybody looked. It reminded me of a kid licking an ice cube tray. Its tongue was stuck, attached to the concrete wall.

"It's a mason's leech," the foreman said.

The hardhats looked at each other and whispered among themselves. Then they backed away from Rick and the pup.

"What's a mason's leech?" I asked.

The foreman looked at me, his face cloudy. "Everybody who's worked with concrete has heard of mason's leeches. Until today though, even I'd thought it was a myth. And I've been in this business 37 years. This is the first one I've ever seen."

I tried to read the faces of the foreman and the others to see if they were putting us on. Their faces gave away nothing. They looked dead serious.

"Heck, till now we all figured it was a myth, didn't we, men?" he asked, and the hardhats nodded. "But this—this is bad news."

"But why?" I asked. "It's just a dead dog, isn't it?"

"I'll tell you what my grandfather told me. He was a stonemason. Concrete takes a long time to dry all the way through, 13 years they say. But just like us, masons fifty years ago had deadlines. So to dry a concrete wall faster they'd take a puppy, infect it with cholera and put it in a wall and seal it up. Called it a mason's leech. The cholera would give it awful diarrhea so it'd get dehydrated in no time. That'd make it thirsty as all get-out, so thirsty it'd attach its tongue to the concrete and try to suck all the moisture out like a sponge drawing water into itself. That thing there I believe is a mason's leech."

I looked at the dog with its tongue stuck to the concrete then looked again to see if any of the hardhats were smiling. No one smiled. "Is it true?" I asked. "Can it be?"

The foreman shrugged. "Don't know. My grandfather said they quit doing it in the 1930s when a whole crew came down with cholera and died."

I knew my mouth was hanging wide open but I couldn't do anything about it.

"So what!" Rick said abruptly. "Somebody's got to bury it." He reached under the pup to pick it up.

"Don't touch it," the foreman yelled again.

A chill ran down my back. I wondered if the germs could still be alive after fifty years in a tomb.

"That's it!" the foreman yelled. "Pack up, men. We're out of here." He waved his arms like a drill sergeant ordering soldiers into a troop truck. They dropped their tools and in less than two minutes they were driving away.

"Hey!" Rick yelled at me when they were gone. "Get a shovel."

I turned to look and there beside the collapsed wall stood Rick, the dog balanced on his upturned palms. I didn't ask how he got the tongue loose.

"Rick," I said. "Didn't you hear the man? Cholera."

"Oh, sure, right. Cholera. You believe that crap?"

I hated it when Rick did that, made me feel stupid. "Look," I said, "I know it's far-fetched. But the man seemed convinced, really convinced. And didn't they all scatter fast? You think they'd take that much trouble for a joke?"

Rick's lip curled in a doubter's smile.

"Hey," I said, "Even if it's not true about sucking the wall, even if that's crap, it's still possible the dog's diseased, ain't it?"

Rick stared at me as if I were an idiot then laughed. I didn't laugh with him. I was worried. Then, holding the dog as if offering some strange sacrifice, he said, "Hey, this dog's warm."

I looked at him waiting for him to say April Fools.

But he didn't. And he didn't drop it. He said, "Here, feel it," and held the carcass toward me.

I shrank back.

"I'm serious," he insisted. "It's warm, almost like it's alive. C'mon, feel it."

I don't know why he didn't drop it then. I was a nervous wreck. But the pup really did look like anybody's regular old pet asleep on a porch. So I put out my fingers towards its flank—to show Rick I wasn't scared, not because I wanted to. I don't know if I was more afraid of it feeling cold or feeling warm. I flinched when he pressed it against my fingertips. I wondered if germs could jump like fleas.

"It is warm," I said, disbelieving my own words.

"Told you. Getting warmer all the time."

I looked around at the road to see if anyone else might verify it.

"Oh man, it's breathing," Rick said.

I snapped around, not believing my ears.

"Look at its side," he said. "It really is breathing."

It did look like it was breathing but I tried to convince myself and Rick otherwise. "That's your hands shaking, that's what's doing it."

Rick looked me straight in the eye. "It's not me." He licked his lips like they were suddenly chapped. "This freaking dog is breathing. It's alive."

I glanced at the pup's face. An eyelid was half open. That's when I noticed the layer of skin from the top of its tongue was gone, no doubt still attached to the wall. But what was odd was that its tongue, despite the missing skin, was now moist. Its black nose seemed to glisten with moisture—but moisture from where? My heart leaped as I felt the terror rising in me.

"This dog's not dead," Rick blurted out, a funny smile on his face, licking his lips yet again. "Really, it's alive."

Rick had to be confused, although I wasn't sure of anything myself at that moment. One thing I did know—that dog hadn't been alive 10 minutes earlier. It was dead, dead, dead—for over 50 years.

"Oh, look," Rick said, wetting his lips with his tongue again. What was with the dry lips? He looked tired, pale now. "The puppy moved its head." He sounded like a kid oohing over a cute Christmas gift.

I looked back to the pup. Its eyes were fully open, moist, and it strained to raise its head the way an old dog on its deathbed does.

Rick's arms trembled, tired from holding the dog on his palms. He pulled it to his chest, cradling it on his forearms the way he might a child. He gazed down into its eyes and for a second I thought, "This is amazing, this really is a cute puppy."

Then it snapped at Rick's face, gluing its tongue to his lips. Rick yanked his hands from under it but the dog hung from his mouth by its tongue.

Rick looked at me, his face a mask of horror. His eyes pleaded help me but no words came from his mouth. He could only grunt. He leaned forward pulled down by the dog's weight, frantically trying to pull the thing off his face. But it was hopeless, like an elephant trying to remove its own trunk.

I ran. I'm ashamed to admit it, but it was the only thing I could do. I deserted my best friend Rick, left him kissing a dog from Hades that wanted to suck the moisture and life out of him the way it dried concrete. I ran home and hid in my room for two days.

Eventually the cops showed up asking questions. They'd found Rick's body at the demolition site, his skin black as a rotten banana peel and barely hanging on the bones. *Deflated* was the word one of the cops used. *Crushed,* the other said, collapsed like a beer can with the air sucked out of it. I thought about his lips drying out when the dog was on his palms. It had started leeching him right away. Then I pictured the dog sucking at his face, drawing the saliva from his mouth and the moisture from his whole body.

I told the two cops what I'd seen, but no dog was found. Tracks leading away from Rick's body, yes, dog tracks—but no dog. The story is far-fetched, they said, but they have no other possibilities.

So now I go from the house to the car then drive to the store and back, making sure I'm out in the open and exposed as little as possible. I spend most of my time inside with the doors locked because when I'm out I'm afraid I'll turn and it'll be on me, snarling and sucking, going for my mouth the way it did Rick's.

The worst is the nighttime. I was washing my hands 100 times a day and now I'm up doing it as much at night. I can't help myself, I have to do it. I have to do it because I touched it on that breathing, freaking flank. Rick made me touch it, he did, and now I don't know if I'll get whatever the pup had. All I know is, tonight I'm thirsty again, thirstier than last night or the night before, and I keep picturing a blackened banana peel with the banana sucked out. So I'm drinking water, water, water all the time and praying to God the thirst is only my imagination.

Garden Plot

I visited Vermont when I was ten. I'll never go back.

That was the summer I went to stay at Grampa Burt's farm. He lived in Bethel out on the back road that runs along next to the White River. Everybody called it the Injun Path because there had been a couple of Indian settlements there around the time of the Revolution. Grampa said they were always turning up arrowheads in the fields after a hard rain or after plowing.

Every day I walked the two miles to town along the Injun Path, if not for the mail then for tobacco for Grampa.

A woman lived halfway between Grampa's and town. Folks said she was descended on the one side from the Abenaki Indians and on the other side from runaway slaves. She spent all her time tending a garden on the back corner of her property, a piece of river bottomland where the river oxbows and the land in the loop is shaped like a thumb.

The garden had a low stone wall around it and a tall scarecrow in the middle. Grampa said every year that woman would shine up a couple of metal pie tins and hang them from the wrists of that scarecrow so the reflecting sun would scare off the crows.

Nobody I talked to had ever seen her face.

I noticed when we drove by her place that no matter how hot it got the old woman would always be dressed in dark clothes. She had a black veil—more of a hood, really—that covered her head so you couldn't see her face. Grampa said she was superstitious and wore it to ward off the spirit-stealers so they couldn't look her in the eye. That, he said, was the only way they could possess you. Once they looked you directly in the eye your soul belonged to them. Grampa also said spirit-stealers couldn't cross water.

A few months before I arrived the Congregational Church had hired a new minister, Reverend Clarke. He made a lot of enemies in a short time. I sort of liked him, though. (My father died when I was young and there weren't a lot of male figures in my life.) Reverend Clarke was a character and with that black suit and black broad-brimmed hat he wore he could've doubled for Ichabod Crane in *The Legend of Sleepy Hollow*.

I went to church with Grandma Burt most Sundays that summer but Grampa only came along once. Grandma believed you should go whether you liked the minister or not and always said: *You go to church through thick and thin or heaven'll come and you'll not get in.*

Grampa disagreed and after one sitting under Reverend Clarke's sharp tongue he swore he'd never go back.

But it wasn't only the preaching that turned Grampa off. It was that Reverend Clarke didn't take Grampa seriously. When Reverend Clarke came to dinner the two of them got into a discussion about souls. Grampa brought up spirit-stealers saying that his father and grandfather had cautioned him about them.

Reverend Clarke pooh-poohed the notion, in the process belittling Grampa in front of Grandma and me.

So as if to issue a parting challenge when Reverend Clarke left that night Grampa said, "I'll tell you somebody who can give you an earful about spirit-stealers—the woman down the road. Why don't you stop by and chat with her some afternoon? Maybe you'll convert her."

Reverend Clarke huffed back at Grampa, "I may just do that, Brother Burt. I do believe I may."

Two days later I was walking to town. When I passed the old woman's place I could see her standing out near the back of her property by the bow in the river, her regular black outfit on, bent over her garden. I could make out the scarecrow with its broad-brimmed straw hat, red plaid shirt, and black pants. Two pie tins hung from its wrists, glints of sun ricocheting off them.

Now who should come walking up the road but Reverend Clarke in his minister's suit and black hat? We talked beside the road for a minute and he said he was going to see the old woman. I told him I'd seen her in her garden then I went on toward town.

It was late afternoon when I started for home. Still plenty of sunlight but I'd have to hustle to get back in time for supper. I approached the old woman's place and saw she was still out there bent over, weeding. At first I thought nothing of it then a feeling came over me like a cold breeze on the back of my neck. I looked behind me. No breeze and no one watching.

Something was wrong. When I turned to look at the woman she was gone. Had she collapsed in the garden? I squinted but still couldn't make her out so I walked fast toward the stone wall. I still couldn't see her and broke into a run, scared I'd find her dead and scared to death I'd find her alive. I stopped at the wall. She had to be inside. There was no gate. Something—*dread*—stopped me from climbing over the wall. It was waist high so I looked over it.

It wasn't just a garden. Mixed with the snap-peas and knee-high corn were stones, markers with faded writing on them. A bone yard. A burial ground. *She was tending a grave garden.* The cold chill pricked my neck again.

I glimpsed a movement to the right—sensed as much as saw it—something black and fast ducking behind the corn. Then a rustling but not the wind. Water. Rippling. The river. The sound brought me back to myself.

Something moved.

I glanced at the scarecrow and, my God, it wasn't wearing its usual broad-brimmed hat—now the hat was black. I looked into its face and, saints preserve me, it was Reverend Clarke, eyes popped wide, mouth gaping as if trying to scream a warning. But no sound came out.

Suddenly I glimpsed a reflection in the pie tin on the scarecrow's—the minister's—arm. A head. In a hood. No face. More like oil on pond scum. She was behind me. Her icy breath pricked my neck and a horrid odor invaded my nostrils. I shut my eyes and held my breath to keep from vomiting and as I did Grampa Burt's warning about eye contact came back to me. *If I turned around she'd have me.*

I sighted in on the water, shut my eyes tight and lit out for the river—leaping, sobbing, swatting at the back of my neck, all the while shouting out a prayer, "Now I lay me down to sleep, now I lay me down to sleep." With who-knows-what riding my shoulders and chewing my neck I plunged in darkness through the reeds and clawed my way across the shallows, cutting and scratching my knees. Finally deep water. I stayed under longer than I ever have and let the current carry me downstream, coming up only a few times for air and always with my eyes clamped shut. I felt and floated my way down river to town and when I climbed onto shore near the town bridge whatever had been on my back was gone.

I have no idea what happened to Reverend Clarke. The constable couldn't find him. Grandma said he had likely left town before the church could ask him to resign. As for me, I begged so hard to go home that Grampa put me on a train early the next morning.

I haven't been to Vermont since or even to the country for that matter. My nerves wouldn't take it. At least here in the city I feel somewhat safe. Even so, though, if I see an old lady coming down the sidewalk with a scarf over her head I'll cross the street to avoid her. Just the thought of having to look her in the face—in the eyes—*brrr*, it gives me the creeps.

Captain James's Bones

My name is Ben and my sister is Gracie. We never play practical jokes any more, not since that night in the graveyard with the old captain's bones, because even today we feel somehow responsible for what happened to Mr. Finkle.

It started when we moved to New Harbor, Maine and the school year began. Gracie started sixth grade and I started fourth. Fitting in at a new school was hard. Kids picked on me because I was small for my age so Gracie felt she had to defend me, which didn't win either of us any friends. As new kids we desperately wanted to fit in.

The week before Halloween we were sitting at lunch when Danny Gamage, an eighth-grader, started talking about the ghost of Captain James who had perished in a shipwreck nearby at Pemaquid Point.

Gracie's and my ears pricked up. All the other kids knew the story, but upon hearing Danny tell it again their eyes grew wide. The story of the shipwreck was one locals knew by heart. In fact it had been one of the first stories we heard when we moved to town.

Captain James' sailing ship had foundered on the rocks off Pemaquid Lighthouse one stormy night and his crew and family had drowned. People on shore tried to rescue the captain but couldn't get to him. Pinned to the rocks in his yellow rain gear and yellow Sou'wester foul-weather hat, he was dashed to bits by the pounding waves. His body was never recovered.

That part we'd all heard. The part we hadn't heard, the part Danny Gamage was telling, was about the Captain's bones searching for their proper resting place. "So every Halloween when the veil between this world and the next is thinnest, the grisly bones of Captain James rise up out of the waves at Pemaquid in search of his grave. His marble headstone stands in the old Pemaquid bone yard—but he's not under it. The stone is nothing more than a memorial because they found no corpse to plant."

Danny knew he had a spellbound audience. "So now every Halloween the poor Captain's bones clank up from the rocks by the lighthouse and clatter down the road to the bone yard seeking their rightful rest at the empty grave."

"And how do people know?" gasped Mary Poole, a sixth-grader. "How do they know his bones are on the prowl?"

"They know," Danny said in a loud whisper, "*from the trail of rotting, stinking seaweed leading from the road into the bone yard*." We all held our breath. "It ends . . . *at his grave!*"

Gracie and I gasped. After a moment she said, "Poor guy. It's like all he wants to do is be where he belongs. He wants to go—"

"*Home*," I finished.

"You're right," Danny said and everybody agreed. "Can't blame the old guy, can you?"

Brian Daggett said, "Too bad somebody can't be there to help the old captain into his resting place."

"What do you mean?" Gracie asked.

"Well, maybe if somebody met him there on Halloween, say, with a wooden crate, and accepted his bones—"

"Sort of like signing for a UPS package," Danny interrupted.

"Yeah," Brian continued. "Maybe if somebody accepted his bones, stopped them from roaming, the town fathers could bury them in the empty grave the next day."

"Sure," Danny said. "On All Saints Day. It follows All Hallows Evening—Hallow E'en. It could be a sort of purifying thing."

"Making things right," Brian said. "After all these years."

"But who'd do it?" I asked. "Who'd meet the ghost with the bones at the cemetery?"

A deathly silence fell over the group then all eyes turned on my sister Gracie. She fidgeted. "Ben, don't fall for it. There's no ghost." But she didn't look 100% sure to me.

"Okay, Gracie," Danny said. "If there's no ghost then there's no need to be *afraid*."

That last word did it. *Afraid.* He had backed my sister into a corner and before we knew it the plan was set. On Halloween night we'd all go to the caretaker's shed at the old Pemaquid cemetery. Danny and Brian and Gracie and I would carry the wooden crate to the Captain's grave and wait for the ghost to arrive then "invite" him to hand over the bones. Once we had them in the crate we'd call the others and haul the remains to the Town Office.

Danny, Brian, and the other kids figured Gracie and I would keep mum about the bone yard caper but we didn't. We mentioned it to Mr. Finkle, the school's gym teacher. He was the handsome, muscular, black-haired man every girl in school had a crush on. He told us the Captain James shipwreck story was true but that the searching bones story was the set-up for a Halloween prank, a trick played on some unsuspecting newcomers. Mr. Finkle said he had an idea for turning the tables on the other kids and asked us if we'd help him.

Halloween night was chilly, dark, and damp. The clammy air made my flesh crawl. Ten of us met by the caretaker's shed.

"Ready, Brian?" Danny asked, getting a nod. "How about you two? Gracie? Ben?"

We gave him the thumbs-up sign.

"Wish us luck," he said to all our friends who were staying behind, and the four of us headed off along the road toward the grave yard's front entrance.

Brian stopped short. "Hey, what's that?" He pointed at the ground. Long strands of brown seaweed formed a trail at our feet.

"Uh-oh," Danny said. "It's the Captain. He's already here."

"You mean we're too late?" Brian asked.

"I don't know," Danny answered.

"Let's catch up," Gracie said and Danny and Brian looked at her with surprise.

"You sure?" Danny taunted. "You're not *afraid*?"

"Let's go," Gracie said, leading the way. "We don't want to miss him."

Not far ahead we spotted what had to be the Captain's gravestone. I reminded myself it was only a marker stone and that they had never found a body to bury. But now covering the grave site was a white sheet that practically glowed in the moonlight. It looked like a freshly made-up bed. We crept toward it cautiously.

"What's with the sheet?" Gracie asked.

"I haven't the foggiest idea," Danny Gamage said. "How about you, Brian? Any idea?"

"Nope," Brian said. "No idea whatsoever." The two of them couldn't have sounded phonier.

We drew even closer to the grave. The sheet wasn't flat at all.

"There's something under the sheet," Danny said.

"Or some*body*," Brian added, stressing the word *body*. The two of them set the wooden crate down.

"Maybe we should take a look under it," Danny said, trying to make his voice sound spooky.

In the darkness around us I heard movements and caught glimpses of shadows shifting. One of the voices sounded like Mary Poole who was supposed to be back at the caretaker's shed with the others. Our classmates were hiding out of sight in anticipation of the lifting of the sheet.

"You grab one side and I'll grab the other," Danny told Brian. "Gracie, you and Ben open the lid of the crate. If his bones are there, you grab them quick and shove them into the crate and close the lid."

And that's the moment I'll remember and regret to my dying day. Danny and Brian yanked back that sheet from the grave expecting to see—as they had set up the prank every year—*a skeleton*. Not the skeleton of Captain James but the borrowed, *plastic*, life-size, science-room skeleton from school. It's what they used for the practical joke to scare the dickens out of newcomers like Gracie and me, trying to get us to believe the captain had arrived with his bones. Mr. Finkle had prepared us.

This time it would be him lying there, dressed like the captain in a yellow raincoat and rain hat. He would slowly sit up and move his arms like a zombie, scaring Danny, Brian, and the kids hiding around us.

But when the sheet was peeled back, what we all saw was neither the school skeleton nor a sitting-up Mr. Finkle. What lay there was a bloody-faced body in yellow rain gear, covered in seaweed and stiff as a board. Gracie and I waited for Mr. Finkle to sit up and act scary. He didn't.

The color drained from Danny's and Brian's faces. Then finally the body began to spasm as if awaking and their eyes grew wide as saucers. Their mouths dropped open. Ours dropped open, too. This wasn't the way Gracie and I had rehearsed it with Mr. Finkle.

The Captain's mouth opened and closed as he struggled to sit up, his voice struggling to croak and crack from deep in his chest, but no words formed.

Danny and Brian screamed in honest terror and so did all the kids hiding around us in the bushes and behind graves. They cried out as they scrambled for the road.

Gracie and I held our ground, still expecting to enjoy a laugh with Mr. Finkle once he took off the yellow raincoat and hat. He had gone beyond the call of duty with this performance.

But the body on the ground before us shuddered in the raincoat, convulsed, and lay still.

My blood froze. Gracie shined her light toward the grave. "Mr. Finkle?" she asked, the flashlight shaking. "Are you okay?"

A ball of pale light arose from the body and hovered above it for a moment then burst like a soap bubble, releasing a pinprick of light that slowly floated skyward until it disappeared far above us.

Gracie looked back over at me. I could see the panic filling her eyes. We turned back to the body.

"Mr. Finkle?" I asked, my throat dry as dust, my voice a whisper. "Mr. Finkle, you're scaring us." And for a moment I thought he might be on Danny and Brian's side, helping them pull their prank on Gracie and me—double-crossing not them but us.

That's when the stench, the foul but sweet odor from the body, hit our noses.

"Oh God, that seaweed stinks," Gracie grimaced, and focused the flashlight directly on the body in front of the gravestone. Something like a mist—no, *steam*—hissed from the arm holes of the raincoat and the ankle holes of the rain pants.

She pushed me to take a step closer but I couldn't, so she eased forward. "Mr. Finkle?" She shined the light where our gym teacher's face should have been, winced, and choked out a gagging sound like *argh.* Then she began to dry heave. I couldn't help myself then. I leaned closer to see what she had seen and aimed my light at the body's face under the rain hat—*except there was no face*—only a moving mix of worms and maggots. I gasped out something and fought the urge to heave, too. "Come on, Gracie!" I said, and grabbed her by the wrist. "We've got to get out of here." We turned and ran for the road and for town.

What the police found at the grave was a yellow rain hat with a skull in it, and a yellow raincoat and rain pants full of bones, a human skeleton—not a plastic one—covered with rotting seaweed. No worms or maggots left, just fresh bones picked clean of all flesh. The soil at the grave site had warmed and softened so the bones, skull, and raingear had begun to sink in. They roped off the grave with crime scene tape. But by the time the coroner arrived everything had sunk out of sight as if the ground were quicksand.

The next day everything—bones, skull, raingear—was exhumed from the otherwise empty grave. The skull was covered with a shock of thick black hair and the identification in the wallet belonged to Mr. Finkle. Dental records and x-rays later confirmed it was him.

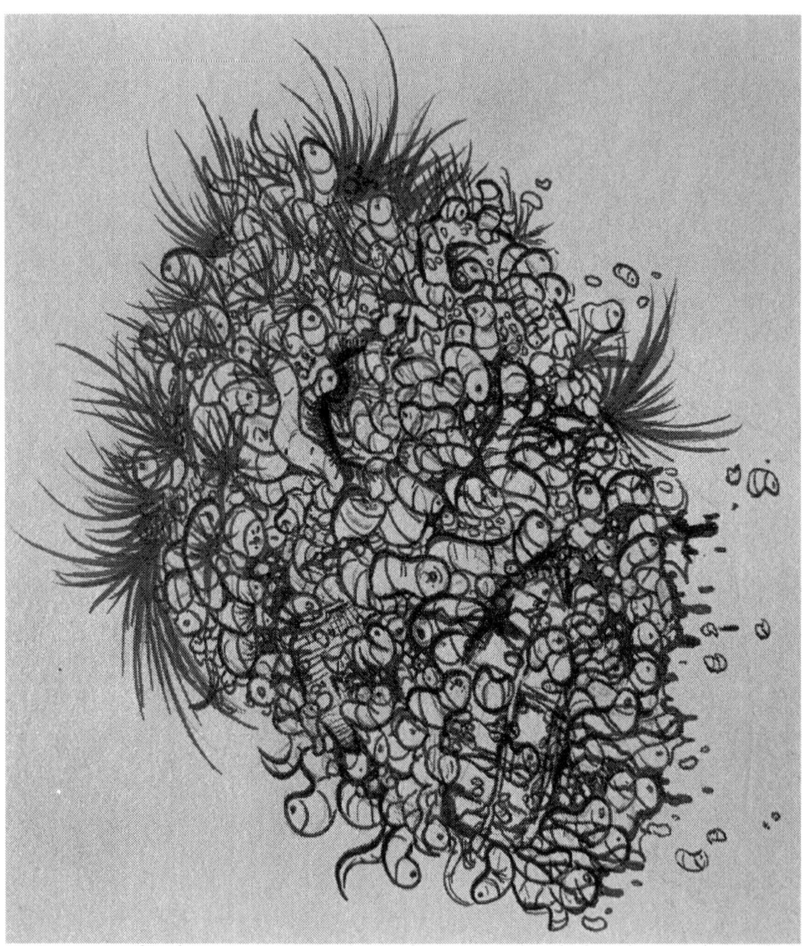

No one had an answer, though I now look back on that night and believe Captain James was real—but he wasn't coming to *deliver* his bones, as the story went, but to *find* some bones—a living person's bones—that he could use to free his troubled earthbound spirit. That's what the bubble and the rising point of light had been—*him*, finally freed. Gracie and I had been the only two to see him make the transition—at poor Mr. Finkle's expense.

We don't understand how it could have happened, but Gracie and I both feel at least partly responsible. The only thing I can say today is: *Captain James, if you're up there, you're welcome. And Mr. Finkle, if you're searching for bones this Halloween to free your earthbound spirit, please forgive us.*

Lighthouse Moths

I was sitting at the front desk daydreaming when the screen door clapped shut and a very tall man stepped into the lobby area. I didn't recognize him at first. He was gaunt and looked exhausted—a bone-weary, sleepless-nights, haunted sort of exhaustion. He reminded me of a fifty-pounds-lighter version of someone from the past whom my mind couldn't quite draw a bead on. But my gut told me the man I was trying to recall was more affable and outgoing. This man by the door was a shadow of somebody I once knew.

"Hello, Mr. Duncan," said a vaguely familiar voice, but one without much timbre or resonance. This man's voice sounded timid, beaten down, lacking any real—energy? No. Life. This voice lacked life. He crossed the room and set his suitcase on the floor beside him.

"How've you been, Dunc?" he said, shifting to the nickname everyone used. He straightened closer to his full height, about six-five. That's when I recognized him.

"Roger," I said, thrusting my hand toward his as I slid from my stool. "Roger Angleford. I'll be damned. I wasn't expecting you."

That's what I said: *I wasn't expecting you.* But I thought: *Roger Angleford, you poor sad tormented S.O.B., I never expected to see you again—not ever. Not after your daughter's death here three years ago.*

Angleford smiled a weak, mouth-only smile, no sparkle to his eyes. Beneath his dark-circled eyes hung puffy bags of skin, the result of a weight drop, I figured, whose underlying cause must have been unrelenting grief.

"You look good, Roger," I lied. "Dropped a few extra pounds."

Angleford ignored my idiotic pleasantry and I felt stupid for even uttering it.

"So, what brings you to Pemaquid?" I asked, making sure not to say back to Pemaquid. I needed to proceed with caution; God only knew, this poor man's nights—days, too, no doubt—had been Hell on Earth, filled with pain, soul pain, after the tragic loss of his only child. He had returned not just to Maine, but to Pemaquid Point where, on a windy afternoon in late August, the day after a hurricane grazed Cape Cod and pounding surf drew sightseers to the shore all along the Maine coast, a huge wave—a killer wave, the papers had dubbed it—had swept his beloved eleven year-old daughter from the rocky peninsula below the lighthouse.

He gazed past me at a painting of Pemaquid Light on the wall behind me and said dreamily, "Couldn't help myself. Something ... drew me."

While Roger Angleford stood transfixed by the painting, my own mind called up a snapshot I had taken of the Anglefords their next-to-last summer at Pemaquid Inn. They mugged for me on the porch while I used their camera to take a family photo. There stood tall, muscular Roger making a goofy face under his off-kilter golf cap, thick hands clapped around the shoulders of the two women he loved: his petite Asian wife Suki grinning and sticking her tongue out through the strings of her tennis racket, and their sometimes precocious, always curious daughter Cara looking into the camera through a pair of binoculars, her frizzy flame-red hair poofing out from under a tan straw sun hat. Oh, that red hair—one couldn't forget that burning red hair. Later they mailed an extra print to me from Connecticut, with a hand-lettered caption: American (Vacation) Gothic.

"I know, it's short notice, Dunc," Angleford said, forcing us both to come back down to Earth. "And I understand how busy the inn is this time of year, but ... any chance you've got an empty room? Say, for three nights?"

I felt like Angleford had just guessed the King of Spades hidden behind my back.

"Roger," I said. "Incredible as this may sound, a couple from Massachusetts had to leave on short notice this morning. A death in the wife's family, so they had to drive back to Massachusetts to make funeral arrangements."

"Wow," he said, but without any real enthusiasm in his voice.

"It frees up a room for three nights," I said, wanting to whistle a few notes from the Twilight Zone theme song. But I didn't, because Angleford's reaction was flat.

"I'll take it," he said, handing me his charge card as he reached to fill out the register. "Twenty-eighth, -ninth, thirtieth."

When I heard him say the dates out loud, it struck me that this was the final week of August, his week, their week, the Anglefords'. A question I didn't dare ask formed in my head: Did Cara die on the thirtieth or the thirty-first? I couldn't remember, and knowing the answer wasn't essential, but it was one of those things that'd gnaw at me until I found out. I was sure it was one of those two days, though. Was that why he was here, to mark an anniversary date, to mark it with a memorial service of some kind?

"Suki?" I asked, wondering if perhaps she was in the car waiting to hear if we had a vacancy. I knew the answer to my question as soon as I asked it. She wasn't with him. She wouldn't return to Pemaquid. Nor would it have surprised me to learn the Anglefords had divorced or were divorcing, citing as cause a three-year wedge of grief.

"Suki's home," he said. "Coping much better than I am. She's got every door and window in the house open. Screens off, too." Then, noting my puzzlement, he explained.

"Old Chinese custom. At certain times of the year—festival days, anniversaries, you know—they open up the home so their departed ancestors can come visit."

"Cara?" I asked.

"No," he said, his eyes two deep wells of pain.

For a moment I feared Angleford had misunderstood the meaning of my question. Had he misheard and thought I'd forgotten Cara was dead, thought I was asking if she'd be staying the three nights, too? If so, he'd think me worse than forgetful, he'd judge me to be horribly insensitive. But when he continued, I knew he had understood.

"Not yet," he said. "Parents, grandparents, aunts, uncles, Suki says. Not Cara."

Angleford pocketed his room key, picked up his luggage, and nodded a thank-you-and-good-day. He started up the stairs toward his room, trudging like a man mounting a gallows. Was it the past three years or was it this particular pilgrimage back to Pemaquid Point that was draining him so?

I thought about Suki welcoming the dead as houseguests, and how Roger Angleford had reported No Cara as if it were a simple fact, like saying there's no mail today. I tried to imagine a gauzy, lace-like Christmas-angel version of Cara Angleford drifting in through a window on the breeze. It was then that I remembered her body had never been recovered from wherever the undertow dragged it. For her funeral they had used her school photo on an empty casket.

I saw Angleford again around suppertime—mine, not his. He passed the dining room on his way out the front door, looking less haggard, perhaps from a nap and shower. He waved and called, "Dinner out. Don't wait up."

I didn't. Roger Angleford was a grown man. Nevertheless I noticed he hadn't returned by ten-thirty when I went to bed.

Next morning I sat in the dining room, sipping my coffee and reading the Lincoln County Weekly. The chair opposite mine scraped the floor and I glanced up to see Roger Angleford sliding onto the seat.

"Lighthouse moths," he said, skipping any early morning pleasantries.

"What?" asked, expecting at least good morning.

"You know," Angleford said, slowly and distinctly enunciating each syllable, giving each the same weight the way an impatient teacher speaks to a child. "Light house moths." His eyes bore into me.

"Geez, Roger," I said. "Lighthouse moths? You've visited here enough years. You know about it. A myth. An old wives' tale. Tourist malarkey."

"Come on, Dunc," he pressed. "There's more."

"What more?" I said. "Are you referring to history—Captain James's schooner smashing on the Pemaquid rocks in a storm with the loss of all hands, including his wife and daughters and crew? Hell, Roger, that's all in the Bristol Town records and a dozen other library books. Every person in this town and most of the tourists know the shipwreck story."

He didn't relax his gaze.

"Look, Roger," I said. "Who've you been talking to? Jacko? Not Jacko Landon? At the lounge, right? Cripes, Roger, he's the town drunk. He's a clown. A whopper swapper. Loves an audience and anybody who'll buy him a drink. Spreads more manure than a dairy farmer. Oh sure, he's a spellbinder. But the one about the lighthouse moths? Don't you see? Jacko. John O. Landon. Jacko Landon. Get it? Like jack-o-lantern. Campfire tales go with his nickname. Halloween, ghosts, goblins, witches."

I thought I had ended my tirade emphatically, but Angleford kept a steady gaze on me and I could see he wasn't convinced. The man was hurting and desperate, and I felt sorry for him, but I didn't want to help Jacko kindle false hopes in Roger. I hated to see him make a fool of himself. Yet I also saw before me a different man from the day before, a Roger Angleford much more animated.

"Okay, Roger," I said. "Lighthouse moths. Captain James's shipwreck is a fact. Lighthouse moths are fiction, the made-up part, the add-on myth that keeps it interesting. Some say they're huge moths, others say disembodied spirits, lost souls, attracted to the beacon in the lighthouse. Jacko probably told you the most common version—that it's the ghosts of Captain James, his family and crew, right?"

"Actually," Angleford said, "Jacko says it's only three of them—Captain James, his wife, and one of the daughters—the three whose bodies were lost to the sea."

"Oh," I said, beginning to see where this was going. I tried to stay with the germ of the myth rather than go back to Cara's death. "I suppose Jacko mentioned it's only on the full moon? Or did he tell it this time as harvest moon, or blue moon, or wolf moon?" I had never put any stock in ghost stories and refused to take them seriously now.

"Blue moon. The second full moon in the same month," Angleford said in defense of his new-found bar buddy, Jacko. "Swears he's seen them swirling around up there dozens of times."

"That's crap," I said. "When?"

"Like he said, on the second full moon of the month. Dozens of times—maybe more—over the years."

"That's what I've heard, too," I said. "Second full moon. Not that I believe Jacko's seen anything. I was just making sure you had the straight story."

Angleford nodded as if I had just offered an apology.

"Want to hear my theory?" I said, and he nodded again. "I think in the summer there are always moths in the lighthouse, regardless of the moon. But at night when they fly around that thousand-watt bulb, it projects their shadows out through the lens, and it magnifies their shadows. Kind of like a slide projector, as I see it. Simple as that. Moths, yes, but regular size ones. With giant shadows. And no Captain James, no wife, no daughter—no ghosts. That's tourist fodder, helps sell souvenirs."

After a moment he said, "Thanks for the theory, Dunc. Makes sense." He stood and went up to his room.

I carried my breakfast dishes to the kitchen and set them in the sink. As I ran some water over them I glanced at the calendar next to the wall phone. The thirty-first would be a full moon, the second full moon in August. The gnawing came back into my brain then. Which day had Cara drowned, the thirtieth or the thirty-first? If it had been the thirty-first, why hadn't Angleford asked for four nights instead of three? Was he planning some sort of symbolic letting-go service for the last morning, after which he'd drive home to Connecticut?

Suddenly Angleford's head appeared in the doorway to the kitchen.

"Dunc," he said. "I need your help. How can I get into the lighthouse?"

I couldn't help shaking my head in disbelief."You can't," I said. "You know that, Roger. The Coast Guard took it over from the old Lighthouse Service and maintains the tower and beacon. The keeper's house has been turned over to the Town of Bristol, which maintains Pemaquid Point Lighthouse Park. Downstairs is the Fisherman's Museum, which I'm sure you've visited on past vacations, and the upstairs is an apartment that's rented to a nice couple. But it'll take the Coast Guard to get through the tower door, which is inside the back room of the museum. The Coast Guard isn't likely to offer you a guided tour."

"But people get up there," Angleford said.

Members of the Lighthouse Preservation Society. Special—"

"You're a member, aren't you?" he interrupted.

"Yes," I said. "But, as I was trying to tell you, the Coast Guard takes them up, and that's once a year on their fall tour. You need reservations, and it's not until October, I think. Not even members of the Preservation Society have keys."

Angleford harrumphed and stood with his arms crossed, then tried another tack.

"What's the name of the people in the apartment?" he asked.

"I really don't recall, Roger," I lied, hoping he'd let it go at that. I didn't want them to think I'd sent Angleford over to pester them.

"Roger," I said, changing the subject. "What day did Cara—" I found I couldn't say die or drown.

"The thirty-first," he said, his words casting a pall over the moment. "Why?"

"Oh," I said, "I was just wondering if you were planning a little private memorial service to mark the date. Because if you were," I said, surprised to hear the words come out of my mouth, "I'd be happy to share in it with you."

"Thanks, Dunc," he said, his mouth tightening as he fought back tears. "Thanks, no."

I wasn't clear if he was saying no to my offer or no, he wasn't planning anything.

* * *

"Good morning, Dunc. I need a favor."

I looked up from my morning coffee and saw Angleford towering over the table.

"Something to eat, Roger? Coffee?" I motioned to the chair opposite me.

"No, thanks," he said. "I've got to get to town and pick up a few things. Just one item you may be able to help me with, though, if I could borrow it."

"What is it, Roger?" I asked.

"A ladder. An extension ladder." Angleford smiled a rubbery Dick Van Dyke grin, a Stan Laurel grin. "Pretty please?"

I stared up at him. "It's not for what I think it's for, is it? You're not planning to scale a local castle wall or parapet, are you?"

"Dunc, I just asked to borrow a ladder. If you wanted to borrow one from me, would I give you the third degree? Yes or no?" he asked, giving me a shaming look.

"It's in the second barn, the yellow Victorian with the colored lobster buoys hanging all over the front of it," I said. "Once you're in the garage door go to the right. There's an aluminum extension ladder hanging from wall pegs. Just put it back when you're done."

"Thanks, Dunc," Angleford said, straightening up from his crouch. "You're a friend."

"Roger," I said. "You may be able to reach the outer catwalk of the lighthouse, but you can't get inside to the inner catwalk. There are huge thick window panels all the way around, and the only way to the inner catwalk is to come up the spiral staircase."

"I know," he said. "I've read up on it and spoken to a couple who know the lighthouse. I just want to look."

"Today?" I asked.

"Tonight," he answered. "I've got stuff to get in town."

Angleford returned and had supper at the inn that night for the first time. He said nothing about his business in town nor about the evening mission he intended. He went out to the barn before dark, strapped the aluminum extension ladder onto his car roof, and quietly turned out the driveway toward Pemaquid Point Lighthouse. For a moment I thought about phoning his wife, Suki, but decided against it. I half-expected to receive a late-night call from the State Police, saying they had Roger Angleford in custody and could I vouch for him. But the call never came.

I tried to forget about Angleford and slept fitfully, finally getting up at two-thirty. I looked outside and saw that his car wasn't in the parking area. Nor was my extension ladder on its pegs in the barn. But a light shone from the two windows of Angleford's room. Had he walked back to the inn on foot? I climbed to the second floor hallway and knocked lightly on his door.

No one answered. Sound asleep? I doubted it. I put a hand on the knob, twisted it and pushed the door lightly. It swung open.

"Roger?" I whispered. Then louder, "Roger, are you all right?"

The bureau lamp and the two lamps on either bedside table were on. On the bed, bureau, desk, and tables were photos, albums, scrapbooks, Father's Day and birthday cards. Angleford had created a shrine to Cara, his tribute, his way of remembering her. Three teddy bears and two dolls sat with their backs against the headboard of the bed.

I felt worse than an intruder. I was violating someone's sacred ground. But before I could back out, movements caught my eye, shadows where two walls came together with the ceiling near one of the bedside table lamps.

Moths! Moths darting and fluttering around the light bulb, their shadows projecting onto the surfaces around them. I glanced at the other lamps in the room. They all had moths beating themselves against their hot bulbs. Where had they come from?

The windows. The open windows. I crossed the floor and saw that not only were the windows up, but the screens were, too. The moths were flying in from outside, attracted to the lamps in Angleford's shrine to his daughter. I reached to lower the screen, then decided not to. Roger would know I'd violated the sanctity of his room. Instead I backed out, closed the door behind me, and tried to go back to sleep.

At 5:30 a.m., my usual time to get up, I put on a pot of coffee. Shortly after first light Angleford's car pulled into the parking area. He got out, replaced the ladder in the barn, and came inside.

"Ladder's back, Dunc," he said with an honest smile that showed a few teeth. There was a faint sparkle, a sign of life in his eyes that showed even through his exhaustion. I was certain he'd not only been out all night, but up all night.

"Hungry, Roger?" I said, hoping to hear what had happened.

"No, thanks. I'm beat," he said. "Time for a little shut-eye. Checkout still 11 a.m.?"

I nodded, and upstairs to his shrine he went.

* * *

At 11 a.m. Angleford was plopping his luggage in front of my registration desk and handing over his room key.

"Dunc," he said. "I can't begin to say how much I've appreciated your patience with me these couple of days." He added in a choked voice, "And your caring," and clasped my hand between his hands in a warm handshake.

"You're welcome, Roger," I said. "I know it's been hard."

He nodded and backed away, luggage in hand, his lip trembling. I watched him load his suitcase into the back seat of his car and climb in. When he got to the end of the driveway, he didn't turn toward the mainland. He turned toward Pemaquid Point. A final goodbye before heading home to Connecticut and Suki? It was none of my business. Roger Angleford had checked out and was on his own. A part of me felt sorry, but I was also relieved to see him go. I didn't think I could stand another day of his pain.

Around five o'clock the phone rang. It was the woman who lived in the apartment above the Fisherman's Museum. She said the man who had knocked on her door two days before to inquire about the lighthouse, the man who had claimed he was a friend of mine and was staying at my inn, had been parked outside her apartment all day, watching her place through binoculars. Her husband was away and, although she assured me she wasn't frightened, she admitted Roger's surveillance made her a bit nervous. She asked if I thought she should call the police. I explained Roger's situation and recapped Cara's death, then promised I'd go and speak with him. I said I could almost guarantee he'd be home in Connecticut the next day, but she thanked me and said she'd just as soon spend the night at her sister's in Newcastle.

I phoned Charlie, my 83 year-old relief clerk, and asked him to cover for me so I could go look for Angleford. My plan was to convince him to join me for dinner at one of the restaurants in Damariscotta.

The sun was about to set when I trotted into the lighthouse parking area searching for Angleford's car. The cars were hard to distinguish in the dusk. A couple near the lighthouse looked similar in shape and color to Angleford's—but they lacked Connecticut plates. I swung my arms and toured the dirt and gravel lot, pretending I was speed walking for exercise. Finally I saw Connecticut license plates on a silver Honda at the lower end of the lot, the view overlooking the rocks Cara had been swept from.

"Roger," I said, pulling up beside the driver's side window. I puffed as if I were out of breath and acted surprised. "I thought you'd headed home to Connecticut." The binoculars hung from a strap around his neck and rested on his chest.

Angleford peered up at me, his eyes puffy and red.

"This is a difficult place to visit, isn't it?" I said.

With lips pressed tight together he nodded.

I had no idea what to say after that, so I squatted down next to the driver's door and the two of us simply watched the sun disappear behind the horizon the way a puppet drops off stage. We didn't speak for what felt like ten minutes, during which time half the cars in the parking lot left. I was about to invite him to dinner when he broke the silence.

"You don't really power-walk, do you, Dunc?" He looked slyly at me and I half-expected him to wink.

"No," I said.

"You were just watching over me, weren't you?"

"Yes."

"Well, I'm okay, Dunc. Really I am," he said. "You can go back to the inn now."

A new set of headlights drove into the park.

"Are they for enjoying the sunset, Roger?" I said, pointing to the binoculars.

"Take a look," Angleford said, pulling the strap over his head and handing me his binoculars. He pointed at the lighthouse. "Focus on the catwalk."

I held the binoculars to my eyes and pointed them at the glass window panels around the lighthouse beacon. The light blinded me immediately, and I had to close my eyes.

"Oh, sorry, Dunc," Angleford said. "Watch out for the light. It comes around every five or six seconds. You'll learn to time it."

After a few rotations of the beacon I had the hang of it and squinted through the binoculars at the upper level of the white tower.

"Damn!" I said. "Isn't that something? It really does look like giant moths."

Something—no, some things, shadowy things—appeared to be fluttering around up inside the glass-paneled lighthouse. Fluttering like moths caught under a jar. Or were they like moths attracted to a lamp?

"So what do you think, Dunc?" Angleford said. "Still betting they're giant shadows?"

Whether they were giant shadows or giant moths, I counted four of them bobbing and dancing up-and-down and side-to-side. When they caught the moonlight I realized they were translucent. Shadows weren't translucent. Shadows were projected onto something. What was I seeing?

I heard the car door open and turned to see Angleford climbing out. He stretched away his stiffness, then walked around and unlocked the car's trunk. He reached in and withdrew what looked like a set of pruning shears. Bolt cutters! Then he pulled out a small crow bar. He slammed the trunk shut and started across the dirt and gravel.

"Roger," I called in a half-whisper. "Where do you think you're going?"

He ignored my question and kept walking for the back of the Fisherman's Museum. I didn't want to follow him, but I couldn't help it.

"Wait for me, Roger," I called, and hurried after him.

By the time I caught up, Angleford had the crow bar wedged between the museum's back door and doorframe.

"This is breaking and entering," I said, my words reminding me that I had always been a fraidy-cat in school. But with a loud crack the door popped open. In a moment we were in the back room of the museum, standing outside the padlocked door to the lighthouse itself. Angleford snapped on a disposable flashlight.

So these were the things he had picked up in town earlier in the week—burglar's tools.

"The light switch is right here, Roger," I said, reaching for it. His strong hand gripped my wrist and held it.

"Don't," he said, shining the flashlight in my face. "I'm afraid it'll scare them."

Scare who? I wanted to say, but didn't. I was pretty sure I knew who.

"Hold the light," he said. A moment later the bolt cutters bit through the steel U of the padlock and Angleford pulled open the heavy door to the tower. The moonlight reflecting off the white inside walls revealed a set of wide stairs that spiraled around a center support up to the inner catwalk and beacon. Not needing the flashlight, Angleford led the way. We inched upward until Angleford halted me with a hand on the shoulder.

"Roger—" I started to say.

"Shhh," he whispered firmly, his fingers digging into my shoulder like a claw.

It was then that I heard them for the first time. *Whoosh-whoosh-whoosh. Whisk-whisk-whisk.* A soft fluttering like rustling silk, then like the wind breathing through fall foliage.

I tugged on Roger's belt. He turned and said quietly, "Stay here."

Before I could object, he slid onto the catwalk on his stomach and rolled slowly onto his back, inching farther around the circular walkway like a prisoner escaping under a fence. The full moon, a huge orange pendant now, seemed to be waiting and looking right into the lighthouse through the huge glass window panels. I crouched on the top stair.

There they were, four of them—rising, dipping, wobbling, weaving—not moths, but beings, like peanut-shaped soap bubbles, shimmery, wet-looking. I could see—both through them and inside them. It was like looking at a drop of water on a glass slide, except that these were two or three feet tall. Like embryos, I thought, it's like looking at a very pale, shadowy embryo in a sonogram.

Angleford lay on his back and raised his hands, then called, "Cara."

They began to move, no longer up and down, nor randomly, but purposefully, slowly organizing, getting in synch with one another, the four lighthouse moths. They moved sideways, the way the beacon rotated, circling slowly like horses in a carousel, they passed over Angleford, his hands passing through them. He kept calling "Cara. Cara. Cara."

They sped up—slowly, slowly, getting in step as if working together, creating a balance, the four of them like the four points of a compass or the wings on a windmill. They rose and sank and I heard a whine, a whine which, as they moved slowly sounded like the night wind strumming the rope of a flagpole; then, as they circled faster, its pitch increased to the sound of summer's-end cicadas; and faster until they practically shrieked—Angleford all the time chanting Cara, Cara, Cara faster and faster—until finally they sang one note like the sound produced by rubbing a wetted finger around the rim of a crystal wineglass—just before it shatters. In trying to call Cara back, was Angleford agitating them?

He stopped calling her name, looked my way and said, "I know why I'm here now."

I plugged my ears. The moths circled the lens at incredible speed, yet they created no draft—only the ear-splitting note and a fine line of light that glowed like a hot filament wire in a toaster. Their movement had created something like a jet's vapor trail, except this wasn't straight or flat, but curved up and down ever so slightly like a sine wave. Was this as close to materializing as they could come?

Then he raised his hands again and called, "Cara, I love you. Cara, I love you. Cara, I love you." As he changed his chant, repeating this new one, they slowed down, slower, slower, until finally they rose and fell like a swelling sea, circling at the same speed as the rotating beacon. Their sound eased to a low, pleasant hum. Slow, rhythmic, peaceful. Calm, calm, calm.

Then the beacon's beam shone right through one of the moths, spotlighting it. It was like light shining through a soap bubble, and the moth, revolving in perfect synch with the light now, appeared to be resting, riding the beam. Was it the beacon, maybe the moonlight—I swear I caught a flash of flaming red—red what, red hair?

Angleford stood up, the revolving moths passing through him—or vice versa—as if he wasn't there. He approached the beacon and Roger Angleford reached in and clamped his hands around the burning hot bulb.

"Roger," I cried out, wincing. But I was helpless, frozen in place.

Angleford screamed, screamed but held on, held on as if his life depended on it. "Cara, I love you," he forced himself to utter one more time.

The moth in the light beam suddenly glowed bright then burst. And as it burst, the full moon—I swear it looked like a laser—the huge smiling full moon hovering near the lighthouse shot forth a beam and drew the moth up to itself, called it home right through the plate glass window panel.

Angleford collapsed face-up on the catwalk in front of me, the stench of his seared flesh immediately assaulting my nostrils.

"Roger," I said, grabbing the front of his shirt and shaking. "Roger, are you all right?" I listened for his answer, but instead heard a fluttering above the catwalk. The other three moths, their balance upset by the departure of the other moth, had fallen out of synch. Something whooshed past me down the spiral staircase. Then another and another. The lighthouse moths were gone, and I sat in silence, the beacon flashing in a slow circle above me.

I felt Angleford's neck for a pulse. None. The big man's chest didn't move. He wasn't breathing. I wanted to pound on it, breathe air into his mouth and lungs, but I knew he wouldn't want that.

As the bright orange moon shone in on us, I rested my hands on the body of Roger Angleford. I knew in that moment that I would deeply miss him. My heart hurt and I put my head down and began to weep.

"You were a good man, Roger," I said. "I love you."

Suddenly something, something peanut-shaped and translucent, not much bigger than a bag of groceries, bloomed from Roger's heart—bloomed in the way a soap bubble blooms to life from the bowl of a bubble pipe. It didn't rip his shirt or tear his skin. It simply appeared.

It rested a second, then brightened to a glow and burst. And as it burst, I felt a faint spray on my arms and face, a warm mist that felt like a light ocean spray on a warm summer evening. Then, as the first moth had done, this lighthouse moth shot out quietly through the window panel—drawn home to the bosom of the moon, leaving me by myself.

I walked home to the inn and phoned Bristol's First Responders, offering the more believable explanation that I had gone looking for a grief-stricken Angleford and, following my instincts, had eventually found his body up inside the lighthouse. I promised to return and meet them at the scene.

Then I dialed Suki Angleford. I recognized her by her accent as soon as she picked up. She sounded wide-awake.

"Suki," I said, my throat tight. "It's about Cara—" Why did Cara pop out of my mouth when I meant Roger?

"Cara here," Suki said. "Gone now."

"Wait," I said, thinking Suki was preparing to hang up. "I meant to say Roger. He—"

"Here, too," she said. "Gone now," she repeated. "Cara fine. Roger fine. Thank you, Dunc." Suki hung up.

I don't recall if I whispered goodbye, but I remember even now the feel of her voice, how relaxed she sounded. Oddly, I felt that way, too—at peace.

A light breeze had come up, so I grabbed a windbreaker and stepped onto the porch. It was September first, and the evening air had that melancholy feel of approaching New England autumn. I set off toward the lighthouse, pale moonlight washing over the road and me and the leaves that would soon fall. As I walked down the center of the blacktop road, I could already hear around me the rustle and flutter—the rustle and flutter of the leaves. Probably the leaves.

The Strand

Each summer from age nine to fifteen I traveled to Maine and stayed a week with my great-aunt Victoria at Ocean House, her twenty-room "cottage" on the Nubble. Widowed early when her husband Archibald's plane went down in the Atlantic, she was incredibly wealthy.

As I got off the train for my fourth vacation—just turned twelve—something occurred to me: I knew where I would find Aunt Victoria. I knew what she'd be doing when I got to Ocean House. Alfred, her only resident servant, would meet me, offer his stiff, formal handshake, and tell me Aunt Victoria was in the parlor and I'd have to wait until dinnertime to greet her. Which meant, I then saw, that Aunt Victoria was in the parlor in gown and pearls—never without a strand of pearls about her neck—entertaining a new suitor. It had been so my first three visits, and it would be so that year and each year thereafter.

At the end of my seventh stay, the summer I turned fifteen, I knew I could never return there again.

The first year I was met at the train by Alfred, who had been my aunt's manservant for thirty years, since shortly before she was widowed. After collecting me at the station, Alfred gave me a walking tour of the harbor town, pointing out the places a boy needed to know about—Post Office, candy store, Harbor Cafe, and the boarding house (if bad weather prevented my reaching Ocean House). He asked those questions adults feel obliged to ask. What grade are you in? How do you like school? Has your summer vacation been enjoyable? I could see Alfred wasn't comfortable with children. He was polite but not enthused.

Alfred seemed distracted. He checked his pocket watch often. Finally he tugged the watch from his pocket and pronounced, "Close enough. Let's go, Master Robert."

Off we traipsed, walking a worn dirt path away from town, beneath a canopy of tall pine trees, then among shorter, scrubbier ones. For more than a half mile we picked our way among rock outcroppings until we emerged onto a bluff with a breathtaking ocean vista. Not a ship or island in sight, nothing but bobbing gulls and lobster buoys riding easy swells. Before I could absorb it, Alfred interrupted.

"The Nubble," he declared, motioning downcoast. "Ocean House at the center."

There in the distance, a half mile from us but barely two hundred yards offshore, loomed an island. I didn't recognize it as an island at first, because it blended into the curve of coastline behind it. But once Alfred pointed it out, I could see it was indeed separate from the mainland. Ocean House, built on a hill and embraced by the island's gray rock-ribbed perimeter, looked like a weathered castle.

"But there's no drawbridge, Alfred," I said. "How do we get out to it? Boat?"

"There," he said, pointing to a strip of dark gray running between the blue-green water of the seaward side and the blackish water of the mainland side.

"A sand bar?" I asked.

"The Strand. A natural bridge of sorts, a ledge of rock exposed by the glacier. Up close you'll see gouges and stripes, like giant claw marks. It connects the Nubble with the mainland."

"But it's underwater."

"Yes, most of the time. When tides are normal it's passable two hours before low tide and two hours after. By the time we get down there, it'll be almost dry enough to cross."

Fifteen minutes later we stood on the shore of the mainland among pink and purple beach roses. We were ahead of schedule and I could see the waters draining back from the Strand. In the twenty minutes we waited for it to become crossable, Alfred told me what I needed to know about the Strand, the Nubble, Ocean House, and Aunt Victoria.

I'd never met Aunt Victoria before, and our getting acquainted over dinner was awkward. It may have been due to her lack of experience conversing with nine year-old boys, but it was also largely due to the attention she accorded her dinner guest, Mr. Belden, the suitor from the parlor. But if Aunt Victoria neglected me in conversation, Mr. Belden worked to include me.

"So, how do you like school, Robert?"

"Fine."

"Favorite subjects?"

"History and Reading."

"Like sports?"

"I love baseball, and I'm learning to play basketball."

"Planning to fish while you're here?"

"Don't know. I've never fished in the ocean, only in ponds and streams back home. Who would take me?"

"Well, that's the great thing about fishing—if you know how to fish, you can go by yourself. It's not a team sport; you can do it alone."

I must have perked up at that, because Mr. Belden picked up a clam on the half shell and said, "And there's clamming. Another activity you can do alone. Why, I'll bet at low tide it's great clamming along those mud flats inside the Strand."

"Absolutely not!" Aunt Victoria piped. "Mr. Belden! The boy will stay away from those flats. A rising tide could catch him with his feet in that muck and drown him." Then to me, "The Strand is for crossing, young man. And that's all—crossing. Understand?"

I spent most of the week either exploring the Nubble or learning my way around town. Whenever I crossed the Strand either direction, I heeded my aunt's stern warning, picking my way quickly across as if running a gauntlet. Something about her voice had frightened me deeply. She'd created an image I couldn't shake, a mental picture that began to appear as a nightmare, of myself mired in the black mud flats, gasping upward as waves lapped in and the tide inched above my mouth and nose. The first few crossings I ran like the wind.

It was week's end before I ran into Mr. Belden again. "Thank you, Victoria, for your gracious hospitality," I heard him say as the parlor door opened. "I hope you'll give my proposal serious consideration."

I didn't know if his word—proposal—described a business deal or an offer of marriage. But the image that sprang to mind was Mr. Belden on bended knee looking pleadingly up into my aunt's eyes, her hand resting on his as he popped the question. Had he made the offer in the old-fashioned way, with a diamond ring? Or had Mr. Belden been astute enough to break tradition and present a worthy pearl?

In the twelve months following, no wedding announcement came.

Over the years suitors flocked to the Nubble like geese to grain, including a dashing black-haired Frenchman named Guy LeFochaud, a widowed Maine lumber baron named Dearstyne, and an eligible bachelor named Dr. Toffler, who had retired from a New York City hospital. No wedding plans ever came after the visits, though. Was romance a game my aunt played, or was there simply no suitable candidate, no man who lit her up the way her dear departed Archie had?

* * *

That first year was the only year anyone met my train. After that I was on my own, the path between town and Ocean House quickly becoming so familiar that there was no need for anyone to accompany me. Beginning my second year, I arrived by train alone, lugged my suitcase through the pine barrens alone, and negotiated the Strand alone.

After the first year, as my confidence grew, my crossings of the Strand became more leisurely. I explored the sand apron along the ocean side. I played tag with the waves and timed my crossings closer and closer. One day in my second or third year I got briefly stranded on a boulder midway across. I quickly realized the water would only get higher and I had little choice but to get wet. I ripped off my shoes and slogged the rest of the way, the water at my knees by the time I climbed onto the Nubble. I had beaten it. I sat on the grass, victorious. But then the picture which always hung in the background of my mind—the gasping boy with water filling his mouth—flashed in my head and made me shudder. I had beaten it—this time.

My fifth year I climbed off the train as a nor'easter hit, forcing me to take lodging in town. The storm blew itself out overnight. Next morning as I sat eating my breakfast at the Harbor Cafe, I heard everyone jabbering about storm damage—trees down, power lost, boats beached, lobster traps smashed on the rocks, tons of seaweed washed ashore. The storm's fury had touched not only what we could see—land, air, water's surface—but it had also churned up what lay beneath.

When I got to the Strand that morning, even though the tide tables listed dead low tide as nine-fifteen, several feet of tidal water covered the rock pathway and angry whitecaps washed rhythmically over it. The storm had created higher than normal tides and the Strand was impassable. I either had to stay another night and try again next morning or I could wait ten or twelve hours for the next low tide, just before dark.

A half-hour before sunset I returned from town and pulled my suitcase from its hiding place in the pines. The full moon was rising even as the sun settled toward the horizon, and the waters covering the Strand weren't deeper than a foot in most places. It would be dry in less than half an hour, so I sat on my suitcase to wait, certain I'd be able to cross in the moonlight.

Something caught my eye way off in the mud flats, close to the Nubble. It looked like a person, thigh-deep or even waist-deep in the water, bending over, then straightening up again and again. With both sunlight and moonlight playing tricks on the water it was difficult to see clearly, but I felt certain it was a man clamming. If someone could clam, I could cross.

I picked up my bag and clambered down to the beach. The Strand's first fifty yards glistened with moisture but it was dry enough to walk on. Part of the crossing, though, would require wading, so I removed my shoes and trousers, stuffed them in the suitcase, and stood shivering in my undershorts.

The sun had slid halfway over the horizon so that between the shadows and the distance I still couldn't clearly make out the clammer. Was Aunt Victoria aware of it? How long had this been going on?

I slung my suitcase under my shoulder and set out. My bare feet slipped on the cold wet strands of seaweed the storm had dumped across the travel surface. Fifty yards along I saw a tangled wire cage, a lobster trap, dashed on the rocks. Near it lay a clot of buoys on a snapped-off tether. The nor'easter had stirred up the ocean bottom and driven ashore plenty of debris. I stopped in puddles of chilly water, and by the time I came to the place where I'd have to begin wading, my feet were already numb. There was almost no wave action now, only a gentle licking, and I was sure if I stayed on the Strand's main path it would get no deeper than my knees. I switched the suitcase to the other shoulder and waded in, ankles aching as soon as the icy waters closed around them. I'd forgotten how cold Maine waters were, even in summer.

The sun disappeared and the area around me was suddenly bathed in moonlight. Trouble was, I couldn't see below the surface, and the path was no longer visible. I had to feel my way with my feet, try to sight in on the Nubble and work from memory. At least the water was receding, and soon I'd see the dry portion of the path at the Nubble end.

Suddenly it grew dark, a fleece of clouds over the moon. I froze in place, unsure of my bearings, afraid to slip and fall. I dared not move forward without some marker.

A flashlight snapped on, the clammer not far off.

"Hullo!" I yelled, and the beam swung in my direction. "Can you help me?"

The flashlight moved toward me.

"Master Robert?"

"Alfred?"

I was never so glad to see anyone. In less than a minute Alfred, clad in chest-high rubber waders, was taking the suitcase from my shoulder and walking me the rest of the way across the Strand.

"What were you doing out there, Alfred?" I asked once we were on dry ground. "I thought you were a clammer."

"Clamming? No clams along the Strand," he said. "Checking for storm damage. I was just preparing to come in." Then he chuckled.

"What?" I said, shivering in the cool air.

"Perhaps you should remain here a moment before greeting your aunt," he said, setting my suitcase down on the grass and patting it. "I trust your trousers, socks, and shoes are in here. I'll go tell her you've arrived safely." And off he waddled in the waders.

That year the man who stayed at Ocean House during my week wasn't a suitor. He visited only two days, and his business with Aunt Victoria seemed to be just exactly that—business. He was Eli Goldman, a New York City jeweler. He arrived with a trunk containing more than a hundred tiny compartments, each housing felt-lined jewelry cases. For two solid days—with the exception of polite conversation at meals—he and my aunt spoke of nothing but pearls and settings.

One afternoon I walked in on them in the dining room and saw tables laden with necklaces, rings, bracelets, watches, brooches, and near Aunt Victoria, bowls of loose pearls that looked like breakfast cereal awaiting milk. One bowl held pears the size of golf balls.

"Let me show you these," Aunt Victoria said, and reached into a huge cloth knitting bag. She withdrew a pearl the size of a bowling ball, waited for Goldman to gasp, then produced another, slightly larger, and when he was totally speechless and wide-eyed, pulled out a third the size of a basketball. She set them on the table and let the jeweler examine them.

"Unbelievable," he said, shaking his head again and again. "I've never seen anything like these. Not even from the South Seas. How do you get them so large?" (Not where, I remember now, but how.)

"Special culture," Aunt Victoria said. "Special culture."

I had no idea whether my aunt was buying pearls, selling pearls, or selecting settings.

* * *

The seventh summer, my last, I finally dared to ask Alfred, "Do you think the right man will ever come along again for Aunt Victoria?"

"Who can say?" he shrugged. "Maybe this summer. Maybe next. Come inside and meet Professor Cassiday."

Professor Cassiday was a retired university educator from the Midwest. The first thing that struck me about him was his bulbous red nose, which reminded me of W.C. Fields and Karl Malden. With his bushy eyebrows, Cassiday more resembled Malden. He seemed quite smitten with my aunt, gallantly kissing her hand every time they met. I wondered if he'd be the one.

On my final night at Ocean House I was startled awake by the awful nightmare about the mud flats. I hadn't suffered it in two years. But I knew I'd been gasping in my sleep. My throat was sandpapery, my mouth cottony. I padded toward the kitchen for a glass of milk. As I tiptoed past my aunt's bedroom I heard giggling and laughter, one voice my aunt's, the other voice a man's. I hesitated in the hallway, wondering if Cassiday and my aunt were engaged in a romantic interlude. It was difficult to imagine the thick-browed professor nuzzling Aunt Victoria with that huge red nose.

"That was wonderful," I heard her say. "You make me feel young."

"My pleasure," the man said. "Always."

The voice wasn't Cassiday's. It was Alfred's. I tiptoed quickly back to my room and climbed back into bed.

New England
Seaside, Roadside, Graveside, Darkside

The next morning after Alfred served breakfast to Professor Cassiday, Aunt Victoria, and me, I said my goodbyes. My train wasn't until after noontime, but I wanted to get going. Low tide came around eleven, which meant the Strand was crossable between nine and one. I was eager to leave. I couldn't look Aunt Victoria or Alfred in the eye.

I spent the morning roaming around town, and at noon found myself in the Harbor Cafe preparing to order lunch.

"So," said the waitress. "How many more days before you go home, Robert?"

"About two hours from now."

"No suitcase?" she asked.

I looked beside my chair. No suitcase. Where had I left it? Not at the train station. Not along the path. I didn't recall lugging it across the Strand. Damn! I had stopped on the downhill between Ocean House and the Strand and sat on a boulder to tie my shoe. I'd set the suitcase in the shadow of the boulder, where it still sat.

I bolted out of the cafe, knowing I barely had time to catch the Strand dry both ways. I would sprint across, grab the bag, and sprint back. If I could make the Strand, catching the train wouldn't be a problem.

The gauntlet was fifteen feet wide when I reached it, the waters closing. I hurried, knowing the return trip would be slower with the suitcase. But the ruts hampered me—I couldn't risk twisting an ankle—so I picked my way across as nimbly as I could.

Midway across I looked toward Ocean House to catch my bearings, and out of the corner of my eye saw a movement on the mud flats, a figure bent over at the waist in the water—almost the same scene as the evening I'd spotted Alfred checking for storm damage, except that now he had an inner tube with a basket set in it tethered to his waist. But I saw no clam rake.

"Alfred? Is that you?" I cried.

The man straightened, looked my way.

"Master Robert?" Alfred called. He had on the chest-high rubber waders. "Don't come—" he started to say once he recognized me. But as the words left his mouth, he stumbled and had to struggle to regain his balance. I couldn't help reacting—I was afraid he'd fall—so I stepped toward him, prepared to wade in if necessary.

"No!" he barked as he straightened up. "No!"

"But Alfred," I said, wanting to tell him I was only trying to help if he needed it.

Alfred saw me looking toward the inner tube and basket. Something about his eyes changed in that instant, as if he were making a mental shift, a decision. But I failed to sense the rising menace in his voice.

"Master Robert, come here," he said, more ordering than cajoling. "Come closer."

"My clothes," I said, something inside telling me to resist. "They'll get wet." His request made no sense. He had recovered his balance.

"My foot," he said. "It's—it's stuck."

I saw something in his eyes then, the first hint of what—pain? Or something else—a sudden idea, a new ploy? He put his hand to his chest and grimaced.

"Master Robert, come quickly," he pleaded. "My heart."

And before I could think, I clambered into the water and slogged toward him.

"Hold on, Alfred," I called. "I'm coming."

I reached him in moments, and as I did he suddenly straightened to his full height, jaw tight, eyes bulging. He clamped his hands on my shoulders and pressed down.

"What? Alfred! No!" I cried.

But his strong arms pushed me under and held me down. I struggled against him, but I had no leverage for my hands, no purchase on the muddy bottom for my feet. My mouth opened for air and instead took in a gulp of seawater, which for a moment had an oddly calming effect. I relaxed, either growing weaker or resigned. My eyes opened and I found myself staring directly into a huge open oyster shell, a shell the size of a Revolutionary War tombstone, and from the center of it

someone stared back, grinning lifelessly. It was a head—no body—just a head in the oyster shell, as if it were the mollusk itself.

In my terror I flailed my arms and grabbed at the only thing I could reach—the chest of Alfred's rubber waders—and pulled down. Seawater spilled in and I felt him pitch forward in the water. He released his grip on me as he fought to keep his own head above water. I pushed out from under him and burst to the surface, greedily sucking down breaths of air.

Alfred floated almost flat for a moment, head craned up for air, hand stretched toward me for help. But then the water completely filled the waders and he sank beneath the surface. Part of me wanted to save him, but then I glanced at the inner tube tied to him. Gaping up at me from the basket in the tube was a face, a face whose bushy eyebrows and bulbous nose I recognized. I tried to push the tube away, but it was tethered to Alfred and wouldn't go away. I scrambled for the Strand, half-running and half-swimming, vomiting seawater and lunch as I went. The Nubble was closer than the mainland, but I ran for town.

An hour later, weak and shivering in a police car, I told a Trooper my story. And while I called my mother from the Harbor Cafe, more police arrived and they started the investigation. But by the time anyone could get down to the Strand, the tide had come in, and things didn't get into full swing for another eight hours. They did manage to get a boat out, though, and found the inner tube with Cassiday's head in its basket and Alfred's body anchored below. They couldn't check out the mud flats then, but they did drop a marker buoy. Then they beached the boat on the Nubble and walked up to Ocean House to tell Aunt Victoria about Alfred. She broke down and cried.

The next morning, while I waited for my mother to arrive in Maine with the car to drive me home, police divers found the giant shells, five of them. Each was between three and four feet from hinge to tip. They dug them out of the mud flat, brought them ashore, and opened them. They shells actually contained live oysters. And in the mouths of four of them were nested four huge pearls, the pearls varying in size from that of a bowling ball to that of a good-sized pumpkin. The fifth oyster, they said, contained not a pearl, but a head, with a thin, almost caramel-like coating around it. The oyster hadn't yet had enough time to spin much substance around its irritant, so the veil was thin.

That's when they asked me to look and see if I could identify the victim. That face that grinned through was Dr. Toffler's.

They cracked open the other pearls and found heads entombed in them as well. Black-haired Guy LeFochaud, Mr. Dearstyne, a man I didn't recognize, and Mr. Belden, who had shown me a clam on the half-shell. Seeing them that way turned my stomach. I was never so glad to return home as I was after that. Thank God they didn't call me to come back.

Eleven decapitated bodies were dug up on the Nubble that summer. Aunt Victoria still had two huge pearls in her possession, apparently having sold or otherwise disposed of several others over the years. She cooperated in surrendering the remaining two to authorities. The smaller of the two, when smashed, contained another unidentifiable head (at least Aunt Victoria wouldn't identify the man). And the larger of the two, by far the largest of all the pearls, the pride of her collection, when cracked, yielded Archie, Aunt Victoria's late husband.

Aunt Victoria admitted Alfred had been her lover for many years—a lover who presented her with fabulous pearls quite regularly, yet a lover it would have been beneath her station to marry. She denied any complicity in Alfred's crimes or any knowledge at all. She had no idea where the pearls came from, she said, and didn't ask.

"It would have been impolite," she said.

And when questioned about the men who disappeared, she explained that Alfred must have murdered them after they had made their goodbyes and headed for the mainland.

"Alfred usually escorted them to the train," she said. "I always wondered why they never came back the next summer."

I never went back to the Nubble and I never again made contact with my aunt, who married Eli Goldman, the New York jeweler, two years later, and died a decade later.

But even now, one or two nights every summer, always during the week I visited Maine, I suffer the nightmare. Except it's a variation on those I had back then. Now I wake up gasping, mouth dry, sandpapery, and I gag—always gag—because I find my tongue curled around a firm little wad of mucus and hair. I get out of bed, dry heaving as I go, and stumble to the toilet, where I spit again and again until the wad is out. I flush it away and—irrational as it is—brush my teeth and rinse my mouth three, four, five times. I can't help it. I have to get rid of it, the wad in my mouth, and the taste, that bitter, choking taste of salt water.

And then I sit up awhile, fretting, wondering if I should have mentioned to the police my aunt's comment to Goldman the day she showed him the huge pearls. I ask myself how much she might really have known, while her voice echoes in my ears: "Special culture. Special culture."

The Witness Tree

When the monstrous tower bell at Old South Church started humming of its own accord the week before Halloween, Dutch Roberts, the town constable for Norwich, Vermont, called me and Devaney to check it out. He didn't call us to evaluate the bell, not in the operational or scientific sense—we're not structural engineers. And he didn't call us to investigate it—we're not ghost busters, either. He called us to get us to check out the story—we're reporters, plain old, garden-variety, small-town reporters for *The Valley News*, the daily serving the Upper Valley of the Connecticut River, which forms the border of western New Hampshire and eastern Vermont.

I say we're reporters. Actually, I'm the reporter. Devaney's my father-in-law, a retired high school history teacher who's an inveterate shutterbug. He shoots pictures to accompany my stories. Most of the shots are of fender-benders, or a nursing home resident turning a hundred, or a pig-tailed girl riding on her father's shoulders at a parade. Not that I couldn't shoot my own photos, which I did before Devaney became my sidekick, but he's decent company, and working part-time as a stringer photographer keeps him out of my mother-in-law's hair.

So when the two hundred year-old tower bell started humming, Dutch called me to ask if I wanted a Halloween story with a local angle.

The story swallowed a lot more time than anyone imagined it would.

The day after Dutch called, Devaney and I drove to Norwich to meet with him and Reverend Halliday, Old South's pastor. The four of us stood in front of the church, staring up at the steeple as Reverend Halliday recounted the story, Dutch filling in details here and there.

The bell had begun humming ten days earlier, on a Sunday night around the middle of the month. A handful of teenagers in the church's Youth Group had noticed it first, when they were playing hide-and-seek around the church and one of them had sneaked up into the belfry. The lad reported the deep hum to the Youth Group chaperones, who further reported it to the building sexton who, unable to find any source for the bell's vibration, consulted Reverend Halliday, who called in several of the Buildings and Grounds Committee. No one had an answer, only such theories as "mild, sustained earthquake" and "static electricity." Eventually the tale of the mysterious humming bell got around to Dutch Roberts, who investigated and suggested the church call a structural engineer, which they did. The structural engineer uncovered nothing.

As we stood craning our necks to look up at the bell, I could faintly hear a sound deep and low, about the frequency of distant thunder. Except that it was a steady tone, like monks chanting a single mantra, an Om, deeper even than the hum of a transformer on a light pole.

"Can we go up?" I asked as Devaney snapped a couple of 16mm shots from the sidewalk and across the road by the white board fence surrounding the village green.

"Be my guest," Reverend Halliday said. "Dutch can show you the way up. My asthma prevents my climbing that ladder."

"Someday you ought to come up, Reverend," Dutch said. "The view from there is in-spire-ing." Dutch laughed at his own joke after he said it.

"I'll just have to imagine it, Dutch," the pastor said humorlessly, waving goodbye as he walked toward the manse next door. "Enjoy the view. Good to meet you gents."

Except for the low hum of the bell, we found nothing out of the ordinary. It was cast iron, made in Boston by the famous Colonial silversmith Paul Revere, and measured nearly five feet in diameter. It no longer swung and tilted to operate the clapper as once had, but was now fixed and had a hammer that struck it on the hour to give the ringing sound. The hum we had heard from the sidewalk below wasn't much louder than it had seemed earlier—in fact, we could comfortably talk over it when we first climbed into the tower. Nor was it painful to our ears—at first. After awhile, though—I suppose because we were standing directly beside it—the steady vibration began to annoy my ears and then hurt them. It reminded me of my pup's annoyance whenever I hummed in his ear, how he'd tolerate it briefly, then give a twitch of his ear, and finally walk away from me.

"No kidding about this view," I said, scanning the town from my bird's perch. "This is an amazing vantage point. You can see everything."

"And look at the view of the green," Devaney said, focusing for a long-distance shot, then for a zoom. "Oh, imagine what this bell has seen in two hundred years. The stories it could tell."

"Parades and church fairs and carnivals and kite flying," I said.

"Kids making out on the green on warm summer nights," Devaney chimed in.

"More than making out," Dutch added. "I've had to throw cold water on 'em more than once."

The three of us laughed and turned back to the ladder. Our inspection had lasted less than five minutes. I noted that though the bell hummed, nothing vibrated, not the decking we stood on, not the stairs of the ladder, hardly even the bell when I felt it. Even though I was no engineer, I had passed my science classes and knew sound was produced by vibration, and if the bell was vibrating at all, there had to be a source. But neither I nor others who had checked earlier for a source could locate it.

Devaney and I thanked Dutch for the tour and told him we wanted to look around the village proper, perhaps interview a few locals about this strange phenomenon. He volunteered the names of the Youth Group teens in case we wanted to talk with them. So off we went on a walking tour of this quaint New England village.

We learned something right away, something which could easily have proven irrelevant. But because I was searching for something that might tie into a Halloween theme for a story, I took notes on even the seemingly unrelated.

Such as: The first things a visitor notices upon leaving Interstate Route 91 at Norwich, Vermont, are the neat, black-shuttered houses which are so quintessentially New England. Then comes the historic village green, which you look through, as through a camera's viewfinder, to see Old South Church fifty yards beyond the far side of the green. The white board fence around the green perfectly centers Old South for pictures, which explains why the church has graced more Christmas cards, calendars, and coffee table books than any other church in Vermont.

On the edge of the green, beside the roadside turnout where visitors park in order to take pictures, a large blue and gold plaque proclaims Norwich's downtown to be on the National Historic Register.

But under that plaque is yet another plaque, erected by the Friends of Norwich, which tells the story of the Norwich Witch.

In 1793, ten years after Norwich was granted its charter, and a hundred years after the Salem, Massachusetts witch trials, Hester Glynn, a young woman thrice widowed, was accused of being a witch. Her accuser was a seventy-five year-old minister, John Ogletree, not from Norwich but from across the Connecticut River at Hanover, New Hampshire, home to Dartmouth College.

Influenced by the stories of the Salem witch trials told him in his youth by his hellfire-and-brimstone minister/grandfather, Ogletree became convinced that the widow Glynn—"thrice widowed, so beware becoming her fourth," he cautioned—was responsible for a "veil of evil" which hung over the village. Ogletree actually preferred charges against Mrs. Glynn, but his accusations were laughed out of court.

Then one morning Widow Glynn's body was found at the back corner of the village green, beneath the spreading arms and heart-shaped leaves of a more-than-hundred year-old linden tree. Her throat had been slit, and dark blood soaked the ground around the linden tree's roots. The Reverend Ogletree was nowhere to be found, and rumors circulated quickly that he had fled the area. An arrest warrant was issued, but folks were certain he'd never show his face again, and there was no pursuit. So went the legend of the Norwich Witch.

After a bit of rummaging for information, Devaney and I learned that on July 4, 1976, to commemorate the nation's Bicentennial, the Friends of Norwich had planted a blue spruce on the back corner of the green, practically in the shadow of the roughly three hundred year-old linden tree where Widow Glynn's body had been discovered. I surmised that though the Friends of Norwich wanted to commemorate the Bicentennial, there was perhaps a dollop of superstition present, too—perhaps the notion of good cancelling out past evil? Devaney snapped a photo of the Friends of Norwich plaque, then took a zoom of the blue spruce with the huge, spreading linden behind it. The tree was known far and wide for its heart-shaped leaves.

"Shame about the grass," said Devaney, putting away his camera. I nodded my head. Both trees—the linden and the spruce—were healthy and flourishing, but around the base of the linden was a rough, barren patch spreading some twenty-five feet from the tree in every direction. "Looks like they could do with some fertilizer."

Mrs. Corcoran at the Town Hall advanced the story of the blue spruce for us, explaining that from the 1976 planting grew not only a tree but a tradition—the decorating of the blue spruce, the Norwich Christmas Tree, on the first Sunday in December. Then, a couple of weeks after the decorating, on the Sunday evening before Christmas, the townsfolk and visitors would gather around it to sing O Christmas Tree. Afterward everyone would cross the green to Old South Church, gather in front of the outdoor manger scene, sing O Little Town of Bethlehem and Silent Night, and go inside for hot chocolate and mulled cider. It had become a tradition which young and old alike looked forward to. Devaney took a picture of a smiling Mrs. Corcoran sitting at her desk with the phone to her ear.

The next day we interviewed the Youth Group kids after school. Their theory about the humming tower bell was that it was receiving a signal from space, either from a far-off galaxy or maybe from something closer, like a satellite.

"After all," one of them said, "if your teeth can pick up radio stations in the fillings . . ."

Devaney got the kids to pose on the manse steps for a group portrait.

The newspaper published my local-interest story and Devaney's photos in the edition which appeared two days before Halloween. Because it was still basically a story about an unexplainable humming bell, with no scientific testing or analysis to report, I related it in a straightforward manner. There just didn't seem to be a way to get a spooky angle on it. We figured the paper would sell well in Norwich because of all the photos of local folks, making for paste-ins for family scrapbooks, that sort of thing. I figured that was the end of it.

On All Saints' Day, November first, the morning after Halloween, Dutch Roberts phoned me at home. "Six reports of missing dogs last night," he said into the phone. He sounded to me like he was trying to keep his voice even.

"Six?" I said. "Dognappers? Halloween prank?" I let the question hang in the air.

"Dammit, Hoagie," Dutch said. "This is serious."

I apologized for sounding flip.

"The six dogs all belonged to families who live within a block of Old South," he said.

"I take it the dogs weren't on leashes?" I said. "People in Florida have been known to lose pets right off the leash. Alligators, you know."

"Hoag!" Dutch said, squeezing his voice so that a yell came out at an almost normal tone.

"Okay," I said. "I'll get Devaney and we'll be right down."

A half hour later we walked into Dutch Roberts's constable's office. About fifteen people sat or stood there. Their squabbling dissipated when we stepped in. Even though it was November, the small office was warm and muggy from so many people breathing and talking in it.

I wanted to ask Dutch, "So why'd you call me?" But I held my tongue.

"So, folks, please," Dutch said. "I know you're upset, but try to remain calm. I've notified the Vermont and New Hampshire State Police. They'll be on the lookout. And we'll put out the word around town to keep an eye out for your pets. If you have pictures of your dogs, please bring them by sometime today."

Then, nodding toward me and Devaney, "I'm sure Mr. Hoag here will help in any way he can by doing a newspaper story on this situation." Several people started to talk at the same time, but Dutch stopped them by saying, "Please, friends, could you excuse us for a few minutes? I've got to meet with Mr. Hoag and Mr. Devaney. You can talk with him after that." He gently shooed them from his office, closed the door, and invited me and Devaney to sit. Dutch closed his eyes, made a steeple with his fingers, and hooked his thumbs under his chin. He let out a tired sigh.

"They're scared some satanic cult sacrificed their animals last night," he said. "In a Halloween ritual." He opened his eyes and caught my questioning look. "I assured them there have been no reports of cults operating in this area," he said.

The three of us sat silent for a moment. Dutch scratched his head.

"Think that it's local kids, neighborhood kids?" Devaney volunteered. "Their own kids, maybe?"

Dutch shook his head. "Nah. Most of the kids were home and in bed already. The younger ones had done their trick-or-treating and the older ones were finished hell-raising. No, as was usual for these dogs, they were all let out to pee after nine o'clock. Five of them go out and do their duty on their own, then return after five or ten minutes. One gets walked by his master near the church."

"And?" Devaney asked. "Did the person see where his dog went, or what happened to it?"

I could see the veins in Dutch's temples throbbing. "As a matter of fact, the man saw his dog wandering along the fence next to the green. But he says when he turned to look up at the tower clock, the dog disappeared. He whistled and called and searched for it for an hour and a half."

"So the dog disappeared right on the hour?" I asked.

"No, fellow said it was around ten-fifteen or ten-thirty," Dutch said.

"So why'd he look up at the clock?" Devaney interrupted. "It wasn't striking the hour. What got his attention?"

Dutch looked blankly at us, then picked up the phone. He dialed a number scrawled on his desk pad.

"Ronald? Yeah. This is Dutch at the constable's office. I forgot to ask you—what made you look up at the tower clock when you did?"

Devaney and I looked at each other, shrugged our shoulders and made faces that mockingly said this was a story for The Twilight Zone.

"Didn't hear or see anything else, then?" Dutch continued. "Just the hum getting louder?" A few more nods of the head and Dutch said, "Call if you think of anything else," and hung up.

Our faces must have said, "Well?"

"Ronald Trask. He says when the dog walked away from him to go do its duty, the hum of the bell increased in intensity a notch."

"You mean it went up a decibel? Got louder? What was he saying?" I pressed.

"Those are Ronald's words: 'It increased in intensity a notch.' He said it wasn't the same as getting louder, but it was more intense, more urgent."

"More urgent? Those his words, too?" I asked. "More urgent? For Chrissakes, Dutch. It's a bell, a stupid freaking bell!"

"Calm down, Hoagie," Devaney said, placing a hand on my wrist. "Let Dutch tell it. Whaddya say, Dutch?"

"The guy just lost his dog. In looking back on what happened, he believes the bell was trying to tell him something," Dutch said.

"Like warn him?" I asked impatiently.

"Look, Hoag," Dutch said. "You can interview the guy if you want to. Hell, you can talk to the other dog owners who lost dogs last night, too. You can interview everybody who's got a dog, cat, or parakeet if you want to. Go ahead. You have my blessing."

The three of us sat a couple of minutes, Dutch and me trying to cool down. We weren't mad at each other. We simply had a mystery that was frustrating us both.

"If it was a satanic thing," Devaney said, "you know, a sacrifice, don't you think they'd have just used one dog? My money's on dognappers. I heard they grab healthy animals and sell 'em to laboratories for experimentation. Halloween night'd be a perfect time. It's a great cover."

Rather than mire ourselves in further discussion and conjecture, we seemed to agree by either consensus or default that Devaney's dognapping theory carried the most weight for the time being. We left Dutch in his office chair and I went home and typed up the missing-dogs story, which was simply a short news item.

The following Friday Dutch called me again. Curt Chase, the custodian at the Elementary School which bordered the green, reported to the constable's office that the earth beneath the linden tree at Witch's Corner, close to the blue spruce, had become even barer than before. The radius of barren ground had widened to thirty-five feet from the tree's base. Sure enough, when Devaney checked the shot he'd taken from the green and compared the bare ground in his photo to the bare ground Curt Chase reported, it had grown ten feet in its radius. Something was killing the grass, Curt Chase noted, but he also commented that neither the linden nor the blue spruce seemed adversely affected.

"In fact," Curt said when Devaney and I caught up to him for a quick interview outside the school, "the trees appear healthier than ever, the way a houseplant perks up and shines after you give it some plant food."

Devaney took a couple of close-ups of the two trees at Witch's Corner. When he developed the film later in the day, he compared them to the telephoto shots he had taken of the trees the day we had read the Friends of Norwich plaque. Although we couldn't be absolutely certain, the trees did indeed seem to look healthier, which was strange because the peak of Vermont's colorful foliage season had passed nearly a month earlier, so the linden's leaves should have been shrinking back, not expanding.

The next day Dutch called and said he had a dozen reports of cats missing, plus two more dogs, several chickens and roosters, and a Vietnamese pot-bellied pig. These I gave more space than a news item—this was Page Three stuff—relating the past Norwich animal disappearances as well. I also interviewed people on the street in Norwich, finding that many people believed the hum of the bell had grown either louder or more intense—but that was a separate news item.

Meanwhile Devaney and I pored over the church records, town records, and the public library's historic documents, all in search of any background information we might use in future articles. Whenever we found a page or paragraph we thought would prove helpful later, Devaney photographed it. We became fairly adept at deciphering the cursive script of our seventeenth, eighteenth, and nineteenth century ancestors.

Over the Thanksgiving weekend, when my wife Carol and I were at her parents' house for the traditional roast turkey dinner, the family got to looking at old photo albums. After an hour or so we worked up to more current pictures that Devaney had taken—the new roof we'd put on his garage, Carol and her mother on a porch swing together, a colorful shot of the changing leaves on the tree behind the house.

"Oops," Devaney said. "The rest of these are from last month's Norwich trip, Hoagie, when we went with Dutch Roberts up into the bell tower at Old South. I had a couple of exposures left on that family roll."

We fanned the pictures across the dining room table. Dutch and me with the bell behind us. A distant shot of the green taken from the steeple.

"Hey, what's that?" Devaney said, pointing to a zoom shot of the green.

We both looked closer. "What is what?" I said.

"There," Devaney said. "By that huge tree, the linden, in the Witch's Corner. Looks like a rope coming from the base of it."

I examined the picture again.

"Looks like a dead groundhog or a possum out at the end of it," I said. "Like the rope's around its neck."

"So the other end's tied to the tree?" Devaney asked, looking puzzled.

"Can't tell," I said. "Your picture doesn't quite show it. You're shooting downward and these branches obscure the base of the trunk."

"Maybe there's somebody behind the tree, holding the rope," Carol offered.

"Kids?" my mother-in-law said.

The four of us sat pondering a minute.

"No," I said thoughtfully. "The kids were in school when we were there. Besides, it looks to me more like the rope goes right to the tree, not behind it."

"Maybe some kids tied the animal to the tree during recess or lunch," my mother-in-law said. "Or maybe it's a pet, a dog that looks like a groundhog. Maybe they came back for it later."

"That's a mighty thick rope," Carol said. "Hairy, I'd say."

Devaney pointed to the photos he had taken after we descended the bell tower, the ones by the Friends of Norwich plaque. The blue spruce and the towering linden tree were prominent in the background.

"Look here," he said. "I took these pictures not long after the tower shots. Look at the green in the background, and the trees. There's no rope in these pictures. And no groundhog."

"So you're saying that these kids removed the animal and the rope while you were climbing down from the church tower?" my mother-in-law asked.

"Ma," Carol said impatiently. "Nobody said it was kids."

I put my hand up, symbolically stepping between mother and daughter.

"I don't know what we're saying," I said, "except that this rope and animal aren't tied to the tree in the later pictures."

The next day we looked at the photos with Dutch Roberts. He concluded that our rope looked more like a thick vine, the kind we had swung on as kids, the ones which snaked up into trees in swampy areas. He was certain the animal was a groundhog, though he referred to it as a woodchuck. He refused to revisit Devaney's Satanic-cult/animal-sacrifice theory, though he wasn't about to dismiss it either.

"It'd be too hard to catch a wild woodchuck," he said. "And why bother if you've got access to tame pets?"

On the first Sunday in December, with the help of the Highway Department's backhoe tractor, the Friends of Norwich decorated the Norwich Christmas Tree as usual. They hung colored lights all over the blue spruce and attached foil-wrapped gift boxes to its branches. Although there was no story for me to write, Devaney wanted to shoot pictures of the tree-trimming, so he talked me into accompanying him for a change.

Later that same day the Old South Youth Group set up the manger scene in front of the church. The kids remembered Devaney and me, and rewarded him with schleppy poses for pictures.

During both events, the tree-trimming party and the manger scene set-up, the tower bell hummed the way a dog growls at a stranger. And for the first time I understood what people had been describing. I felt it. The intensity, the growing urgency, the warning.

A stray cat living under Marciano's Italian Ristorante disappeared that night. I wouldn't have known except that Marciano himself called two nights later to tell me, knowing I had been on top of the pet-nappings. Everyone in town was tuned in to it. Marciano didn't really notice the cat was gone, he simply observed that over the next few days the scraps he put out weren't being eaten. This from a cat that had eaten at Marciano's rear door every night for two years.

Oddly enough, no roadkill carcasses were reported on any of the Norwich streets—no skunks, no possums, no raccoons, no cats. In a normal autumn the town's animal control officer or the Highway Department would get two or three cleanup calls a week.

The Sunday before Christmas arrived, and with it came Caroling Eve, which Devaney and I decided we'd attend. By four o'clock, with daylight fading, the caroling began, as always, at the Witch's Corner with O Christmas Tree. Another carol followed. Just as it got dark, someone threw a switch and the strings of colored lights blinked on. Everyone, especially those with toddlers, oohed and aahed. Then the crowd meandered across the green toward Old South's manger scene, singing as they strolled. Devaney and I lagged behind so he could snap a few pictures of the Christmas tree.

About that time Jim and Tanya Hathaway, one of the couples we had interviewed when their Doberman disappeared, missed signals on who was watching Joshua, their three year-old. Jim had Eric, and Tanya had Etta. Each assumed the other had Josh. From where Devaney and I were standing, we could see what happened.

Josh's attention span for the tree-lighting ceremony had been short. He'd discovered a great place to push his little dump truck around, under the huge three hundred year-old linden tree. His playground was a bare patch of ground as calloused as an oiled Vermont dirt road. The truck wheels moved so freely, and the tree lights made it so easy to see. Devaney and I had been so caught up in the picture-taking that we had failed to notice him at first.

Josh had gotten deeply involved in his play and failed to notice that the singers, including his parents, had drifted across the green toward Old South, whose humming tower bell grew steadily more urgent. It drew my attention the way Ronald Trask said it drew his on Halloween night, when he lost his dog while walking it. I could feel the bell growling a warning.

As Devaney snapped pictures of the Christmas tree, I glanced over at little Josh playing innocently with his dump truck under the linden tree. That's when I saw the movement he didn't see—the root, brushing, swishing, sweeping. I not only saw it—I was certain I heard it, too, even over the rising hum of the bell. It swished softly like a tail, deceptively caressing the ground the way a feather duster brushes the surface of a table, the root all the while slithering toward the unknowing boy.

"Josh!" I heard, but it wasn't my voice. It was his mother's scream, and for a moment my gaze left the boy as I turned my head to look toward Tanya Hathaway as she raced across the green. Her husband Jim and their two other children stood by the manger scene in front of the church, looking confused as she ran from them.

The bell above started to tremble and rumble. From a hundred yards away I could hear it throbbing. Then the ground under our feet began to shake, and I heard someone near the church yell, "Earthquake!" People dropped to the ground.

"The kid!" It was Devaney's voice behind me. "Hoagie, get the kid!"

"Josh!" Tanya Hathaway screamed as she raced for him. "Josh!"

The root swished side to side, closing within five feet of the child. I had no idea if it had lightning speed and struck like a cobra or if it slowly strangled its victims like a boa constrictor. Maybe it could do either. It could surely have its way with this prey, a clumsy three year-old.

As I started toward him, Josh heard his mother's screams and looked up, realizing for the first time that he was alone. He clapped his hands to his ears, not to shut out his mother's voice, but to escape the deafening din of the bell, which sounded like a boiler about to explode now. As it crescendoed, I could make out dogs howling all over town as if a fire siren had sounded.

I think Devaney's flash went off behind me then, because I caught a momentary glimpse of the base of the linden tree. In that bright moment, I swear, I could clearly see the whip-root emerging directly from the tree's trunk at ground level. In that split second I was reminded of the rabbit hole, the White Rabbit, and Alice.

The root coiled itself near the child now, like a rattlesnake.

"Josh!" Tanya screamed, the two of us six feet from the boy. The boy held out his arms to her, and I held up the only thing I had—my spiral reporter's notebook—between the child and the ready-to-strike snake-root.

Crack! A line of electricity-pure energy, Devaney later told me, arced from the sky to the church bell then—not soft summer heat-lightning, but a vivid, violent, terrible-swift-sword sort of lightning, thunder-cracking lightning, the lightning of judgment—sizzling as it shot forth from the heavens. It refracted off the bell, never touching the square steeple that housed it, crackled high above the green, and grounded itself in the rabbit hole, the open throat of the linden trunk.

Kaboom! The tree exploded, shooting out of the ground like a rocket at Cape Canaveral, trunk clearing the ground, roots trailing like a nest of angry snakes. The tree disintegrated in mid-air, shattered into a million tiny fragments, a blood-curdling scream filled the air as it blew apart.

The blast threw Josh, his mother, and me twenty feet out onto the center of the green. When I sat up, I saw Tanya lying near me, crying hysterically and clutching her babbling child. Soot rained everywhere like volcanic ash. Foil-covered gift boxes, blown off the adjacent blue spruce, lay scattered all around us.

"Holy maracas!" I heard Devaney say. "Talk about fireworks!" When I looked to where his voice had come from, I saw him lying on his side near the white board fence, camera beside him.

The crowd from the manger including Jim Hathaway and his two other children made its way across the green to Tanya, Josh, Devaney, and me. Dutch and the others stood staring at the crater where the linden tree had stood. The hole was seven feet deep and fifteen or twenty feet across the center. All around the green were splinters and small pieces of the tree, though no single piece was longer than two feet. The lightning strike had practically pulverized it.

"Hey, look down there!" someone yelled. "In the hole!"

While Jim Hathaway and several others comforted Tanya and Josh, a group of us peered into the crater. Flashlights shone on someone in the crater, crouched in the center.

"What the—" Dutch said. "Who is it?"

No one answered. The figure, as far as we could see, was clad in a black suit and black hat. I didn't recall anyone reported missing.

"My Rusty!" Ronald Trask yelped, pointing down into the crater. There beside the person lay the carcass of a dog, its neck wrapped in a hairy root.

Rusty wasn't the only lost pet in the crater. We made out the carcasses of dozens of dogs, cats, and other animals in various states of decomposition, each with a root strangling it, the roots all leading back to the body.

Nobody, not even Dutch Roberts, the constable, wanted to jump down into the pit, which was beginning to stink of rotting flesh. Finally Devaney stepped past me and, before I could stop him, jumped in, camera in hand.

"Shine those lights on his face," Devaney ordered, pointing to the black-suited man who appeared to be sitting. Devaney lined up for a shot.

"Who is it?" I called down. The odor drifting up from the crater was beginning to turn my stomach.

"Can't tell," Devaney said. "It's mostly hair and clothes on a skeleton. Long gone. Looks like his hands were tied by the tree roots."

"And what about all those other roots?" Dutch said. "The ones wrapped around the animals?"

Devaney examined the scene more closely.

"Geez," he said. "Those roots all lead back to the skeleton's mouth."

"To its mouth?" I asked. "Not its hands?"

"Looks like it," he answered. "To the mouth. Throw me a flashlight and I'll make sure."

Dutch tossed one down into the hole, but Devaney missed catching it. The heavy flashlight bounced off his hand and struck the root that had strangled the pot-bellied pig.

"Cripes," Devaney said. "That gashed the root. It's oozing." He bent over and retrieved the flashlight, shining it on the damaged root.

"Well?" Dutch asked.

"Looks like blood," Devaney said.

The foul odor wafting up out of the hole was getting to me, and though I wanted to jump in to get the story, I couldn't. I pinched my nostrils and breathed through my mouth.

"Move over, Devaney," Dutch yelled. "I'm coming down."

In a second Dutch was in the hole, standing beside Devaney. He prodded the root near the gash, then pressed the sole of his boot down on the root between the potbellied pig and the gash. The root oozed a little more.

"It's like a transfusion or something, I think," Devaney said.

"See if the root taps into the pig's skin," I called down.

Devaney pulled a pair of gloves out of his coat pocket and put them on. Dutch, not having gloves, pulled a handkerchief from his back pocket and wrapped it around one hand. Together they grabbed the part of the root coiled around the pig's neck.

"Ooh, geezum," Devaney said, making a face of disgust. "It's squishy, like a—"

"*Tongue*," Dutch finished for him as they both pulled their hands back. "It's like grabbing a tongue."

"Yeah," Devaney agreed.

"Okay, okay," I said. "So it feels like a tongue. Does it break the pig's skin?"

Devaney stripped off his gloves and handed them to Dutch.

"You check it," he said to the constable. "I'll shoot the pictures." His fingers returned to something they felt more comfortable with, his camera.

Dutch unwound whatever it was that had wrapped itself around the small pig's throat. He shined the light close around the dead animal's neck.

"No," Dutch said. "It was just coiled around. Maybe strangled it. But no broken skin that I can see."

Devaney snapped a couple of shots.

"Now the other end," I said in my nasally voice.

"The ass?" Dutch said, looking up at me with genuine puzzlement his face.

"Not the other end of the pig," I said impatiently. "The other end of the root."

I heard Devaney chuckle. Down there in the midst of that carnage and stench, he was able to chuckle.

"Oh," Dutch said, swinging the beam of his flashlight around toward the black-suited skeleton. I watched the light move from the restrained wrists to the skull's mouth.

"This is weird," Dutch said.

"What is?" I asked.

Devaney and Dutch looked at each other, and Devaney said, "It could actually be a tongue, Hoagie."

"What do you mean, a tongue?" I said.

"A tongue," Dutch answered. "It looks like every one of the roots that are wrapped around these animals are coming out of this skeleton's mouth."

"Then what's holding the skeleton's wrists?" Devaney said, continuing to click away with his camera.

"The tree's roots," Dutch answered, touching the wrist restraints with his gloved hands. "These are live roots, tough ones. Different from the squishy stuff that came out of Mr. What-s-his-name's mouth. They looked the same in the dark, at least they did from a distance, but they're definitely different. Tree roots holding the skeleton's wrists, and the skeleton's tongue holding the dead animals."

While I stood there pondering what it might mean, I noticed that everyone else had withdrawn, probably because of the stench. I had no idea how long there had been only the three of us there alone. I also noticed that two police cars and several firetrucks were screeching up in front of the church. At least the tower bell had stopped its humming.

"Cops and fire department are here, guys," I said down into the hole. "They're coming across the green. Do a quick check and see if there's any I.D. on the skeleton."

Dutch took off one glove and patted down the loose-hanging suit.

"No pockets in these old trousers," he said. "No zipper, either. And no side pockets or vest pockets in the suit coat," he said.

"The hat?" I heard Devaney ask, and saw Dutch lift it. A sheet of paper fluttered from under it.

"What's it say?" I asked. "Hurry! They're coming."

"I can't read it," Dutch said. "It's that old kind of writing. Like in George Washington's time."

"Give it here," Devaney said sharply. "I can read that stuff pretty well now." He glanced over it. "It says: I have decided to tell the truth."

"But it's not signed," Dutch said.

That's when the police and firefighters descended upon the scene of destruction. They helped Dutch and Devaney out of the crater, then took statements from the three of us, along with everyone else who had been around that night. Thank God they moved us into the manse for the interviews, getting us free of the stench of rotting animal carcasses. And thank God for small-town police work, because no one ever thought to ask Devaney for his camera or the rolls of film he shot that night.

I worked all night on the story while Devaney developed the film in his darkroom, so we had one heck of a scoop for the wire services the next morning. I wrote it as straight as I could, just reporting, not concluding anything. Other papers sent reporters who picked up the story after the fact, but they either headlined it "Norwich Christmas Miracle," emphasizing the disaster element and the fact that no one had been injured, or "Steeple Smites Christmas Tree," pitting the church and Christmas's true meaning over against the commercialism symbolized by the Christmas tree (even though the bolt of electricity had destroyed the linden tree while missing the blue spruce, liberating only its foil-wrapped boxes). All the stories listed "rare winter lightning" or "static electricity" as the cause.

Since there was no injury, loss of human life, or crime against a person committed (only against pets)—it being fairly clear that the skeleton was very, very old—the police sealed off the scene around the crater, but opted to wait until daylight to bring in the State Police investigators. The hole in the ground, the skeleton in the chair, and the rotting, stinking animal carcasses could wait six or eight hours.

The next day the investigators found "no tongue-like root wrapped around any animals, as bystanders claimed they saw the night before." They only found the dead animals. They did, however, find "the skeleton's wrists bound by the roots of the linden tree, which must have encircled the ulna and radius bones over a period of years." They also "located no scrap of old paper, which Mr. Roberts and Mr. Devaney claimed to have seen and which Mr. Devaney claimed to have read."

Unfortunately, Devaney had neglected to take a photo of the scrap of paper. The pictures from the crater—of the carcasses and the skeleton in the chair—showed what could have been a vine, a root, or even a rope, wrapped around the animals' necks and protruding from the skeleton's mouth, though whatever showed in the photos had miraculously evaporated by the next morning when investigators checked the crater. When we showed the shots to the police later, since their investigators had found no tongue-roots in the crater the morning after, they said they feared a hoax and would say so if we made the photos public.

The official report offered no conclusion, nor would the authorities speculate as to how the skeleton, a male's—estimated to be from around 1800—got under the main trunk of the tree. One interesting side note: the linden tree's age was estimated by a Forest Service expert to be three hundred fifty-four years old.

* * *

"Look, Hoagie," Devaney said to me a month later, after the police closed the books on the case. "We saw the lightning ricochet off the bell and splinter that tree, didn't we?"

I nodded my head.

"And I know what me and Dutch saw down in that hole," he continued.

"I'm with you, Devaney," I said, continuing to nod agreement. "Even from up on the green I'm pretty sure I saw something wrapped around those animals. And I think it led to our friend, the skeleton's mouth."

We'd been over the story a hundred times.

"And Dutch saw the note under the hat, too," Devaney said.

"Yup," I agreed.

"And I know what I read."

We sat silent a moment.

"So what's your theory?" I asked.

"Probably same as yours," Devaney said.

"You think the bones are old Reverend Ogletree's, don't you?" I asked. "From 1793."

"Yup," Devaney said. "He's the one who slit Hester Glynn's throat. Agree?"

"I agree," I said. "They were having an affair and she threatened to expose it and ruin his reputation, or maybe he was having an affair and she found out and threatened to tell about it. Something along those lines."

"So he killed her at night," Devaney said.

"On the back corner of the green," I added.

"And then what?" Devaney said. "You think a small group of townspeople took the vigilante route, grabbed Ogletree, and planted the tree on top of him to mark the spot?"

"That theory wouldn't be bad," I said, "except that the linden tree wasn't two hundred years old years old, Devaney. Remember? The forester said it was three hundred fifty-four years old. So that tree was already a hundred and fifty-plus years old and extremely well-rooted when Hester Glynn was murdered in 1793. It must have been fairly formidable even then."

Devaney looked totally puzzled.

"So you're saying the townspeople didn't bury Ogletree and plant or move the tree on top of the site?" Devaney said.

"Correct," I said. "Besides, even if it were a handful of vigilantes, or even the whole town and they agreed to keep silent, why would they go to all that trouble to bury the murderer under the tree?"

Poor Devaney's face was a question mark.

"But you do agree the skeleton is old Ogletree, right?" he said. "And that Ogletree killed Hester Glynn because she threatened to expose him for some reason, whether it was an affair or something else?"

"Yes, to both questions," I said. "I think that mystery's solved."

"Then who buried him under the tree?" Devaney asked in frustration.

"The tree," I said, thinking of the heart-shaped leaves.

Devaney simply stared open-mouthed at me.

"I know this sounds crazy, but it's all I can figure. No one saw the horrific murder there on the back corner of the green except the tree. The tree was the only witness, and it knew there would be no justice, so the tree dragged Ogletree down and held him."

"Which explains the roots binding his wrists," Devaney said. "But what about all those dead animals? Dragged down by the tree, too? Why would it do that—to feed Ogletree?"

"No," I said. "Ogletree dragged them down—to sort of feed himself, although I don't think he was alive in the human way, living and breathing. I think all that was left was the evil, or the insanity, his essence. And that's what the tree had to hold captive for two hundred years. But, like the Bible says, no one has ever been able to tame the tongue. The tree could only restrain his hands and feet. The problem was, the evil was growing stronger again and Ogletree kept dragging more live bodies—animals—down beneath the tree. First it was small animals, then pets and larger animals—"

"And then," Devaney interrupted, "it went after a small person, little Josh Hathaway."

"Correct," I said.

"Which is why the lightning struck," Devaney said, even more animated now that more pieces of the puzzle were fitting together for him. "The bell began humming as the evil grew stronger, the way a dog growls, a sort of warning. And when Ogletree went for the kid, the church bell directed a lightning bolt at Ogletree."

"Yes, I think so," I said. "Either that or the lightning bolt used the bell. In any case, it appears the lightning and the bell coordinated their efforts."

"And zapped Ogletree," Devaney said.

"Exposed Ogletree," I said. "Or exposed the evil, at least, and put a stop to the stalking. But I doubt the evil is destroyed. It never is."

"Like that Bible story," Devaney said. "About the evil spirits Jesus cast out of a man. He didn't destroy them. He sent them into a herd of pigs. But better in the pigs than in the man, I suppose."

"But Devaney," I asked. "Remember what happened to the pigs?"

"They went nuts and committed suicide. Stampeded off a cliff into the sea," he said.

"So where'd the evil spirits go after the pigs drowned?" I asked.

Devaney was stumped. "I don't know," he said. "Into the fish?"

I simply shrugged my shoulders. Where had the evil in Ogletree gone? Where does evil escape to, and where does it reside while it seeks a new host?

Perhaps there is no answer to that. Perhaps the best we can do is to pray. Pray for more linden trees. And preserve the ones we have.

The Ice Fisherman

Cornelia watched from her parlor window, waiting for her brother Paul to appear on the frozen lake. He always walked onto the ice from behind the pines that made up the boundary between her land and his. They'd lived there all their lives—she, at seventy, occupying the family homestead she'd inherited thirty years earlier, and he, at sixty-eight, in his log cabin on the land their father had given him when Paul came back disabled from the war in Europe in 1945.

A dozen fishing shacks dotted the ice near the middle of the lake. Paul's was the light green one with the fluorescent orange door. Six or eight more fishing shacks—shanties some folks called them—rested on the far shore on dry ground. Their owners either hadn't gotten them on the ice for the winter or had begun pulling them off early, anticipating an early thaw.

Paul's shack had been a more conservative color when he inherited it from their father, a dull brown, weathered with age. Except for the three years when her brother was away in the Navy and the year of his recuperation (not just from the physical recuperation but getting over the nightmares, one of which he claimed had begun recurring again recently after a forty year hiatus), Paul hadn't missed a winter of ice fishing on the lake since he was six. Fifty-eight years of fishing.

A snowmobile crossed the lake, coming first as a speck from the far shore where two dozen year-round camps had sprung up. There had been only two when Cornelia and Paul were growing up—one Uncle Freeman's, the other a rental cabin—and those used only in summer.

From behind the thermal-paned window Cornelia couldn't hear the whine of the snowmobile. Fine with her. She agreed with Paul that snowmobile racket shattered the peace of the place. Cross-country skiing was all right, but not noisy snowmobiling. Peace was what Paul loved more than anything, a sense of peace.

The snowmobile crossed the center point of the lake, weaving its way among ice fishing shacks as if negotiating an obstacle course. Once through the maze, it sped toward Cornelia's small dock. The driver was a boy—what, nine or ten—too young, she thought, to be riding the dangerous machine alone. She could hear their mother's voice railing against the evils of motorcycles in the 1930's, when Paul bought an old "hog" for the dirt roads.

"You be careful, Paul" Cornelia could hear her mother cautioning. "I want you home for supper in one piece."

The snowmobile slowed and veered before reaching the dock, then cruised parallel to the shore as if on drill parade. When the boy's hand went up in a wave, Cornelia's hand started up, too, in answer, but then she saw that Paul had emerged from the pines and was waving at the boy. A shadow crossed the ice between them—clouds overhead, no doubt—and Paul continued on toward his shack as the snowmobile kept following the shoreline and grew smaller.

Paul made his usual beeline for the orange-door shanty, pulling his ancient Flexible Flyer sled behind him. He limped in his usual way, first on his good leg with the insulated engineer's boot, then on the wooden one, mahogany from the knee down, saw-toothed heel plate on the end of the peg so it'd bite into the ice. He'd hobbled to his ice fishing shack thousands of times that way.

Cornelia smiled and shook her head as she thought once more of the irony. Paul's ship had been sunk in the North Atlantic by a German sub, and he'd had to adapt to a wooden leg. Yet here she sat day after day with two legs, each weak and unsteady, while her brother trekked onto the lake daily to fish.

Paul turned, looked Cornelia's way, and waved. She returned it, their daily visual litany, a comfort. Only today's wave—what was there about it? Perhaps a heaviness, a tiredness she sensed rather than saw?

Her brother had never married. Cornelia had, but her husband Rudy has passed on fifteen years earlier. They'd never had children. Now it was just her and her brother.

Paul stood outside his shack, near where the white ice turned greenish-blue. A spring fed it from below, which was why Paul set his shack there year after year. Their father had said the Indians believed the swirling spring was made up of spirits. Paul didn't know about that, he simply claimed the spring made it the best part of the lake for fishing.

"Springs are life-giving," he said, "like circulating your blood."

She watched him disappear inside. It wasn't cold; in fact, the sun was bright and the lake's surface had been warming for days. Cornelia knew Paul wouldn't light the kerosene heater he kept inside the shack.

She knew her brother's routine, could picture him unfolding and setting up the blue canvas director's chair he kept on a nail. He'd use the rusty hatchet to break up any new ice that had formed over the hole in the night. Then he'd drop in his lines, settle back in the chair, and reach for the well-chewed cigar in the pewter ashtray on the shelf. He'd work the cigar around until it fit his lips and teeth with the snugness of a marble settling into a hole on a Chinese checkers board. He never smoked the cigar, didn't even chew it. Just held it there in his mouth most of the morning and afternoon, removing it only to eat the sandwich and cookies in his lunchbox. When he left at mid-afternoon, he'd rest the cigar in its cradle on the lip of the pewter ashtray for next time.

"Don't hurt me if I don't smoke it," Paul would argue whenever she and Rudy had kidded him about the cigar. "Besides, unsmoked, a good cigar will last a week, maybe two."

Paul hadn't actually smoked a cigar since the day Kennedy died in Dallas, and he never said why he'd quit then. Unless he'd told Rudy, that is, Rudy who'd been not only his brother-in-law but his best friend. But if he had told Rudy, Rudy had taken the secret to his grave with him.

The sun cleared the peak to the east, and the thermometer outside Cornelia's parlor window read forty degrees. If it got much warmer and stayed that way, the ice above the springs would soften. It was already beginning to melt around the edges of the lake.

Cornelia felt a seed of worry. She'd seen it happen before, the melt above the spring. Shacks sank into the ice as if in quicksand, tilting this way and that. Sometimes the lake would refreeze and the owners wouldn't be able to free them. Or if the shacks sank at final thaw of the season, they'd wait a month or two and retrieve them by boat, towing them home like dead whales.

Paul's had sunk only once, when he and Rudy had driven to Virginia for a Navy reunion. Things had warmed up unexpectedly. She could still remember how it chilled her to watch the coffin-shaped shanty sink gradually into the ice over those four days. In the end, only the roof was visible.

"I can always get another cigar," Paul had joked upon his return from Virginia, when he discovered the submerged shack.

Cornelia had wondered if it didn't remind him of the war and his ship's sinking, after which he and a group of his shipmates had spent two days adrift. Everyone but Paul had eventually slipped into the icy waters while awaiting rescue. Frostbite had claimed his leg and several fingers. He'd been decorated but insisted he didn't deserve to get the same medal the others got, which was why Cornelia kept the framed medal on her wall. Paul wouldn't allow it in his house. He spoke to no one about the sinking or his comrades' fate except Rudy, who confided to Cornelia that he thought Paul carried a load of unnecessary guilt.

The boy on the snowmobile zipped along the far shore, drove up the bank to a small frame house with smoke trailing from its chimney, and disappeared inside. Could he be done for the day? It was barely 9:30.

Another fisherman appeared three cabins east of the snowmobiler, wearing an insulated coverall outfit, fluorescent pink with black trim. If he hadn't walked toward a shanty, Cornelia would have thought him a jogger. He disappeared inside the shack farthest from Paul's. The sun felt warm streaming through the window and made Cornelia sleepy.

* * *

The Regulator clock above the piano read one-thirty when she awoke. The sunlight that had put her to sleep had moved around to the other side of the house, and she felt cold. She moved to the kitchen for tea and a jelly sandwich, spreading butter on the bread before applying jelly, the way their mother had always done it. Paul had done it that way, too, until his heart problem, so now he skipped the butter.

"Hard to believe," he had said in honest disbelief. "A bum ticker. How can that be, with all the fish I eat?" Nevertheless, he had heeded his doctor, cut down on his fat, and lost weight. It was all he could do, since he wasn't a good candidate for bypass surgery.

Cornelia returned to the parlor window, sweater around her shoulders, lap blanket over her knees. Forty-eight degrees outside, and that from a thermometer reading in the shade. A gnawing returned to her stomach. She sipped her tea to calm it, and as she looked up from her tea cup—just for a second, the briefest moment—she was sure she saw Paul's friends standing together and looking at her, smiling, from a distance. She swallowed hard, almost choked, then she realized it was a reflection she was seeing in the window, a reflection of the World War II black-and-white photograph of Paul and his buddies that sat on the small table behind her. Except that Paul was in the photograph behind her. Had he been in the reflection she'd mistaken for the gathered group on the lake?

The jogging-suit fisherman stepped from his shanty and started the walk home. A string of small fish dangled from his hand. His free hand went up in a wave, and Cornelia saw that the snowmobiler had come back onto the lake and was waving. The boy showed a burst of speed the way young boys did in front of men, then headed straight across the lake toward her, bisecting it. From so far away, he resembled a teardrop dripping down her windowpane.

He turned the machine and put it into a skid before reaching Cornelia's shoreline, spitting up ice shavings as a figure skater did upon pulling up short. As he did, she felt the tiniest breath of air, chill air. A draft through a tightly shut window? It caressed her cheeks and a frisson of dread tingled along her spine. She drew her sweater tighter around her. Then the boy was flying across the ice again the way Cornelia had seen her father do sixty years earlier in his iceboat. This machine seemed less graceful, less fluid.

Paul stepped from his shack, stretched like someone awaking from a nap. He glanced toward Cornelia, then reached back in and pulled out a double string of fish, ten or a dozen. He held the strings up as if he were an Olympic athlete displaying a medal.

Cornelia smiled. So did Paul, and for the first time ever she caught a glimpse of sunshine reflecting off his gold-capped eyetooth. She was amazed to think she could see it at that distance. Was it because he hadn't smiled that broadly in a while, or that the sun and the angle had never been right? It reminded her of an old movie she'd seen, where the hero's eyes and smile had flashed from the screen. Her brother, the hero.

That's when the snowmobile crashed through the ice. The boy went down, clutching the controls of the heavy machine. It never floated, not even for a moment, something it might have done had it been a four-wheeler with air in the tires. This was all metal and treads, and it simply disappeared down toward the bottom where the spring fed in. He must have let go the controls once he was underwater, and his snowmobile suit, perhaps because of the air trapped inside it, buoyed him to the surface.

He thrashed his arms. Cornelia could see his mouth opening and closing, but she heard nothing. Her eyes searched the far shore for the jogging-suit fisherman. He was gone, probably in his cabin.

She saw Paul hobbling fast toward the boy, booted foot on his good leg slipping, metal-toothed heel on the wooden peg gripping, biting the ice. Fifty yards to the boy, but Paul was closing the gap fast. The boy foundered and the snowmobile suit that had buoyed him now took on water, changing from life preserver to anchor.

The pink and black fisherman appeared in his doorway, perhaps to retrieve the fish from his porch. He glanced at the lake, dropped his fish, and broke into a run. He had two hundred yards to cover.

Paul was almost to the boy now, dragging his Flexible Flyer sled. He pulled up short of the ice break, swung the sled the way a muleskinner side-arms a whip. The sled snapped toward the hole and splashed into the water in front of the boy's outstretched arms.

"Grab it!" Cornelia screamed. But the boy was too panicked and continued thrashing wildly. She pounded the windowsill, yelled again, "The sled! Grab the sled!"

The man in pink and black looked like a runner now. A hundred yards to cover. Cornelia could see his mouth moving.

The boy flapped his arms twice more, looking the last time as if his hand might strike and grasp one of the runners of the sled. But the icy water turned his clothing to lead. He went under.

Paul let go the sled rope, planted his metal-tipped wooden leg as a pole-vaulter plants the pole at take-off, and catapulted into the opening. Cornelia screamed as her brother vanished beneath the surface. The other fisherman reached the hole and stood staring blankly into it. Cornelia held her breath.

Suddenly the slushy water exploded as a head broke the surface. Two heads. In the midst of that upward thrusting, breaching-whale motion Paul's strong arms heaved the boy out and onto the ice. The man in pink and black clutched the boy, then dragged him back from the hole. Paul rested his arms on the edge of the ice, and Cornelia saw him smile. The sun caught the gold-capped tooth again as he glanced her way. A second later she glimpsed the pain, the excruciating pain, as Paul's face contorted. His heart.

The other fisherman could do nothing. Cornelia could do nothing. Then she saw Paul's hand come up—a salute perhaps—before his face relaxed and he slipped backward, backward into the icy water with his comrades, backward into the chilly sleep. She couldn't see him, but somehow she wasn't afraid either. She could picture him—drifting, drifting slowly downward, like a leaf in autumn, freed from the tree, drifting slowly downward into his comrades' open arms, to rest, to rest in the life-giving spring.

John Flynn's Banshee

John Flynn—everyone called him Jack—stepped away from the window. He'd seen the hearse cruise by two or three times now, an older black one. This wasn't the first time he'd seen a hearse in the Irish section of Nashua. It made him nervous. When the hearse came around in the evening—it was now six o'clock—it wasn't for a funeral, it was always to pick up a body. It meant someone had been called in. Usually the police cars were at a house first. Perhaps someone had died in bed or been found on the floor, an older person with a hip broken in a fall who had stayed there for a day or two with no way to call for help. A newspaper carrier or a mail carrier might have noticed the newspapers or mail hadn't been picked up for a couple of days and phoned the cops. That was the only reason an old black hearse would come cruising through the neighborhood this time of night.

Jack took his seat at the supper table as his wife began putting out the various dishes: a thick beef stew, coleslaw, and biscuits. While she dished it up, he rifled through a stack of mail. He had only gotten home from his factory job a few minutes before—after the usual stop at the bar for a few drinks and a couple of games of darts with the boys—just in time for supper. Jack passed the John Flynn mail across the table to his father and kept the John Flynn II mail for himself.

The white-haired man across the table was in his eighties, but he certainly wasn't on his last legs. With his crooked pug nose and scar over one eyebrow from a pub brawl, the old man still looked tough as a tree stump. When Jack was young, the old man had beaten him with a belt, a coat hanger, a wooden paddle, even a barber's thick razor strop. He'd been a tough disciplinarian who had whipped his son until he was eighteen. And then it was as if Jackie was suddenly an adult—Jack—and the old man stopped hitting him.

Now Jack was 50 and had a young wife of 30, Tina. Tina stood by the stove cooking, with their toddler Maria on her hip. The girl was their firstborn and started out colicky, something Jack took to be simply a terrible temper, which enraged him. But he found ways to keep her in line. Not the strop yet—it was too early for that—but the bare hands on the buttocks and the little finger flicks—plink, plink—on the face. She was learning.

A cry came from the bedroom. The four-month-old was awake now, John III. Johnny, they were calling him, to distinguish the father, the son, and the grandson: John the first, John the second, John the third—John, Jack, and Johnny.

When everything was on the table, Tina deposited Maria in her high chair and sat down at the end. No one moved. They all knew the routine. It was time for grace, something John the patriarch—King John I, Maria called him behind his back—would pronounce. He did it every night. If anyone made the mistake of reaching for a biscuit or started to serve the stew or the coleslaw before the grace, it meant a whack on the hand, either from John—King John I—or from Jack—King John II. Jack was the heir apparent, although nothing seemed that apparent, for although old King John I had suffered a heart attack only a few months before, he didn't appear any closer to departing the earthly realm for the heavenly, if he had a chance of going there at all.

"I might prefer to go where it's warmer," he'd often said jokingly, except there wasn't much humor in his voice. It was the humor of a tyrant. And yet, tyrant that he was, Jack felt something for his father. He didn't know whether it was love or fear, but certainly not admiration.

Then again, perhaps it was admiration; the old man had held the family together when Jack's mother died when he was barely twelve. She had taken a fall down the stairs late one night when she and Jack's father came in from a night of drinking. The two police officers beat the coroner to the scene seemed to think there were more bruises around the woman's cheeks and eyes than would have come from a fall. If she had been killed in the fall, it seemed to them, the blood would have stopped flowing and the bruising wouldn't have occurred. But perhaps because Jack's father knew one of the police officers—and the sergeant and the captain at the station were drinking buddies—no autopsy was performed. No investigation followed, and it was quickly deemed an accident and filed as such. Still, Jack had always wondered.

King John I said the grace and the food began its rounds, beginning with him, of course. It was all sort of medieval, the master of the house getting the best cut, then the next in the pecking order and so on down the line. Tina had learned that if she wanted to assure herself and little Maria of a meal, she had to make plenty of everything each time."

That granddaughter of mine is the cutest thing," John Flynn said. "She's got my eyes."

"Maybe your temperament, too, Dad," Jack said, flashing a quick smile and holding it, hoping his father would latch onto it, too, which he did.

"Nah, I don't think so," the old man replied, and for a moment he looked almost benevolent. "Well, maybe she does. She is pretty sweet." He laughed at his own joke and the rest of the family dutifully followed.

A light shone through the shades and Jack felt a chill run down his spine. Their street wasn't all that well traveled, it was off any of the main roads in a rural section. One never saw Volvos or Mercedes out here; if anything, it was more likely to be dump trucks or pickups, and then only during the day. Any night traffic would be quite late, high school couples going parking or under-aged kids looking for a place to share a bottle of blackberry brandy.

Jack took a mouthful of stew and burned his mouth. He sucked in his breath. "Damn, that's hot!" he snapped, shooting an angry scowl at his wife. "Why didn't you tell us it was so damn hot?"

Tina averted her eyes and said quietly, almost under her breath, "Your dad said he liked the food hot. That's what he said last night."

Just for an instant, Jack's eyes and his father's locked and he shot his father an eye dagger. But King John's gaze didn't flinch or drop, and the old man showed no fear. So Jack turned a withering gaze back onto his wife. She was looking down into her food, head bowed, shoulders slumped. She knew better than to give him an opening, any opening. Jack's anger smoldered with no place to ignite.

Headlights flashed across the window shade again, this time from the opposite direction.

"Who in hell is that out there going back and forth?" Jack snarled, standing up fast. The feet of his chair scraped the wooden floor, the chair nearly tipping over. He walked to the window, placed a finger inside the curtain, and pulled it aside slightly. It was black outside, almost total darkness save for a streetlight fifty yards down the street.

He was about to let go of the curtain when he saw the headlights returning. The old black hearse cruised by slowly. But when it passed under the streetlight he noticed it wasn't the familiar hearse. This one was very old and looked like a '59 Cadillac, the one that had the huge tailfins and looked like a Batmobile. Only this wasn't a Batmobile; it was clearly a hearse and older than 1959. Could this be something an 18 year-old motor-head had bought and custom-painted so he'd be the envy of his school friends? No doubt such an 18 year-old would sport tattoos like Jack's father and Jack had. For a moment he relaxed, his imaginings allowing him to identify with the car's owner.

"Who is it, Jack? Who is it, son?" King John called from his chair at the end of the able.

"Oh, it's just some old beat-up hearse," Jack said. "Looks like the Batmobile."

"The Batmobile?"

Jack heard something in his father's voice he'd never heard before—fear.

"You sure it looks like a Batmobile?"

Jack glanced out the window again. The hearse sat parked under the streetlight, driver's door and passenger door both open. Two huge men in black suits and white shirts stood on the curb. Even at the distance Jack was certain they were wearing sunglasses and the stovepipe hats that reminded him of chimney sweeps.

"They look like Ackroyd and Belushi in The Blues Brothers," Jack said.

"Agh, damn!" his father cursed. "Damn it! Damn it! Damn it! Is there a skull and a crossbones painted on the passenger door?"

Jack squinted. "There's something on there. Could be. Too far to tell, but it sure looks like it."

"Damn!" his father said again. "It's the banshee."

Jack turned. "What?"

"The banshee."

"You mean, like in the movie Darby O'Gill and the Little People—where the phantom stagecoach of Death comes down from the sky to take Darby away because he sold his soul and it is collection time?"

"Yes, basically," the old man said. "I don't know if it's someone surrendering his soul on collection day, as you put it, but it does mean someone here is going to die. The banshee has sent the hearse for it."

Jack thought something in his father's voice sounded false. But he did recall his mother telling him about the banshee before she died.

John Flynn stood up from the table, walked to the gun cabinet in the corner, and withdrew a shotgun and a box of shells.

"Are they here for you, Dad?" Jack asked.

His father cracked the gun's double barrels and plugged a shell into each, emptying the remainder of the shells into his side pocket.

"Dad?"

"Grab yourself that shillelagh by the door, boy," the old man said, pointing to the gnarled wooden stick in the umbrella stand. When Jack didn't move quickly enough, his father's voice grew nasty. "Grab it, boy. Grab it, I said."

Jack's hand closed on the twisted cane his father had used on his back and backside many times.

"Pick it up, boy," his father said. "We may need it."

Jack picked it up, hefted it in one hand, and slapped it against his palm the way his father had done so often when threatening him. Doing it now sent a surge of adrenaline flowing in his system.

"We have to defend ourselves," his father said, and Jack, despite finding it hard to believe that the hearse was anything other than this-worldly, found himself nevertheless responding to his father's orders as if there was no question this was a hearse from hell and the two men the banshee's henchmen.

"Take the girl," the old man commanded Tina. "And get in the bedroom. Hunker down under the covers. We'll let you know when it's safe to come out."

Jack's wide-eyed wife scooped up the toddler in her arms and disappeared into the bedroom.

"Where are they now?" the old man said.

Jack peeked out. One man smoked a cigarette, the other stood looking at his watch. The kitchen clock said 6:29. The two men climbed back into the hearse and its headlights came on with a flicker. It rolled slowly toward the house.

"They're coming!" Jack said.

His father turned the recliner to face the door, sat in it, and drew a blanket up as if he was about to take a nap. He slid the shotgun under the blanket, aiming it at the door.

"Hang onto that shillelagh, son," he said. "This could be the fight of our lives." It was the first time Jack could remember him calling him son.

The hearse had pulled up in front. Its headlights went out and both men got out and walked toward the house.

"They're almost here, Dad."

"Wait for them to ring," the old man said. The old man clutched his chest and popped a nitro pill into his mouth.

The doorbell rang.

"Just a minute," Jack called, gripping the shillelagh so he could do some damage.

"Who is it?" Jack said.

No one answered.

"Who is it?" he said again, still not opening the door.

“We’re here for John Flynn,” said a voice from the other side.

"John Flynn?” Jack said. “He lives somewhere else. He moved.”

“I don’t think so, sir,” said a deep voice from the other side. “This is 804 Back Bonnet. We’re certain John Flynn has not moved. We have instructions to pick him up.”

Jack’s face went white. He looked at his father, whose face had also gone pale.

“You can’t come in just now,” Jack said, stepping back from the door in case they tried to kick it down.

Suddenly the two men were standing inside, though the door hadn’t moved. They were right in front of Jack, as if he had blinked and they’d materialized.

“Who are you?” Jack said. “How’d you get in here?” He gripped tight the shillelagh.

Both men wore black gloves, so Jack couldn’t see their hands. Their sunglasses were oversized and Jack couldn’t see through them. Their hats were pulled down, their collars turned up. What little bit of facial flesh he could see looked more like tanned leather than human skin. The mouths moved weirdly as the men spoke their words.

“John Flynn,” one of them said. “This is a pickup. 6:30 p.m. February 21.”

“February 21 be damned,” Jack yelled, brandishing the shillelagh like a cudgel. “You’re not getting him!”

“Oh, we’ll have him,” the second man said. “We always do.”

“But why?” Jack said. “What’s this all about?”

The first man’s lips moved woodenly. “We have orders to pick up John Flynn.”

“And who do you represent?” Jack said. “Are you with a funeral parlor?”

The second man said in his deep voice, “You might say that.”

The first man raised his voice, “Where is John Flynn? It’s time.”

Jack looked in terror toward his father and saw the blanket move by his knee. His father nodded and Jack backed away. The cover rose slightly and suddenly the shotgun roared. The blast made Jack's eyes squeeze shut, but when he opened them the two men were still there. A second blast pockmarked the door with holes. Cold air blew in through the shattered window, the flapping shade in shreds. The men were unscathed.

"John Flynn," the hearse driver said slowly and deliberately. "John Flynn."

The old man gasped for breath and clutched his chest, his face whiter than ever.

Jack swung the shillelagh with all his might. It cut through the men as if they were fog and struck the front door. The two men never flinched.

"Now!" boomed the voice of the second man. "John Flynn! Now!"

Jack backed closer to his father. "Are you all right, Dad?"

His father looked up weakly, eyelids half-closed with pain.

"Do you need another nitro, Dad?" Jack said.

His father nodded, and Jack grabbed the pillbox from the side table. He slid a pill under his father's tongue.

"Get the hell out of here!" Jack screamed at the ghouls standing over them. "You can't have him."

"John Flynn," the driver said firmly. "Now!"

Jack looked first at his father, then at the bedroom door where Tina and the children lay in hiding.

The men in black raised their right hands then and, for an instant, Jack saw them clearly—or was it his imagination? He was staring into the faces of two skeletons, two skulls under two hoods, two Grim Reapers. He began to cry and shake.

"John Flynn!" their voices boomed in unison.

Jack raised his own bony finger then and for a moment, a fleeting moment, he had a heroic thought. I'm John Flynn, he would say, and his father would finally be proud of him. I'm John Flynn. Take me. But instead he gazed down at his father cowering in the recliner, this old man clutching his chest and wincing in

pain, this old man who had beaten him so many times, dominating him all his life.

"Father, forgive me," Jack said. He made the sign of the cross with one hand and pointed to the bedroom door with the other. "In there's John Flynn. He's in the crib!"

Caretaker

It was one of the first signs of spring: Uncle Warren preparing to mow the graveyard.

The cemetery was an unusual one. There were more than a dozen other graveyards in town: the Catholic cemetery, the small Jewish cemetery, the Congregational cemetery behind the church, another behind the Baptist Church, and many all-purpose cemeteries. Then of course there was a pet cemetery, not in the scary Stephen King *Pet Sematary* sense but a place where people's dogs and cats and parrots were laid to rest—or their ashes, if cremation was the preferred method of disposing of a body—and (thankfully) stayed at rest.

The one Uncle Warren took care of was the Potter Cemetery, a unique graveyard set up by the State of Maine. There were only 25 graves with room for more. Those buried in there, he always told me, were there because no one would claim the bodies. All were men, no women among them. Some had been found dead beneath underpasses or near railroad tracks or in alleys. Their common link was that they had been persons no one, society or individuals, seemed to want. The other link, he told me for years, was that many of them had died violent deaths and those deaths cried out for justice but received none. So his version went.

Uncle Warren, now six months shy of 90, had been tending Potter Cemetery since its inception in 1944. For his labors—mowing, pruning, filling in low spots and keeping the white picket fence around it painted every couple of years—he received the sum of four thousand dollars a year and the free use of a 1954 12'x 25' house trailer which he heated primarily with wood with a kerosene stove backup. For an 89 year-old man he was still tough as a stump and could swing a hammer, handle a light axe or hatchet, and wrangle a lawnmower.

But this year Uncle Warren broke his foot in a fall on the ice around Valentine's Day, so he asked me to come help him with the first mowing or maybe two. I'm 21, three years out of high school and not sure what I want to do with my life. I figured he was joking when he said I should try out for the job of bone yard apprentice.

So on a Friday night in mid-March I went to visit him at his trailer carrying a pint of blackberry brandy that I knew he'd appreciate. Not to say he was a drunkard, not by any means, but he did appreciate a nip or two a couple times a week especially on cold winter nights. He wanted to give me an overview of the plans for mowing the next day. I figured he was starting to get confused, since it was only mid-March in Maine and there'd be no grass for six weeks or more.

"The mower's all gassed up and set to go, Vinnie," he told me. "I cleaned it this week, gapped the spark plugs, sharpened the blade, greased the wheels, and put fresh oil in the crankcase. It's in the shed itching to go."

"You got pruning shears?" I asked, humoring him. "Oiled and sharpened?"

He took my comment as serious. "Don't need those for a while. Won't be trimming the trees and bushes for another month or more. For now it's just mowing."

"And how about a shovel so we can top off any graves that may have settled over the winter?"

"We'll do that next week. No need to worry about that now. Tomorrow we just do the first mowing."

I took a sip of my brandy and asked the obvious. "Uncle Warren, why are we mowing now? There won't be any grass for at least a month."

"Because you've got to get this first mowing in right now, Vinnie, before they get out of control."

I was pretty sure I'd misheard him, thought he'd meant: before it gets out of control, not they. "But Uncle Warren, grass and weeds won't be getting out of control for quite a while."

"Well," he said, tipping back his shot glass and draining the rest of his brandy. "It's more of a mulching project, really. You know, sticks and branches come down over the winter. If you get them now they're not a problem later."

"Then why don't we just take a couple of rakes? Now. Before the grass comes in. Shouldn't be too hard to collect up all the twigs and branches, rake them into piles. We can either burn them or cart them away."

"Nope, nope. That's not the way I do it, that's why. There's a certain way things have to be done here and you've got to learn it. If you've got any idea of taking this over from me in the future—I hadn't said a word to him about this—you've got to learn to do it the right way. I know I can't do it much longer and it's going to take a special person. Being the groundskeeper at Potter Cemetery isn't a job for just anyone."

I fought hard not to giggle. I didn't want to insult my uncle but in my head something as simple as keeping a little one or two acre cemetery in shape didn't seem like it'd require any special talent. But I didn't want to blow the prospect of a job for myself, especially if there was a chance that it might later offer a trailer to live in, too.

"Am I hearing you right?" I asked. "Are you seriously proposing an apprenticeship—helping you, then taking over when you—" I didn't know how to finish the question, so I said, "retire?"

"Something like that. When I die, retire, whatever. For now I need a little help but it's also a good time to train you. I talked to the powers that be and found the State and Town together will kick in a little extra to cover you. Eventually you'll take over from me. They can see it's easier to start this now rather than go through a long process of advertising and interviewing. They know that if I go down, things will get out of hand fast while they waste time interviewing."

He could see I was ready to listen a while longer.

"I think it'd be a good idea if you did learn it whether you stick with it long-term like I did or not. But you've got to pay attention and you've got to do it my way. Agreed?"

I agreed.

"Fine then. We'll see you tomorrow morning, Vinnie. Around 8:30. Come get me here at the trailer."

I downed the rest of my blackberry brandy, grabbed my hat, and said goodnight.

The next morning Uncle Warren and I looked out across the cemetery.

"Well, we caught them just in time," he said.

I had no idea what he could mean. It looked to me as if there was plenty of time. The grass wouldn't be up for weeks and whatever mulching he was talking about could be done over the next month.

"It looks fine to me," I said.

"That's because you don't know what you're looking for. Let's go a little closer. But be careful where you walk here. Leave the mower where it sits."

I stepped from behind the big mower that had been designed for golf courses, a huge beast of a machine with handlebars and grips like a motorcycle. The two of us moved to the very edge of the graveyard.

"Vinnie, you'll need to watch your footing here," Uncle Warren said, "or they'll grab you. You sure as heck don't want to trip and fall down around here." He pointed off to his right a couple of feet. There, sticking out of the ground was a bony wrist and hand. No skin, just bones.

"What is it?"

"It's exactly what it looks like. Just watch for a minute."

We stood over the skeleton hand and I could feel my mouth hanging open. The thumb and fingers flexed—very slowly, to be sure, but they flexed.

I gasped.

My uncle put his hand on my wrist and said softly, "Just wait. Watch."

A moment later the fingers tried to clench again very slowly then straightened out.

"What the devil's going on, Uncle Warren? Is this robotic? Battery-operated? Put here to scare somebody?"

"Vinnie," he said, clutching a little tighter on my wrist, "this is no joke. Look over here." He pointed to his left.

Another bony hand, small enough to be a child's, had broken through the soil as far as the back of the hand but hadn't yet exposed the wrist. There was only the faintest movement in the fingers, nothing more than a twitch.

Ten feet ahead of us I could see two large hands poking through the ground, one a left hand, one a right, about eighteen inches apart, both no more than bones, the skeleton of someone long dead. The fingers and thumbs were wiggling madly as if being jolted every millisecond by electricity.

"That's why we've got to mulch now," Uncle Warren said. "If you don't start now when the ground first softens up, in the mud season they'll get ahead of you. You've got to keep them down early. And like I said, God help you if you fall down."

I scanned the graveyard from where I stood and saw more skeletonized hands, fingers, and wrists poking through the sod.

Uncle Warren tapped me on the arm and pointed to a far corner of the cemetery. "There's a big fellow over there by that tombstone with the greenish moss on it. He killed two little girls in 1956. He's a big strong bugger and you'll want to mow over there at least once a week."

"But—"

"But why doesn't the State do something about it?" Uncle Warren finished. "They tried. They lost two caretakers the first eight months. So they called me in, showed me what was going on, and I told them I'd take care of it. That's what I've been doing ever since 1944—I've been taking care of it. The State people who originally hired me for the job have long since died themselves or retired and moved away. The point is, anyone with any memory of what really happens here is long gone. But the State keeps the checks coming and the amount is so small for taking care of a tiny cemetery that even the biggest budget-cutters don't bother looking to give it the ax. And me? Well, you might think I don't raise the issue because I have a vested interest, thinking I've been feathering my nest all these years, which to some extent is true. But it's also true that there's a lot of accumulated evil here and it wants to manifest itself in some ungodly way from beyond the grave. It's given me a sense of mission, of purpose. And that, as much as anything else, is why I do it."

"But what about the bodies of those calling out for justice—that story you told me so many times over the years?"

"Well, son, it ain't true," Uncle Warren admitted. "I said it because I needed a cover-up. Truth is, once you look at all those graves and markers you'll find they're all between 1944 and the end of the death penalty. They're all full-grown men with the exception of one midget there whose hands look like a child's. And they all committed the most unspeakable crimes. It looks like only 25, but it's 31 because six ain't marked. I've got them all plotted out on a map in the trailer so you can keep track. Each one was put to death by the State. Most of them were legally executed. A few however had unfortunate accidents at the Big House just after the death penalty was declared unconstitutional by the State."

I was too stunned to speak and my uncle saw that. He took advantage of the silence. "This foot of mine—I told you it was a broken foot and that I slipped on the ice. That's close to the truth."

He sat on a boulder and pulled up his pants leg then took off his shoe and sock. "This here's why I've been laid up. Four broken bones, one a compound fracture of the little toe, the other a compound fracture of the big toe. And over 100 stitches." He rubbed his foot. "It's cold most of the time, too, damaged the nerves. I was lucky to break free of him and get help before I could bleed to death."

He read the shock in my face. "That's right, Vinnie. It was him." He pointed an accusing finger out over the cemetery at the pair of huge hands. "And them." He made a sweeping hand gesture that covered the whole graveyard. "I'm—I'm afraid I'm getting too old and weak to fight them off."

He looked me square in the eye and I swallowed hard. I knew what was coming next.

"You might have taken over if it was a cushy job with just a little cemetery to mow. But what about now? Are you up to it, Vinnie?"

I said nothing. My heart was pounding fast. I felt like he'd asked me to charge an enemy machine gun nest alone. He saw the fear written across my face.

"I'm sorry, nephew, I know I've placed you in an awkward position. And you don't have to say yes or no now. But promise me you'll think on it, Vinnie. Think on it and let me know. If you say no I've still got time to try and find somebody else."

I nodded weakly. "I'll think on it, Uncle Warren." I started to walk away.

"Wait a minute, nephew," he called out. "You can't leave just yet. We've got to get this first mowing in and it's got to be today. I need you even if it's only for today. Help me today and then let me know tomorrow. That'll give me time to get somebody else."

Out of the corner of my eye I saw several bony fists clutching and releasing. The giant set of hands seemed to beckon me. My own hands trembled.

"Just this once," I said. "I'll help you out this once, Uncle Warren, because of your foot. I doubt I'll say yes. In fact, I'm sure I'll say no. But I'll call and give you my answer in the morning."

"Thanks, son," Uncle Warren said with a grin. "I appreciate it, Vinnie. But don't be surprised if you find it's more fun than you thought."

I fired up the engine, engaged the deadly blade, and put the big mower in gear. For a brief moment as I looked out over the twitching, clutching field before me, my heart was in my throat and I was afraid. But then once I advanced upon the graveyard and heard the crack and crunch of bones, twigs, and branches, the fear subsided and I felt a rush of adrenaline, a thrill of pure power.

"Chew them up good, Vinnie," Uncle Warren yelled to me from his perch on the boulder. "Chew up as many of those wretches as you can, son. Lay into them." He sounded insane, almost gleeful. "Don't forget, though, they come back up again and again like the grass and the weeds—all fresh and new and nasty."

I turned the mower in the direction of the giant hands and took aim. The hands opened and closed like pincers as I bore down. I knew right then that I didn't need until morning to give Uncle

Warren his answer. I'd tell him when I finished the first mowing. I felt giddy. And to think they'd pay me to do it.

Beneath the Streets

There was only one little movie theater in town and nothing playing that we wanted to see. So Jake, Luca, Spider, and I dug out our slingshots and walked toward the docks. After we blasted or sank all the soda cans we tossed in the water we headed for the big cement drainpipe everybody called The Tunnel.

It really wasn't a tunnel but was a huge cement culvert that served as the outlet for the business district's underground storm drain system that was buried beneath the streets. When it rained the water would run along the curbside gutters and disappear down the street grates to enter a maze of these giant concrete pipes. The flood would spill through the system toward The Tunnel and gush out the end over the sand and into the bay. Much of the time, if there'd been no rain for a while it was either damp or dry.

At least that's what we figured. We really didn't know because none of us—and nobody we knew—had ever gone in farther than the first straight 100-yard stretch we called The Tunnel. After that the system made a right turn into unknown territory—a new dark block-long tunnel that ran from Third Street to Front Street where it made another right turn. Or so we estimated based on the gutter drain-grates we had seen on the downtown streets. The Tunnel was round and about four feet in diameter, hard to stand up straight in. The four of us had never gone far past the first right turn, nor had anybody else from what we'd heard.

"You looking for Tom Thumb?" a voice asked from the boardwalk that ran above the entrance to The Tunnel. We all flinched. Luca and I stepped out of The Tunnel and looked up.

It was one of a group we called the Scary Kids. This guy had dropped out of school in eighth grade and worked at a local junkyard. He must have been 16 or 17, maybe older.

Jake and Spider came out and looked up, too.

The Scary Kid repeated, "You looking for Tom Thumb?"

Tom Thumb was less than four feet tall, in his 30s or 40s we guessed, and would be described today by two terms: little person and street person. He was very short with a tight little face and beady eyes. And nobody knew where he lived. No matter if it was winter or summer he wore a navy blue ski cap so we couldn't tell if he was bald or had a rat's nest of hair under it. He had a heavy scraggly beard, a plump body, and looked like a fat-cheeked rodent: a groundhog or a beaver. Our parents had cautioned us to steer clear of Tom Thumb.

One time Jake and I had gotten near him at a convenience store. He reeked of body odor. As we finished paying for our gum, Tom Thumb whispered hoarsely, “A penny apiece for any frogs or salamanders you git me.” He didn't say *get* me, he said *git* me.

We averted our eyes, not answering, and walked out.

“No,” Luca said to the Scary Kid. “We weren’t looking for anybody, and certainly not Tom Thumb. Why? Did you lose him?” Luca laughed at his own wise-guy joke and so did we but the Scary Kid didn't catch it.

“Not hardly. But I been sitting over there on the dock for three hours fishing. I seen him go in there right after I set down to fish. He never come out.”

“He never came out?" Jake asked. "You sure? Maybe he came out while you were pulling up a fish or baiting your hook?”

“Don’t think so. I still got the same piece of squid on my hook that I started with. Wasn’t nothing biting so I just been keeping my eye on The Tunnel. I’m telling you, he ain’t come out. He went in but he ain’t come out.”

“You going in after him?” Spider asked him.

“No way. I ain’t going in there. Heard too many things about The Tunnel. Besides, I ain’t got no flashlight.”

“I've got one,” Luca said, pulling a penlight out of his pocket. He hadn't mentioned to us that he had one, maybe because he was afraid we'd suggest going into the dark maze.

“I've got one, too,” Jake said, and pulled one out on a key ring that had no keys.

“Well then, you guys go in looking, if you want," Scary Kid said. "I wouldn’t go in there if you paid me.” He turned and walked away.

“All right, what now?” Spider asked. "We've finally got a couple of flashlights. No excuses left."

Trying to sound practical and not wimpy, I said, "Well, it’s already 3:45 and I’ve got to be home by 5:30 for supper. Doesn't really leave enough time to go exploring today. Besides I’m not worried about finding that Tom Thumb weirdo. Mom and Dad said to stay clear of him.”

“What if he’s in trouble?” Spider asked. “What if he broke a leg and needs help?”

“If he broke a leg," I replied, "he'd yell up through one of those grates to somebody on the street.”

“Maybe he’s out cold,” Luca said. “What if he hit his head and can’t yell? He could be unconscious.”

“Whoever found him and saved his life would be heroes," Jake said, "and get their picture in the newspaper and be on TV.”

I could see the tide turning against me. “Maybe we should do it tomorrow, when we’re not so rushed.”

“But what if he really is hurt?” Spider pressed. “That’d be a whole day’s delay getting him to a hospital.”

“What if he’s not hurt at all?” I countered. “Maybe, just maybe *he lives in here* in a little apartment.”

Jake, Luca, and Spider stared at me. They knew a lame argument when they heard one.

“I think we better get in fast,” Spider said. “A half hour in, a half hour out, and we still have fifteen minutes to get home. Deal?”

“Deal,” Luca and Jake agreed. They crossed their arms and waited.

“Oh, alright, deal,” I said reluctantly.

It took only a minute or two to get to the first right turn. We headed up Third Street, only needing the flashlights for the dark stretches between overhead grates that let sunlight in.

Along the way we found junk that that had been swept down from the gutters: twigs, branches, straw, dead grass, bottles, cans, paper, wads of newspaper, cupcake wrappers, a plastic doll's head, and plenty of loose stones and sand left by the runoff water. We reached the junction with Front Street, the main drag through the business district, and followed it a ways until we reached First Street. We had two choices then: continue straight on Front or take a left on First. First Street looked darker to me, more ominous.

"Left," Spider decided for us. "Let's take First. It's only a short block to Adams, which is behind the department store. Maybe there's a grate we can lift off so we can climb up to the street. It'll save walking all the way back bent-over in these tunnels."

"Or we could just turn around now and retrace our path," I suggested. "Nobody down here but us. We've seen what there is to see and we've probably explored farther than—"

A high-pitched squeaking stopped me mid-sentence. Not a screeching but a squeaking—coming from somewhere in the darkness down First. Nobody moved. After a minute frozen in place we relaxed a little and lowered our voices.

"Too big for a mouse," Jake said.

"Way too big," Luca said. "Unless it's got a megaphone."

We laughed nervously, quietly.

"Well, it doesn't make any difference," I whispered. "It's time to head back. We agreed on a half hour."

Still no one moved.

"Come on, you guys," I pleaded, trying not to sound whiny. "Remember? Half hour in, half hour out, fifteen minutes to get home."

After a moment Jake seemed to shift over to my side. "We did say that."

Spider started to object but clammed up when we heard the squeak again. It was followed by several softer, slightly different squeaks.

"Could it be alligators?" Luca asked. "I heard about people bringing them back from Florida—baby ones that grew too big to keep so they got flushed down the toilets."

Jake shook his head. "Alligators don't squeak. "Porpoises or dolphins maybe, but not alligators."

"You think it's the guy?" Luca asked. "Tom Thumb?"

"He doesn't squeak either," I said. "Jake and I heard him in the convenience store. His voice isn't that high."

"What about if it *is* him and he's hurt?" Spider asked.

"If he was hurt he wouldn't be squeaking," Jake said. "We'd be hearing words."

"Whatever it is," I said, "we've got to—"

"Hold your horses, for crying out loud!" a voice far down the tunnel cried. It wasn't exactly a yell but it was loud, not quite commanding but forceful. And deeper, raspier than the squeaks.

"Now *that* sounded like Tom Thumb," Jake said.

I thought of Tom Sawyer and Huck Finn trapped in the cave with the escaped murderer Injun Joe. Everything about this underground tunnel screamed *get out, get out while you still can.*

"Hey!" a voice warned in the distant darkness. "Slow down, I said! Wait your turn! Don't shove!"

I began backing away from the junction but Spider started up First toward the voice. Jake and Luca were a step behind him, drawn to the mystery, I suppose. I gave in and brought up the rear.

Almost immediately we came to the junction Spider had figured was there, Adams Street, the short dead-end. That seemed to be where the noises were coming from. Jake and Luca snapped on their flashlights but kept them shielded and pointed down by their feet. They inched forward toward what looked like a blank wall at the end of Adams.

Spider reached it first. There was another junction we weren't expecting, this one to the right. Above his head was a small grate that let a little light through. He hugged the wall and carefully peeked around the corner. I heard him gasp. He tried to back away but Jake, Luca, and I pressed forward. We had to see. There, in what looked like a huge nest made of straw, beach weed, leaves, and trash, lay a rat the size of a full-grown hog. It was on its side, and suckling at its swollen breasts were many smaller rats. I say smaller but that was in relation to the big one. Each of the smaller ones was three times the size of the largest sewer rats I'd ever seen.

These were as big as small dogs and there were eight or ten of them.

The mother rat had large eyes with black centers but she didn't seem focused on us. They were rolled back in her head. I had seen kittens and puppies nursing before, pushing and scrambling over each other to reach the lifeline, but it never occurred to me that rats might behave the same way.

The closer I looked, the more I realized that these were not baby rats with closed eyes and untrained muscles. These were adult rats that hadn't yet attained the size of the giant mother feeding them. These were capable, dangerous adult rats that could turn on us at any time. We backed away from the corner before they could spot us.

And then we heard the voice again. "Wait your turn, I said! Wait your turn!" We sneaked another quick glance and saw what we had overlooked at first glance: in the midst of the suckling rats was Tom Thumb on his stomach, partially covered by the others as he jockeyed for position at the mother's swollen breasts. The squeaking we'd heard had been coming from his—what were they—half-siblings or step-siblings. Tom Thumb's was the only human voice in the litter.

I grabbed the back of Luca's and Jake's shirts, got their attention, and motioned *let's go* with my thumb. They nodded. Spider drew back from the corner then and whispered, "I think they were sniffing the air. Go. Go."

We crept as quickly but quietly as we could to the First Street junction and turned toward Front, making a quick check of the corridor behind us as we went. I thought I saw a dark mass clogging the bottom of the Adams Street tunnel where we had been standing watching the hungry brood. The dark shadow was advancing slowly, perhaps following our scent. They knew someone had spied on them.

"They're coming!" I whispered, trying not to shriek. "No sense trying to move quietly. They're onto us. Go!"

We turned the corner of Front Street and started scrambling through the long straightaway that would take us to Third Street and the homestretch to The Tunnel.

Occasionally when we got near a shaft of light from above Spider would try pushing up on a street grate, hoping we could climb up and out sooner. But they were all either stuck or had a parked car's wheel on them.

"Keep moving," I croaked. "Faster."

But the cement drain pipes were too low for us to sprint. It was like running inside a barrel. We knew we needed to put distance between ourselves and the army of rats pursuing us, but the best we could manage was an awkward, hunched-over straddle-run that was exhausting. None of our pursuers was as tall as the cement pipe.

It seemed likely they hadn't actually seen us yet but had either heard or smelled us and were advancing cautiously from Adams into the tunnel for First. But once they swung from First to Front's long straightaway they'd spot us and give chase faster.

"Okay, here's the plan," Jake said as we ran. "The next turn's the left onto Third. Start picking up rocks for the slingshots. Put some in your pockets but not so many as to slow yourself down. When they start to catch up to us, turn and fire. Hopefully that'll slow them down."

We moved fast up Front scooping stones as we ran. Spider and I brought up the rear. Halfway to Third I heard loud hissing and squeaking. A voice behind us in the distance yelled, "Hey, you!" They had seen us. Tom Thumb had seen us. Was he leading the charge? I glanced back and saw a shadowy blob moving faster now, chasing us.

We passed under the curbside grate by the movie theater—the last grate before the Third Street left turn. We had 100 yards to cover to get to it. The rats were 50 yards back and gaining, squeaking loudly now.

"Jake! Luca!" I yelled. "Go for Third. Spider and I will cover your retreat. When you get there, don't make the turn. Stop and set yourselves up to give the two of us cover fire. Shoot ricochets at the walls beside us so you don't hit us. We'll catch up and pass you. When we get a ways down Third, you pack up and run while we stop and cover you the same way. We leapfrog back to The Tunnel in pairs."

No questions asked they took off. Spider and I turned and fired our slingshots as fast as we could—five, 10, 20 times each—all the time waddling backwards.

The horde slowed its unrelenting advance only slightly.

"The turn's right behind you," I heard Jake yell. "Get out of the way and we'll let them have it."

Spider and I ducked down and then dodged into the Third Street tunnel as Luca and Jake began releasing mad volleys. Then with Spider and me barely 25 yards into the tunnel they fired a final volley from their position and ran after us.

With us in the Third Street tunnel and the rats still in the Front Street straightaway, we were temporarily out of their line of sight. It was a momentary comfort but it also meant we didn't know exactly how close they were.

"I hope you two have some ammo left," Jake yelled as he and Luca caught up to us. "We're almost empty."

"We're out," I said. "But there's a pile of stones by the final turn. Spider and I will stop and set up there while you two squeeze past and run for the beach. There'll be plenty of stones at the mouth of The Tunnel so you can cover us. We won't be far behind."

Suddenly the squeaking reached a fever pitch.

"Look!" Luca yelled. "They've made the turn! They're in this pipe and closing fast!"

"Keep moving!" Spider ordered. My legs felt like rubber.

The next thing I knew Spider and I were at the rock pile by the last turn. We set up, each of us on one knee with nature's ammunition pile between us.

"It's dark," I yelled to Luca and Jake. "Move single-file in the center of the tunnel with your flashlights in front of your mouths so we don't hit you."

Two lights rose from waist height to face height, centered in the pipe.

“Let them have it!” Spider said, and we began firing stones off the walls to the side of the flashlight beams.

The squealing and screeching told me we were scoring some hits. A voice—not Jake's or Luca's—growled, “Ow! Why, you little—"

Jake and Luca came into view then passed us, making the final turn into The Tunnel. With them out of the way Spider and I were able to fire our volleys straight down the middle into the dark blob advancing on us. The pack couldn't be more than 75 yards away.

“Time to scoot," Spider said, and grabbed my arm. We ran, hearing Jake and Luca yelling “Come on! Move! Move!” as they took up their position outside the mouth of The Tunnel.

The squeaking rose again now that Spider and I weren't hitting them with anything. It was down to a foot race but I sensed we could win it. We were more than halfway out when the rats turned the last corner where Spider and I had made our rock-pile stand. We slowed and turned to look back at them just as Luca and Jake shined their little flashlights toward them.

The advance stopped and they ceased their squeaking. There were 10 or 12 of them about two feet up, their pink eyes glowing as they reflected Jake and Luca's flashlight beams. And there another two feet above the rat pack was another pair of glowing pink eyes, Tom Thumb’s.

“Should we keep firing?" Luca asked.

"No," Spider answered. "They've had enough for one day. And we're all safe."

Tom Thumb and his half-siblings or step-siblings, whatever they were, turned and disappeared back into the darkness of the Third Street tunnel. The four of us lay on the beach exhausted, like Jonah in the Bible story after the whale vomited him up. When we caught our breath and felt strong enough, we headed home.

We told our parents right away and the police later that night. A cop and two Road Department guys pulled up the Adams Street grate and dropped down into the culvert where we had seen the nursing mother and her brood. They said that what we had described as “a huge nest” was actually no more than a strewn-about mess of branches, straw, grass and leaves. *Ruined by Tom Thumb so his family would escape detection*, I thought. No rats anywhere, the men said, no sewer rats, no triple-size sewer rats like we had said, and certainly no giant mother rat the size of a hog.

They never bothered checking out Tom Thumb, because the idea of him being part of a family of giant rats was ludicrous. Still, we were surprised he didn't leave town now that we knew about him. His staying around made things awkward for us. We did our best to avoid him and only ran into him once after that in front of the bowling alley. He was sitting on the steps when we walked past on the sidewalk.

"Hey, kids," he said, not looking up at first. "A penny apiece for frogs and salamanders." Then he looked up, stopped himself cold, and stared at us with those beady eyes. I swear, for just a second—when they caught the sunlight—his pupils glowed pink. His nose wrinkled and he sniffed the air around him.

We backed away.

"Free advice, boys," he growled, and shot Luca and Jake a leer that exposed a picket fence of rotten teeth. "If you and your friends here know what's good for you, you'll stay above ground. Next time you won't be so lucky."

The Camp

A simple break-in, that's all we planned. We were looking to get some money to buy booze and cigarettes, so we figured a basic home invasion was the way to go. Well, not a real home; we'd break into a summer camp. Might be a little cash in a drawer. Nobody ever left any expensive jewelry or anything, but usually there was something we could pawn off pretty quick—stereo, microwave, TV—to make fifty or a hundred bucks. Then, of course, since we were minors, we'd need somebody else to buy the beer and cigarettes for us.

So we targeted Squanto Pond, because we knew nobody would be up there so late in the year. If anybody was around, it'd just be for ice fishing. Even so, the camps weren't much in use; the ice fishermen tended to come in by snowmobile and went out the same day.

There were about fifty camps around the pond. Some were nice, some pretty ratty, some you wouldn't put trailer trash in.

The lake was maybe a mile end to end. We parked just off the access road and hoofed it in. It didn't occur to us that if we picked up anything big, like a stereo or a microwave, we'd have to lug it all the way back out to the car. Chalk that up to our inexperience. We'd only done a few break-ins and my partners weren't known as the sharpest knives in the drawer.

Benny dropped out of high school when he was a freshman. And Gregor—whose real name was Gregory, but Gregor sounded cooler than Greg—had dropped out when he was a sophomore. I hadn't dropped out; I was just hanging around with these guys, taking another day off from the grind of tenth grade. If my parents knew I was skipping school, they'd have been mortified, and it they knew why I was skipping, *yeouch*.

We walked past three or four prospective targets. When we got to a red cedar building about forty feet by thirty feet, with a nice deck overlooking Squanto Pond, we knew it was the place. There was no smoke from the chimney and we didn't see any tracks going into or out of the place. The snow was hard and crunchy enough that we didn't worry too much about our own tracks. It would likely be spring before any break-in was discovered, and if it was reported at all—many of the camp-owners didn't bother, they just complained, because the follow-up from the police wasn't so good—by the time anyone investigated, the snow would be melted and any tracks gone.

Gregor used a small pry bar to pop the back door, then put his shoulder to the inside door to force it. It didn't take much. It was one of those simple locks, and when the door popped, there was hardly any damage. In fact, we were able to close it behind us, the latch barely catching.

What surprised us was that it was warm inside. The place had electric heat, and the power hadn't been turned off. We snapped on the lights. The clocks on the microwave and on the wall were both running. The place had a nice kitchen and looked like it could have been lived in year-round. The thermostat read 68 degrees.

"Crap," Benny said. "You think somebody's living here?"

We spread out, took a quick look around, but didn't see anybody.

"Doesn't matter," Gregor said. "Let's take what we need and get out. And if there is somebody living here, maybe there's some cash or jewelry."

"This just doesn't feel right," I said. "It's one thing to burglarize a summer camp, but a place where somebody's living? What if they come back while we're here?"

"They won't," Gregor said. "There were no tracks in or out, no sign anybody's been here for awhile. My guess is, somebody left in after foliage season and forgot to turn off the electric and drain the pipes." He lifted a finger and pointed at the kitchen sink, which had a slight drip.

"Or maybe a renter skipped out without telling the landlord," Benny said.

We stood looking at each other for a minute. Things didn't make much sense, no matter how much Gregor and Benny tried to explain them.

"I think we ought to just get out of here," I said.

"We're already in," Benny said. "We may as well take advantage of it and then get out. Spread out."

There were four rooms and a bathroom, so it was easy to check out. Benny took the bathroom and the kitchen/dining area, Gregor took the two bedrooms, and I took what looked like the family room. Mine was the largest in the house, with a fireplace, sofa, three easy chairs, and a pool table. There were paintings of naked women on the wall. They weren't pornographic or obscene; they were nudes in the sense of the Greek or Roman paintings, although they weren't from those times. These were modern nudes—eight of them.

I made my way quickly from one painting to the next, checking behind them for a safe—as if I'd have known what to do if I found one. Unless it was unlocked, I'd have no chance of getting into it. It didn't matter; there was nothing but wall behind the paintings. I spotted a huge television, but I knew there was no way I could lug it out; even the three of us together would find it difficult. I checked the drawers of the end table, the coffee table, and the buffet next to the fireplace.

"Find anything?" Gregor called from the bedroom doorway.

"Nothing but a well-used microwave," Benny said from the kitchen. "It's filthy."

"No jewelry in the bedroom. No cash either," Gregor said. "Anything in the big room?"

"Nothing I can find," I said, and proceeded to look for change in the couch cushions.

"Never mind that," Gregor said. "I don't mean chump change. I mean something of value."

Suddenly the paintings caught their eyes.

"Wow!" Benny said. "Look at those."

"Far out!" Gregor said. "Who do you think these broads are?"

"I don't think they're broads," I said. "I don't think they're locals at all. I think these are paintings of models who sat for famous artists."

"Oh really, Mr. Smarty Pants?" Benny said. "Looks to me like they're all painted by the same person."

I looked at the paintings again. He was right. All eight paintings had a similarity to them, something that connected them, a style, a brush stroke, the way the women were posed, a similar sense of color, something that said they were all painted by the same artist.

"They were done here," Gregor said. "In this room. Look at the backgrounds."

He was right. Each had been painted somewhere in the room, near the fireplace with a fire going.

"So now we know, whoever who owns the place is a painter," Benny said.

"Maybe," Gregor said. "But I didn't see paints. No easel, no canvas. Nothing about it says a painter lives here."

"Maybe the painter shoots photographs here," I said, "and then paints from the photographs elsewhere. My Uncle Harry does it. With the sun is always changing, it's hard to paint at some locations, so he shoots a picture. Or if he's traveling and sees something he wants, he takes a snapshot he can paint from later."

"Makes sense," Gregor said.

The two of them walked over to the pool table.

"Want to play?" Benny asked.

"We haven't got time," I said. "We've got to get out before somebody comes back."

"Nobody's coming back," Gregor said. "Let's play. Benny, you rack. Round-robin nine-ball."

"Wait a minute," Benny said. "Look at those paintings. I heard somebody say this about the Mona Lisa, that famous painting—her eyes follow you all around the room. That's what these do. Look at them. Wherever you go, they watch."

We began moving around the room.

"Yeah," Gregor said. "Ain't that weird?"

"It's pretty neat," I said. "I don't know if it's a painter's trick or what, but it seems pretty cool."

"Yeah? Well, it creeps me out," Benny said.

"Aw, come on. Let's shoot some pool," Gregor said impatiently. "It's warm in here. Nobody's around. We can hike out later. This way the day won't be a total loss."

The three of us walked back to the pool table.

"Grab the corners on that cover," Gregor said. "Peel it back to this end and throw it in the chair."

Benny and I each grabbed a corner of the huge sheet covering the pool table and pulled it back.

"Holy crap!" Gregor said.

We stopped and caught a glimpse of the terror in Gregor's eyes as he stared at the exposed table. There lay a naked man, white as a sheet, face-up in a bath of silvery liquid. There was no green felt cover like on a normal pool table; there was nothing but the liquid with the man floating in it. The only parts of him above the surface were his toe tips, fingertips, navel, and face.

"What the—" Benny swore.

We stood there as if our feet were glued to the carpet. I wanted to scream, but I couldn't take my eyes off the man who looked like he'd been frozen in the ice. Except this wasn't ice. It was some kind of silvery liquid. Not water. Mercury? Not exactly mercury, either, because it was clear enough that it had to be partly water.

"Who do you think he is?" Gregor asked. "Is he dead?"

"I don't know," I said. "Benny?"

"I don't know," Benny said. "I can't tell. He doesn't smell."

"That's because he's underwater," Gregor said.

"What are we supposed to do?" I asked. "Should we call the police?"

"No," Gregor said. "We don't want to get involved in this. If we call, they'll come out and investigate. And if we call anonymously—before our tracks melt away—they may figure out who we are and connect us with it, think we did something. It won't work. We just need to get out of here."

I couldn't take my eyes off the body in the pool table.

"He couldn't have pulled the cover over himself," Benny said. "Somebody else must be involved."

"You're right," I said. "So somebody could be coming back. Let's cover him up and get out."

Benny and I pulled the cover back over the pool table and arranged it the way we found it.

"Wait," Gregor said. "We can't leave the cover. It's got fingerprints now. We'll take it with us."

"But what about everything we touched?" Benny asked.

"We haven't touched much. Remember where you went and start wiping," Gregor said. "There's a roll of paper towels there by the sink. We'll take the paper towels and pool table cover when we leave."

We spent five minutes wiping down every surface we could remember touching. After I had wiped the end tables, coffee table, and buffet, I went to the paintings and wiped the frames all the way around. Each time I moved a painting, in the back of my mind like I heard a tiny *eek*, a little scream, no louder than a mouse. I was in a hurry and didn't have time to think about it. But each picture I went to, gave out that *eek* sound. When I finished, I stood in the center of the room, looking for any spot I might have missed. I felt the eyes of the women on me.

"You guys," I said. "Come here."

The two of them came back into the big family room.

"You done?" Gregor asked. "We finished ours."

"Just stand here a second," I said. Listen. See if you hear a noise, even a very faint noise, coming from the paintings."

The three of us stood there a full thirty seconds but heard nothing.

"Okay," I said. "Now go up to one of those paintings—use your sleeve so you don't leave a fingerprint—and try moving the frame. Move it a little and see if you hear anything."

Gregor walked to a painting and moved it. "I see what you mean," he said. It's like a squeak. The painting's not on a hinge, so it's not that kind of a squeak. It's almost like a—"

"*voice*," Benny finished, moving a picture frame. "It sounds like a voice."He and Gregor touched another painting.

"I don't know what it is," I said. "But it's pretty creepy. It's time to hit the road."

Gregor and Benny headed for the door.

"Wait a minute," I said. "The paper towels. Put them in a bag so we can take them with us. And what about the pool table cover?"

"Maybe we could just wipe it," Benny said as he threw the paper towels in a paper bag.

"No," Gregor said. "Take the cover. We'll burn it later."

"But if we take it," I said, "we've got to—you know—*look at him again*."

"We'll make it fast," Gregor said. "Rip it back, fold it up, and get the heck out. Ready? Go!"

Benny and I grabbed the cover, peeled it back quickly and folded it once, then again and again, trying not to look at whoever or whatever was under it. We never folded a sheet or a blanket as fast in our lives. I stood there with it under my arm.

"Oh geezum," Gregor said. "Did you feel that? The temperature must have dropped ten degrees just now."

He was right. And it hadn't dropped slowly, as if we'd changed the thermostat; it dropped while we were folding the cover.

We stared down at the man in the silver pool whose surface rippled now. His eyelids snapped open, the centers of his eyes looking like my grandmother's cataracts, huge and cloudy. He didn't blink.

We all tried to yell out, but before we could, chaos broke loose as women began screaming around us, wailing and crying "Oh no!" and "Help!" and "Save me!" from the paintings which trembled and shook, tilting this way and that, wooden frames clattering as they threatened to loose themselves from the hooks they hung from. The silvery liquid rippled wildly, as if an earthquake was gaining strength somewhere deep below.

I looked at Gregor and Benny, who had clapped his hands over their ears.

"Get out now!" I shouted, and we were out the door in a second, sprinting across the snow in our heavy boots.

When we got to the car, Benny had the bag of paper towels, but I didn't have the pool table cover. I don't know if I carried it some or all of the distance or if I dropped it on the floor in the big room. I have no memory of it.

We drove as fast as we could for twenty minutes, then stopped at a diner to warm up with coffee, get rid of the jitters, and talk about what we'd do. After an hour we decided to call the police. They sent an officer to talk to us at the diner. He called for a second person to go to the camp with him. We wouldn't go, but gave the cop our names and addresses.

They found the paintings on the floor where they had fallen and they found the pool table with its holding tank—the cover over it—but there was no body in the liquid. Wet footprints led out of the room to the porch. But that was as far as the footprints went. The person had vanished into thin air.

There were no bodies, no blood, no crime scene except for our breaking and entering, which was by our own admission. If the man's fingerprints had been on the paintings, I had wiped them off. We later got off with a misdemeanor.

The paintings matched the photographs of eight women reported missing over a four-year period. A recording on the message machine at the camp asked respondents for the Models-Wanted-to-Pose-for-Artist ad to leave their names and phone numbers, and the artist would get back to them. Two women had left their information. When the cops checked on them, they were safe. So maybe we saved a couple of them. No bodies were ever found, either the eight women's or the man's.

Gregor and Benny started a trash hauling business.

I returned to high school and finished. Then, surprisingly, I went on to become a minister. I figured if there really was a cosmic battle of Good and Evil going on, I wanted to be closer to the one side than the other.

The Power of the Pen

They had always been close, this brother and sister. But then, too, they'd always been competitive, and for the most part in their growing-up years she had bested him. Now they were in their thirties and each living comfortably on the inheritance from their deceased parents.

She continued to live in their hometown of Salem, Massachusetts, writing her poetry and venturing out only occasionally for church or to attend a meeting of the Board of Directors for Salem's Witch Museum. He, on the other hand, had moved away to a small town near Lancaster, Pennsylvania, in Amish Country. He hadn't joined the Amish, but he did appreciate their simple lifestyle. So, although they had gone in different directions, this brother and sister still had some similarities, preferring the simple, reclusive lifestyle.

They had not seen each other in a number of years. Was it four? Or five? But they kept in touch by letter several times a week. Time and distance had helped them forget some of their differences, and in an odd way, not seeing each other regularly had perhaps deepened their relationship. Perhaps.

Thursday, September 2
Dearest sister,

My job at the library goes well, even if only part time. I enjoy being amongst the books and find that I love the relative quiet of the place. The interaction I have with patrons is pleasant. There is of course the usual small talk as they bring in books or check them out. And because I'm only there 16 hours a week, this being a small-town library, I find the demands of the job not too taxing. The obvious bonus is, I become familiar with more books than I would if I were only a patron of the library. My only regret must be that my life will surely end before I can read all the books I'd like to read. For the first time in a long time, I feel happy, almost content (and perhaps that too will come).

I appreciated the last poem you sent. It was an excellent piece of work and conveyed much deep feeling. If I were to critique any part of it, it would be the last line, the sense of which may be a bit unclear to the reader. That occurs, I think, because of the forced rhyme on the last word. I know you are sensitive about your poems, but I trust this comment will help your work to be even finer than it already is.

I hope your work with the board at the Witch Museum continues to be fulfilling.

Your loving brother,

Robert

Wednesday, September 8

My dear little brother,

I am happy to hear that your new job at the library suits you. While it may be a basic clerk's position, there is no shame in that. If anyone were to ask me, I would assure them that our parents' fortune provides you with more than adequate income, and that the library position is more a public service on your part, much the same as my agreeing to sit on the Board of Directors at the Witch Museum.

I will take your critique of my poem's last line under consideration.

Yesterday several of us from the Board of Directors attended a lecture and demonstration given by a modern witch at the Museum. The woman looked to be a hundred years old and claimed she was closer to two hundred. She cast a few spells. There was quite a large group from the public in attendance and the spells were a hit.

My only regret is that I sat in the front row. The room was warm, so we had the overhead fans on. During one particular spell the fan above me blew some of the powder in my direction, causing me to sneeze seven times. I have never sneezed seven times in succession in my entire life, and when I sneezed the seventh time, the witch gave me the strangest look and said, "Seven. Seven only. Seven." I have no idea what she meant, and when I pressed her about it afterward, she refused to explain further.

The sneezing episode brought to mind how sick you were from the influenza that winter you were eight and I was nine. Oh, how I worried about you then. That same year, you'll recall, in the summer and fall, we played croquet with Mom and Dad almost every afternoon. After what must have been five hundred games, you finally beat me for once. You played well, though I recall that you won by a lucky shot, your ball striking a rock that diverted it into the final post. Then you crowed mercilessly about your victory the entire rest of the day.

I will send another of my poems, but not with this letter, perhaps with the next. I have a little tweaking to do on it first.

Your loving sister,
Elizabeth

Monday, September 13
Dearest sister,

So strange, you sneezing exactly seven times. (I've been sneezing a lot lately, too, and may have a touch of the flu.) Obviously the witch's powder was an irritant to your mucous membranes. You don't think it was in any way toxic, do you? Has it continued? Have you manifested other symptoms? Perhaps you should consult Dr. Mather, just to be certain there are no long-term effects. I hate to be a worrywart about your health, but you know I've always been a bit of a hypochondriac myself. Please take care of yourself.

Me? I'm healthy as a horse, finally. I'm trying to learn to be more social, but it's not easy. At my boss's suggestion I tried out for a bit part in a small skit we're doing as a fundraiser here at the library. Guess what? I got the part. It's only two lines, but all the same I'm excited about it. Imagine, your brother, the thespian!

I look forward to receiving another of your poems.

Your loving brother,

Robert

Saturday, September 18
My dear little brother,

No need to worry, the sneezes stopped at seven. Thank you for your concern.

Good luck with the little play. I'm surprised you tried out for a part (and more surprised you got it). Until now the only acting I'd ever seen you do was acting innocent, like the time Mom accused me of stealing her pie from the windowsill. You let her punish me instead. Good luck with the acting. As they say in the theater, break a leg.

I've enclosed the new poem I promised you. I like it quite well myself.

Your loving sister,
Elizabeth

Friday, September 24
Dearest sister,

Sorry to be so long answering your letter, but the day I received it I actually broke my leg. I tripped over a footstool during rehearsal and tumbled off the stage. It was a nasty compound fracture, the shinbone protruding through a bloody mass of flesh. But the doctors set it and it's in a cast. After a couple of days in the hospital, now I'm laid up in my apartment. Luckily, friends from the library look in on me daily and bring in meals. They've gotten another fellow to take my part in the play. Such a brief career on stage, eh? Oh well. The upside of it is, I'm learning what community is really about.

I loved the poem you sent, though I found it hard to focus at first (because of my leg pain mostly, not because of any problem with the poem). I wonder if it wouldn't be stronger if you switched the second and fourth lines of the fifth stanza. It would keep the rhyme scheme the same, but it would clarify the point about the barns. I read it aloud to one of the women who stopped by with a meal, and she agreed.

The leg is starting to ache again, so I'll sign off for now.
Your loving brother,
Robert

Wednesday, September 29
My dear little brother,

Thank you for the suggestion you and your woman friend made regarding my poem. In the future, please don't show my work to anyone else.

A broken leg? You should have had someone notify me when it happened. When you're out and about and have a little time, please file some papers regarding next-of-kin and all that, just in case something happens. I have already done it on my end. And I have had Mr. Higgins, Mom and Dad's lawyer, draw up a will for me.

Do you remember Mrs. Merritt's husband Lester who lived two streets behind us? Three weeks ago he fell in the barnyard and broke his leg, too, a compound fracture, just like yours. He had been recuperating at home but gangrene set in (the wet, not the dry, so there was not only infection but fear of blood poisoning). They took him to the hospital to treat him. But so much of his lower leg was dead flesh they had to amputate it at the knee.

I'm glad you're becoming more sociable, though I'm sorry it took a broken leg for you to get to know your neighbors.

Your loving sister,
Elizabeth

Friday, October 8
Dearest sister,

I've developed gangrene and am writing this as I wait for an ambulance to come and transport me to the hospital. They're going to try massive doses of some drug on me, but the doctor has confided that there's a good chance they'll have to amputate my leg at the knee. I'm devastated at the thought but also thankful they can do the surgery here (if needed) on short notice. I'm keeping my fingers crossed that the drugs will work. But if I must choose between my leg and my life, let them take the leg.

This will be my last letter from the apartment for a while. I'll have someone pick up my mail and will send you the hospital address soon. Telephone me there after you get my letter. I don't know the number.

Your loving brother,
Robert

Wednesday, October 13
My dear little brother,

I telephoned you at the hospital last night, but the nurse on duty said you were sedated so you could sleep. (Better than being in a coma.) She said you'd had the surgery for amputation at the knee, and that it was a success. But she said you'd be experiencing a lot of pain during recovery (which reminded me of you laughing cruelly when my throat was so sore after the tonsillectomy). This is all so hard to take. Gangrene. Losing part of a leg. It's very upsetting to me. I'll mention you during our prayer meeting at church tonight.

The nurse suggested I try phoning you today at noon, that you might be awake at lunchtime. I'll take her advice and will try. In the meantime, I'll keep doing what I know best, writing. At least I can keep up my end of the correspondence.

The postman is due any time, and I want to get this in the mail. I've enclosed a new poem. I'd appreciate your comments.

Your loving sister,
Elizabeth

Wednesday, October 13
My dear little brother,

My second letter today. I'm worried. When I telephoned a few minutes ago, the nurse put your doctor on and he said you had slipped into a coma. He said a coma is the brain's way of protecting the body while it heals. I asked the doctor if I should come and be by your bedside; he said to give it another day first. He promised to phone me tomorrow.

In the meantime I'm a wreck. I feel like I did when we had that picnic on the Charles River, when Mom made me watch over you. You disappeared and I called out for you again and again until I was hoarse. I begged you to stop hiding, to stop being so mean to me, but you wouldn't come out. When you finally did, you were laughing, you were horrible. I know this is a coma and it's serious, but you'd better not be toying with me again. Sometimes you make me so angry.

I'm off to town for groceries, so I'll mail this at the Post Office.

Your loving sister,

Elizabeth

P.S. Poor Mr. Merritt died a couple of days ago. His funeral was yesterday.

Thursday, October 14

My dear brother,

I can't go anywhere for fear I'll miss a call from your doctor. I'm too worked up to read a book or work on a poem. There's not much to do while waiting except to write another letter. I tried knitting, but as I knit I find myself counting to seven over and over. It only serves to remind me of the seven sneezes. I've been trying to remember how many letters I've written you since the sneezes. If you were awake, you could tell me.

As I promised, I lifted up your name at prayer meeting last night. Afterward, Rev. Decker asked if I'd like a pastoral visit. He had been planning to see Mrs. Merritt this morning anyway and said he could swing by. He just now telephoned from the Merritts' to say he's on his way here now. I've got to put on the tea kettle, so I'll close this letter and put it out for the postman.

Your loving sister,

Elizabeth

Friday, October 15

My dear brother,

When the doctor called yesterday morning to say you had died, I couldn't believe it. My mind refused to grasp it. I felt a wave of guilt. Did I somehow contribute to your accident, your infection, your coma? Your death? I never even said goodbye.

Since then I've dwelt upon the witch's words. Seven, she said, seven. And so, this letter (I believe) being my seventh since the spell was cast, and having no other hope, I offer you the words Rev. Decker shared from scripture this morning: He rose from the dead.

Love,
Elizabeth

She sealed the letter and carried it to the front porch for the postman to take. Then she went inside and waited for the phone to ring, for the doctor to call and babble on about a miraculous recovery.

Instead, she heard heavy footsteps on the porch. Her skin broke into goose bumps as a terrifying image flashed across her mind. Her heart fluttered errantly for a moment and she put a hand to her chest. The other hand she placed on the deadbolt and unlocked the door. She could picture the letter where she had hung by a clothespin from the mailbox. Could she still snatch it and tear it up? Would it make a difference? She turned the knob and tried to prepare herself for what she might see, praying to God it was only the postman, an hour early.

Steve Burt

The Praying Man

Every morning my friend Steffy and I would walk to middle school together. To get there by foot we had to walk a long way around one particular bad neighborhood near the railroad tracks. It was either that or take the shortcut through it which we often did.

One Monday we took the shortcut and came to the first run-down house across the tracks. An old man was in the window sitting at his kitchen table, hands clasped in front of him. His head was down and his forehead was resting on his knuckles as if praying. Steffy and I had seen other people do that before and had even done it with our own families before Thanksgiving, Christmas, and Easter dinners. But except for asking for help getting out of tight spots, Steffy and I weren't big on prayer.

Steffy made a joke about it. *You suppose he's praying for a bigger house?* We spotted a couple of kids coming in from a side street a block ahead so we stretched our legs to catch up, forgetting all about the man in the window.

Next day about the same time we passed the little frame house again. The man was back there at the table, head bowed, hands clasped, elbows on the table, forehead on his knuckles. We were pretty sure his eyes were closed—we tried not to be too obvious when we looked on our way past—and I supposed he might be bent over his morning newspaper reading the way my father often did while having a cup of coffee. As I recall I made some comment about the *praying mantis* in the window then we headed for school.

On the third day when we saw him there again I jokingly said maybe we should put a mirror in front of his mouth to see if there was any breath, a trick I had seen on an old TV mystery show.

"If he's still there tomorrow maybe we'll try that," Steffy said, and rolled her eyes.

On Thursday the old guy was there *again*—or maybe *still*—praying or reading his newspaper or examining his cereal, whatever. Curiosity got the better of Steffy and she walked up close to the window.

"Get out of there!" I whisper-warned in a raspy voice.

She raised her hand and rapped on the glass a couple of times. The old man didn't move.

"Maybe he's deaf," I said.

She rapped again then flapped her arms. Still no movement. "He's deaf, all right," she said sarcastically. "Or a very sound sleeper." She rapped a third time. "Maybe, just maybe," she said, "the guy is dead."

"Well, if he is it's his business not ours. Look and see if there's a newspaper on the table. Maybe he really is deaf and is reading his paper at the same time every morning. Could be he's simply engrossed."

Steffy stared in through the window. "Matter of fact there is a newspaper. And a green coffee mug. And a piece of toast. And a jar of jelly. And a butter dish. But I can't see inside the butter dish. It's got one of those covers that looks like a little coffin."

"Not funny! Now come on! Let's go! Forget about him. You can check him on the way home." This would be the first day we'd pass the little house on the return trip, because on the first three afternoons we had taken a different route home so we could play sandlot baseball. But nobody played on Thursday.

By mid-afternoon the sun was reflecting off the window so we couldn't see inside until we'd almost passed the house. Our deaf man—or dead man—was still there.

"I think we better call the police," I said. "We need to report this."

"Not yet. Let me check one more time. I've never seen a dead person close up. This morning didn't count because I wasn't sure he was dead. If he is, I want to see. You come with me."

Her words froze my blood. I just wanted to call the police and get it over with. If Steffy wanted to buy a little time, fine, but I didn't want to go with her. The thought gave me the creeps. But I couldn't look weak in front of her so I said, "Okay, but just for a minute. Then we go home and call the cops."

A minute later we were at the window gawking. On the table sat the green coffee mug, the toast, the jelly jar, the coffin-shaped butter dish, and a vase of wilted flowers.

"Everything's where I saw it this morning," she said. "I'll bet it's been exactly like this all week, maybe longer. You know what's happened, don't you? The old man died reading the paper and drinking his coffee. He balanced in that position for a while and rigor mortis set in. I don't know how long it takes for that but it set in and now he's stiff as a board. They'll probably have to carry him out in that position like furniture movers loading a statue."

The man's lap moved.

"Cripes!" Steffy cried, jumping back, her hand flying to her chest. "Did you see that?"

"Bet your butt I did. Let's go home."

"No, wait. Look. Look closer."

There from under the edge of a small blanket on the man's lap twitched something rope-like, black and white. *A tail.*

"It's a cat," I said. "The guy's dead but his poor cat won't leave him. We gotta go call the cops."

"Wait. What if there's something else in there—like other cats or a dog or something?"

"What if there is? That's where the police come in. That's not our problem, Steffy."

She ignored my logic. "Let's check the door and see if it's open. We can call from his phone."

Then it hit me what this was about. "It's not the cat you want to save, is it, Steff, or any other animals? You just want to see the dead guy up close. That's it, isn't it?"

"No," she lied. "That's not it, not really. If I wanted to *see* a dead person, this would be close enough right here, wouldn't it?"

"This is close enough for me," I answered, falling into her trap.

"From here we can *see* but we can't be certain, can we?"

"Oh no," I said. "No, no, no. You want to *touch* him, don't you? You want to go in so you can *touch* a dead body."

Her face reddened. "As a matter of fact, yes. I do. And there's nothing wrong with that. Kids our age are inquisitive, curious. And what's the harm?"

I didn't know how to answer that. It was a good question. What would be the harm?

"Besides," she said. "What if there are photographers.later? We want to be here if they take pictures, right? Can't you see the headlines? Two seventh-graders discover dead body, rescue animals. They'd have newspaper clippings of us posted all around school."

She had me off balance now and the only thing I could think to say was, "We have to knock first." I realized it was stupid as soon as I said it.

"Of course we'd have to knock," she agreed, and we moved onto the little porch. She knocked a half dozen times. No answer. She turned the knob, found the door was unlocked and pushed it open. "Hello. Anybody home?" Steffy stepped in and I followed.

The place smelled like garbage. It was a pigsty. Hundreds of newspapers, three-foot stacks of magazines, coffee table piled high with dirty TV dinner trays, crusty silverware and dusky glasses, clothing strewn over the couch, chairs, and end tables. The only sound was the hum of the refrigerator.

"Smells worse than the dump," I commented.

"Not surprised. My dad said my grandfather's apartment was like this when they found him last year dead in his bed. He had turned into a packrat and lived on TV dinners, soup, and Spaghetti-O's. We hadn't seen him in a while. He lived next door to us for years before he moved away. When he was close by I visited him every day."

"Was that your first funeral?"

"First funeral? No, I've never been to one. My parents wouldn't let me go because they thought it'd be too traumatic. They left me with my aunt for the visiting hours and the funeral. I never saw my grandfather dead, never got to say goodbye."

We waded through a sea of trash-filled paper bags to reach the door to the small kitchen where the praying man sat with his cat.

Steffy reached the doorframe before I did and stood there staring at the old man's back as I stared at hers. I didn't want to look up. I was glad she was there in front of me to block my vision. I was in no rush to get to the kitchen and see him.

"What do you think killed him?" I asked.

"Old age. Same as my grandfather. Body just wore out. Or his heart, lungs, something. Like an old car that won't go any more."

The two of us stood in silence a minute.

"Well, what're you going to do?" I asked. "You going to touch him or not?"

Steffy didn't answer for a long time. Then softly, very softly she said, "No. I don't think so."

"But are you sure he's dead?" I pressed. "I thought you wanted to touch him to make sure."

"There are flies all over the toast. Pretty sure he's dead."

"What about the cat? Wasn't that one of the reasons you made me come in?"

"I thought it was, but it wasn't." Her voice was thick, choked, and emotional. I could only see the back of her head, not her face, but I knew she was crying.

"You okay?" I asked, half-afraid she'd turn and face me.

She tried to clear her throat and compose herself. But she didn't compose herself. Her shoulders shook as she sobbed.

I placed a comforting hand on one of them and with a knot in my own throat, said, "It's alright. It's okay." I wanted to pull my hand away, but I left it there.

On the wall to Steffy's left I saw a black telephone with a long tangled cord. For just a moment I thought about calling the police who would arrive in no time. But I didn't. "Let's go," I said. "We can call the cops from my house. We don't have to tell them we came in."

We waded through the garbage, closed the door and went home to make the phone call. There was no photographer, no story, and no mention of the squalid living conditions. All that appeared in print was an obituary: three paragraphs about an old man who loved his children, his grandchildren, his church, and his cat. We agreed that what was in the obituary was all that needed to be said. That was the last time Steffy and I mentioned the praying man in the window.

Shadow Meadow

Doris and I were on the way home from school one Friday afternoon when we decided to take a shortcut. The route would mean sprinting the Interstate and crossing a meadow we'd heard was haunted. We'd never gone that way before.

It was a day with a little bit of fresh snow on the ground. A few of the school bus drivers reported patches of black ice on the roads. But we figured the shortcut would save us 20 minutes getting home, maybe even a half hour. The detour would take us behind the school through a stand of pine trees to the Interstate. Once we crossed the highway we'd pass through a break of trees that enclosed a large open meadow.

People swore the meadow was haunted by the spirit of a Revolutionary War drummer boy of 12 or 13. Some said he marched back and forth, others said he chased trespassers. But he had never actually harmed anybody, at least not so far as we could determine, so we weren't really scared.

Doris and I headed through the pines behind the school and found the ground a little slick underfoot, but for the most part we simply left tracks in the snow. As we walked along we talked about the school dances coming up and the history test we'd just survived, nothing heavy or consequential.

The Interstate was thick with tractor-trailers flying by. The pavement looked dry. We braced ourselves, waited for a lull in the traffic, and when the coast looked clear we lit out across the lanes toward the snow-covered median. Since we were at full tilt anyway we did a quick on-the-run scan of oncoming traffic in the far lanes—saw a couple of semis in the distance—and made a snap decision to keep going all the way to the opposite shoulder.

But the two semis were barreling at us faster than we'd calculated and we couldn't see the black ice in front of us. Our feet shot out and we slid on our butts and backs, clunking our heads on the pavement as we skidded to the side of the road. I felt the breeze from the tractor-trailers as they blew past.

"Whew! That was close," I remember Doris saying with a nervous laugh. We got to our feet.

"Too close for me," I said. "But I guess we made it, didn't we?"

She looked me up and down then patted herself as if double-checking. "Apparently." The two of us laughed.

"You hurt your head on the pavement?"

"Don't think so," Doris answered. "You?"

I felt the back of my head. "I cracked it pretty hard but I think I'm okay."

Doris felt her own head and shook herself out to see if she had any bumps or bruises on the rest of her body. "Nothing I can see. We were lucky, I guess. Not cutting it that close again, though."

A minute or two later—maybe it was 10 or 15 minutes, time seemed a little funny—we found ourselves in the meadow surrounded by trees. It looked to be two football fields across and about the same distance long, nearly a perfect square. We could see several worn paths. The one we took went through the center of the meadow and forked into a Y. According to our calculations we needed to take the path to the right if we were to come out on Yondel Circle. From there it'd be six or seven blocks home.

As soon as we started across the meadow I spotted the shadow of a squirrel on the snow. The shadow moved almost parallel to us and was going the same direction.

"Must be a squirrel above us," I said matter-of-factly.

Doris glanced at me, puzzled. "What do you mean—squirrel? There aren't any trees out here in the meadow. You mean a flying squirrel?"

"No. Look," I pointed. "See the shadow?"

She looked. "Oh. I didn't see it before." We stopped. "I don't know where that shadow could be coming from. There's nothing above us, no trees, no poles, and no power lines. Where's the squirrel that's casting the shadow?"

"I have no idea," I answered. "When Pete told us about this shortcut, didn't he say folks call it the *valley of the shadow*?"

“Yeah, that and *shadow meadow* or shadow something. But shadows don’t exist on their own.”

When we looked again at the snow in front of us the squirrel shadow was gone. But then the shadow of a bird appeared as if there were a vulture tilting and whirling above us, circling. We looked up—nothing—then back down—the unmistakable shadow. But the dark shadow was the only thing soaring—no vultures.

"What's going on?" I asked. "This can't be."

“I don’t know. It’s strange but that doesn't mean the place is haunted. Still, I think we better get across fast. Something's not right about it.”

We pressed forward, trying to move fast, but the snow cover ahead was slick and slowed us down. More and more shadows began appearing: raccoons, possums, deer, more squirrels and plenty of birds of all sizes. But we couldn't see anything alive casting the shadows.

"Is this starting to scare you?” Doris asked. “It’s like road-kill heaven."

“Scared isn't the right word, but I feel a bit spooked." After I said that, I thought to myself: *It's true, I’m not scared. I should be, but I’m not. Everything about this situation tells me to be scared, and yet I don’t really have a lot of feelings about it—except maybe curiosity. I'm actually feeling kind of flat about it all.*

As we advanced more shadows appeared. Ahead the path disappeared into a small cluster of trees at the far edge of the meadow.

Suddenly I did feel scared—it came on me fast—but I didn’t know why I felt that way. “Let's get out fast. Now it's getting to me." My sense of feeling—both physical feeling and emotional feeling—was coming back.

“That’s odd,” Doris replied. “I’m actually feeling calmer, less scared, almost relaxed enough to go to sleep.”

“Go to sleep? You're kidding, right?" I was remembering *The Wizard of Oz*, when Dorothy and her dog Toto and their three new friends started to cross the poppy fields toward Oz. The poppies put Dorothy, Toto, and the Cowardly Lion to sleep. An alarm went off in my head and I felt a chill run up my backbone. Something was wrong but I couldn't put my finger on it.

When we got within 50 yards of the tree-line somebody appeared walking right toward us—a boy. He was no bigger than we were. Nothing about him was distinct. He looked like all the other shadows had except he had slight shades of color, not just black and white, and appeared to be wearing a bluish-gray uniform with a little billed cap on his head. The cap reminded me of a picture I'd seen of an old-time train conductor.

"It's the drummer boy," Doris whispered, and we stopped.

The shadowy boy halted 10 feet from us. I had the feeling he was looking right at us but I couldn't make out his eyes.

"Welcome," he said, his face not clear enough for me to see his lips move. "It's good to have company."

Doris and I looked at each other. I thought my eyesight was going, because I was seeing her through a haze even though she was beside me and a foot away.

"This is a strange place. Where are we?" I asked. "We saw animal shadows but not the animals making them."

"All shadows here," his voice answered.

Doris laughed as if the idea were preposterous. "Well, *we're* here. *We're* flesh and blood. We're not shadows."

"Look again," the drummer boy said.

I turned to Doris. Her outline was less distinct than a moment before and her color—clothing, body, hair, all coloration—had faded to half its brightness. I looked down at myself and saw that my own colors were fading—not as fast as Doris's but mine were perhaps half as dull as hers. Something was dreadfully wrong.

"Before long you'll be like me," the drummer boy said, his voice lacking any life.

"But why?" I asked.

"How?" Doris wanted to know.

"Don't you understand? The animals died. Their shadows are left."

"What are you saying?" I asked, hearing some animation in my own voice again. "Are you a ghost? Or a shadow?"

“I’m not sure. Perhaps one or the other, maybe both. I was killed in this meadow by a musket ball.”

“But we're not dead!" I protested. "We—" Doris and I exchanged a glance. She had faded more. I could barely make out any clarity and there was no color to her eyes, no sharpness to the iris. I glanced down at myself. I hadn’t changed much since my last look, not at the rate Doris was washing out.

“It was the truck, wasn't it?" Doris asked. "One of those two semis?"

The drummer boy shrugged what had once been his shoulders. "I don’t know. I wasn’t there. I was here in the meadow. Sounds like you were in the old part of the meadow that became a road."

“Doris, we’ve got to get out of here.” I tried to touch her on the arm but my hand passed through her. I motioned and begged. “Come on. We need to go now!”

The drummer boy turned back toward the trees he had come from and she started to follow.

“No, Doris. Not that way. Back where we came from.” She ignored me so I turned, my body heavy as a log. I began to retrace my steps. It was slow-motion as if I were slogging through chest-high water. It took every ounce of strength I had. I looked over my shoulder and made one final attempt to convince my friend. “Doris, this way. Let’s go.”

But she didn't turn and I heard nothing from her. Something told me I couldn’t afford to call to her again, I had to take care of me. I forced my way forward—backward, actually, toward the place where we had entered the meadow. As I did, everything seemed to be like a movie running in reverse. I saw the shadows of the raccoons and the deer and the vultures and the first squirrel again as if time and motion were going backward.

It took me I don’t know how long—hours or days, it seemed—to make it to the edge of the woods. I stepped over what felt like a finish line at a marathon. I felt myself grabbed by some sort of a huge suctioning force, a gravitational pull that yanked me back at the speed of light.

After that I have no recollection until I felt the pain of light in my eyes as I opened them in a hospital room and saw my mother and sister and a nurse. Mom and Sis burst into tears and hugged me. I ached all over and somehow knew my legs were broken.

“Where am I?”

The words tumbled out of their mouths. I had been in a terrible accident, run over by a tractor-trailer on the highway. The driver had seen Doris and me skid on the black ice in front of him. I’d been in a coma for four days, my survival touch-and-go.

“Where’s Doris?" I asked, afraid to hear the answer but needing to know. "What about Doris?”

The pain in my mother’s eyes told the story: Doris hadn’t made it.

I was too numb to sob. That came later in waves.

Three months later, after I had told my mother and sister about shadow meadow, the three of us went there. We didn’t come in from the highway side as Doris and I had. We came from the Yondel Circle side—close to where the drummer boy had appeared.

We stood on the spot where I had last seen Doris—or Doris' shadow. There was no snow now and the grass was beginning to sprout as everything in the meadow fought to come alive again. The sap was flowing and the trees were budding.

We saw no separate shadows like the ones I had seen with Doris. There were only normal shadows: a shadow of a tree extending out from its base and the grounded shadows of gulls, hawks, and vultures flying overhead. Everything was normal and beautiful and for a moment I thought: *what a great place for a park.*

"Seen enough?" Mom asked.

“Could you two just leave me alone for a minute?” I answered. She and my sister stepped away. I closed my eyes and tried to recall Doris's face, but it wouldn’t come to me. I concentrated harder. Nothing. Finally I opened my eyes. In front of me I saw three shadows. The closest was my own stretching before me from my toes. The other two, a drummer boy and an eighth-grade girl, neither of whom got to become adults—lay flat on the ground 10 feet away, shadows not tied to physical bodies. Doris's shadow held out its arms to me.

On the ground before me I could see my own shadow's arms quivering and trying to rise, wanting to respond to Doris's shadow's outstretched arms. My flesh-and-blood arms wanted to lift and respond to her, but I forced them to stay at my sides, refusing to let the shadow arms make the choice.

Were Doris and the drummer boy trying to pull me across or did she simply want to make one last connection? Had I cheated death that day Doris and I took the shortcut? The meadow had a hold on me right then and even though I thought I was physically stronger on this visit, I wasn't sure I could resist the way I had the day of the accident.

"Peggy!" my mother's voice called from some distant part of my brain.

Despite the coolness of the air I could feel the sweat of exertion on my forehead as I fought to resist Doris's call. I was losing the battle, being drawn somewhere. Where, I didn't know.

"Peggy, are you ready to go?" Mom asked, right behind me. I felt her hand on my arm then my sister's on the other arm. Their added weight broke the spell. My arms relaxed and I had control over my body again.

A cloud passed in front of the sun and the two shadows that had been on the ground vanished. When the sun appeared again, the only shadows were my mother's, my sister's, and mine. We turned and walked out of the meadow.

Doris still visits me occasionally in my dreams and beckons me to join her, but I find it easier to resist now. I try to answer her, though, let her know I'm not saying no. *Someday, Doris, someday, old friend. But not yet.*

The French Acre

Devaney took the phone call about the crows. It was Fourth of July weekend. My wife Carol and her mother were off at church and I was relaxing on my new redwood chaise lounge with a mug of French Roast and the Sunday funnies. My father-in-law Devaney, whom Carol and her mother called my partner-in-crime, came back from the living room with the portable phone in his hand. He set it on the end table between us and plopped heavily onto his patio chair.

"I'll leave it out here," he said. "That way we won't have to run in and get it every time it rings."

I tried to go back to reading *Hagar the Horrible*, but Devaney interrupted before I could start it.

"Don't you want to know who that was?" he asked.

I didn't look up, but out of the corner of my eye I could see him scratching with his pen in his little notebook, playing cat-and-mouse with me. This was exactly why my mother-in-law appreciated me—I kept her retired-history-teacher husband out of her hair. But I had to admit, he wasn't always annoying, and he was a pretty fair amateur shutterbug. He had shot some darned good photos to accompany the feature stories I wrote for the *Valley News*, the daily that serves the small Vermont and New Hampshire towns within a forty-mile radius of White River Junction.

"Is there a story in it or not?" I asked, trying not to look up. But I couldn't keep my mind on *Hagar*. I looked up.

Devaney smiled, a big cat-ate-the-canary smile. "Remember *The Birds*? Hitchcock? Suzanne Pleshette? Rod Steiger? Peck, peck, peck?"

I nodded. "It was Rod Taylor, not Rod Steiger. What about it?"

"Not *it*! Not *it*! *They*! The birds! They're here!" He made his eyes go wide, puckered his lips, and began whistling the *Twilight Zone* theme song.

Ever since we'd investigated Norwich's humming church bell and the Witness Tree on the green, people had been phoning us—

me and Devaney instead of the police—when something a little out-of-the-ordinary came up. A cow couldn't just get lost; it disappeared, maybe got beamed up. So they phoned us. And a day or two after we met with the person calling it in, the cow would wander home or be found by a neighbor.

Or the lights in a Florida snowbird's house mysteriously came on and went off at odd hours, with no burglars to be seen anywhere near the place—so someone speculated that maybe ghosts were afoot in the haunted house. Devaney and I in turn called the snowbirds in Florida and learned that the lights were on automatic timers—but these were on a special irregular timer so burglars wouldn't easily spot a nightly pattern.

Sure, there were several other truly odd cases, but most of the calls were petty. Nevertheless people kept calling me and Devaney, as if we were the Upper Valley's sleuths of the paranormal or psychic detectives or something.

"Okay, which Looney Toon called this time?" I asked.

"Nelda Potter. In Norwich. Remember Zack Potter? Used to have that farm stand beyond the curves on the way up to Beaver Meadow—that place where we got the pumpkins ten, fifteen years ago?"

"The dairy that became a Christmas tree farm?"

Devaney nodded.

"But Zack died," I said.

"Of course he did," Devaney said with a scowl. "I know that. But she didn't. She's the one who called. I was just dropping his name to help orient you." Devaney rolled his eyes.

"Fine," I said, annoyed. "So Nelda Potter—Zack Potter's widow—called. Is she holed up in her house with swarms of starlings pecking through her wooden storm doors and shuttered windows? Rather than call 911, she chose to call the Psychic Detectives Hotline, right?"

"Closer to the truth than you think. But it's not starlings. It's crows—hundreds of them."

"And?" No story I could pick out so far.

"And they're not attacking her house. They're roosting on that high wall around the French Acre."

Still no story that I could see. "You have a punch line to this?"

"Yes, I do." He paused for effect. "Nelda says there's never been a crow on those walls before, not ever. Birds won't go near it."

I looked at my father-in-law blankly.

"She says the crows showed up when Charlie Rivers started clearing the French Acre two weeks ago."

The French Acre was a walled-in acre of land whose overgrown interior was reported to be an almost impregnable thicket of bushes and trees. Legend had it that before the Revolutionary War, the acre of pastureland had been bounded by a waist-high stonewall. But something happened and the Norwich townsfolk added rocks and mortar, raising the wall's height to nine feet. Oddly, they left no gate and no door.

"You mean clearing brush around the outside, right?" I said. "Outside the walls, like cleaning up after the accident?"

Devaney and I had been at the French Acre two weeks earlier to cover the story at an accident scene. I'm a garden-variety reporter, a generalist, not an investigative reporter. Most of my stories are about high school graduations, charity cow-flop drops, 100th birthdays in nursing homes—local stuff, features, human-interest pieces. But when the editors were shorthanded, my stories included the occasional accident.

Four teenage boys in a pickup—all four packed in across the front with no seatbelts—had died when they slammed into the wall at the French Acre. The impact punched a small hole in it, and I remembered someone at the scene trying to shine a flashlight in. Holy mackerel, the guy had said. The brambles and trees are so thick in there you couldn't swing a hatchet.

"No," Devaney said, bringing me back. "Nelda said he wasn't clearing brush outside; Charlie Rivers was clearing it inside, inside the French Acre."

I felt the short hairs on the back of my neck stand up. "What time'd you tell Nelda we'd be out?"

“One o’clock.”

“Call her back,” I said. “And get your camera. Tell her we’re on our way.”

* * *

We passed Dan & Whit’s Country Store, turned left at the Norwich Inn, and headed out the back road toward Beaver Meadow. Nelda Potter’s farmhouse was only two or three minutes from the Inn, and the French Acre was along the way. I wanted to catch a glimpse of it in daylight. The last time I’d seen it, the night of the accident, its walls had been bathed in the light of emergency vehicles.

“Holy crow!” Devaney said as the walls of the French Acre came into view. “Pun intended.”

Nelda Potter had been right. The high wall around it was rimmed with crows, hundreds of them. I pulled the car onto the dirt shoulder and we sat watching and listening.

“Notice anything?” I asked after a minute or two.

"Yeah. They’re quiet.”

The lack of noise wasn’t what I’d been getting at. But he was right. The crows weren’t cawing. Not a single one of them. And they were all facing inward, looking down from their perches into the Acre, watching. Devaney pointed his camera and took a couple of shots of the birds.

“No. Look. The hole in the wall is bigger now,” I said. “And there are brush piles along the outside, stuff that’s been cleared out.”

Devaney snapped another shot or two, this time of an opening that looked like an arched doorway to a ruined Scottish castle.

Just then a small blue pickup with a utility trailer pulled around us and stopped in front of the opening. A wiry older man got out, eyed us without waving, and began loading brush into the bed of the pickup and onto the utility trailer. His long gray hair was tied back in a ponytail. He didn’t bother to shoo the crows.

“Charlie Rivers?” I asked Devaney.

"Looks like him. Want to talk to him now?"

"No, not yet. Nelda's waiting," I said, starting the car. "Besides, when we come back this way, Charlie should be loaded up and gone. If he is, we can take a look inside for ourselves."

"And I can shoot some pictures."

We gave Rivers a polite New England nod and a wave as we eased onto the road. The man in the blue jeans and chamois shirt nodded and went back to work.

Nelda Potter's white-clapboarded farmhouse sat on the opposite side of the road, less than a half mile beyond the French Acre. She waved from her porch rocker as we pulled into the driveway. Five minutes later we were in her parlor with teacups on our laps.

"So, tell us about the crows, Mrs. Potter," I said. "And what you know about the French Acre."

"Well," she started. "There's been a lot of deaths there."

"Four," I said. "Teenage boys. A terrible waste. We covered the story for the Valley News."

"Besides those four, I mean. There's been ten or a dozen over the years. I remember young Henry Corbett in the 1950s. The Tucker girl and her boyfriend in '63. Mary Grady's twin boys from up the road, around '67, they crashed on Graduation night. Then others in the seventies, eighties, nineties. It's a bad spot—and there's not even a curve there; that's what I don't get. They just wind it up on the straightaway and hit that damned wall—pardon my French."

"And the birds?" Devaney asked. "You said there have never been birds on the wall of the French Acre?"

"Mr. Devaney, Mr. Hoag, I'm 80 years old. I've lived on this farm for 60 of those years, and my husband lived here all of his 78. His family went back seven generations here. Everybody on this road knows that no crows—no birds of any type, not a robin or a sparrow—go near that cursed acre. There's been nothing live there except trees and brush that have grown up inside and died and rotted there, then grown up again. There's something wrong with it."

"Any idea what?" I asked.

"Well, they call it the French Acre, supposedly—Mr. Devaney, as a former history teacher you may know this—because a contingent of Lafayette's soldiers camped there just before or during the American Revolution, 1774 or 1776, sometime thereabouts. It was a pasture then, with a low stonewall around it. At least that's the way I've always heard it—Lafayette's soldiers."

"But something happened," Devaney interrupted.

"Yes," she said. "They died. All of them. It's the how that's a mystery. But whatever happened, people felt the need to wall up the Acre."

The three of us sat quiet a minute.

"I'd heard this before," Devaney said. "There's speculation it was disease. Or bad food or poison water."

"But why build a nine-foot wall around it?" I said. "With no plaque or historical marker. Did they die overnight? Or was it over several weeks or months? Was it a quarantine situation? Is that why they built the wall? There's got to be something written down somewhere. Town records. An old diary. Something other than word of mouth."

"And what's it got to do with crows?" Devaney asked.

"I don't know," Nelda Potter said with a shrug. "What's it got to do with Mr. Rivers?"

Devaney and I looked at each other, then back at Nelda.

"Who hired him?" I asked. "To clear out the brush."

"I have no idea. Maybe the Town? As far as I know, there's no Society or Association that looks over the site, not like a cemetery association or historical society. Nobody's ever tended it."

"Maybe the families of the boys who were killed hired him," Devaney said. "Or their insurance companies?" But that didn't make sense.

"So why is Charlie Rivers down there bush-hogging it out?" I asked her. "He must have been hired because he's a handyman, a yard cleanup guy, right?"

"I have no idea. I've talked with all my neighbors on the road and nobody seems to know who'd hire him for it, or why."

"And what do you know about Charlie Rivers?" I asked.

"Well, he lives a few miles north of here, past the Beaver Meadow Chapel where the road goes from paved to dirt at the Norwich/Sharon line. He's always been quiet. He's in his seventies, eight or ten years younger than I am. He's part Abenaki Indian—name's actually Charlie Three Rivers. Worked a bunch of different jobs over the years, including helping me and my husband in haying season, but mostly he makes his living mowing cemeteries in Norwich and Sharon. If you need to know more, you could check with Dutch Roberts, the Norwich town constable, and Oscar Bell, the Town Manager up to Sharon."

After we said our goodbyes to Nelda Potter, we drove back to the French Acre and pulled off the road. No sign of Charlie Rivers or his truck. We got out and stood in front of the newly enlarged breach in the wall.

"It's dark in there," Devaney said, snapping a picture. "Like a cave."

I stepped through the opening and almost fell forward. I caught my balance by putting a hand on the wall, and found myself standing ankle-deep in soil.

"You okay, Hoag?" Devaney called from behind me. He shone his flashlight in.

"I'm fine. But watch your step. It's soft. I think it's silt and loam from years and years of rotting vegetation."

"Geez," Devaney said, stepping in behind me. "You can hardly see the sky in here. It's really thick overhead. Charlie Rivers has barely made a dent in it."

He was right, Charlie Rivers hadn't cleared a hundredth of it yet. But he'd begun. The word thicket came to mind. What was left was an impenetrable woven thicket. I doubted anyone could successfully crawl from one wall of the French Acre to its opposite wall.

"So, what do we see?" Devaney asked. He handed me his flashlight and I did a quick search.

"Nothing out of the ordinary. You see anything from back there?"

"Nope. You've got my flashlight."

"Hear anything?"

"Nope. Not even the crows."

"Smell or taste anything?"

Devaney said nothing for a moment, and I thought maybe he hadn't heard my question. Then he answered. "Death, I think."

"You mean like rotting leaves?"

I shut up and breathed it in through my nose. Yes, it was layer upon layer of rotting vegetation. But it was also something hard to pinpoint. Devaney was right. Whatever it was, the smell made the word death appear in one's mind. And it gave me goose bumps.

"It is death," came a voice from behind, startling us. We turned toward the light of the doorway. A thin man's shadowy profile leaned on the wall.

"Charlie Rivers," Devaney said. "Didn't hear you sneak up."

"Didn't sneak. I parked the truck by your car and walked over to look inside. Tried my best to not scare you."

"The Acre's scary enough," I said. "Especially the inside of it."

"Oh, it's not so bad once you get used to it. Would you prefer to come outside in the light and talk? I figure you've got questions. And you can empty your shoes out, so you don't track it all over your wife's carpet."

We stepped out.

"Devaney and Hoag," I said, and the three of us shook hands.

"*Valley News*," Rivers said. "I've read your stuff. Especially liked that piece on the Norwich Witch a couple years back."

Rivers was friendlier and more outgoing than I'd expected. He dropped the tailboard of his utility trailer and extended an open hand. Devaney and I sat down. Rivers stood.

"We got a call about the crows," I said. "The caller said it's the first time a bird or beast has come near the French Acre. Is that true?"

"Could be. I don't keep watch over every little thing along this road like some of the busybodies do. But still, there's a ring of truth to it."

"So what's your part in it?" Devaney asked. "Somebody hire you to clear it out?"

"Nope," Rivers said, looking down at the ground. "Nobody's paying me. And nobody asked me to do it."

"Then why?" Devaney asked.

"It couldn't be put off any longer, not after those four boys. And that's when it opened up."

"Opened up?" Devaney asked.

Rivers motioned toward the new entrance through the wall. "I've got to take care of it before someone else is killed here. It's just something I've got to do."

"If you're intending to clear that entire Acre, it'll take you a year," I said. "With only that one small opening you can't get in with a bulldozer or a backhoe or anything very mechanical."

"It's got to be done pretty much by hand, anyway," Rivers said. "You can't bulldoze." He looked up at me and said, "And no, I don't need help. It's something I've got to do alone."

"And just what is it you're attempting to do?" Devaney asked. "Is it about the French soldiers, the ones who fell to the disease?"

"Who said anything about disease?" Rivers jumped down off the trailer. He grabbed an ax and a shovel and walked toward the opening. "Devaney, Hoag, nice to meet you. If you'll excuse me, I've got to get back to it if I'm to finish in less than a year."

After the holiday weekend Devaney and I visited Dutch Roberts, Norwich's town constable, at his office. We'd known each other awhile and he'd always been helpful when I needed information for a story.

"Charlie Rivers has been the groundskeeper for three or four of our smaller Norwich cemeteries for about thirty years now," Dutch said. "He mows and trims, fills in graves that have settled, resets the stones that tip or fall, that kind of thing. Does the same thing for Town of Sharon at two or three of theirs. Put it all together and he makes a basic living part of the year."

"What's he do the rest of the year? Go to Florida?" Devaney asked, chuckling.

"I think he hauls firewood and plows snow. One winter he went to work for Henry Mason over at the funeral home."

"He's not trained or certified as a mortician's assistant, is he?" I asked. "That'd take some basic education and licensing."

"Well, no," Dutch said. "Not quite at that level. Not assisting with embalming or anything. Charlie was more of a fill-in to help wheel in the bodies and open doors at wakes and help with funeral parking."

"Does he still do it?" I asked.

"Nah. That was six or eight years ago. Henry let him go after a month. Charlie told him he was getting vibes from the stiffs."

A half hour later we were in Sharon, chatting across the desk with Oscar Bell, the Town Manager.

"A reliable worker, Charlie is. Been taking care of four of our cemeteries for years. He even found one up in Beaver Meadow, a cemetery we didn't even know about. It was terribly overgrown, neglected for a hundred years. No idea how he located it. It wasn't until he'd cleared it all out that we even found it on one of the old maps."

"You know anything about his history—like his family, education, jobs?" Devaney asked.

Devaney knew we shouldn't be asking the question, and I knew it too. What's more, Oscar Bell knew it. But he wasn't a stiff bureaucrat, he was also a friend. He went to a file cabinet, slid open a drawer, and fanned his way through a sheaf of papers in a manila file.

"Pardon me while I think out loud," he said. "High school grad. Odd jobs. Never married. Supported his mother, one of the last of the Abenaki medicine women, who lived with him until she died about five years ago. That's about it." Oscar turned back to face us.

"Sounds like Charlie Rivers you're talking about," said a voice from the doorway. Devaney and I turned in our chairs and saw a bent-over old man leaning on a cane.

"Well, I'll be damned. Alton Brock," Devaney said, rising to greet the man with a handshake and a slap on the shoulder. "Come in, come in, my old friend. Hoag, you remember Alton Brock, don't you, the unofficial mayor of Sharon, the man who single-handedly raised the money for the new school?"

I nodded, shook hands, and Devaney motioned Alton Brock toward a chair.

"Oh, I can't stay, Devaney," Brock said. "I've got a meeting down the hall. But I couldn't help overhearing you three when I was walking by."

"You know Charlie Rivers?" I asked. "From some cemetery association meeting, right?"

"Oh, I know him," Brock said. "But not from that. Many of the old-timers here in Sharon know him—if they're drinking water. When he was young—I doubt he's done it in forty years or more—Charlie Rivers was the best apple-branch dowser around. If you needed a well, you called Charlie. He could locate water with a divining rod in places you'd never believe you'd find it. And he was always right. Never saw him fail. Charlie Rivers had The Sense."

"The Sense?" I asked.

"Well, sure," Brock continued. "You know, the sensitivity. Not everybody can do it. It's a combination of the apple-branch and The Sense. My mother—God rest her soul—told me it was like mind-reading the earth. That's what Charlie Rivers could do."

* * *

I had a restful evening at home that night, because there was no story to write. It just wasn't there. Instead I made notes about what I knew so far. And I asked Devaney to do a little research on the French Acre, Lafayette's troops, and what else was going on around Norwich around the time of the Revolution. Then I called Nelda Potter back to get the names of the accident victims she'd spieled off. It wouldn't be difficult to check the Norwich Town cops and the State Police for accident reports connected to the French Acre over the last 40 years.

Two days later Devaney called to say he'd hit a dead end. In fact, he found no evidence of French soldiers being in the area before or during the Revolution.

"I checked Dartmouth's library with a fine-toothed comb," he said. "Despite the spot being called the French Acre, there's nothing to support the idea that French soldiers came anywhere near Norwich. Several British contingents passed through and likely camped here, but no French."

It took me two weeks to find and go through all the Town and State accidents reports. Eleven people had been killed at the French Acre since 1935. They had all been coming from the same direction at a high rate of speed and, based on the sketches and photos in the files, the vehicles had all impacted the wall in practically the same spot.

When I told Devaney what I'd found in the reports, he looked pensive.

"Were there also accidents without fatalities?" he asked. "I mean that's a lot of deaths. Didn't anybody ever walk away from one?"

"Nope."

He was right. Not a fender-bender in the bunch. No one with a broken arm or leg, no one ever hospitalized.

"All fatalities," I said. "What are the odds?"

"The wall's like a death magnet," he said.

I had enough background material to do a first story on the French Acre, a curiosity story. But because of the recent accident resulting in the four boys' deaths, I decided against it. A curiosity piece could wait. No matter when it saw print, it would reopen old wounds, but right now the wounds were too fresh. I let it rest awhile.

* * *

The leaves were starting to turn—golds and early reds—when we drove to the French Acre to see Charlie Rivers again. Hills of dead and dying brush had begun to pile up outside the wall. Charlie's truck and trailer were nowhere in sight. Hundreds of crows perched on the wall.

"Looks like he's given up hauling it to the landfill," I said.

"Maybe he wants to spend all his time and energy clearing," Devaney said.

We stepped through the opening in the wall.

"Hey, Charlie, you in there?" I called, not expecting to find him. We were amazed to see the progress Rivers had made.

"Wow," Devaney said. "He's really gaining ground."

"Literally and figuratively," I said. In the five weeks since the crash he'd cleared a quarter acre.

"What's that?" Devaney asked, pointing.

"A chainsaw."

"No, not that. That. *Those.*"

Before I could answer, Devaney had his camera in front of his broad face and was snapping pictures. In front of us were reflectors, red ones on aluminum rods, the sort you'd see marking the edge of a driveway. There were seven.

"What do you think they're there for?" I asked.

"No idea. A couple are close together, but then there's one way over there, another out that way. And nothing connecting them, like string or crime scene tape. I don't know, Hoag. Bodies, you think?"

"Maybe. If there really are bodies here. If there are, how would he know where they are?"

"He has The Sense. And didn't Oscar tell us the man's a dowser?"

"A dowser, yes. But a dowser of the dead?"

We heard the crunch of gravel along the road, then the sputtering sound of an engine that didn't want to shut off. We stepped back out into the full daylight.

"Hello, Hoag, Devaney," Charlie Rivers said.

"Hi, Charlie," I said. "You're making great progress, I see. That's damned backbreaking work. You're twice the man I am. I don't have the stamina for it at my age."

"And I sure don't," Devaney said with a laugh.

Charlie reached into the back of his pickup and pulled out a handful of the red reflectors on aluminum rods.

"Those things help you keep your bearings in there?" Devaney asked.

"Gotta use 'em," Charlie Rivers said. "Nobody else knows where they are."

"The bodies?" I asked. "Of the French soldiers?"

Charlie moved toward the opening. "After all these years I wouldn't say *bodies*."

"Bones, then," Devaney said. "Bones of the French soldiers?"

Charlie paused at the opening, smiled quizzically and said, "Who said they were French?" He ducked his head inside and stepped through. "Excuse me, gentlemen. I've got to get back to work now. Deadlines, you know, something newspapermen should understand." And he disappeared inside.

Devaney called, "Are you saying they weren't French?"

"Do your own homework," Rivers said.

* * *

It was Monday of Columbus Day weekend and the foliage was at its peak when Devaney called me.

"You on a car phone?" I asked. "You sound funny."

"One of those new cellular phones. It's my cousin Bernie's."

"Bernie's? You're in Connecticut? Or is Bernie at your place?"

"We're in Connecticut. We came down for the long weekend."

"You didn't mention it to me. Carol and I didn't even know you were gone."

"Spur of the moment, I suppose. You know how I sometimes get inspiration. Well, yesterday the thought just jumped into my head—call Bernie, call Bernie. It wouldn't go away. So I called Bernie."

"And?"

"Bernie invites us to spend the long weekend. It's only a three-hour drive, so we pack a bag and head out the door. You know, I never do these last-minute things. But this just felt like the thing to do. To make a long story short, we arrived late last night and didn't have much time to chitchat before we turned in. But this morning

Bernie and I are having breakfast and I mention what you and I are working on—you know, the French Acre—and Bernie says, 'Reminds me of the French soldiers buried in the Revolutionary War cemetery over at Norwich.' Norwich, Hoag. Norwich, Connecticut, he means. He tells me it's only a twenty minute drive, so here we are."

"Here we are? Where?"

"Norwich. Connecticut. The cemetery, Hoag. Aren't you listening? Bernie and I are standing in the cemetery in Norwich, Connecticut. I'm looking at a stone, a memorial to twenty of Lafayette's French soldiers who died in camp here in 1778. It's Norwich, Connecticut, not Norwich, Vermont. Someplace along the way, I think, this story got mixed in with ours."

"Get a picture of the stone, Devaney," I said. "I'll see you when you get back." I hung up and drove straight for the French Acre.

From a half mile away I could see Charlie Rivers' truck. I eased over onto the shoulder a distance away, then walked the last hundred yards. When I poked my head in the hole in the wall, Charlie was standing near the most recently cleared section, facing away from me. He held a small split branch in his hands. I stood perfectly still and watched.

"No sense gawking, whoever you are," he called, not turning around. "Come in, if you like."

"It's Hoag," I said, stepping in on the silty floor of what had become a third-of-an-acre room without a ceiling.

"No Devaney? He sick?"

"Guess you're not clairvoyant after all. He's away for the long weekend." I labored through the soft soil toward Rivers.

"Okay, Devaney's away. What brings you out? It's a lovely day, a long weekend, you should be enjoying yourself, Hoag, maybe doing a little leaf-peeping."

"What brings me out is the soldiers. Devaney did his homework. You were right. They're not French soldiers. That story comes from a different Norwich, the one in Connecticut. Somehow the story of Lafayette's soldiers dying of disease while encamped at a place called Norwich got mixed in, or borrowed, or co-opted, whatever, with something similar here. Right? What we call the French Acre isn't French at all, is it?"

"Nope. It's British."

"British? How do you know that? This whole walled-in crypt may be just another Cardiff Giant, a colossal hoax. We've found nothing written down anywhere that would suggest anything actually happened to a detachment of French, American, British, German, or other soldiers here—or to anyone, for that matter. Maybe it was just a cow pasture. If something happened, don't you think someone would have recorded it?"

"I'm pretty sure I've located thirteen so far," Rivers said, motioning toward the reflectors.

A little leap in the pit of my stomach told me he was right.

"There was a reason no one ever wrote it down," he said.

He was forcing my brain to work hard now. "Shame?" I asked. "Something they didn't want future generations to know about?"

Charlie nodded.

"Like maybe the soldiers were sick and quarantined," I said. "But the Colonists abandoned them—and walled them in?"

Charlie Rivers said nothing, and I stood mulling it over in my reporter's mind.

"Then if none of this is written down," I said, "how did you know?"

"Oral history. Indian. My mother was an Abenaki medicine woman. She passed the story on to me. She said the whites wouldn't tell it, wanted to forget it." Rivers sat on a stump and motioned for me to sit on a log.

"They did not die of disease, my mother said. Shortly after the American Revolution began, twenty of the King's soldiers camped here in the pasture. The men of Norwich who were able-bodied enough to fight had already left to join the armies of the Colonies, so the few males who were left were either young or old or infirm. It was largely a community of women."

"Are you saying the soldiers went into town and raped them?" I asked, thinking I could see where he was going.

"No, they didn't. In fact, if they had, what followed might have seemed somehow justified. But the soldiers were gentlemen. They hired six women to cook for them here at the pasture campsite. But the women feared their militiamen-husbands might meet these same British soldiers on the battlefield. So they obtained a sleeping potion and mixed it with the soldiers' evening meal. While the 20 soldiers slept soundly, the women slit their throats, all twenty of them. They hastily buried the dead where they had bled out."

"But why the wall? To hide the shame?"

"Maybe."

"What're you thinking—that the wall was to keep the spirits in?"

Rivers shrugged. "I don't know. They're here, though."

"And you think that's what's caused the crashes, the deaths—every single one a fatality, never a survivor. You think the spirits inside—on the desecrated ground—drew the vehicles and passengers to the wall?"

Rivers shrugged again, and I glanced at the reflectors.

"So what's your part in all this? What drew you in?"

"The last accident with the four boys. That one finally opened a hole in the wall. For years I sensed something here, but I couldn't tell exactly what. The morning after this accident, when I stood by the break in the wall, I knew what I had to do."

"Mark the graves?"

Rivers didn't answer at first, looked away from me. Then he said, "Yeah, mark the graves."

"You believe that'll make the difference? You think it'll stop the accidents? I mean, wouldn't it be easier to just press the Town to tear down the wall?"

"Crazy as it sounds, it's a historic site," Rivers said. "The parents of the last two kids killed here tried to have it demolished and failed. Anyway, it's a part of people's mental landscape. Too much public sentiment in favor of keeping it."

"But back to my question. Do you somehow believe dowsing the dead and putting up grave markers will put an end to it?"

Rivers mistook my impatience, my reporter-style interrogation, for hostility. “Excuse me,” he said, rising to his feet. “I’ve got at least a half-acre left to clear and time’s running out.” He picked up the chainsaw and fired it up, but even at the eruption of the saw the necklace of crows on the wall never flinched.

* * *

When Devaney got back from Connecticut, I filled him in on my visit with Charlie Rivers.

"What do you suppose he means, time’s running out?” Devaney asked.

“I assume he means time’s running out to get the brush cleared and the spots marked.”

“But what’s this time limit he’s up against? Does he have to finish before the snow flies? Before the year is out? Before Halloween and the witching hour?”

“Maybe before the wall claims any more victims.”

“Oh, come on, Hoag, we aren’t buying into that yet, are we? As far as I can see, what we’ve got is a string of unrelated automobile accidents over a period of decades, an old dowser clearing brush, and thirteen driveway reflectors that *might* be marking some Revolutionary War graves. Heck, you haven’t even got enough to pull together a story on it yet, have you?”

Something Devaney said struck me: *a string of unrelated automobile accidents*.

"They’re not unrelated automobile accidents,” I said. “They’re all related to the French Acre. And they all resulted in fatalities, no survivors. There’s something here, Devaney. I know there’s something here, and it’s got to do with Charlie Rivers’ story.”

“Don’t forget the crows. I don’t suppose you asked Rivers about the crows.”

I hadn’t. I’d completely forgotten.

“Tell you what,” I said. “This week you do a little genealogical research.”

“On who? Or is it *whom*?” he said, rolling his eyes.

"On the car crash victims."

"The four boys?"

"No. On all of them. See if they trace back to Colonial families who lived in Norwich."

"What? What are you thinking, Hoag—that it's a revenge thing, the march of the dead soldiers?"

"I don't know what it is. But if there are ties here—if they're all descendants of the women who massacred those British soldiers—there's enough for a story."

"And what're you gonna do?"

"I'm going out to help Charlie Rivers," I said.

"Help him do what?"

"Clear brush. And dowse the dead."

* * *

For the next three weeks I worked side-by-side with Charlie Rivers. He didn't talk much, and I didn't pressure him. A nominal trust seemed to build between us—or maybe he was simply ignoring me. On my fifth day I noticed several new reflectors in the ground. He must have dowsed at night or before I arrived that morning. Another reflector appeared the tenth day, giving a total of seventeen. That's what we had on Halloween morning, October 31. We also still had a quarter acre of brush to clear.

"Hoag," Charlie said that day as we sat eating lunch from paper bags. "I appreciate your help. I really do."

"Are you disappointed we won't get it cleared by tonight?" I said, remembering Devaney's comment about Halloween and the witching hour.

"No. Why?" Rivers said, looking surprised.

"Oh, I don't know," I said. "I just thought, you know, Halloween, the crows, the deadline you mentioned."

"What about the crows?"

"Well, you never mention them. There are hundreds of them. They've been here for almost four months now. They wouldn't come near this place for decades, maybe longer. What do you make of them?"

"Harbingers of death, I suppose. Don't you think? I mean, most cultures see ravens and crows as symbols of death, right?"

"But the four kids died months ago. These soldiers—if they are indeed under this soil—died hundreds of years ago. Why are the crows still here?"

"You're the reporter, Hoag," Charlie Rivers said, and got to his feet. "I don't explain this stuff. I just sense it."

That afternoon, after we cleared a small patch of brush, Rivers let me watch as he used a split apple branch to dowse it. I'd never seen anyone dowse for water before—certainly never for bodies—and I had a healthy skepticism based on the Ouija board I'd tried using with my cousins when we were kids. But when Charlie stood over a certain spot, the stick did seem to quiver faintly in his rough hands. He had me mark the location with a reflector.

I left early that afternoon to get home for trick-or-treaters. Charlie said he'd stay until dark.

Devaney's genealogy search didn't produce the results I had hoped for. Not one victim had a connection to any colonial Norwich families.

"But I did discover something else," Devaney said. "It looks like every one of them had a trace of Abenaki Indian blood in their veins."

The next day was Saturday. Devaney and I drove to the French Acre right after breakfast, both dressed to clear brush. The crows were there, but Charlie Rivers hadn't arrived. We poked our heads in, then stepped inside and nosed around.

Eighteen markers. Maybe an eighth of an acre left to clear.

"Guess All Saints Day isn't his deadline," I said. "That's today."

We heard a vehicle crunch up on the gravel. A minute later Dutch Roberts stepped into the mostly cleared French Acre. He gave a whistle of surprise.

"Morning, Hoag, Devaney," he said. "What brings you two out on a Saturday? Looks like you're dressed for gardening."

"We're giving Charlie a hand today," I said. "It's a lot of work for one man alone. And what about you? What brings you out? Come to help?"

"Hell, no," Dutch laughed. "Did enough bush-hogging when I was younger. My back won't stand it now. If I laid into it, I'd have to spend the afternoon on the heating pad."

I could see Dutch's eyes sweeping the place, taking in the reflectors.

"The graveyard's grown," he said.

"What makes you think it's a graveyard?" Devaney said.

We hadn't been in touch with Dutch since the week following the accident.

"Oh, just a guess," Dutch said. "Not very orderly rows, though. Maybe it'll all make more sense when you put up the little flags."

"What flags?" I asked. Dutch looked genuinely surprised that we didn't know.

"The ones Charlie Rivers ordered through Dan and Whit's store. They're the size you put on graves for the holidays."

"How'd you find out?" I asked.

"Oh, a bunch of us were shooting the breeze at Dan & Whit's. Veteran's Day came up, which is what—nine or ten days away? The store clerk mentions Charlie Rivers was in the other day and hit the roof because his two twelve-packs of flags hadn't come in. Seems he'd ordered them around Labor Day—a special order—and the clerk had forgotten to call it in. So now Charlie's sweating it. They told him they'd call around to flag stores and distributors."

"But what's the big deal?" Devaney asked. "Charlie can go down to the VFW or the American Legion and get them, no problem."

"No you can't, Devaney," Dutch said. "They're foreign flags, not American flags. French, I'd guess. Makes sense, this being the French Acre. So I'm figuring the flags will take the place of the reflectors on Veteran's Day. Maybe Charlie will have a little memorial service."

I could see Devaney was itching to say, "Or maybe two dozen British Union Jacks," so I shot him a button-your-lip look.

Although Rivers hadn't said the story he shared with me was told in confidence, I presumed it was, so I'd said nothing to anyone except Devaney, who had followed suit. And we didn't tell Dutch then.

Charlie Rivers still hadn't shown up by the time Dutch left, so Devaney and I worked for a couple of hours clearing brush, then drove to Dan and Whit's for coffee and sandwiches.

"We're helping Charlie clear brush down at the French Acre," I said. "I know he ordered some cemetery flags—French, maybe—and I wondered when they're expected in."

"British, not French," the clerk was quick to correct. "And they'll be here in under two weeks."

"So not in time for Veteran's Day next week?" Devaney asked.

"No. But I asked Mr. Rivers about that, too. He said he didn't need them for Veteran's Day. He'll have them soon."

In the car Devaney said, "So if the deadline isn't Veteran's Day, when is it? And why?"

"I don't know," I said. "But I'm worried about Charlie. I'm going to call his house and see what's up."

Rivers sounded puny when he answered the phone. He'd come down with the flu and was worried it would put him behind schedule. I said we'd drop by with some hot soup from Dan & Whit's.

Twenty minutes later we were in Charlie's living room. He lay on his couch, wrapped in a blanket, shivering. On the coffee table sat a jar of yellow powder, a blue bottle, and a bowl containing a bright yellow paste.

"Home remedies?" I asked.

"Abenaki potions," he said. "For big aches and pains." He wasn't kidding. The man was sick. He looked terrible.

"Try an old-fashioned remedy from our tribe," Devaney said, holding out the container of chicken soup.

Charlie smiled weakly and said thanks. After an awkward silence he admitted he was worried about the French Acre, so I volunteered to keep working at it while he was down with the flu. He was grateful.

"Clear, but don't dig up anything, Hoag," he said. "Same as we've been doing it all along. Don't disturb what's under."

"Want us to try dowsing, too?" Devaney asked. This was his first day working inside the French Acre.

"You're welcome to try," Rivers said. "I doubt you'll have much luck. If you haven't sensed water, you probably won't sense the dead. But who knows? It won't hurt to try. Even if you don't locate anyone, I'll be back soon."

We stood at Rivers' front door and I called back to him, "What's the deadline?"

"Umm, night of the twenty-fourth," he said. "It's got to be ready by then."

"Why the twenty-fourth?" Devaney asked.

"You'll see," Rivers called back, then whispered loudly, comically, "It's a secret."

The next day was Sunday, so Devaney and I only put in half a day's work, a three-hour morning. We cleared a twenty-by-ten piece of land that each of us tried unsuccessfully to dowse. Maybe there just wasn't anybody down there. As we gathered our tools together to leave, the two of us stood in the center of what was essentially a huge, high-walled, private cemetery for a very few inhabitants.

"Notice something different, Devaney?" I asked.

Devaney beamed proudly. "Yeah, it's just a little bit bigger now, Hoag, thanks to our efforts."

"No," I said. "Something else." He looked up and his body slowly made the turn.

"Damn," he said. "No crows. Not a single, damned crow. Were they around when we got here this morning?"

"Can't recall," I said.

Neither could he.

We worked the next week, half days only. It was all the manual labor our poor old bodies could take.

Charlie Rivers gained enough strength to make a brief appearance on Friday. When he saw our progress, he split an apple branch and located number 19.

Devaney handed him a reflector to mark the spot. While he stood poking it into the soft soil the crows fluttered back in threes and fours.

"Hoag, Devaney, you guys have been great," Charlie Rivers said. "And I thank you with all my heart. But I know I can handle it from here on. That's 19, so there's one left—probably the sentry. My guess is I'll find him in that last corner. I've got two and a half weeks. Weather permitting, I'll make it just fine. I'll get back to clearing brush tomorrow. Thanks again."

We were pretty tuckered out, so being dismissed didn't feel so bad. We told him we did have stuff to do in our own lives, but we'd check in on him regularly, see if he needed anything. We shook hands, packed up our tools, and left.

It rained 10 of the next 14 days. The whole Upper Valley was one gigantic puddle. The French Acre wasn't immune. Several times when it was coming down hard, we drove by and saw Charlie Rivers sipping coffee in his pickup truck, parked in front of the nine-foot wall, waiting for the rain to slack off enough so he could wade in and fight to get a little chainsaw work done. He made little progress in the two-week stretch. Even if we had wanted to, there wasn't a thing we could do to help.

Monday and Tuesday, the seventeenth and eighteenth, I was tied up with a couple of writing assignments farther south in Springfield and Ascutney. But I didn't need a photographer, so Devaney helped Charlie out for part of the day.

"The guy's killing himself," Devaney told me on the phone the second night. "He's there at dawn and works until dark. And I don't believe he's fully recovered from that flu yet."

I told Devaney I had to make another trip south Wednesday on the Springfield story, but I'd try to help out Thursday.

"Have you found out why the deadline is the twenty-fourth?" I asked.

"He's pretty tight-lipped about it," Devaney said. "Near as I can figure, it's the day before the full moon, so maybe there's a tie-in there."

Wednesday afternoon when I got home from Springfield I had a message from Nelda Potter on the answering machine.

"He's got the whole place lit up," Nelda told me when I called her back. "He's been working the last two nights there, running a generator and electric lanterns. I don't drive at night, but my neighbors told me. They said it looks positively eerie, the light shining through the opening in the wall where the boys hit it, and lit up like a searchlight from inside, shining toward the heavens. The crows stay there at night now. I don't think they did that before."

I phoned Devaney, who had just gotten back from helping Rivers at the French Acre.

"I saw the generator and the lanterns, but I didn't realize Charlie had been staying round the clock," Devaney said. "I'm only on days. We're making headway and, if you help out, the three of us should have it all cleared by this weekend—Monday at the latest, and that's the twenty-fourth. Still, I'm betting we'll get it done and he'll locate the last grave by the weekend."

Thursday morning Devaney picked me up and we drove to the French Acre. Charlie's pickup was parked in front, but when we stepped through the opening in the wall, he wasn't anywhere to be seen. The generator wasn't running and there were no lanterns lit. The area of uncleared brush was down to about thirty-by-thirty. We stepped back out toward the road and looked in the pickup. Charlie was stretched across the bench seat, curled up under an Army blanket.

"I hope he's just asleep," Devaney said, and prepared to rap on the window.

"Don't," I said, grabbing his wrist. "The man's exhausted. He needs the rest. You and I can get started without him."

We cleared brush as quietly as we could for two hours, not firing up the chainsaw. Finally Charlie Rivers appeared behind us.

"Morning," he said. "Thanks for letting me catch a few winks."

"No problem," I said. "No sense killing yourself over a deadline. Besides, we'll make it by Monday night, no sweat. The weather report for the four or five days is good—at least until the full moon."

Rivers smiled. He knew I was fishing.

"More than a full moon," he said, and turned to walk back out of the Acre. "If you two don't mind, I've got to pick something up at Dan & Whit's. Then I've got to hitch up my trailer and pick up a load. Back in a couple of hours."

Devaney and I worked until noon, then knocked off for the day as planned. Using two chainsaws we had made a commendable dent in what remained. Rivers still hadn't returned by the time we packed up and left.

Carol invited her mother and father over for dinner that night, and after we gave an update on the French Acre, my mother-in-law said, "Is this some kind of a special full moon?"

"Good question, Mom," Carol said. "You mean, like a harvest moon, a corn moon, a wolf moon—one of those superstition things? Wolves howling, asylums and emergency rooms filling up, people freaking out? I read somewhere that lunar and lunatic come from the same Latin word."

Before Devaney could roll his eyes, I said, "You know, could be you're onto something. We like to check out all possibilities, don't we, Devaney?"

He rolled his eyes. "Well, it's not a Blue Moon," he said. "That's when you get a second full moon in the same month—like first and twenty-ninth, second and thirtieth, third and thirty-first. I don't know about the others."

While the three of them were having dessert, I went to my study and got on the Internet, planning to do a search for Full Moon. But Devaney's comment about the Blue Moon had stuck in my mind. I typed Blue Moon in instead of Full Moon. A World Book encyclopedia article came up.

The term blue moon was used as early as 1528 to represent an absurd belief. Later, people described uncommon events as occurring "once in a blue moon." Blue moon also refers to rare types of full moons.

Two types of full moons qualify. According to one definition, a blue moon is the second full moon in a month that has two full moons. According to an older definition, a blue moon is the third full moon in a season that has four full moons. The older definition was developed using a calendar in which spring always begins on March 21.

* * *

So a blue moon wasn't simply the second full moon in the same month, as Devaney had said and as I had always thought. There was an older, different definition.

I did a computer search for phases of the moon and came up with charts from the U.S. Naval Observatory. I found the one for the current year, 1996. In the autumn quarter the full moons fell on September 27, October 26, November 25, and December 24—four full moons in a quarter. And the third one—the blue moon—would be on Tuesday, November 25 at 4:10 a.m. It was the definition I hadn't known about, the one that didn't require two full moons in the same month. Charlie had said it was more than just a full moon.

So that was why Charlie Rivers needed to be done by Monday night, the twenty-fourth. Although the date of the blue moon would be Tuesday, the twenty-fifth, because it was in the wee hours of the morning Tuesday, it would seem as if it were appearing late Monday night, after midnight.

I printed out a copy of the article and the astronomical chart to show Devaney. Retired history teachers could be such know-it-alls, but they weren't always right.

"Maybe he figured there was going to be an even worse accident on the blue moon," Devaney said. "So he wanted to clear and mark all the graves with the flags. You know, the honorable thing, thinking it'd set things right and save some lives."

"Sounds plausible," I said. "But who can say? I sure don't know what's in that man's mind. As he said, we'll have to wait and see."

Friday morning we were met by more than a hundred bales of straw stacked at the opening in the wall. Charlie's pickup and utility trailer weren't around, but there was a note pinned on a bale of straw blocking the opening: *Devaney and Hoag. Can you move the straw inside? Don't break the bales apart, just space them evenly around the ground. Back soon. Thanks. C.T.R.*

"Looks like we're going to seed it and cover it with straw for the winter," Devaney said. "We'll have grass in the spring. Old Charlie's gonna give the town a park."

We had lugged the last bales inside and were resting on them when the pickup and trailer pulled up in front and Charlie beeped his horn. Devaney and I clambered out to see what he wanted.

The truck and trailer were piled high with more bales. The three of us unloaded them and, under the watchful eyes of the crows, hauled them inside the compound.

By Sunday noon we had all the brush and trees cut, cleared, and piled outside the walls. It took Charlie less than five minutes to locate the twentieth soldier's resting place. I marked it with a reflector.

"That's all of them, right, Charlie?" Devaney asked.

"Twenty. That's it. But just to be sure, I'll make a final sweep of the place after lunch. That'll be it, guys. Your work is done. I appreciate all the time and labor you've put in."

"But what about the straw?" I asked.

"Yeah. Where's the grass seed?" Devaney added. "Don't you want us to help you seed it?"

Charlie stared at us. "Oh, the seed? Umm, I haven't picked it up yet. I'll get it tomorrow—and I'll rent a spreader—it'll be light work. I can handle it myself. Can't spread the straw until the seed's laid down, but the straw will be light work, too. You two have done more than enough. Thanks."

"But I thought you had a deadline of tomorrow?" Devaney asked.

"And what about the flags?" I asked.

Charlie Rivers looked sheepish.

"Charlie, you didn't bust your hump to clear this place out by tomorrow just to create a town park. It's about them," I said, motioning around us at the reflectors. "It's about the soldiers."

"Yeah, Charlie," Devaney added. "Why don't you spill it?"

Rivers looked uncertain for a moment, measuring us. Then he said, "Tomorrow night. Come after midnight, right around three-thirty in the morning. Nobody else. Just you two. I'll take care of everything between now and then. Don't come beyond the opening in the wall, though. Stay outside."

"Okay," I said. "Three-thirty, not before. Just the two of us. Can you tell us what you're going to do?"

"No, I can't," Rivers said. "And Hoag, Devaney, promise me—no cameras. Promise. No cameras."

"Promise," I said, Devaney standing dumbly beside me.

The rest of that day and all of Monday we honored Charlie's request and left him alone. Twice on Monday we drove by and saw his vehicle there. On our first pass we noticed he'd picked up another load of straw, which he carried in without help. On the second pass we saw him carrying ropes and two-by-fours. But we didn't stop.

Devaney came by after supper and we half-watched a couple of TV shows. Our minds weren't on TV, they were on Charlie Rivers and the French Acre. We rehashed all the information we'd collected, went over everything we'd seen and done. But, except for the idea of a memorial service, we had no idea.

"He said no cameras," Devaney said. "But he didn't say no tape recorders."

"I've got two in my coat," I said. "One in each pocket." We each had heavy winter coats, scarves, gloves, and hats. It was going to be a very cold, frosty night, the forecast said, but no wind chill.

We watched the ten o'clock news on one channel, the eleven o'clock news on another, and a late-night talk show. When we couldn't stand it any longer, we went out to an all-night truck stop for bacon and eggs. At 2 a.m. we paid the bill, walked out into the parking lot under what seemed to be a full moon and slowly made our way toward the French Acre.

We rounded the last curve onto the straightaway and could see it. With the light of a full moon above and lantern light inside, it looked eerie, like a huge crown that was glowing on top. It wasn't yet 2:30, so we pulled off the road two hundred yards before it. Devaney pulled out the thermos he'd filled at the truck stop and we drank a couple more cups of coffee. We saw Charlie make a couple of trips to the truck, the last one for a ladder.

I heard Devaney's door open.

"Just got to step out and pee," he said. "Get rid of some of this diner coffee."

When I looked out his window a minute later, I saw a camera in front of his nose. I pressed the button and lowered his window.

"What are you doing?" I asked. "I thought you were peeing. We promised Charlie no cameras."

Devaney clicked off a shot, turned his head toward the open window, and whispered loudly, "I am peeing. A good photographer has to be able to do two things at once. And I heard Charlie to say he wanted no cameras *inside*. And, regarding no cameras, I believe he said *after 3:30*."

Sometimes Devaney could split hairs and mince words better than the teenagers he'd taught. This wasn't the time to argue with him.

"Hurry up," I said. "The cold air's pouring in."

He climbed back in and closed the door as quietly as he could. I hoped Charlie hadn't heard the noise or caught a glimpse of our dome light while the door was open.

"So what've you got besides the camera?" I asked. "Video surveillance equipment?"

"As a matter of fact, I've got the mini-video cam in the bag behind me, and a collapsible tripod. I know we can't take it inside, but I figured we could set it up just before 3:30 outside the hole in the wall. It's the only way I'll get any shots to compare with the others I took."

Devaney had shot dozens of rolls of film the past several months, both inside and outside the French Acre. The walls of his study bore witness to the gradual success of Charlie's brush-clearing efforts.

At 3:15 I started the engine and we eased behind Charlie's utility trailer. The light shining in the French Acre silhouetted the hundreds—maybe thousands—of crows on the wall. We could see the moonlight shining off the feathers of the ones closest to us. They seemed to glow an iridescent blue-black, as if they had auras.

Devaney opened his door and started to climb out.

"Hey, what are you doing?" I asked, putting a hand on his arm. "It's early."

"Relax," Devaney said. "I'm simply going to see if everything's okay with Charlie. Maybe he needs a little last-minute help." Then he added, "Besides, I figured I'd get set up." He reached for the mini-cam on the back seat.

"Just wait," I said. "Give him until twenty-five-after, anyway."

Devaney gave me a pouty look and reluctantly slid back into the car. I pulled out my two miniature tape recorders and tried them. Both worked fine.

"A little nervous?" Devaney asked. "Eager to get down to brass tacks?"

Before I could answer, a truck pulled up behind us. I sighted along my outside mirror and saw a large figure in heavy clothing get out. He walked straight toward my driver's-side window. He approached like a cop on a traffic stop.

"Hoag? Devaney?" a deep voice asked as I lowered my window. I tried to look up at the man, but he shone a flashlight right in my eyes. "You're both under arrest," he said, then started to giggle, "for idiocy!"

"Dutch? Dutch Roberts?" I sputtered. Well, what the—" Both Dutch and Devaney were laughing now. "Devaney," I said. "Did you tell him we'd be here tonight?"

"Yes, he did," Dutch said. "He called me during The Tonight Show."

"Hoag, I know nothing's going to happen," Devaney said. "But we could be walking into an ambush, and nobody else knows we're here."

"Ambush? You think Charlie's taken almost three months to set us up for an ambush? What's he going to do—scare us to death?"

The two of them kept chuckling.

"All right, Dutch, get in the back seat, damn it. But first," I said, catching a glimpse of the holster on his hip, something he almost never wore, "please put that pistol in your glove compartment. There's nobody here but me, Devaney, a sick old Indian dowser, and a boatload crows."

Dutch obliged.

When it was time, we all got out and approached the wall.

"Look at that," Devaney said. "He must have seeded it all by himself."

Dozens of kerosene lanterns hung from spikes pounded into the inside walls. Every inch of ground had been covered with loose straw. But the layer of straw was far too thick to be protecting newly sown grass seed. The straw looked to be more than a foot deep. The driveway reflectors were gone. In their places were small British flags taped to the ends of long, straight branches.

"What in the hell is that?" Dutch said, pointing toward the center of the French Acre.

Something like a tree fort, a cross between a duck blind and a giant rattan barstool, stood eight feet above the ground on poles. The wooden ladder we'd seen earlier was leaned up against it.

Charlie Rivers sat cross-legged in its center, head down, forearms on knees, palms upturned.

"What's he doing?" Devaney whispered. "Yoga?"

"Some kind of meditation," Dutch said.

Devaney set up his tripod and mounted the mini-cam on it. He panned across the Acre a couple of times, wanting to capture the bluish-gold color of the straw, which looked like an ocean. He zoomed in on Charlie in the tower, then panned around at the faces of the crows, every one facing the tower.

"Has he got his eyes closed?" Dutch asked.

"Of course he does," Devaney said. "He's meditating."

A moment later Charlie Rivers began removing his clothing.

"It's ten-to-four," I said into the tape recorder. "After a period of what appears to have been meditation, the man we're watching has started taking off his protective clothing. Hat, coat, boots, shirt."

"Damn, he's got to be freezing," Dutch said. "Is this a man in his right mind?"

Charlie's striptease went on for ten minutes as if it were a ritual thing until he had nothing left but his long underwear and tee shirt. At four o'clock I reported into my tape recorder that he was sitting buck-naked on the platform.

"Oh-ah-wa-hay-ye-ah," Charlie chanted. The tape player was too far away to pick it up, but I repeated into it what I thought I heard Charlie saying. He sang it like a mantra, kept repeating it the way I'd heard Native American rain dancers do it in Arizona.

A cloud passed across the moon and I felt a chill run down my spine. It was 4:05 when I mentioned the cloud and my chill on the tape.

"It's some kind of purification ceremony, ain't it?" Dutch asked.

Neither Devaney nor I answered.

Rivers had lit six lanterns and arranged them on the platform around him. He prepared what looked like a smudge pot on his lap and began streaking his face. At first I thought of war paint. Then I thought of Ash Wednesday, the first day of Lent, and my mind conjured up a memory of my wife Carol returning from the worship service at church with a smudge of ash on her forehead, a sign of repentance.

"What time is it, Dutch?" Devaney asked.

"Four-oh-nine," Dutch said, and before he could say more the crows moved—just slightly, ever so slightly—all of them. We heard their feathers rustle, all of their feathers together.

"Jeezus," Devaney said, and we all shivered. "What was that about?"

"Four-oh-nine, as I said," Dutch answered. "Four-oh-nine and going on the witching hour."

Charlie stood up on the platform with his arms raised, with what appeared to be leather thongs around his biceps. He continued chanting to the skies, maybe to the gods. Or was it to the moon? To the blue moon?

We saw the crows move again, heard the sea of feathers rustle.

"What happens now?" Dutch asked.

"I don't know," I said. "Four-ten. Full moon. Wait and see."

Charlie stopped chanting. He turned around in a circle once, twice, three times, and reached for the lanterns. He swung in a softball pitcher's windup and flung them toward the corners of the compound. One. Two. Three. Four. Five. Six. The lanterns landed, some without breaking, others with the sound of shattering glass chimneys. The loose straw quickly caught fire around each lantern.

"Rivers!" Dutch yelled. "What in hell are you doing? You damned fool, get out of there." He sprang through the opening but immediately floundered in the loose straw and fell over.

"Dutch, get back here," Devaney screamed. "You can't get to him now."

The two of us grabbed the constable and dragged him back to the opening.

Charlie stood chanting wildly. In no time the entire surface of the compound was engulfed in flames. The crows stood their ground, moving their wings in wider sweeps now—fanning the flames—bringing in oxygen from outside the wall. They cawed, a cacophony that mixed with but didn't drown out Charlie Rivers' insane chanting. The six separate fires from the lanterns connected and moved toward the center, bound for Charlie's tower. We saw the twenty British flags disappear in the hungry flames.

"Oh my God, oh my God," we would later hear Devaney say on tape.

A moment later the heat was so intense we had to back away from the opening. Even above the snapping and popping, though, we heard the tower come crashing to the ground, and Charlie's screams.

The crows lifted off *en masse* then as Devaney and I stood transfixed, watching stupidly as they flew across the moon and out over the deep dark woods.

Dutch ran to his truck to call the Fire and Police Departments. By the time they arrived the French Acre was nothing but a smoking black smudge. The only flames they could douse came from the support poles of Charlie's tower.

Devaney and I sat weeping while the Town and State Police asked us questions.

It was days before we could bear to check the audiotapes and mini-cam footage. We were pretty sure we knew everything we had said on the audiotape. But right after we pulled Dutch up from his fall into the soft straw, as Devaney was saying, "Oh, my God. Oh, my God," we could hear Dutch say, "See them? Soldiers. Blue smoke soldiers." With the intensity of the moment, and with Devaney saying, "Oh, my God. Oh, my God," neither of us recalled Dutch uttering that. And upon questioning, Dutch said he couldn't remember saying it, either. Nor did he remember seeing it. Even when we played the tape, he swore it made no sense to him. Nothing, no blue smoke soldiers—nothing at all—showed up on the videotape to corroborate it.

"So what do you think it was all about?" Devaney asked as we tried to piece it all together in my study. "What'll you put in the story?"

Another *Valley News* staffer had already written up the basic fire story—I was too caught up in it—but there was space reserved in the weekend supplement for the special report I'd be delivering.

"Well, we can tell Charlie's side of it," I said. "We can clear up the misconception that it's Lafayette's French soldiers, explain about Norwich, Connecticut. It'll be interesting to bring in Charlie's background—Abenaki, cemetery groundskeeper, funeral parlor assistant, dowser. We've got the part about the British flags bought at Dan & Whit's, the decades of automobile fatalities, your time and my time working with Charlie. What we saw the night of the blue moon. The crows. Everybody on the road had been talking about the crows. There's plenty here for a story."

"I know that, Hoag. I know there's plenty. But what was it all about? Was it a purification ceremony? Give the soldiers a funeral with honor?"

"Well, sure, obviously it had to be some of that," I said. "But—"

"But what?"

"My guess is, Charlie Rivers didn't tell it all to me, because if he did, he'd have tipped me off that he was going to die in the process, and he knew I'd try to stop him. You see, he told me those Colonial women obtained a sleeping potion they mixed in with the food they fed the soldiers. Charlie didn't say a drug, he said a potion. Remember how he used the same word—potion—when we took the chicken soup to him? The word potion suggests to me it's a pass-down story, handed from generation to generation of Abenaki medicine men and medicine women. That's how his mother got it. He said she was a medicine woman. A potion is something you get from an herbalist, a naturopathic specialist who knows natural cures and remedies—a medicine woman."

"You mean a long-lost, distant relative of Charlie Rivers?" Devaney asked.

"Maybe. But it probably doesn't matter if it was a blood relative or not. It's an issue of honor for the entire tribe."

"Is that what the accidents were about?" Devaney asked. "Remember how the victims all had Abenaki roots? Was the French Acre calling for Abenaki blood?"

"Charlie may have recognized that all along. But it wasn't until the wall opened up after the last accident that he sensed it in his unique way, when he went past the scene the morning after."

"You think Charlie felt it was his duty to do penance, to atone for his tribe's sin?"

"Sin's more a Judeo-Christian word," I said. "I think Charlie's people would say dishonor."

"But it was the colonial women who slit the throats of those soldiers," Devaney said.

"True," I said. "But it was Charlie's Abenaki ancestor, the medicine woman, who supplied the potion. So, whether she knew how the sleeping potion would be used or not, she had a hand in the murder of twenty men."

"But why did the act of atonement—this making right—have to coincide with the blue moon?" Devaney asked.

"I'm not sure. Maybe if we ask an Abenaki medicine person, we'll learn the answer to that. Or maybe it was just something Charlie sensed—you know, with that sixth sense he had. Maybe he just knew that's when it would work."

"What do you mean—work?" Devaney asked.

"Apparently the ceremony, Charlie's sacrifice, worked. I think that's what Dutch—or somebody, maybe Charlie through Dutch—was telling us on the tape. Blue smoke soldiers? Blue smoke, blue moon? Think it's a stretch?"

"I don't know, Hoag" Devaney said, shaking his head. "Maybe. It's a theory. Good thing is, the mystery's solved."

The following spring a team of forensic anthropologists unearthed the remains of twenty men. Buttons and other evidence indicated they had been British soldiers who died during the Revolution. Attempts to determine causes of death were inconclusive. The remains were returned to England.

Two years later the Town dismantled the wall and built a Little League field on the French Acre. Now, for the first time in two hundred years, the French Acre teems with life. The park has been aptly named Soldiers Field.

Night Train to Plantation 13

I kept my eyes averted, not wanting to meet the UPS driver's gaze as I signed for the two packages from Maine. He couldn't have missed the return addresses: a funeral home on one and the Augusta Mental Health Institute on the other. Light bulbs had to be flashing in his head. I figured he'd recognize the heavy smaller box as cremation ashes, an item he'd no doubt delivered before. Not every UPS package required a signature, but a box containing a person's remains, even if only ashes, would surely require one for legal issues.

The second parcel, the one from AMHI, apparently required a signature for a different reason. It wasn't because it exceeded any particular dollar value—I had an idea what was inside and doubted the contents were worth fifty dollars—but likely required delivery acknowledgment to satisfy the sender. *Official Business*, AMHI had stamped it. As if those two words and the return address—a state mental hospital—weren't accusing enough, some social worker had penned in red ink: *YOUR FATHER'S EFFECTS*. I felt the driver's eyes burning into me as I scrawled my signature on the electronic clipboard. I felt embarrassed and ashamed.

Back in the security of my apartment I sat on the couch and stared at the packages. The smaller box from the mortuary seemed less threatening, so I slit it open with my house key. An unsealed envelope lay on top—*Attn: Arnold Burnett*. I opened it and slid out a funeral director's card that identified the ashes as my father's. It also listed a few vital statistics. *Name: Robert Burnett. Age at death: 42*, which I had known. *Place and date of death: Augusta, Maine*, which I had known. *Marital status: never married*, which I had known. *Place and date of birth: Plantation 13, Maine*, which I had not known. My father had never spoken of his hometown except to mention Bangor, Maine, where he had spent his early years with his own father.

Beneath the card sat a thick-walled plastic bag that reminded me of the potting soil I had bought in Wal-Mart, its top puckered and tied off like a belly button. The bag filled the inside of the box completely the way milk spreads to occupy a carton. I opened the top of the bag and touched the ashes, feeling both the softness and the grittiness between my thumb and fingers, letting it sift through. I recalled a line from a soap opera's opening credits: *like sands through the hourglass*, then dug my thumb and fingers deeper into the ashes as if I were clamming a beach below the low water line.

My middle fingertip met something hard, a tiny foreign object that wasn't ashes, and when I worked it free I realized it was a fragment of bone that hadn't been totally incinerated. I felt around and discovered more bits of grit and gristle. I had read that this was common, but this was first-hand and it unnerved me to be sitting on my couch with my father's remains on my fingers and under my fingernails and in the wrinkles of my knuckles. I set the ashes box on an end table and went to wash my hands in the kitchen. My father wasn't going anywhere. I could handle the disposition of the ashes later.

When I got back to the couch, I opened the AMHI box and spread its contents—my deceased father's officially itemized personal effects—on the coffee table. There wasn't much: the clothing he'd been wearing when they checked him in—a pair of black socks, a pair of tan work boots without laces (no doubt removed for his safety), white underpants and white tee shirt, a pair of Lee blue jeans (38W x 34L), a blue chamois work shirt (large), a worn black belt (probably taken from him when he was institutionalized, then returned to me after his death, unlike the disappeared shoe laces), a pair of soft brown work gloves, a hand-knit green-and-white ski cap. In a clear plastic bag I found a promotional pen from the Portland Savings Bank, a dime and three pennies, a Swiss Army knife, and an apartment key. Another plastic bag contained a worn leather wallet shaped by my father's buttock, a ten and three singles. Thirteen bucks. What a lucky guy.

Inside the wallet, a plastic photo insert held his driver's license, social security card, and a snapshot of me in his arms at age three. Even then it had been obvious that I was his kid. We had the same wild hair, flaming red, the same freckled faces, and the same broad, toothy grins.

Another similarity was our eyes. His left eye—which was a glass eye—was a mesmerizing green, an almost perfect match for his right eye, which was a match for my right eye. But the similarity ended there, because although he had a glass left eye, I had no left eye, none at all. What people saw when they looked at me—until the year I turned five and started wearing a black eye patch—was flesh: a sealed eyelid that they mistook for a gigantic skin graft. I had no left eye and, thankfully, no open left socket. This drew unwanted attention, countless intrusive questions, and caused me great embarrassment. People asked why the lid had been sewn shut, and my father would explain that it wasn't stitched but was a congenital defect—the skin had always been that way, there was no functional eye behind the lid, no optic nerve, and corrective surgery would not restore my sight.

When I set my father's wallet back on the coffee table, I caught myself rubbing the eyelid hidden behind the patch. I felt something stir inside me. At 21 years-old, for the first time in my life, I experienced something I had never felt in my teenage years—a deep yearning to be with someone of the opposite sex. I sat a few minutes trying to make sense of it. This was new to me, yet I found I was clear about what the feeling was, though not about what it meant or how to respond to it.

The last item on the table was a purple velvet bag with black drawstrings, a poke bag like a prospector might use for gold dust or a school kid for marbles. The bag hadn't been mine, but I felt it trying to trigger a memory. I'd seen it before, but where? Someone had pulled its strings tight and pinched a sticky label around the top to seal it. I fingered the label, smoothed it out, and made out my father's handwriting: *For Arnie.* I squeezed the bag like it was a Christmas present the contents of which I was trying to guess. A marble, a big one. And something papery, maybe a letter. I sat back on the couch, heart fluttering, hands trembling.

I had seen my father only once in the last two years, and that was when AMHI had the Maine and Connecticut State Police track me down in Connecticut to say he was in the State Hospital in Augusta. He'd had a breakdown. His diagnosis was bipolar disorder with adult-onset schizophrenia. The prognosis sounded bleak. I was devastated.

The one time I visited him he was withdrawn, non-communicative, fragile—shattered. When I saw him curled up on a mattress on the floor of his room, I could hardly bear it. Trite as it may sound, the phrase *a shadow of his former self* perfectly described the man I saw that day. I was confused and ashamed, and in my weakness and isolation I cut him out of my life, exorcised him. I left my father stranded in the mental ward. With absolutely no relatives and very few friends, it was all I could do to take care of myself.

But although I had deserted him, he hadn't abandoned me. Here he was in my living room.

I ripped off the gummy label and loosened the mouth of the bag, half expecting steam or smoke to spew out and a genie to appear. Then, heart on tiptoe, I tipped the bag. The huge round object slid out the bag's throat and plopped against my palm. I stared at it then started to giggle and to laugh. A minute later I was crying and laughing at the same time. There, staring up from my palm, lay not a marble but my father's green glass eye. I hadn't recognized the bag at first, because he used it only once in a blue moon for storage, like the week he was fighting an infection of the socket and couldn't wear it. Most often the bag sat in the drawer of his bedside table.

"Someday it'll be yours," he'd said a couple of times when I was young, but never explained.

I'd always wondered why I might want it, since I had no socket in which to place it. Why would he pass it on to me? But here it was, my bizarre inheritance.

I lifted my eye patch and held the glass eye against the web of flesh, imagining myself inserting it into an empty socket the way my high school friends had popped in their contacts. Would I then look as normal as my father had? I walked to the bathroom and gazed into the mirror. The green eye was an almost perfect match for my good eye, and for a moment I fantasized gouging out the socket with a teaspoon so I could force it in.

A wave of melancholy washed over me—was that it, melancholy? Melancholy for the days when I'd been young and my father had been alive and active in my growing up? Or was this a feeling of sadness and grief at losing him, at feeling lost now, suddenly an orphan?

As I rolled the glass eye around with my thumb, it struck me that it was neither. The feeling was neither nostalgia nor grief. It was more like homesickness, but it wasn't about yearning for a place I'd been before; this was an instinctual pull toward someplace I'd never been, this was a primal feeling like birds get when it's time to migrate.

I set the glass eye on my father's folded white tee shirt on the coffee table, picked up the purple bag again, and drew out a folded piece of paper. It was a letter from my father dated two years earlier, two nights before he had been committed to AMHI.

Dearest Arnie, my son,

Please forgive me for disappearing last month, but I had no choice. I prayed that the breakdown and the mental disintegration would never come for me, but I knew in my heart it would. I even knew when. My cycle is just like my own father's, 42/21, and his father's, and his father's father's. No doubt it's yours, too. Our family line pays a terrible price to continue, always hoping things will be different, better, less cruel for the next generation. So far, though, nothing has changed.

I cannot explain what may lie ahead for you. If you follow my footsteps and my father's and his father's, it will be both an adventure and a curse. I will not tell you what to do or not do, just as my father did not tell me. We make our own choices. I can only tell you this, if you resist the deep yearning awakening in you now, you may live to old age. If you feel you cannot, if you do as I did, you'll find incredible joy, but only for a short while. I have always loved you, my son, and I have never regretted my own choice.

Your loving father,

Robert Burnett

Paper-clipped to the bottom of the letter was an old punched train ticket from Maine. Passage was from Bangor to Eagle Lake to Plantation 13 and back. The ticket had been used 21 years earlier, on the day I was born.

* * *

Two weeks later, during my college's weeklong break, I boarded a bus in New Haven and headed for Maine. Since my father's ashes and letter had arrived and I'd held his glass eye against my eyelid, I had found it impossible to concentrate on class work. My heart ached. At 21, I was finally feeling like a lovesick teenager. Throughout my teens I had been, for all practical purposes, asexual. Neither males nor females had turned me on. I simply had no interest. But now I yearned, I felt desire. But although my eyes wandered after women, it wasn't for just any women, it was women pushing strollers and carriages and carrying their infants in slings across their bellies.

It took me awhile to clarify it, but I soon saw that it wasn't the women I wanted, it was the babies I coveted. I was like a middle-aged woman whose biological clock was ticking too loudly. Not having a child led me to unexpected fits of weeping that caught me off guard. They crept up and blindsided me, and often I sat sobbing at the preciousness and beauty of life, marveling at the miracle of one generation being able to pass itself along to another. Something deep, something primal, was drawing me to northern Maine to my father's home of origin. And though I had never been given a birth certificate, I was sure that his home of origin was also mine.

That afternoon around 1:30 I found myself in the Greyhound station in Bangor, asking where the railway station was so I might catch a train north.

"Ain't no passenger trains out of Bangor, not for years, just freights," the aged ticket agent said through the grillwork of his cubicle. "If you're going north to Millinocket, Houlton, Fort Kent nowadays, you drive or take the bus."

"What about Plantation 13?"

"Plantation 13?" he asked, a note of incredulity in his voice. Then he turned on his stool and called to the fat man sitting behind him at an office desk, "Hey, Charlie, a second one for Plantation 13."

Charlie the manager creaked back heavily in his swivel chair, rose, and edged in beside the older man at the ticket window."Okay, here's the deal," he said. "I'll tell you the same thing I told the other young man."

I pulled off my ski cap then, and my hair caught the two men's attention, momentarily diverting the conversation.

"You two brothers?" Charlie asked, furrowing his brow.

I shook my head. "Don't know any others. Why?"

"You're both redheads," he said. "And same black eye patch."

"And the other kid is going to Plantation 13, too," the old ticket agent added. "He came in last night, must have taken a hotel. His bus leaves in half an hour."

"Bus for where?" I asked.

"It's the Houlton run, but the driver'll drop the kid off at Eagle Lake. They still run an old log train from there out to Plantation 13."

"So Plantation 13 is a town?" I asked.

"Well, yes and no," Charlie said. "You see, a plantation is a sizeable geographical area with no formal government. The land is largely uninhabited, usually cared for by the big paper companies that contract to log them. The only people that far out in the boondocks work in the logging operations."

"What you refer to as Plantation 13," the ticket agent interrupted, "is no more than a cluster of shacks that threatened to blossom into a village shortly after World War II. But it didn't work out. It was too far off the beaten path to support gas stations and supermarkets. What's there now is little more than a ghost town for fifty or a hundred die-hards who are too stubborn to leave."

"Definitely no hospital, right?" I asked.

"Houlton would be the closest," Charlie said. "Why do you ask that?"

"I was wondering where babies would be born."

"Home, I expect," he said. "Unless they plan ahead and stay with friends or relatives in Houlton about the time they're due."

My father's birthplace hadn't been listed as Houlton. The card had read Plantation 13.

"Will I have to piggyback a ride on a log car?"

“No,” Charlie said. “The log train has an engine, a coal car, one or two log flatcars, and a caboose. You and the other kid will end up riding in the caboose with the conductor. It’s not heated, but it’s out of the wind.”

“How come there’s no passenger car?” I asked.

“Because,” said the ticket agent, "that train has two purposes: to get supplies from Eagle Lake to Plantation 13 and to haul logs from Plantation 13 to Eagle Lake. Strictly speaking, it’s not supposed to carry passengers.”

“But I can get a ticket, right?”

“At the café in Eagle Lake they’ll sell you a ticket,” Charlie said. “But it’s a wink-wink sort of thing, not strictly legal. So the waitress will give you is one of the old train tickets they sold twenty-five years ago. Just buy it and give it to the old conductor and he’ll let you ride in the caboose with him.”

“So when does it run? Tonight or tomorrow?”

“It only runs the first and fifteenth, and today’s the fifteenth,” the ticket agent said. “It’s an odd arrangement that has them run two roundtrips today. The locomotive, coal car, and caboose belong to Eagle Lake, but the log cars are the lumber company’s and stay in Plantation 13 so they can load them. They leave Eagle Lake and haul supplies to Plantation 13 in the morning, hook up to the log cars, bring them back to Eagle Lake, then make a second trip back so they can return the log cars, and then run empty back to Eagle Lake.”

“So the train’s already gone today?” I asked, alarmed.

“On the supply run, yes, and to bring back the logs,” Charlie said. “But after supper they’ll leave Eagle Lake, drop the empty cars at the plantation, and come back at midnight.”

“So I have to go to Plantation 13 and ride back the same night?” I said, wondering how I could track down any relatives or get any information in a couple of hours.

"Yep," the ticket agent said. "Unless you want to stay two weeks. Your ticket'll be punched anyway, so it's up to you. You don't have to decide beforehand."

"So it's a couple of hours or two weeks?"

The two men nodded.

"Is there a hotel?"

The two men shrugged and Charlie said, "We're not travel agents. All we can do is sell you a bus ticket to Eagle Lake."

"You in? We've already phoned to say the other kid is coming," the ticket agent said.

I bought a ticket and as I walked away I heard the ticket agent say to Charlie the manager, "Happens every year around this time, doesn't it? Like the swallows returning to Capistrano."

* * *

On the bus trip to Eagle Lake I sat with the other redhead. Tim was from upstate New York, stood four inches taller than I, and spoke in a deeper voice. He also had ruddier skin and more freckles. Except for our height, weight, and skin tone, we had a lot in common. Our unmanageable, flame-red hair looked like we'd both dyed it from the same bottle and our green right eyes matched perfectly. We were 21, born the same day, just as our fathers had been born the same day and died at age 42 the same day in separate mental institutions. Neither Tim nor I had known our mothers nor ever thought to ask about them. Under our eye patches we had the same congenital defect, the sealed eyelid.

In talking we discovered we were both loners, not because we chose to be, but because we felt a natural separateness from other human beings and didn't feel a strong attraction to anyone, either male or female. But we had both found a deep primordial longing, a magnetic attraction toward our roots that seemed to have awakened in us right after the deaths of our fathers. We were like moths drawn to a flame, and I doubt either of us could have abandoned the quest. Something was pulling us, something stronger even than the need to discover our history and origin. We were experiencing feelings so intense that we couldn't begin to fathom them.

We also had in common our fathers' glass eyes. Tim's lay nestled in a hard plastic jewelry case that had been made for a ring. He kept it in his breast pocket close to his heart. Mine lay warm and secure in its purple bag in my side pocket, the bag's drawstrings tied to my belt.

* * *

"We get the train tickets for Plantation 13 inside, right?" Tim asked the driver after we clambered down the bus steps at the Eagle Lake Café.

The driver shrugged, the door shut, and the bus chugged away.

"Better get inside and grab a hamburger, boys," said a voice behind us. "Train leaves in 15 minutes."

We turned and saw a man leaning out the café's front door. Judging by his furrowed face, he was well past retirement, but still he wore the black uniform and hard-billed hat of a railroad conductor. Protruding from under his hat was a thinning layer of not gray but flaming red hair. I could see by the light of the porch bulb that he wore a black patch over his eye. When he caught us staring at it, he flipped the patch up and revealed a fleshy eyelid sealed like mine.

"Food and tickets in the café," he said, and walked inside.

The café was warm and its only waitress hospitable. I wanted to sit at a table and ask questions of the conductor, but all six tables were taken, one of them by the conductor, engineer, and brakeman Tim and I would have preferred to speak with the conductor privately, since neither the engineer nor the brakeman was a redhead. And they each had two eyes.

“We’ll talk on the train,” the old conductor told me.

Tim and I sat at the counter. We ordered hamburgers, fries, and milkshakes, which we wolfed down as if this was our last meal. The waitress sold us two roundtrip train tickets.

“We usually close at nine, but this being a special occasion, we’ll be open all night,” she said. “Those who get back after midnight usually drink coffee or nap with their heads on the tables until the morning when the bus pulls in at 7:30.”

The train crew got up before I could ask what she meant by special occasion, so Tim and I stood too. We left enough for the bill and a good tip and followed the men outside to the train. While the engineer and the brakeman climbed up into the cab of the locomotive, we followed the conductor into the caboose.

* * *

“I’m sure you’ve guessed by now,” the conductor said as the train pulled out, “that we come from the same stock.” He removed his cap and ran his fingers through his hair—except on top where he was bald. He looked like a monk, and for a moment I thought it might be a disguise, a skullcap like an actor might wear. He saw our surprise at his baldness.

"My apologies, gentlemen,” he said, relaxing in a chair. “I forgot that you’ve only seen your own hair and your fathers’ hair.” He pulled out a pipe and tamped tobacco into it. “Those of us who live past 42 tend to go bald around 50. I’m 73. I’ll likely live to be 100, possibly 105. It appears that longevity is the reward for celibacy in our line. A dubious reward, I’d add.” He removed his black eye patch and set it on the table.

I stared at the conductor’s eyelid, wondering if somewhere he had a green glass eye that his father had passed on to him.

"When we get to Plantation 13," he said, "nobody's going to force you to get off the train. When I was 21, I came here same as you. There were three of us, and I didn't go into town when the other two did. I stayed on the train with the fellow who was the old conductor then. Believe me when I say there's no shame in staying on the train. Even now, I stay aboard when we're in Plantation 13. I've never seen the town, so I can't tell you what's out there. And the boys who make it back don't speak of it. So I don't know, I just don't know. And because I haven't paid my dues, I haven't earned the right to know."

We sat rapt, listening to him.

"But one thing I can say is this: when midnight comes, be on this train, because it pulls out whether you're on it or not. If you're close, I'll pull you aboard if I can. Trust me, you'll want to be on the train. Nobody who's missed it has made the next one two weeks later."

* * *

After an hour's train ride through rugged terrain, the train slowed, and my eyelid began to itch. I was still rubbing it when we pulled to a stop in a broken-down, mist-covered railroad station.

"Plantation 13," the old conductor said from the back porch of the caboose. He made a sweeping arm gesture. "All ashore that dare go ashore," he said without stepping out onto the station platform himself. "If you'll excuse me, we've got to decouple the log cars on the side track, then do an about-face for the return trip. Stay or go, it's up to you, gentlemen. You've got roughly three hours. Remember what I said. Midnight."

I hesitated a moment, thinking about the bald conductor who expected to live to be a hundred, and about my father—and Tim's father—dying insane at forty-two. Deep inside me, logic battled instinct. I was sure Tim was wrestling with the question, too. After a moment we looked at each other and seemed to draw strength from our new relationship. We climbed down from the train and walked toward the dim streetlights that promised some semblance of a downtown.

Plantation 13's business district was a cross between an Old West ghost town and a 1940s movie set without any automobiles. Main Street was dirt, with a couple of side streets off it. No sidewalks, twenty street lamps total, the downtown's wooden buildings needing either paint, patching, or a wrecking ball. A sign in one window proclaimed a bar inside, another a pool hall. One block contained a hotel, a dry goods store, a hardware store, a drugstore/soda fountain, and a barbershop. As we walked down the center of the street I felt like Burt Lancaster and Kirk Douglas pacing through Tombstone on the way to the gunfight at the OK Corral.

On one corner appeared two women dressed like saloon girls in heavy eye makeup. Three others stepped from the shadows of a side street and slunk toward us, waving, teasing. From the door of the bar came two more, with scarlet feather boas around their shoulders and matching feathered Mae West hats. I could sense others closing the gap behind us, and when we turned, we were surrounded by women. They could have formed a chorus line. They all had flaming red hair like ours, and bewitching green eyes—not one eye but two each. These women were beauties—at least they appeared beautiful to me—captivating, *desirable*.

"Hey, sweetie," one called kittenishly to Tim, linking her arm with his as if he were her beau. "Movie starts in ten minutes."

She and a half dozen others raised their hands and pointed to the movie house on the next corner. It said MAJESTIC THEATER. Half of the bulbs of its marquee were burned out and nearly all of the letters had fallen off, so that it was impossible to make out what the movie was.

Two women, one on either side of me, clasped my hands in their warm palms and ushered me toward the theater. One looked to be around eighteen, the other fortyish, but both made my pulse race. I could hardly catch my breath.

Tim had his arm around the shoulder of a knockout and was veering toward the theater. We had a huge crowd of women following closely. There was no animosity among them, no possessiveness or fighting over us. It reminded me of World War II, when the men were away and Rosie the Riveter could play. Where were the men who did the logging? But perhaps this was simply ladies' night on the town, my mind said, trying to convince myself, and these women were treating us like soldiers and sailors at a USO dance. Whatever was up, the women of Plantation 13 were definitely glad to see us.

The ticket booth at the theater entrance was dark and empty, so we walked right in, all of us, close to 75 by then. The concession stands were dark and cobwebbed, the carpets dusty. But inside, it was just like any old theater. The floor slanted toward a stage, above which hung a huge curtain that would soon uncover a screen when the movie started. The aisles were lit by lamps hidden low on the outside seats, and tarnished brass numbers marked the armrests of the seats.

We poured into the center section of the movie house the way teenagers sometimes do, *en masse*, only with Tim and me suddenly the most popular kids in school in the very middle of it all. Dozens of us squeezed into the plush but worn flip-down seats. The only thing missing was popcorn and sodas. And conversation.

I glanced to my right at the younger woman holding my hand, and as I did, I made a mental note of the red EXIT signs that glared at me from either side of the stage.

"Lorraine," the woman purred, as if anticipating my question. "What's yours?" She lightly rubbed my forearm.

I could hardly form words, my mouth was so dry, but finally I croaked out "Arnie."

"Arnie. That's nice," she said, moistening her lips and flaring her nostrils.

The lights dimmed and the curtain opened. In the row ahead of us I heard Tim say, "I'm Tim" to one of the women beside him, and a woman's voice answered, "Tim. That's nice." She lay her head on his shoulder.

A projector lamp flickered behind me somewhere as the curtain in front of us parted, and as it did, a hand caressed the back of my neck. I felt a mix of alarm and pleasure. A moment later the MGM lion roared and the screen came to life as the opening credits rolled. I felt many hands on my arms and shoulders, stroking, massaging, touching lightly. Fingers teased my hair. As my heart raced and the blood pounded in my ears, Lorraine turned to me with longing in her eyes. She opened her lips slightly and her face drew close to mine. I gasped, breathless, then leaned in and met her kiss. It was the most exciting moment of my life.

I couldn't see Tim, but I had no doubt that he too was in the throes of a passionate kiss.

Lorraine's tongue probed my lips and I opened them slightly for her. My entire body was burning up. She slipped her hands behind my neck and drew me to her and I wrapped my arms around her and held her close. My eyelid felt warm and pulsed in time with my heartbeat. Her wet tongue teased mine. I couldn't get enough of it. In that dark theater in Plantation 13 that night, I found myself in another world.

Then suddenly—this is the only way to describe it—more of her tongue slithered past my lips, and more of it, and more. It filled my mouth completely, the tip of her tongue gripping my own tongue at its base as if with pliers—holding me prisoner—so that I had to inhale and exhale rapid shallow breaths through my nose. I opened to my eye and even in the dark could see her green eyes had gone pink, bright pink. They were wide open, glowing, concentrating.

One part of my brain told me I had to remove my arms from her, but another part, something deep down, something instinctive, told me to hold on, and I did. As she filled my mouth with her tongue, I held on for dear life. The movie went on in the background, but it was like being trapped in a dream unable to wake up. It was like hearing and seeing underwater. I had no idea what the movie was about and I didn't care. I was in a state of euphoria, alternately terrified and thrilled, and I lost any concept of time. In that moment I didn't care about the rest of the world.

As the words THE END came on screen, Lorraine broke free as quickly as she had come on to me, her arms cool and clammy now, her tongue recoiling rapidly the way a vacuum cleaner cord rewinds. My mouth sucked down air in big gulps like a newborn babe spanked to life in a strange new atmosphere.

The entire room breathed then, I could hear it. A collective sigh of relief. Or exhaustion. As the lights came up slowly, I could see everyone relax as if they were about to fall asleep after laboring all day in the hot sun.

My eyelid itched and the left side of my head felt heavy, weighted, off-balance. When I put my left hand up to feel my cheek, the cheek was swollen. So was the eyelid. It was puffed out so far that my right eye could see its paunchiness over the bridge of my nose. I felt a migraine building in my head.

From the next row Tim turned and looked up at me. His eyelid was huge, too, as if a bee sting had caused a severe allergic reaction. We looked hideous.

The clapping began. The horde of women started slowly, politely, then gathered intensity and concentration. A rhythm developed and as they clapped their hands together faster and faster and faster, it was like the beating of bees' wings. The sound was hypnotic, and though something told me to rise and run, something else—a voice from eons past—told me all was as it should be.

Lorraine and the woman with Tim clapped, too, then joined their voices in a high-pitched chant, hands moving with blurring speed now. The others blended in, mouths open, their throats producing a *hreee* sound over and over, like nineteen-year locusts on a summer night.I felt my eyelid stretching and straining, the flap of skin struggling to contain the swelling behind it. My head and eyelid were about to explode. Suddenly a bolt of pain shot through my cheek and struck a hot nerve deep down behind my empty eye. Then another pain and another. I couldn't stand it. I yelped and screamed. So did Tim. I stood up. Tim stood up. We wailed together in our agony.

The women ceased their clapping and chanting. The houselights brightened. The entire left side of my face went into a cramp and spasmed.

Suddenly my eyelid burst. So did Tim's. They exploded like piñatas, spewing forth something like wet rice kernels—maggots—that hit the warm air of the theater and metamorphosed into dozens and dozens of tiny bat-like creatures. They grasped the gift of flight instantly, instinctively, and swarmed around Tim and me. The warm air agreed with them, and they grew bigger as they swarmed, so that in no time they were each the size of a thumb. And as they expanded, I could see they had faces—human faces—with tiny wisps of red hair, and legs and arms that began to sprout from their bodies.

Most had two green eyes, but a dozen or more had only one—a right eye, the left one hooded like mine and Tim's. I wasn't afraid of the newly birthed creatures. In fact, I stood in awe. I felt an attraction, an affinity—love.

One landed on my shoulder, a one-eyed creature whose arms and legs had just emerged, and it stared up at me like a pup in a shelter, terrified, eye begging.

The women of Plantation 13 went berserk, scratching and clawing and biting one another to get at the new births—not at the ones on the floor and on the seats that were molting their wings as their lungs filled with oxygen, their bodies swelling and shaping into plump-cheeked, red-haired, two-eyed baby females—but to get at the one-eyed males, grabbing the poor things like chicken legs, ripping them apart with their teeth and swallowing them in quick bites.

Suddenly I knew why I was there.

I curled my hand around the pitiful creature on my shoulder, pressed it inside my shirtfront, and began pushing and punching my way through the crimson-mouthed women in their feeding frenzy.

A steam whistle sounded, barely audible over the din in the theater.

"Tim!" I shouted. "The train!"

He shoved two struggling males inside his shirt, and with elbows and fists fought his way through the hysterical mob. As we started uphill for the lobby, four or five women scuttled over the seats and beat us to the rear door, blocking our retreat.

"There are exits by the stage!" I shouted, and we straight-armed our way through the crowd to the red lights.

Tim flung open the door and a rush of cold night air whooshed in.

"Down there!" a woman a few paces behind us screamed. "They're stealing them."

We stepped out into the chilly night and Tim slammed the door and held it with his shoulder. The steam whistle sounded again, twice this time. I glanced at my watch. Three minutes.

We ran down the alley, and I heard the door crash open behind us. I knew the women were pouring out of the building behind us and we had less than 20 yards on them. As we rounded the corner of the Pool Hall building, we glimpsed another horde of flesh-starved women spilling out the front of the Majestic past the ticket booth.

The steam whistle blasted impatiently. Thank God neither group of women had been able to cut us off from the train. We could see the station and it all came down to a footrace now. All we had to do was outrun them.

"Here they come! Get them!" someone screamed, and four women stepped out from behind the station platform to block our escape.

"Go through them!" Tim shouted, and we tried to knock them down like they were bowling pins.

Tim went down clutching the precious cargo in his shirt. I had two hands free and punched wildly.

"Get up and fight, Tim!" I cried. "Use your hands."

But they piled on him too fast and the other two groups of women were almost on us.

"Come on! Run!" I heard the conductor shout. "You're the only one with a chance now. Run!"

The whistle blasted six or eight times in rapid succession then, and I could see the train moving slowly away. It was no longer struggling to overcome its own inertia, now it was rolling steadily forward, picking up speed. I put a hand to my shirt, made sure that my own cargo was still there, and lit out for the tracks. It looked like it was moving away faster than I was running.

"Run!" the conductor yelled again. "Run!"

I heard the women's voices behind me but didn't dare turn to look. Puffing and panting, I managed to match my pace with the train's forward movement then reached out for the old man's open hand. For a moment I was sure the train had gotten just beyond my reach, but then the old conductor grabbed the handrail, swung himself as far back as he could and clamped his hand around my wrist. I gripped his wrist, too, and he swung me to safety. I looked back and saw my pursuers abandon their footrace.

The conductor ripped up a white sheet for us to use as swaddling cloths and, clearly envious, spent as much time as he could rocking my son. Or perhaps it had been Tim's I had scooped up. I don't know why, but we didn't speak of Tim on the trip back to Eagle Lake. The child cried and slept like any other baby and by the time we reached the Eagle Lake station, he had plumped up enough that he was pink and fleshy and—except for his webbed left eyelid—looked just like any newborn.

The kindly conductor swabbed the sticky afterbirth fluid from my eye socket and covered it with gauze. He cautioned me not to insert my father's glass eye for at least two full weeks.

"Twenty-one years is what you've got, Arnie," the conductor said the next morning as I boarded the bus back to Bangor, "if you don't count the year or two of insanity at the end. I wish you and your boy the best."

We waved goodbye and I wondered if the balding conductor—nearly four times my age, like a doting grandfather who doesn't get to see his grandchildren often enough—was happy with his own life choice. Was there a chance he'd still be the conductor in 21 years when it was my time to become ashes and my son's time to take the night train to Plantation 13?

My eye socket itched under the gauze bandages. But this time it was a different kind of itch. Now it ached for the symbol of fatherhood that had been my father's and my grandfather's and my great-grandfather's: the glass eye. As soon as the socket was healed and ready for it, I'd put it in. And when my time came, as it no doubt would, I would pass on to the beautiful son who now lay so content in my arms.

* * *

I nearly named the boy Robert, after my father. But then I wondered who I'd been named after, and why, and eventually I decided it was more fitting to name him after Tim, the friend and comrade we'd left behind at Plantation 13. As my father had written: our family line pays a terrible price to continue.

Steve Burt

The Cave

Butterflies? Yes, butterflies! The cave was filled with them, hundreds, thousands of them. Alex had never seen anything like it in all his years of spelunking—exploring caves and collecting rocks, minerals, and pieces of ore. Imagine! A cave filled with butterflies.

The cave was thick with them. They weren't just hanging on the walls. They fluttered around filling the air, covering the floor, creating a cloud around Alex's head. He kept his mouth closed and breathed through his nose. Only the light from his headlamp and flashlight held them at bay. When he walked across the cave it was like parting a curtain, the creatures dividing where his headlamp and flashlight shone. He wasn't sure if it was because of the light or the heat.

The cave wasn't totally dark. Around the edges it was black and shadowy, yes, where the walls and floor met. But the center of the room was brighter, a column of natural light streaming down a large natural funnel in the cave's roof. This cavern he'd climbed up into, this almost perfectly circular room, reminded him of a giant freestanding Scandinavian fireplace. A chimney rock, the Indians would have called it in earlier times. So long as the sun was high in the overhead sky the chimney let some light in.

Alex gauged the height from the floor to the lowest part of the chimney hole to be 12 to 15 feet. The throat of the chimney extended another six or eight feet to the earth's surface. The room's curved walls reminded him of a geodesic dome. He guessed it to be 100 feet across.

But it didn't make sense, butterflies congregating in a cave. They'd be drawn to the light, wouldn't they—or was that moths? And didn't butterflies need the leaves and vegetation outside for a food source? Yet here they were, thousands of them—maybe tens of thousands—living inside this cave. How could it be? What did it mean? Why didn't they flutter up the chimney to the warm air and sunshine?

Alex's headlamp caught a rainbow of colors, the full spectrum, the predominant ones being black and orange. *Monarchs*, which made sense. They were the most common species of butterfly in this region. Butterflies weren't his specialty but the monarchs he was sure about. Just the idea that he recognized one of the many types comforted him.

There was no wildlife in the cave that he could see. No bears, thank God, but then again this wasn't hibernation season nor was there any obvious way for them to get in or out. He expected a few bats, considering the perfect entrance and exit the chimney offered, but when he probed the ceiling with his flashlight he saw no sign of any.

He snapped off his headlamp to save it and used just the flashlight to examine the overhead. How perfectly rounded the cave roof was, how smooth. *Limestone,* judging by its color, which would make sense for this area.

He shone the light on the floor. As he had suspected from the roughness and striations underfoot: *granite*. One look confirmed it. But that didn't make sense. *Why would the cave's floor be granite and its dome limestone?* He pictured his wife's cheese server: a wooden cutting board with a glass cover. The two materials didn't necessarily have to be the same, did they?

Alex sat perfectly still on the rough floor trying to count the different kinds of butterflies. He wasn't actually sure about species but he could differentiate colors and patterns. By the time he reached 10, many more landed on his hands and arms. In no time he was covered with them. *They have weight*. Individually it wasn't so noticeable but there was a cumulative effect. He shook them off and shone his flashlight upward again. *They have barely enough airspace to hover*. The cramped creatures had to be beating against each other with their wings.

He aimed the light at the floor and hundreds of butterflies lifted off. Others hovering above them immediately took their place.

They're taking turns, flying in shifts, resting in shifts. There's cooperation here. They're working together.

Alex snapped off his light and relit the headlamp. He wanted to examine the area where the floor and walls met—something felt odd about it, wrong. That meant crawling on hands and knees away from the natural light toward the dark corners where the ceiling curved lower. He started forward through a cloud of beating wings, feeling as much as seeing his way.

His right hand struck something, knocking it forward. It made a familiar sound as it scraped the granite floor. He felt around until his fingers grazed it. *A headlamp.* With his free hand he dusted a cloud of butterflies out of his face and focused his own headlamp on it. *Identical to his own.* Someone had left it behind. But who would do that? No cave explorer he knew. He clicked it on but it was dead.

He edged forward again and his hand grazed something else. He felt it, not even having to shine his headlamp on it this time. *Another headlamp. Dead.* Beside it lay a flashlight also dead.

Alex got to his feet with both the flashlight and the headlamp on, hoping more light would dispel the fear gnawing at his gut. He swatted his way through the cloud of butterflies, keeping the flashlight beam aimed at the floor ahead. Headlamps, flashlights, and fanny packs—caving gear lay scattered everywhere.

He stopped. Something was wrong. *Why had so many cavers visited the domed chamber only to leave their equipment behind? Was it a shrine? Was it like visitors leaving pictures and flowers and personal items at the foot of the Vietnam Memorial Wall in Washington, D.C.?* He recalled the names of a half dozen missing cave explorers he'd read or heard about over the years: Ray Jackson, Henri Toulouse and Martha Jameson, Frank and Barry Montgomery, and, of course, his own brother Hal whose disappearance was one of the reasons he'd come exploring here. A shiver ran through his body. *Hal?*

Alex stepped back under the shaft of sunlight streaming down the chimney. Had the hole he'd come up through been under the spotlight or just beyond it? Something told him it was time to leave, that the hole he'd come in by might be his only way out. It was near the center of the cave, he was sure of that, and it was only slightly wider than his shoulders. It had been a tight squeeze. He had to find the hole.

But the question nagged: *limestone walls and a granite floor?* He needed to return to the dark recesses and check the joint where the wall met the floor. Turning back toward the outer darkness he waded through even more caving gear until his head almost banged into the wall. He knelt down and leaned forward into the tight V. Something odd here. He unhooked the rock hammer from his belt and tapped the wall expecting a *chink-chink* rock-chipping sound. But that wasn't what he heard. He rapped in several more places high and low then to the right and the left. Same sound—*metallic.* He smacked as hard as he could but couldn't break through, the sound reminding him of banging a wrench on thousand-gallon fuel tank at his uncle's house. The walls were cast iron or steel or some alloy. They'd been made to *look like* limestone.

He shone the flashlight where the wall met the granite floor. The floor was notched, channeled so there was a groove all the way around. The metal wall fit precisely in the groove as if it had been lowered into place, fitted there. The image of the cheese platter came back to him.

He crab-walked sideways to the left checking the seal as he went, hoping for a break or an imperfection or a hatch door, even a manufacturer's logo or part number—who knew what might be there? But it was engineered perfectly. Did it have a rubber O-ring seal, too? What was going on here?

When Alex was sure he'd gone full circle he stopped then returned to the sunlight. He gazed up at the chimney. The sky was clouding over. His watch said it was 2:10. Even though it wouldn't be dark outside for a few hours the cave was losing the light as the sun sank. He needed to get out.

A low, slow, grating sound came from floor level to his right—*like a cement block being dragged over another cement block. It was moving rock. The hole was closing!*

Alex scanned the floor but saw no hole, only solid granite. The cloud of butterflies felt thicker, denser, as if they were purposely blocking his vision. He flailed away at them and searched the floor trying to fight the sense of panic rising inside him.

He decided to try a grid search to be sure he didn't miss a spot. He set the flashlight on the floor at the edge of the sunlit oval then backed away until he was at the oval's far edge. He removed his headlamp so he could mark that spot, too, its beam aimed upward. Using the line between the two lights as his compass Alex paced back and forth like a plowman harrowing a field. *No hole.*

He widened the grid search beyond the oval. Still nothing. The hole wasn't within the sunlight circle nor was it around the outer edges of it. He struggled to catch a deep breath but his chest felt the way it had when he'd had allergies as a child. He tried to tell himself to relax. He could make it a while with shallow breaths. *Save your strength while you figure out what to do next. Don't give in to the fear.*

Alex sat down to relax and think. *Had the hole moved?* No. The grating sound could have been the hole closing, of course, though he preferred to not believe that, for it would add to his—*don't mention fear*. Besides, he hadn't actually seen a slab slide across to cover a hole—at least not within the bounds of the sunlit oval—he had only heard it. Then it struck him: *the hole didn't move, the sunlit area did. It had been a circle when he entered the cave, an oval now.* Of course, as the sun shifted across the sky, the lighted area changed. *But had the previously lighted area—if that was where the hole was—had it been beyond the flashlight or the headlamp he'd used as markers? How far beyond?*

He glanced up the chimney shaft. The sun moved from east to west, from low in the sky to directly overhead at noon then to low in the sky on the opposite side later. Which meant the spotlight effect when he'd entered the cave must have been farther to the right than the current area. He stretched his arms and began searching farther to the right beyond the lighted oval. Two sweeps, three, four. *Nothing*. He tried not to think about the grating sound. *It was him against the cave, wasn't it?* To think it might be him against the cave *and something else—something more intentionally insidious*—that was too much to bear.

He looked up the chimney again. Something wasn't right about it. He felt around for a rock but there was none to be found, nothing but caving gear. He gripped his hammer, wound up like a softball pitcher and let it fly underhand as hard as he could. It went straight up the center of the chimney—*thunk*—and fell back down, striking the floor close by. What in blazes had it hit—a plexiglass ceiling, a thick plastic window, a force field? Or was it his imagination?

No wonder the butterflies hadn't left. *They couldn't.* They were imprisoned in a huge sealed terrarium.

His chest felt tight again, his breaths shallower and more labored. He sat down and crossed his legs in a lotus position, wrists over thighs so he could practice the yoga relaxation technique he'd learned. *Deep breath in through the nose, hold it, exhale through the mouth.* He felt butterflies on his bare upturned palms, his shoulders, all over. He didn't bother to retrieve the still-lit headlamp or the flashlight. The relaxation technique was what mattered now.

Alex's hair grew damp and sweaty and butterflies landed on it, their fluttering wings tickling his ears. One landed on his nose but he kept his eyes shut and didn't attempt to brush it away. A few more touched down on his cheeks and forehead, on his eyelashes and eyelids, on the dimples beside his mouth, on his lips. They didn't feel threatening, they were simply there, wanting to alight, to rest. *As he wanted to rest.*

Even with his eyes closed he could feel more butterflies landing on top of the first layer covering his body and a moment later another layer on top of that, a thickening blanket of butterflies. He concentrated on relaxing, breathing in through his nose and out through his mouth, his thoughts no longer about escape or rescue, only about relaxing.

He heard a hiss, the finest hiss he'd ever heard, like gas escaping. But it wasn't gas, at least not from some outside source. This was right next to his ears.

He relaxed more deeply—*I'm going numb*—as the sheer weight of them—*it's the butterflies hissing*—forced him onto his back on the dark floor. *This feels like Hal pinning me on the mattress. Relax. In through the nose, out through the mouth.* He heard a delicate flutter, thousands of wings—fanning, cooling—and the hiss again, ever so fine—*anesthetic*—and then their tiny nicking, clicking teeth, first on his ears and his nose and then—when he was screaming and his mouth was filling with them—on the papery film of his eyelids and on his tongue.

The Chambers Crypt

"Well, well. If it isn't Devaney and Hoag, couch potatoes," my wife Carol said as she and her mother came in from church and took their coats off. My father-in-law and I knew better than to engage her. It was close to lunchtime and experience had taught us if we didn't antagonize her, she and her mother would make us all lunch.

"You've got to get out more often boys," my mother-in-law said. "We got out today, maybe that's why we scooped you."

Devaney and I turned away from the television and our wives flashed those smug, cat-that-ate-the-canary smiles.

"What do you mean, scooped us?" Devaney asked.

"Well," Carol said. "If you'd go to church once in a while, you might be there when a story breaks."

I'm a reporter for the *Valley News*, the daily that serves both White River Junction, Vermont and Lebanon, New Hampshire, and the small towns clustered around that part of the Connecticut River's Upper Valley. Mostly I write local news, human-interest stories, and features. My father-in-law, Devaney, a retired history teacher, is a pretty decent amateur photographer who keeps me company and shoots most of my pictures.

"Yeah, like a lot of stories break out at church," Devaney guffawed, seemingly unaware he was killing our chances for lunch.

"As a matter of fact, Mr. Smarty," my mother-in-law said, "a story did break in church today."

Devaney smiled a tight smile, rolled his eyes with feigned disinterest.

"What story?" I asked.

Carol paused, pretending she might not spill it. But she'd obviously been dying to tell us since she got in the door.

"Ghosts," she said, letting the word hang.

Devaney and I sat up.

"Oh, come on," I said. "You're talking about the *Holy* Ghost, right? Church talk. On the third day rising from the dead, that kind of ghost."

Carol looked at her mother, then back at us. "No, we're not talking about church stuff, although these are church-related. We're talking about ghosts, real ghosts. In Norwich."

"Norwich?" Devaney barked out. "Where? Who saw them?"

My father-in-law and I had accumulated a number of stories—*cases*, he prefers to call them, but since I write them up for the paper, I call them *stories*—inand around Norwich, Vermont. Ever since we'd gotten involved with the Norwich witch and the Witness Tree on the green there, locals had begun treating us not just as reporter and photographer, but as psychic detectives (though neither of us is psychic). Some folks even use the terms ghost busters, though we've never busted any ghosts. Now, whenever something weird or out of the ordinary happens—a cow or pet disappearance, a freshly cracked or toppled tombstone, an eerie mist over a swampy area—we get phone calls. Not from my editor (except on special occasions), but directly from townspeople, sometimes in the middle of the night.

"Gee, Mom, I don't know about you," Carol said. "But I'm getting hungry. Must be close to lunchtime." I could see a twinkle in Carol's eye. "Sure would be nice to have somebody else fix Sunday lunch for a change, wouldn't it?" My wife stared right at me and waited, close-mouthed.

"That would be a real treat," her mother said. "Maybe you men would consider preparing lunch and serving us on this Sabbath day of rest." She stared at Devaney exactly the way Carol was staring at me.

Twenty minutes later the four of us sat around the kitchen table, a plate of my tuna-with-celery sandwiches in the center along with a saucer of dill pickles. Bowls of tomato soup and glasses of iced tea sat in front of us.

"Okay," I said, plunking a bag of potato chips on the table as I sat down. "Lunch is served. Now it's your turn, ladies. What's this about ghosts?"

"Ahem," my mother-in-law said, folding her hands. "Perhaps we could offer thanks for the meal first. It's been awhile since we've done that, I believe. What do you say, Carol?"

Carol nodded and turned to me. "Honey, would you say grace?"

Devaney exhaled heavily at the blackmail. I simply smiled and we all bowed our heads. I thanked God for the food, the hands that had so lovingly prepared such a masterpiece, and for the loving spouses we all had. Devaney said Amen and we divvied up the sandwiches.

"Well," Carol started. "Everybody at church was talking about what happened up at the Congregational Church in Norwich, the one on the green."

Devaney and I had been there before, for our first "case." When the church bell began humming of its own accord, Town Constable Dutch Roberts and we had met with Reverend Halliday, who let us go up inside the bell tower to investigate.

"It seems there was a Junior Youth Group meeting in the church last night. The children are fifth and sixth graders. The leaders, two couples in their thirties took the kids for an after-dark hike down the road to the River Bend Cemetery."

Devaney shot me a look that said we'd given in too early on fixing lunch. It was obvious where this story was going—youth group, ancient graveyard, black of night.

"Well, nothing happened at the cemetery. They went for their hike—eight of them and their four advisors—then came back. Around eight o'clock they all went to the minister's house for hot chocolate. The minister wasn't there, he was away for a conference, but his wife was there. She had a roaring fire in the fireplace. While they were sitting around it, one of the girls saw something in the fire—people, she said, four of them. The other kids swore they saw them, too."

I cast a sideways glance at Devaney. He was looking at me out of the corner of his eye in the same doubting way.

"But here's the kicker," my mother-in-law said. "The adults saw them, too."

A chill ran down my spine. The chill never failed to alert me to a real story.

"That's right," Carol said. "The kids, the four advisors, and the minister's wife—13 people—all swear four people were calling to them out of the flames."

I looked at Carol and saw she wasn't trying to pull the wool over our eyes. We didn't know what had actually occurred, but she and her mother seemed convinced there was something to the story. And I had my chill—my hunch—to rely on.

"And what were they calling out, these four ghosts?" Devaney asked.

"I don't know," Carol said, glancing around at her mother, who shrugged her shoulders, too. "I guess nobody got that part of the story. You think it's important?"

"Important? I'm not even convinced anything really happened," I said, only half-lying. "At least, anything to do with ghosts. But it seems to me, if they were calling out something, they might like us to listen to whatever it is they're trying to tell us, don't you think?"

Carol and her mother agreed, and we rehashed the details several times over lunch. Then Devaney and I called the minister's wife in Norwich and arranged an interview for three o'clock. She gave us the names and numbers of the two couples who were the advisors, and we set up meetings with them for four and five o'clock. If the story seemed like it was worth pursuing further, we'd get information on the eight kids and interview them separately over the next couple of days.

* * *

"Of course we were frightened, all of us," Mrs. Halliday, the pastor's wife, said as we stood looking into the parsonage fireplace. The embers from the evening before had long since burned out, leaving a pile of cold gray ashes. "But it wasn't the spirits that scared us—they weren't aggressive or threatening. It was the experience itself that frightened us—the fact that we'd never before seen or heard or had anything like it happen. I mean, when it first happened, we all ran out of the room. But then we came back in, a couple of us at a time, until we were all in the room again."

"Did the ghosts—there were four, I believe you said—did they reappear?" I asked.

"I'm not sure they ever disappeared," Mrs. Halliday said. "At least not while the fire was going. When we came back into the room, they were still where we'd last seen them."

"In the flames?" Devaney asked.

"Yes. In the flames."

"Did they speak?" I asked. "Earlier you said you heard."

"And what did they look like?" Devaney asked.

The pastor's wife gestured toward the huge stone fireplace. The opening stood nearly six feet high and six feet wide, with a beehive oven built into the left side.

"The kids had piled plenty of wood on it, so the flames were pretty high. We were reading a Bible passage—about Daniel in the fiery furnace, of all things—when suddenly we heard faint voices, squeaky, distant voices. At first I thought it was hissing logs—you know how they sound. But one of the children said, 'Look. There's somebody in there, in the fire!' We all looked and, sure enough, there was a face—a man's face—with a long beard. It was like he was part of the flames, and his image rippled and distorted as the flames moved, kind of the way an image moves when you disturb the surface of a pond. He seemed to be calling for help—his mouth was moving urgently, but we couldn't really make out what he was saying."

"But weren't there four of them?" Devaney asked.

"Yes. A moment later a woman appeared, then two young boys, teenagers or younger."

"Were they dressed in suits, work clothes, anything with color?" I asked.

"They were the way people look in school portraits—head or head-and-shoulders shots. I don't remember any color, but my impression was that I was seeing black-and-white Civil War photos, like tintypes or daguerreotypes of famous generals. Not with uniforms, I'm just saying I was reminded of that era."

"Did they fade? How long did you sit and watch them?" I asked.

"They faded as the fire burned down. They might have stayed longer if the fire had kept going, I suppose, but we were afraid to throw more wood on it. As for how long—from the time we first saw them and ran out of the room until the time they disappeared—that must have been about an hour and a half."

Devaney shot a couple of pictures of the fireplace and the room.

"Anything else you can add?" I asked. "Any theory on what they wanted?"

"Mr. Hoag," the pastor's wife said. "Late last night I phoned my husband at the conference he's attending. When I told him about it, he said it was probably a case of mass hysteria, that all thirteen of us were predisposed to a group experience like it because we'd come from the cemetery. I reminded him I hadn't gone to the cemetery, but he ignored that. He wasn't here. I was.

And I believe someone—*four* someones—tried to communicate with us last night. I don't believe it was a hallucination or hysteria. I plan to light the fire again tonight, Mr. Hoag, and if you and Mr. Devaney would like to come by and visit after supper, I'd be happy to have your company."

Devaney nodded his head, so I accepted for us, thanked her, and we all agreed on seven o'clock.

Andy and Diane Hermann, the youth group advisors we interviewed at four, added nothing to Mrs. Halliday's story. Rather than use the term ghosts, they spoke of the four faces in the flames as spirits. Like the minister's wife, they too stressed that while this new experience itself had unnerved them at first, once they "warmed to the spirits," to use Andy's words, they could see the visitors meant no harm. The Hermanns agreed that the four spirits seemed desperate to communicate some warning message, and both Andy and Diane were sorry they couldn't interpret it. We didn't tell them we'd be returning to the parsonage that night to sit by the fireplace with Mrs. Halliday. I wondered if they'd find out and show up.

The other youth group advisors, Bob and Danielle Cassidy, spoke of the apparitions as entities. Their story jived with the ones we'd already heard. They did, however, add two bits of new information.

"All four of the entities seemed to be mouthing the same thing, the same couple of words," Danielle recalled.

"She's right," Bob said. "I'm sure they were all trying to say the same thing. They looked like that famous ghoulish painting of someone trying to scream."

"I think it's called *The Scream*," Devaney said, and the couple nodded.

"Any idea what they might have been trying to say?" I asked.

"Bob and I don't," Danielle said. "But two girls in our youth group, Clarissa and Shawna Jones—their father is Clarence Jones, the new professor of Black History at Dartmouth—thought they heard what the entities were saying. The family just moved up from South Carolina."

"What did the girls think the ghosts—excuse me, entities—were saying?" I asked.

"*Chambers*," she said. "They both thought the entities were saying *chambers*."

"What are they—lip readers?" Devaney asked. "How'd they make out what the ghosts were saying?"

"They heard them," Danielle said. "Both girls said they heard them."

"And did the girls think *chambers* meant a place—like in the judge's chambers," I asked. "Or was it somebody's last name, with a capital C?"

Bob and Danielle shrugged.

* * *

While we were home grabbing a quick supper before our return to Mrs. Halliday's, I called our friend Dutch Roberts, the Norwich Constable, hoping he'd be able to shed some light on the mystery. His wife Patsy said he and his brother-in-law were out for their usual Sunday evening of bowling.

"He'll be home around 9:30," she said. "Do you want me to have him call you then, Hoag, or will it wait until morning?"

"Tonight, if he doesn't mind," I said.

"Is it about the parsonage ghosts?"

"Yeah. How'd you guess?"

"Elementary, my dear Hoag, elementary. Everybody's talking about it. Dutch took a phone report last night and scooted around the corner to the parsonage right after it happened. But the fire had died down by the time he got there, and the so-called ghosts were long gone."

"Did he interview the kids? The twin girls?"

"Yes. They said they heard the four ghosts say chambers. But none of the others heard it. They only saw lips moving."

"And what did Dutch conclude?"

"Nothing. He has no explanation. But there was no threat, no apparent danger, so he's not worried about it."

"And what about them saying chambers? Has he got any idea what that means?"

"Not yet. I'll have him call you when he gets in, though I doubt he'll have anything to add to what I just told you."

I thanked Patsy, then called Directory Assistance and got the new listing for Clarence Jones, the Dartmouth professor. After the fourth ring a man with a slight Southern drawl picked up. I told him who I was and asked if I could meet with him and his daughters, Clarissa and Shawna, the next evening. He was reluctant at first, but I was persistent without being pushy, promising I'd take only 15 minutes of their time. He finally agreed and gave me directions to the condo he was renting near the college in Hanover. We set the meeting for six-thirty Monday. After I hung up, Devaney and I grabbed coffee and a couple of apple turnovers for the road and headed for the meeting with the minister's wife.

Mrs. Halliday showed us in and lit the fire in the parsonage fireplace.

"I've got fresh decaffeinated coffee and homemade tollhouse cookies," she said, turning back toward the kitchen. "I'll be right back."The woman was so nice, neither Devaney nor I had the heart to admit we'd already had dessert and coffee.

We looked around. Everything appeared the same as when we were there at three o'clock. The fire caught on fast, racing through a very dry pile of kindling Mrs. Halliday had used to start it. Before she got back with the coffee and cookies, we had a roaring blaze. Devaney and I stared into it, half-expecting to see the four ghostly visages appear.

“If they decide to appear,” Mrs. Halliday said softly as she entered the room, “I’m certain they’ll seem quite clear to you. This isn’t like a children’s magazine with a hidden picture in the scene. Either they’ll appear or they won’t.”

“Are you saying you’ve seen them before?” Devaney said. “Before last night, I mean?”

She sat on a flowered Victorian side chair and set a tray on the coffee table between us.

“Strangely, no, even though we’ve lived in this house for eight years. That was my first time. But I knew about them. Apparently a few of the past ministers and their families saw them. They’ve never revealed themselves to outsiders, though, like parishioners, only to the clergy families. And until these two girls last night, no one had ever heard them, so far as I know. They’d only seen them. One minister wrote in the records that he’d been losing his hearing and developed a facility for reading lips. He saw them a number of times and believed they were saying *jaybird*.”

"So the girls’ claim that the voices were saying *chambers* makes sense,” I said. “*Jaybird? Cham-bers?* I can see how that minister might mistake them.”

“Or maybe the girls are wrong,” Devaney said, “and that minister was right. Maybe it is *jaybird*. Or *jail bird*. How far back do these sightings go?”

"Well,” said Mrs. Halliday. “The man who believed they were mouthing *jaybird* was here in the early 1900s. One parsonage journal from a different minister had an entry about the apparitions—not what they were saying, just about their presence—around 1870.”

“Do you mind if we take a look at the written documentation?” Devaney said, sounding very professional.

"Not at all. I figured you'd want to examine it, so I have it laid out on the dining room table."

"Devaney," I said. "Take your camera. I'll watch the fire."

My father-in-law grabbed his camera and went with Mrs. Halliday to shoot the written material.

No sooner had he left than the fire flared up. Four faces appeared in the flames, their mouths working like fish gasping for air. Sure enough, all four seemed to be mouthing either jaybird or chambers, though I couldn't distinguish which. Nor could I hear anything. I felt myself blinking and could hear my brain telling me this had to be an illusion, a magic trick, but I couldn't look away. I didn't feel frightened, and I was more entranced than anything. Something about the way they looked told me that these four souls—or entities or spirits—were clearly a minister, his wife, and two children.

Five minutes later when the door opened and Devaney and Mrs. Halliday came back into the room, the four vanished.

"You okay, Hoag?" Devaney asked. "You look a little washed out."

"I saw them," I said. "Just as the others said."

Devaney looked at the fireplace, then aimed his camera at it and shot a frame.

"They're gone," I said. "They didn't wait for the fire to burn down. They disappeared when you two came in. Maybe you startled them."

"What'd they say?"

"Just what the others told us. They seemed to be saying either *jaybird* or *chambers*, but I'm not certain. It could've been something else, but I had a preconceived idea what it would be, so that's all I could see the lips saying."

The three of us sat watching the fire for another half hour, eating cookies and drinking coffee, waiting for an encore. Nothing happened. I wondered whether the presence of Devaney's camera made a difference, but even after we moved the camera into another room, they didn't show again. Finally, just as we got up to leave, the fire flared unexpectedly. No one appeared, there was just the flare-up. I wrote in my notebook that, although it was probably nothing, the flare-up could have been an acknowledgment, or perhaps a goodnight.

Dutch Roberts phoned right after I got home.

"You actually saw them?" he asked. "Aw, Hoag, you're kidding, right?"

I assured him I was dead serious.

"So what do you know about all this?" I said. "Tell me new stuff, stuff I don't already know, anything—besides Saturday night's incident—that may seem a little weird. You know, past history, other Norwich spook stories, reports of ghosts or apparitions."

"As a matter of fact," he said, "there is one report that's come up time and again for decades. It's tied to the River Bend Cemetery where the kids were before they saw the fireplace ghosts."

"Is this the story about walkers being drawn to the cemetery?" I asked. It was one I'd heard several times over the years.

"Yeah, that's it. I'll bet I've had 40 or 50 fifty people tell me almost the same story—sane, respectable pillars of the community, too, not just winos and wackos."

"They're walking past the cemetery at night," I said, "and something inexplicably draws them in. Then whatever has led them there disappears. Right?"

"Basically, yes. It leads them, or they lead them—some reports tell of two, three, or four spirits. Put it this way—the guiding force draws them to the oldest part of the cemetery."

"And disappears?"

"Yes. Once the guiding force gets them there, it leaves them standing."

"Anybody been able to describe the apparitions?" I asked.

"No. It's like they had more of a sense of whatever it was. A couple of them said it was a faintly glowing shape, like a big drop of water with light shining through it, or through them—one lady saw four."

"And like the fireplace ghosts, there was never any attempt to frighten or harm, correct?"

"Correct."

"Did any of them describe the four spirits—or giant water droplets, or whatever they saw—in a way that sounds like the four fireplace images I saw?"

"Tell you what, Hoag. Why don't you and Devaney come by the office tomorrow morning around eight o'clock. I'll have coffee. You guys bring a bag of Danish pastries and I'll let you look over all the past reports. There's a few photos of the sites, too—not of the spooks, just where the incidents occurred. You can get names, addresses, and numbers if you want to interview anybody."

I told Dutch we'd see him around 8:00 then called Devaney about it, undressed and climbed into bed.

"I'd want to know more about the past ministers who lived in that parsonage," Carol said, as I was lying with my eyes open. "Maybe then you can learn whether the faces were a minister and family."

I made a mental note to call Mrs. Halliday for information. Even if she didn't know, she'd have old records and could put me in touch with her church historian. With Devaney's background as a history teacher, he'd love poring over historical documents.

* * *

Dutch Roberts was at his desk when we walked in the next morning. The wall clock said 7:55. Devaney plunked the bag of Danish pastries down on Dutch's desk blotter.

"There's breakfast," Devaney said. "Coffee ready?"

Dutch motioned toward a counter against the wall. "Our most reliable employee, Mr. Coffee, is on the job," he said, and the popping, gurgling, and perking noises started. "I already drank one pot. Been making copies for you guys since 7:30." He placed two manila folders on the desk in front of us.

Devaney and I plopped down in the visitor chairs facing the desk. We ignored the folders for the moment and small-talked until the coffee was ready, then fixed ourselves a mug each and sat back down.

"That folder has the notes on the different River Bend incidents," Dutch said. "It wasn't hard to come up with, because my three predecessors and I kept a separate file on the cemetery. Whenever we had an incident, it not only went down in the general reports, but we slipped a carbon in that special file. Everett Carlson started it back in the 1920s. I can't give you any of the photos, because they're originals, but you can look over the originals while you're here and take the black-and-white photocopies with you. The other folder is names, addresses, and phone numbers of people involved. I couldn't give you any reports on the parsonage ghosts, because this is the first I've heard of it. I guess ministers and their families wouldn't talk about it or didn't call it in. Not a conspiracy, just that folks probably didn't want to appear insane or be laughed at."

"Or accused of consorting with the devil," Devaney added.

"Thanks for the folders, Dutch," I said. "We'll look them over at home. But boil it down for us. What's your take on the River Bend stories?"

Devaney began shuffling through the original photos.

"There's too many reports from too many credible people to not think there's something going on," Dutch said. "There's something magnetic about that back section of the graveyard. Not magnetic in the lodestone sense, but in the weird sense. People say they're drawn to it. That's their words. Drawn to it. From what I've gleaned out of the reports—the older ones and mine—they don't really see anything. There's no substance. Some suggest swamp gas, others say pranksters. Myself, I've never seen or felt anything in there—and I've gone and sat or stood there for hours. Many nights, when things were slow, I'd park my patrol car in River Bend, drink coffee and read the paper. Nothing. But I don't discount what so many others say has happened. Ghosts, spirits, energy? I don't know. But it's something."

"And what about the parsonage fireplace and those twin girls in the youth group?" I asked.

"Oh, the Jones girls? Yeah, *chambers*. Hoagie, I haven't a clue on that one. That was the first report on that house, so I've only just now started a file."

"You think the parsonage and the cemetery incidents are related?" I asked. "Same ghosts or different ones?"

Dutch shrugged. "Dunno. You suggesting the ghosts have migrated—from haunting the cemetery to haunting the house?"

"No," I said. "Mrs. Halliday says the fireplace ghosts have been there for over a hundred years. It's just that this is the first you've heard of them."

"The kids were at the River Bend Cemetery," Dutch said. "They saw ghosts that night at the parsonage, but not at the cemetery. Could be the same ghosts, or—" Dutch caught himself and laughed. "Geez, Hoag, you've got me doing it now—talking about these ghosts, spirits, entities, whatever, as if they're real, a proven fact. You two may be ready to fall into it, but as an officer of the law I've got to remain a skeptic, stick with hard evidence."

"Then you've already tried a Geiger counter?" Devaney asked, glancing up from the photos.

Dutch Roberts grinned sheepishly. "Yeah, about four years ago. No radiation."

"It was worth a shot," Devaney said, grinning back.

We finished off the pastries and coffee, thanked our old friend, and walked outside and around the corner to the church office to meet with Mrs. Halliday and Arthur Lambert, the church historian. We spent the rest of the morning examining the church's historical documents.

"So the parsonage is on the site of one that burned to the ground in 1858," Devaney said on the ride home. "With Reverend Nightingale, his wife, and two sons inside. You think the fireplace ghosts are the Nightingales?"

"Could be," I said. "The newspaper clippings of the time suggest it was arson."

"Suspected, but never proven," Devaney said. "Makes sense, though. The guy had no shortage of detractors and no shortage of enemies. Reverend Nightingale was outspoken on many issues including gambling, alcohol, child labor, the treatment of Indians, and slavery. He was very well known in abolitionist circles."

"Tomorrow we'll check town and cemetery records, see if a contemporary of Nightingale's—someone with a name like Chambers—died in the years after the fire."

We spent the afternoon in my kitchen, going over Dutch's file of the River Bend incidents. There was a remarkable consistency to the stories, and a hundred years of passersby seemed drawn to the same part of the old burying ground.

"You think the later ones knew about the earlier ones?" Devaney asked. "If none of the people knew about the others' stories, maybe you'd have something. But who says they didn't find out about the earlier stories and report the same thing—whether it really happened or not? What's to stop us from doing it ourselves?"

"We'll find out tonight. We can stop by River Bend Cemetery after we meet with the Jones twins. In the meantime, I'll look over the name-and-address file. You see if you can work out a grid, a calendar, of the cemetery appearances. See if there's a pattern."

"You mean like full moons?" Devaney quipped. "Appearances by Halley's Comet, Pisces-Virgo rising, stuff like that?"

"Whatever you can manage. You're welcome to use the computer in my room if you need the Internet, or the National Weather Service, or the Oceanographic Institute."

"Or Dionne Warwick's Psychic Network," he said. "Hoagie, I was just kidding about that astronomy stuff."

"I know you were," I said. "But once in a while you stumble on a good idea. Maybe this is one of them. Check it out. Could be something there."

I doubted he'd turn up anything, but one never knew. After all, tracking the blue moon had helped us in the case of the secret graves at the French Acre. Besides, this would keep him out of my hair while I sneaked in a forty-minute nap on my recliner.

I heard him returning and was able to look awake when he walked back into the room. For all I knew, he'd caught a few winks himself in my study.

"Nothing," Devaney said. "How about you?"

I looked down. I had the name-and-address folder on my lap. The incident folder was on the coffee table. But here was an incident report staring up at me—from the name-and-address folder. It was an original, not a copy. I scanned it quickly. It wasn't one we'd seen.

"Just this," I said, holding up the report. "When Dutch did his photocopying this morning, he must have misfiled this incident report. It's an original."

"So spill it," Devaney said. "What's there?"

"In July 1985, a Dartmouth College student and her boyfriend biked to the cemetery in late afternoon to do a couple of charcoal gravestone rubbings. When they finished, they rode to Dan & Whit's Store to buy sandwiches. But they forgot one of the rubbings and biked back to River Bend. They weren't drawn inside, as others had been, but the woman had an experience."

"Like what? Did they see the ghosts?"

"No, they didn't. Neither the girl nor her boyfriend saw a thing. But the girl reported hearing a whispery voice. It drew her to the same spot the others were drawn."

"So the voice drew her, not the visions, not some magnetic feeling," Devaney said. "Does it say what she heard, what the voice said? Was it one voice or four? The twins heard four at the parsonage, didn't they? Did this cemetery voice say *jaybird*? Or maybe *chambers*?"

"The report doesn't say. But we've got her name. Let's call her and ask."

"She was a college student," Devaney said. "The address is probably a dorm. I'll bet she's moved out of the area long ago, got married and has a different last name now."

"We'll check the Alumnae Affairs Office. If we can't locate her by computer, we can call the office on campus and sweet-talk them."

I pulled the paper clip off the report. Two Polaroid instant pictures fell onto the desk. They'd been clipped underneath.

"What're those?" Devaney asked, sliding around beside me to look.

The first, like the others we'd seen in Dutch's office, appeared to be a nighttime shot taken in the oldest section of the cemetery. The flash hadn't helped much, but there were enough similarities to the other pictures that we knew it showed the same basic area. The second had been taken in an office, probably the Town Constable's. The names on the back of the photo matched the names in the report. This was the college student who had heard the voice, and her male friend.

"She's black." The words popped out of Devaney's mouth before he could think. Amazingly, although the report had been written in the 1980s, it had not described her race. Her male friend was white.

"And your point is?" I asked.

"I don't know that I had a point," Devaney said. "It just jumped out at me." He stared silently at the photo for a moment. "The Jones twins are black, too."

"I have no idea if that means anything," I said. "But you're right."

We tried to puzzle it out for five minutes and got nowhere, so Devaney went to the computer to track down the former college student through Alumnae Affairs. In less than 15 minutes he had her address and phone number.

"Bingo!" Devaney said. "She lives in California now. She and her husband teach at UCLA. She teaches Theater. I've got her home and office phone numbers."

I placed a call to her home number first and left a message on her answering machine, asking her to call me back collect after her suppertime. Since we were three hours ahead, Devaney and I would surely be home from interviewing the Jones twins by then. Then I tried her office at the university and was surprised to have her pick up.

"Dr. Diana Hanley?" I asked, and when she said yes, I explained the reason for my call.

She had only five minutes left on her lunch break, and gave me a quick recap of the incident at River Bend Cemetery the evening she'd gone grave rubbing.

"Exactly what did you hear?" I asked. "The report doesn't make it clear except to say you heard a whisper. Was it a single voice?"

"Pretty sure it was one voice—a man's. And not exactly a whisper, but a deep, scratchy, hoarse sort of whisper—like someone gasping for air or someone thirsting for water. Croaky."

"Croaky?"

"Yeah. Someone in distress, like a death scene in a World War II movie. You know, the dying soldier cradled in his buddy's arms on the battlefield. A weak voice, fading, croaky."

"And what did the voice say?"

"*Nazareth*, maybe. At least, that's what I think it said. It wasn't perfectly clear. Like I said, the voice was weak. But I'm pretty sure it said *Nazareth*. Or possibly *Naz-rus*."

"Nazareth? As in Jesus of?"

"I don't know if it's Nazareth. As I said, it could have been *Naz-rus*. It's been a lot of years since then."

"You're sure the voice didn't come from pranksters hiding behind a tombstone? You know, from other college kids?"

"Positive. "Nor did it come from inside my head."

"But the police report states that your friend, who was standing beside you, didn't hear any voice at all."

"That's correct, he didn't. But I did."

"Just Nazareth? That's all the voice said?"

"That's it. And not necessarily Nazareth. My first impression was that the voice said Naz-rus. Just Naz-rus. Over time I've started to think maybe it was Nazareth, but initially I'm pretty sure I heard Naz-rus. Might have even been *Az-rus*, for all I know. I remember thinking afterwards that I wasn't even sure I'd heard the N."

"Any chance it was a dialect, somebody saying Nazareth in a way that came out Naz-rus?"

"Can't say."

There was nothing else Dr. Hanley could tell me, and I couldn't think of anything else to ask, so I thanked her for talking with me and hung up.

At 6:20 Devaney and I pulled up in front of a lovely condo near Dartmouth College. We wanted to arrive a little early, since the twins' father had said we could only have fifteen minutes of their time. If we were going to grab a little extra time, it'd probably be easier to sneak it in on the front end of the visit.

"Quite the place, ain't it?" Devaney asked as I pressed the doorbell. "Now I can see where that expression came from—keeping up with the Joneses."

I shook my head and offered my father-in-law my weakest smile.

Two minutes later we were sitting on a comfortable sofa opposite Clarence and Celia Jones and their girls, Clarissa and Shawna. We asked them to tell us what happened at the parsonage on Saturday night. Their version, which took about 10 minutes, matched those of Mrs. Halliday and the four advisors. I was glad we'd picked up the extra time on the front end of the interview.

"But you were the only two who heard voices, right?" I asked.

The girls nodded.

"They were trying to shout to us, but they sounded like people yelling from a faraway hilltop," one of them said.

"And it was like all four of their voices could barely make up one whole voice," the other said. "It took a lot out of them."

"But you two heard them, right?" Devaney asked. "You didn't just read their lips?"

"Oh, we heard 'em, all right," Shawna said.

"And you're sure of what they said?" I asked.

The two girls screwed their mouths into identical funny faces and said, "*Chambers*, I think."

"Anything else?" Devaney asked.

"That's all."

"How about your visit to the cemetery?" I asked. "See or hear anything at River Bend Cemetery? Or on the walk there or back?"

The girls' eyes grew wide as they turned to look at each other.

"We were just talking about that," Clarissa said.

"We didn't hear or see anything," Shawna said. "But we sensed something."

Their father leaned forward on his seat. "This is the first mention of that. What did you sense?"

"Clarence's grandmother had the Sight," Celia Jones whispered to us.

"We didn't see any spirits or ghosts or anything," Shawna said. "But we felt a pull, for sure."

"Someone wanted us to come closer," Clarissa said.

"And what did you do?" their father asked.

"We walked in a different direction," Shawna answered.

"We steered the rest of the group away from it," her sister said.

"Were you afraid?" I asked.

"Not for us. But we didn't know about the others," she said.

"What others? Other spirits?" Devaney asked.

"No. The other kids," she continued. "The kids in the Youth Group, we were afraid for them and for Mr. And Mrs. Hermann and Mr. and Mrs. Cassidy."

"And not *spirits*, just *spirit*, *one force.* Drawing us," she said, and her sister nodded.

"And was it different from the four faces and voices in the fireplace?" I asked.

The twins looked at each other, then nodded. They seemed certain.

"What part of the cemetery were you feeling drawn to?" Devaney asked. "Pretend you're walking with us through the front gate. Describe it for us."

I knew Devaney wanted to ask the twins if they'd be willing to go to River Bend with us—I was dying to ask them, too—but we both knew the father wouldn't allow it.

The girls not only described it, they drew a map on a sheet of notebook paper. The place they had stopped to divert their group was just short of the path entering the oldest part of the cemetery, the area in all the incident reports.

Professor Jones had begun looking at his watch, and I could see from the grandfather clock behind him that it was 6:45. Our time was up. I thanked the Joneses for their time and we eased toward the front door. The question still burned inside me, and apparently it still burned in Devaney, who surprised me by pulling an old Peter Falk/*Colombo* detective's trick.

"Dr. Jones, I know this would be a terrible imposition. I know you and your family are very busy and this has been quite an ordeal, but—" Then he shook his head and looked away. "Oh, never mind."

"What is it, Mr. Devaney?" the professor asked, taking the bait. "Is there some way I can help?"

Devaney turned back and looked Jones right in the eye. "I don't suppose you and your wife and the girls—in the daylight, not at night, of course—I don't suppose you and your family would go back there with us, would you? With Hoag and me? You see, Hoag and I, we don't have the Sight. But maybe you do. Or your girls." Devaney held the eye contact, and I thought I saw Jones cave a little. But I was wrong.

"I don't think so, Mr. Devaney. I'd rather not put the girls through such an ordeal. They knew enough to steer clear of it once, so I think we'll go along with their good sense. It's nice of you to invite us along, though. Good night."

Devaney didn't say a word as we passed through the Dartmouth Campus and drove downhill toward the Ledyard Bridge over the Connecticut River. As the crow flies it's less than two miles from the center of Hanover, New Hampshire to the center of Norwich, Vermont.

"It was a darned good try," I said finally. "I was itching to ask him, too, but couldn't figure a way to lead into it."

"Nothing short of brilliant, you say?"

I looked across at my father-in-law in the passenger seat. He was grinning like a Cheshire cat.

"Just a tad bit short of brilliant. But if it had worked—well . . ."

"Then you'd have conceded: nothing short of brilliant," he finished.

"Maybe. I guess Dr. Jones watched *Columbo*, too."

I picked up Route 5 and followed it north past the Congregational Church and the school.

"So we're going ghost busting, eh?" Devaney asked.

I turned in at the gate of the River Bend Cemetery and parked about 20 feet in. I grabbed my flashlight from the glove box and we got out.

"Should've packed my piece," Devaney said, patting his right hip then his left armpit. Devaney didn't own a gun. As far as I knew, the man had never even hunted deer or rabbits.

I held the twins' map in front of me and shone the light on it.

"We should've come by and checked it out in daylight," Devaney said. "We knew from Dutch's files where to look."

"Shhh," I said.

"Why're we stopping?" Devaney whispered. "You hear something?"

"No. But let's see if we can sense anything. See if we feel the pull."

We didn't. So we proceeded slowly, stopping every 20 or 30 feet to check again. Nothing. Eventually we got to the point where the twins had felt the force before they steered their youth group away. We stood still and waited quietly a full minute.

"Where's Charlie Rivers when you need him?" Devaney finally asked.

Charlie Rivers, an Abenaki Indian in his seventies had been one of the last of the old-time apple-branch dowsers. We'd helped him clear brush at the French Acre. His dowsing skills had applied to more than locating water, and Devaney was right—there wouldn't be anybody more helpful than Charlie at the River Bend Cemetery—except maybe the Jones twins.

We walked into the oldest section of the cemetery, but felt no "presence." Nothing drew us, or pulled us, or summoned us. Devaney and I simply didn't possess the Sight, not in the way Charlie and the twins did. I shone my flashlight on a few gravestones. Nothing. We turned around and headed for the car.

"Come on, Charlie," I said, calling up toward the heavens. "How about a break, old buddy? After all that brush we helped you clear?"

No answer. No clap of thunder or bolt of lightning to illuminate a grave. We walked on.

"Hey, look," Devaney said, pointing at my car.

Directly in front of it stood a deer. I shone my flashlight on it, but it didn't move. When I took the beam off it, it started toward us. We backed off of the narrow dirt drive and watched it amble past us, coming within three feet. I could have reached out and touched it. We followed it. A minute later we were back at the same place we'd been earlier, at the entrance to the oldest part of the cemetery.

The deer kept going. We followed ten paces behind. It wended its way among the graves, gravitating toward the farthest corner, eventually stopping. It had led us to a huge flat weathered stone. It looked as if it measured four feet wide by eight feet long, perhaps six inches thick. The stone must have weighed several tons.

"That's what they call a wolf lid or a wolf stone," Devaney said. "They put those on top in Colonial days so the wolves couldn't dig up the bodies."

"I've heard of them. And seen a few, too, mostly down in Connecticut, around Stonington and Mystic. But they're mostly two or three feet wide by six feet long, two or three inches thick. This one's more than a plain old wolf stone, Devaney. I think it must be the cover to a mausoleum."

I shone a light on it.

"It's worn," Devaney said. "But I think it says *Masters*." He rubbed a hand over the stone's faded letters. "I was hoping it'd say *Chambers*."

"Yeah, me too. But the deer clearly led us here, didn't it?"

"Yeah, it did," Devaney answered. "Hey, where'd it go?"

The deer was nowhere to be seen.

"Think it was Charlie?" I asked.

"Charlie Three Rivers? Could've been. But even if it was, and if I'd have thought to get him on film just now, a picture of a deer in a graveyard wouldn't convince anybody of anything, would it?" He whistled a few eerie notes from *The Twilight Zone* and we walked back to the car.

* * *

The next morning we checked out plot maps for Norwich cemeteries, including River Bend. We found the notation for the plot the deer had led us to: Masters family: James Masters 1747-1809 and wife Grace (nee Roberts) Masters 1754-1818, their daughter Rebecca 1777-1781, their son Albert Masters 1786-1852 and his wife Jenny (nee Russell) Masters 1793-1816 who died in childbirth with son Robert Masters 1816-1816. Albert's second wife Alice (nee Burns) Masters 1801-1851. In small print in the margin someone had added: Grace (nee Masters 1820) Nightingale buried with her family 1858 at North Cemetery, Norwich.

"Nightingale!" Devaney exclaimed. "Same as the minister in the 1858 parsonage fire."

We checked the records for the North Cemetery, a larger and slightly newer cemetery just north of River Bend, and found the Nightingale plot on the map. All four Nightingales had died in 1858: Reverend Frederick, wife Grace (nee Masters), son Robert, son Franklin.

"Still no Chambers," Devaney said glumly.

"Not yet. But we've connected the parsonage site with the River Bend grave. Until now we had two separate and unrelated cases."

"I thought you preferred to call them stories. I'm the one who calls them cases. After all, we're reporters, not ghost busters. Remember?"

* * *

We hit Dutch's office and once again drank his coffee as we shared our Danish pastries.

"So you think the four ghosts in the fireplace are the Nightingales, the minister and family who burned in the fire in 1858," Dutch said. "And Mrs. Nightingale was Grace Masters, whose family is buried—without her—in the oldest section of River Bend Cemetery. And the Fireplace Four, as they'll no doubt become known after Hoagie's front-page story wins the Pulitzer, have been trying to tell us something."

"They're trying to tell somebody something," I said. "But I don't know if it's us they're trying to tell."

"Yeah," Devaney said. "It seems like only black people—I mean people of color—hear them. White people just see them, make out their lips moving."

Dutch frowned at Devaney like he was nuts.

"Where's this only-black-people-can-hear-them stuff coming from, Devaney?" Dutch asked. "The two Jones girls heard them, and they're the only two, right?"

"And Dr. Hanley," Devaney said.

Dutch looked puzzled.

"Diana Hanley, the black Dartmouth student in your incident files," I said. "The one who was there doing the grave-rubbings with her boyfriend."

"I know the incident," Dutch said. "How did you know she was black?"

"From the Polaroid," I said. "It was the only original photo you gave us. If it had been a photocopy like the others, we'd have never guessed. She was very light-skinned."

"I didn't give you any original," Dutch said. "I double-checked everything to make sure I retained my originals. I'm positive I only gave you photocopies of files and pictures. I never even noticed the woman was black."

Devaney shot me a funny look. His lips didn't move, and I half-expected him to start whistling *The Twilight Zone* theme song again. How had the Polaroid come our way? Myself, I was thinking: Charlie Three Rivers.

Dutch went to the cabinet, withdrew a file, and leafed through it as he returned to his chair.

"According to the file, Miss Hanley heard a voice saying Nazareth or something like that. Not *Chambers* or *jaybird*. So you've got two little girls hearing *chambers* and a college student who heard *Nazareth*. And the student heard it in a different setting—if she heard anything at all. Why assume the connection among the three who heard something is the fact that they're black? They're also all female. They're also all students. And they also all lived in Hanover, New Hampshire, have a connection with the college, and visited Norwich, Vermont. If you want to take it to extremes, they all crossed the Ledyard Bridge to get here. Maybe they're all bicycle riders, too."

I sat feeling stupid. I hadn't thought of the other common denominators.

The phone rang. Dutch answered it, looked mildly surprised. "It's for you," he said, handing me the receiver.

It was Carol, who knew where her father and I were. She had just gotten back from her morning walk to find two messages on the answering machine. One was one from Dr. Hanley, who had my number from the message I'd left on her home machine. She wanted me to call her at her office around 10:30 my time, 7:30 hers. She'd just be getting to her office then and didn't have a class until eight. The other was Clarence Jones, asking me to call his condo. Since he had only called ten minutes earlier, I asked Dutch if I could call from there.

"Mr. Hoag," Jones said when I got him on the phone. "My girls had a strange night after your visit. Not exactly nightmares, but they had weird dreams."

"Tell me about it," I said.

"They dreamed they woke up during the night because of a voice. Both girls described the same dream."

"Not the fireplace voices, but a hoarse voice—a man's—right?" I suggested.

"Yes. How'd you know?"

"Just a hunch. Please continue. What did the voice say?"

"They said it was sort of pleading. And they thought it said *Az-rus*."

"Az-rus?"

"Yes, Az-rus."

"Any chance it was Nazareth?" I asked.

"I asked them that, too. They thought it was Az-rus. Two syllables."

"Were they frightened?"

"No. But they said they awoke feeling sad, and sorry they couldn't help."

"Anything else?"

"Yes. A while ago my sister called from South Carolina. You'll remember my wife Celia told you last night that my grandmother had the Sight?"

"Yes. Is your grandmother still alive?"

"No. But my sister Nell seems to have it to some degree, too."

"Go on."

"She had the same dream, the same dream as the girls. Heard the same voice say the same thing."

"Az-rus? Or Nazareth?"

"Az-rus, I believe. She also felt the overwhelming sadness that she couldn't help whomever was calling out to her. What was different from the twins' dreams is, my sister had a sense the voice was connected to her area, South Carolina. Any ideas? What should I do?"

Dutch and Devaney could only hear my end of the conversation, and they were fit to be tied. I wanted to ask Jones again if he'd let Shawna and Clarissa go to the cemetery, but I remembered how he'd responded to Devaney's Columbo ploy. Besides, they'd already heard the voice and the word or name that Dr. Hanley had heard in 1985. They didn't need to go to the cemetery again to verify that. Nevertheless, something told me the twins visiting the cemetery again would be the key to unlocking the mystery.

"I've got another phone call to make," I said. "Can you call me around suppertime?"

"About 5:30?" Dr. Jones asked.

"That'd be great. And would you mind if I called your sister Nell and spoke directly with her about this?"

Jones gave me his sister's last name and phone number. I thanked him and hung up.

"I see from your note that his sister's last name isn't Chambers," Devaney said. "Or Nazareth."

"No such luck," I said. "But we do have another black female who heard the voice. And Dutch, she's not affiliated with Dartmouth College nor has she crossed the Ledyard Bridge." Having made my point, I filled them in on my conversation with Clarence Jones.

I left Devaney going over records at the Town offices and library. He wanted to check all the cemeteries for any names like

Chambers. He had also set up a second meeting with Arthur Lambert, the church historian, for 10:00. I told him I'd meet him at 11:00 in front of Dutch's office, then drove home to call Nell in South Carolina. The man who answered said she worked mornings, but I could catch her at noon when she got home.

At 10:30 I phoned Dr. Hanley in California. She'd had the same dream as Shawna, Clarissa, and Nell.

"I hadn't heard the voice since that evening in 1985," she said. "So this time, because it was on my mind, I listened more closely. I think it said Lazarus—like in the Bible. Not Nazareth."

I told her about the parsonage and the fireplace ghosts, gave her the basics on the twins and Dr. Jones's sister Nell hearing the voice, too. Then I asked her if chambers or jaybird made any sense to her. No luck. I asked her to call if anything else came up and promised I'd keep her updated.

I went to Carol's office and pulled her Bible and concordance off the shelf. The concordance told me where in the New Testament to find Lazarus. He'd been Jesus' friend, Martha and Mary's brother. The sisters second-guessed his death, wondering if Jesus of Nazareth, had he come right away when they first sent word their brother was sick, mightn't have saved Lazarus' life. When he finally did arrive and learned his dear friend was dead, Jesus wept. I remembered the line now: *Jesus wept.* It was the answer to the question: *What is the shortest sentence in the Bible? Jesus wept.* He wept for *Lazarus*. When Mary and Martha took Jesus to their brother's gravesite—in a foreshadowing of Jesus's own Resurrection—Jesus commanded, "Lazarus, come out!" And Lazarus did. He rose from the dead and came out.

I returned the Bible and concordance to the shelf, went to the phone and called Clarence Jones. Answering machine. I left a message.

"Dr. Jones, this is Hoag. Is it possible that Shawna and Clarissa heard the voice saying not *Az-rus* but *Lazarus*? I'd appreciate it if you'd ask them when they get home from school. If you can't reach me or my wife Carol, please leave a message on my machine. I'll chat with you at 5:30 tonight as planned."

At 11:45 I couldn't stand to wait any longer. I called Nell, Dr. Jones's sister, in South Carolina. She answered, and in short order related the story of her dream and the voice.

"And what, exactly, did the voice say?" I asked. "Did it say Az-rus?"

"To tell you the truth, Mr. Hoag," Nell said. "It could have been clipped speech, even a regional dialect, maybe saying Nazareth—or even Lazarus. Plenty of people mix those two words up, not only here in the South but everywhere. And Az-rus, well, that doesn't make any sense now, does it?"

I told her the rest of the story, about Dr. Hanley, the Nightingale family, the fireplace ghosts, and chambers or jaybird.

"Tell me," I said. "If you were to come visit your brother, and if you happened to stop by the River Bend Cemetery, do you think the Sight would be helpful in uncovering the truth?"

"Can't say for sure," she answered. "I don't have it as strong as my grandmother did. It travels through mostly the women in our family, and it's stronger in some than in others. My and Clarence's mother, for example, didn't have it at all. The twins appear to have it, from what I can see."

"Did your grandmother's mother have it?"

"She did, but then she gave it up, refused to use it. She and her husband, my great-grandfather, they were slaves. He disappeared when he was 25. Ran for freedom and was never heard from again. My great-grandmother said she foresaw a horrible death for him. She warned him, begged him not to go. But he went anyway. Promised to send someone to buy the family's freedom. But no one ever came, no one ever heard from him. After that she cursed the Sight and never used it again. At least, she never spoke of it."

No sooner had I hung up than Devaney called.

"No luck on cemetery plots with the name Chambers," he said. "But Arthur Lambert and I found a strong motive to suspect arson in the Nightingale fire. Not only was the Reverend Nightingale vocal in the abolitionist movement, he may also have been helping to fund the Underground Railroad that helped slaves escape the South to the free states in the North."

"Call me back in five minutes," I told Devaney, and hung up. An idea—a hunch, really—was beginning to form in my brain. I dialed Nell in South Carolina again, hoping she hadn't gone out. She answered.

"Nell, it's me again, Hoag in Vermont. When did your great-grandfather disappear?"

"Just a minute, it's in the journal," she said, and the line was quiet. I heard papers rustling.

"April of 1858," she said a moment later.

"1858?"

"Yes. 1858. According to the story passed down in the family, he left at night with a little food, the clothes on his back, and a quilt."

"A quilt?"

"Yes, a quilt. It served as his bedroll, but the quilt was really a map to freedom. The squares contained different pictures and symbols. Each was a clue to the safe stops on the way North."

"The Underground Railroad?"

"Yes. Why?"

"I think your great-grandfather was on his way to see Reverend Nightingale in Norwich, Vermont. But the minister and all three members of his family died in a fire, leaving your great-grandfather without anyone to make that connection."

"So, what happened to him?" Nell asked.

"I don't know. I'll call you back when I have more."

A minute later Devaney called back. I told him I'd be right over to pick him up. I called Clarence Jones and caught him on his lunch break.

"Dr. Jones, I really need Shawna and Clarissa to come to the cemetery," I said. "Please. Trust me. I wouldn't ask if I didn't think it was really important."

"I don't see how it would benefit the girls," he said.

"I think it's about a relative of theirs."

"A relative? Which one?"

"Your great-grandfather, the slave who disappeared. I think whoever or whatever is drawing people to the cemetery is trying to tell us what happened to your great-grandfather."

Jones was quiet on the other end. He didn't ask me to explain it further. Either he trusted me or something in his soul told him there was some truth to what I was saying.

"How about 4:00?" he asked. "The girls will be home from school by then, and Celia will be home from work."

"Devaney and I will meet you in front of the Congregational Church." I hung up and called Dutch Roberts to say Devaney and I would buy him lunch. When he asked where, I said, "At your office. We'll pick up three deli sandwiches at Dan & Whit's on our way over. Roast beef or turkey?" Then I went to pick up Devaney.

* * *

"I can't just authorize a Town backhoe to open the Masters graves," Dutch said as his mouth prepared to clamp down on the sandwich. "I'd need permission either from the descendants or from the State Medical Examiner. Geez Louise, Hoagie, you can't just go digging up people's graves on a hunch."

"I don't want to open up anyone's grave," I explained. "The actual graves—caskets or whatever's in there—are under the crypt, or the mausoleum, or whatever it's called. They're under that huge stone slab. We won't disturb the individuals at all. I just need a look."

"No can do," Dutch said. "If word got out, I'd be up a creek without a paddle. I could lose my job, get sued."

"Dutch," Devaney chimed in. "Think of it this way: It's not about opening a grave or exhuming a body. It's about straightening out that historic lid that's shifted out of place." Devaney winked a couple times to be sure Dutch caught it, then beamed a heck of a stupid grin at Dutch. If he'd had long eyelashes, we'd have seen them flutter.

Despite the free lunch and our best cajoling, Dutch wouldn't relent. He did, however, ask if he could accompany us to the cemetery at 4:00. "To protect the Joneses," he said.

"From the ghost?" Devaney asked.

"No. From you two," Dutch said. "Together, you're a public menace."

After lunch, the three of us scouted River Bend Cemetery, but we found nothing, saw nobody.

"Looks like the place is clean," Devaney said in a TV cop voice.

"Yeah," Dutch answered in a similar voice. "The perps must've wiped the prints."

"You overlooked one thing, gentlemen," I said.

"What's that?" Devaney asked in his best Joe Friday/*Dragnet* voice.

"They left a heckuva lot of bodies behind."

* * *

At four o'clock an SUV pulled up in front of the Congregational Church and Clarence Jones got out. We shook hands and I thanked him for coming.

“When I got home,” Jones said, “I got your message on my answering machine—from this morning. You wanted me to ask the girls if the voice in the dream might have said Lazarus. They weren’t sure.”

The rear window of the SUV wound down and a head popped out. “Daddy, Mom wants to know if we’re leaving the car here.”

“Just a minute, Shawna,” her father said. He looked to me for direction.

“She doesn’t seem frightened,” I said. “How about her sister? And your wife?”

“They’re fine, I think.”

“Good. Let’s drive the cars to the cemetery and park just inside the entrance gate, which will block anyone else from driving in and disturbing us.”

Five minutes later we were out of our cars, walking toward the oldest part of River Bend Cemetery. The twins led, I walked with Clarence and Celia, and Dutch and Devaney brought up the rear.

“This is where we felt it that night,” one of the twins said. “So we got everyone to go that way.” She pointed off to the left at an access road leading back toward Route 5, away from the Masters crypt.

I hadn’t told them where we were going. I preferred they find their own way. Maybe the deer that Devaney and I had followed had been just a deer, and our suppositions were off base.

“Do you feel the force, girls?” Devaney asked.

“This isn’t Star Wars, Devaney,” Dutch whispered loudly.

“Nothing yet,” the girls answered. Then a few steps later, “Yes. It’s pulling us over there.” They pointed toward the Masters crypt.

A moment later we were standing in front of it.

“Here,” one of the twins said. “Under that giant stone.”

“Any voices?” their father asked.

The girls closed their eyes and listened. “No voices,” they said in unison. “Should there be?”

“We don’t know,” I said. “Maybe we just need to stand here and listen a while.”

The seven of us stood quietly facing the Masters crypt. Three or four minutes passed.

“I’m feeling a bit strange,” Clarence Jones said.

“Are you sick, dear?” Celia asked, supporting his forearm.

"Not sick,” he said, his voice growing higher, as if he were about to faint. “Just strange. Let me sit down.” He turned around and sat on the edge of the stone covering the Masters crypt.

“If you feel like you’re going to pass out,” Celia said, “put your head between your knees.”

But Dr. Jones didn’t put his head between his knees. He lay back on the stone cover.

“Do you have any chest pains?” his wife said, a hint of alarm in her voice.

As he shook his head, his cell phone rang, and Celia reached inside the breast pocket of his jacket and removed it. It rang again, and as she was about to put it to her ear, her husband moaned.

“Somebody else answer it,” she said, and lobbed it to the twins, who were closest.

Dr. Jones began to shiver violently and tried to wrap his arms around himself. His eyes rolled back in his head, only the whites showing. His lips moved, something between a gasp and a hoarse whisper, and Celia put her ear to his lips.

“It’s a seizure or a heart attack,” Dutch said. “Give me the phone. I’ll call 911.” He reached toward the girls for the cell phone. But they were talking to someone.

Clarence Jones hissed out something, a phrase or a word, so Celia leaned closer to hear. “*Laz-rus*,” she said. “He’s saying *Laz-rus*.”

The twins stood like statues, as if in a trance themselves, then linked hands, raised them heavenward, and called out together in a loud voice, “Jabez, come out!” Then again they commanded, “Jabez, come out.”

At first I thought they’d said *Chambers*. Or jaybird. Their lips seemed to be pronouncing those words. But they were saying *Jabez*.

The air around us was electric with tension. Still lying on his back the stone, Clarence Jones stretched his arm toward the closest corner of the crypt. And as he did, a vapor squeezed out of the tomb, seeping out where the lid met the sides of the crypt. I could see through it, yet it wasn’t totally clear, and it eerily took the shape of a hand. For a moment the tip of Clarence’s Jones’ index finger strained to touch the tip of the ethereal hand’s index finger. I could feel the tension in my own body, wanting him to make it, yearning on his behalf. Closer, closer.

And then they did. They touched. And I blinked—one of those involuntary blinks like when something explodes, though I don’t remember any sound. Later, when we recounted the experience, none of us would recall a sound, only Clarence’s hand and the ghostly hand and then when they touched, the blink. And in the moments after the blink, we all saw Clarence Jones’ hand—but no other hand—hanging limply over the edge of the crypt.

“We need a doctor,” Dutch said, but with Celia’s help Dr. Jones was sitting up.

“What happened?” he asked. He stood and swatted the dust and dirt from the seat of his pants while Celia cleaned off the back of his jacket.

The twins handed him his cell phone. “Aunt Nell in South Carolina called to tell us your great-grandfather’s name—Jabez," one of the girls said. “She wants to talk to you.”

As Dr. Jones put the phone to his ear and said hello, there—not ten yards beyond the crypt—stood a deer. It gave a quick nod of its head and bounded away through the brush.

* * *

Three days later Dutch Roberts had the Town backhoe in the River Bend Cemetery to "realign the lid" on the Masters crypt. Devaney and I were there. So were Clarence Jones, his family, and his sister Nell from South Carolina.

Before the backhoe realigned the stone cover, though, we got a peek inside. What we discovered, in addition to the coffins of the Masters clan, were other human remains—bones later identified as a black man's. They appeared huddled in the tattered remnants of an 1850s map-quilt. One of its squares depicted four nightingales. Beside the quilt rested an empty water jug.

Later at home, Devaney and I pieced it together this way. The Masters crypt might not have been the perfect short-term hiding place for a slave traveling the Underground Railroad, but the Nightingales' house was under scrutiny and was unavailable. So the Nightingales found an alternative. Who could imagine them hiding Jabez Jones in the crypt of Mrs. Nightingale's ancestors, the Masters clan?

Unfortunately, an arsonist, perhaps angry with the minister for his liberal views, ruined the plan by setting fire to the minister's house, snuffing out the lives of the only four people who knew Jabez Jones' hiding place and could release him from under the heavy slab.

As Jones' wife foretold, her husband would die a horrible death. And despite the fireplace ghosts trying to tell others the trapped slave's name, and Jabez himself calling attention to his plight through the name Lazarus, it would take nearly a hundred fifty years before his great-grandson Clarence and twin great-great-granddaughters Shawna and Clarissa set him free.

"What about the deer?" Devaney said after I'd laid out my explanation. "You didn't explain the deer. Charlie Three Rivers?"

I shrugged. "Don't know," I said. "Sometimes a deer is just a deer."

"And sometimes," Devaney said, "it's more."

I whistled a few notes from *Twilight Zone*.

* * *

Three months later, after the Vermont State Forensics Team released the bones, the Jones clan gathered in a South Carolina cemetery for a very belated funeral.Devaney and I drove down for it.

The stone was simple.

JABEZ JONES
1833-1858
A FREE MAN

Croaker

The Croaker thing started and ended with the North Ferry.

It was a Sunday morning in early August and the four of us—Jake, Luca, Spider, and I—were waiting by the ferry ticket office for the church bus that would take us across the bay to Shelter Island's Camp Quinipet. We lived near the ferry terminal so ours was the last stop for the bus. Once we climbed on it'd be 15 minutes across the bay then a 15-minute drive to Quinipet.

"This better be good," Jake said as the bus pulled into sight. He, Luca, and Spider had never been to camp and my first time had been the year before.

"Can't wait to paddle a war canoe," Luca said, and Jake and Spider agreed.

I had told them about Quinipet's oversized war canoes. One was painted like a South Seas outrigger with a pontoon out to the side, another looked like a birch-bark Indian canoe, and the third was modeled after a Viking long ship. My age group hadn't been allowed to use them the previous summer—something about age and insurance—but I was sure we'd get a chance this year. It was my main selling point in convincing Jake, Luca, and Spider to try church camp.

We climbed onto the bus and found seats. "Hey Ben, hey Gracie," I said to a brother and sister I recognized. I high-fived them and introduced Jake, Luca, and Spider.

"You heard about Croaker, right?" Gracie asked.

Croaker—that's what we called him though his real name was Kroeker, Kroeger, Kroener, something like that—was Quinipet's long-time handyman. He was a tall, muscular deep-voiced blonde who always wore a blue New York Yankees jacket. He had a trace of a German accent and people around the camp swore he was a World War II German soldier trying to lay low and disappear on Shelter Island. He was rude and grumpy to everyone: staff, volunteer counselors, campers, even the Executive Director, Mr. Tinker. The two of them were the Quinipet's only year-round residents.

In return for mowing lawns, plowing snow, maintaining the buildings, and taking care of the waterfront—meaning the swimming float, lifeguard towers, picnic tables, sailboats, and war canoes—Croaker got a salary, the use of the camp truck, and a small caretaker's cottage to stay in. His door said in bold letters: *PRIVATE, KEEP OUT. THIS MEANS YOU.* He meant it. Croaker was a scary dude.

"No, I haven't heard," I answered Gracie. "What about him? Did he die or something?"

"He's gone. Packed up all his stuff in the middle of the night and left. They say it was about a month before the counselors came in for their training. But I guess nobody's sure exactly when. He didn't give notice, he just split for parts unknown."

I was tempted to say *good riddance* but instead I said, "You're kidding!"

Jake joked, "Maybe the FBI got wind of him."

"Nobody knows anything except that he vanished," Gracie went on. "He must have hitchhiked or left on foot."

"What makes you say that?" Luca asked.

"The guy had no car of his own. He used the camp truck but he didn't take that."

"So we should cheer up, right?" Spider grinned. "This is good news?" He pretended to raise a glass. "A toast—to Croaker's replacement. May she be 18 and a swimsuit model." We laughed and everyone pretended to drink. But something didn't feel right.

* * *

"Be sure you've got all your gear from the buses," a voice squawked through a bullhorn. A scrawny middle-aged man stood on a picnic table. He wore a fluorescent yellow windbreaker and held a clipboard under his arm. He was trying hard to look and sound important. The cap on his head was navy blue with a ponytail stuck out the back. Gold lettering above the brim declared him *Supreme Commander*.

"That's Mr. Tinker, the Executive Director," I said to Luca, Jake, and Spider. "He's got this control thing. You can call him Tink or Tinkerbell behind his back but to his face it's Mr. Tinker. Not Tinker. *Mister* Tinker."

"Tink and Croaker did *not* get along," Gracie added. "No love lost between those two." Ben nodded in agreement.

Tinker droned out instructions about facilities, mealtimes, recreation, quiet time, worship time, arts and crafts time, and free time.

Luca raised his hand. "Mr. Tinker, you forgot to mention waterfront. What about swim time, sailboats, and the war canoes?"

Tinker put on a sad face. "I hate to break it to you, kiddies, but don't unpack your bathing suits this week. All summer we've had reports of sharks around the swimming area especially near the float. So in the interest of everyone's safety we've had to close the waterfront for the season. No swimming, sailing, or canoeing." He didn't even say he was sorry.

A collective groan went up and the grumbling started.

"Quiet. Quiet down," Tinker said into the bullhorn in front of his mouth. "I'm sure your parents would prefer this approach to risking their children's lives. Don't you agree?"

Spider grumbled low enough that Tinker couldn't hear, "No war canoes? That's bogus. Everybody knows sharks can't get you inside a boat." He shot me a dirty look as if I had deliberately deceived him. "This is just great, just great."

We were so disappointed we barely heard the rest of Tinker's instructions.

* * *

By Tuesday everyone was sick and tired of Half-a-Camp as Spider referred to it. Yes, softball and arts-and-crafts time were fun. So were the hikes around other parts of Shelter Island, especially the visit to the Old Quaker Burying Ground where we had lunch on log benches in an outdoor meeting circle and poked around a bunch of old graves. But without the waterfront activities it just wasn't camp.

On the hike back from the burying ground we stopped at an IGA to buy candy bars.

Jake jokingly said to the man behind the fish counter, "What? No shark? Figured you'd have plenty in stock."

When the man explained that there wasn't any decent sort of edible shark to be had anywhere near Shelter Island, Jake told him about Tinker's waterfront ban. The fish guy turned to a meat butcher behind another counter. "You heard anything about sharks in the area?"

"Not a thing. And my cousin's the harbormaster. If anybody knew, it'd be him and he'd have told me. It's a small island and word about something like that would get around fast."

"Sorry, kids" the fish guy said. "But between him and me we know all the cops, fishermen, baymen, and Coast Guardsmen. Somebody's either misinformed you or is pulling your leg."

* * *

Our favorite time was free time. We explored every part of Quinipet and a little beyond.

Once we sneaked into Gracie's cabin while she and the other girls were out hiking. We tucked garter snakes and salamanders into their bunks. Then we moved next door to the infirmary where we climbed on the roof and rolled small stones down the roof until the nurse, Mrs. Wesley, came out to see what the clatter was.

On Tuesday afternoon we walked down the road past the Pridwin Hotel to Louis' Beach and bought ice cream cones at the concession shack. Jake asked the teenager at the counter if they'd had any shark problems.

The boy pointed out at the sandy beach and gave us the short answer. "Look out there. Hundreds of people swim here every day. Cops ain't said nothing, Coast Guard neither. If we had shark problems they'd have signs posted everywhere. You see any signs?"

By Wednesday morning we were beyond bored. Without having waterfront activities to burn off campers' energy, the poor counselors couldn't find enough to keep us busy. So they gave us extra free time.

Jake, Luca, Spider, and I went for a walk near the vacant caretaker cottage. When we got close we sneaked up and peered in the window. It was unlocked so Spider raised it and slipped inside then unlocked the door for the rest of us. It was three tiny rooms and a bath.

"Pretty empty," Jake said, testing out a worn recliner next to a small wood-burning stove.

"Check and see if he left a Nazi uniform in the closet," Luca said, pointing to a door.

Spider opened the closet and found three or four shirts hanging alongside two pairs of jeans and some coveralls. Boots, sneakers, and shoes sat on the closet floor and a green winter coat hung on a hook.

Spider grabbed the coat. "Doesn't look like his infamous Yankees jacket. Seems like he left a lot of clothes behind."

"I thought Gracie said he stuffed everything into a suitcase and walked away," Luca recalled.

Jake began opening and closing dresser drawers. “Tee shirts, underwear, socks, and sweaters. Must have been a really small suitcase if he didn't have room for the basics.”

“The man was on foot,” I reminded him. “He probably took what he could carry and had to leave a lot behind.”

“I'd say he was in a real hurry,” Jake said.

The camp bell rang for lunch and the discussion ended.

* * *

Wednesday afternoon we split up during free time.

Luca and Jake filled some water balloons and headed for Gracie's cabin while Spider and I walked out the main driveway toward the waterfront. Before long we were sitting on a cement wall looking out past the famous Quinipet gazebo at the open bay beyond. I knew Spider was imagining himself paddling a war canoe and I expected he'd soon start moaning about not being able to do it. But he said nothing for a while and when he did finally open his mouth he surprised me.

"It makes no sense." I figured he meant the closing of the waterfront, but then he added, "Why would that swimming float be out?”

“What do you mean?” I asked. “It’s anchored in place.”

“Yeah, but if there’s no swimming, sailing, or canoeing this summer, why’s it out at all?” It was a good question.

“Maybe it’s out year-round,” I said, guessing. I had no clue.

“No way. They pull those things out at the end of the season so they won't rot or so they can paint them. They either put it up on blocks or stick it in the barn. When the new season starts they put swimming floats and floating docks back in the water around early to mid-June before camp starts. They're not going to put it out while kids are still in school." That made sense.

“But if Tinker declared a shark alert before the season started," I asked, "why would he put the float out at all? He might as well keep it in storage."

“Tinker wouldn’t have put it out," Spider reasoned. "Croaker would have. He was the caretaker, it was his job. If it took a second person he might have gotten Tinker to help.”

I worked that idea around in my head. “But Croaker was already out of the picture in April, way before the counselor training sessions. So did Tinker do it alone after Croaker left town?”

We mulled that over.

“Know what else is odd?" Spider asked. "There's no other waterfront equipment out. No lifeguard towers. No roped-off swimming area. And no picnic tables by the beach. Why not at least put out the picnic tables for us? Sharks don't attack kids at picnic tables.”

“Good question," I said, but my brain wasn't moving as fast as his.

"Know what I think? I think Croaker quit and left. Then Tinker somehow got the float out of the barn into the water by himself. But he got tired of doing both his job and the caretaker's so he cooked up the shark story as an excuse for not having the waterfront ready for the summer camp season. *There are no sharks*." He let that last idea sink in.

He was right, of course. It was obvious. There were no sharks.

An impish smile crept over Spider's face.

I knew what he was thinking: in 10 hours it would be dark, everyone would be sleeping, and it would be the perfect time to borrow a war canoe.

* * *

Around 8:00 Spider and I were on a log bench by our cabin, counting down the hours. Our plan was to sneak out after 10 p.m. with Jake and Luca then rendezvous with Ben and Gracie. We needed them to help lift the heavy war canoe off the boatshed rack and carry it to the water. Then we'd have to get it back into place on the rack later so no one would suspect we'd been out in it.

Luca and Jake trotted across the yard toward us. "Come with us," Luca said. "You've got to see this."

"See what?" Spider asked.

"Croaker's cabin," Luca replied. "There's a fire in the woodstove."

Jake explained further. "On the way back from telling Ben and Gracie the plan we smelled something burning and followed our noses. It was smoke from Croaker's chimney. We peeked in the window and saw the woodstove door open with a fire inside. But the place is empty."

* * *

We sneaked around behind the caretaker cottage.

"Wait," Luca whispered. "Somebody's coming. Hide." We crept into the bushes.

A shadowy figure came around the corner and stepped in front of Croaker's door. He wasn't very big so it couldn't be Croaker returning. In the moonlight we could see the man fumbling with the lock then we heard a click and watched the door swing open. The firelight from the stove lit up the man's lemon-yellow windbreaker and the gold lettering on his ball cap: *Supreme Commander*. He stepped in and shut the door.

"It's Tinker," Jake said. "What's he doing here?"

"Shh!" Spider said. "Let's go see."

We sneaked forward and snuck a look in the windows.

"What's he doing?" Luca asked.

“Looking in the closet,” Jake answered softly. “He’s got an armload of clothes.”

"This is a weird time to be cleaning out Croaker’s closet,” Spider said.

Jake sneaked another peek. “He’s stuffing the clothes into the stove.”

"Why would he do that?" Luca asked.

"I don't know," I said. "But we’ve got to go. The rest of the cabin will be out looking for us.”

“One more look,” Jake whispered and before we could object he raised his head. “Oops! I think he saw me. Run.”

We took off through the bushes like scared rabbits.

* * *

It was dark but moonlit at 10:30 when we six met at the boathouse. The camp’s fleet of small sailboats along with their centerboards, masts and sails—anything worth stealing—had been locked inside. But on the outside wall under a lean-to roof held up by poles was a three-level canoe rack. The South Seas outrigger was on top but didn't have the pontoon attached. The middle one was the fake birch-bark canoe. The one on the bottom rack was the Viking long ship with the bow that looked like a dragon's head. It was the easiest to reach and it wasn't chained. It was heavy but we managed to lift it off and turn it right-side up on the ground. There were six paddles in it but no life preservers. Working three to a side we lugged it down to the sandy beach.

“Remember," I cautioned, as we pushed off from shore and scrambled in. "It's dark." We don’t want to get so far away from the beach or the gazebo that we can’t tell where to come back in.”

“No biggie,” Gracie said. “It’s an island, remember? We can come in close to shore anywhere and follow along close to the coastline. Eventually we'll get back to the camp." She had a gift for logic.

I also reminded them that we had no life preservers.

"We're good swimmers," Spider said. "Besides, it'd take a tidal wave to flip this heavy thing over." He stood up and intentionally rocked it.

"Knock it off, Spider," Gracie ordered. "Don't be stupid."

Spider laughed and gave a couple more shakes to show he wasn't stopping just because a girl had told him to. Then he sat back down. "Okay, let's paddle. Head for that point of land to the right. Louis' Beach is around the bend."

We started stroking and the war canoe moved forward through the water. None of us spoke for a while. It was magical, mesmerizing hearing only the paddles slicing into and pushing the water to propel us forward. The only light came from the moon and stars overhead. Then as if on cue we all stopped on the same stroke and coasted. It was serene, peaceful, and utterly magnificent. Finally we got our ride in the war canoe.

Twenty minutes later we nosed the bow up onto the sand at Louis' Beach. The ice cream stand and trampoline concession had already closed so no one was around. Jake, Luca, and Ben explored the buildings while Spider, Gracie, and I walked the long beach.

"Hey, check this out," Spider said, pointing to a bright yellow beach towel someone had left behind. On one corner rested a pair of sunglasses and a dark blue baseball cap. He picked up the cap and sunglasses and put them on. "All that's missing," he joked, tapping the brow of the cap, "is *Supreme Commander.*" He draped the bright yellow towel around his shoulders like a cape.

"I wonder who left those things," I said.

"The swimmer who got too close to one of Tinker's sharks," Gracie joked and we three laughed.

"Finders keepers; losers weepers," Spider said, and started back toward the canoe wearing his treasure.

Luca, Jake, and Ben were already in the canoe when we reached it. We pushed off and climbed in, Spider in the bow. He struck a pose and said something about George Washington crossing the Delaware.

“Sit down, Tink," Gracie ordered. "You're rocking the boat." She was on target with the name. With the hat, sunglasses, and yellow towel he looked like Mr. Tinker.

"We'd get you his bullhorn," Jake said, "but you'd probably use it to say *Stroke, stroke, stroke*." We laughed.

We paddled back around the point of land and were soon closing on the swimming float.

“Let’s tie up at the swimming float for a minute,” Spider suggested. “Thanks to Tinker that’s another thing we didn’t get to use this week. And here we are without our swimsuits. Let's at least check it out.”

We held our paddles in the water so the drag would slow us. A minute later we bumped sideways against the float.

"No way to tie up," Luca said. "We don't have any rope."

“Somebody stays in the canoe to hold it to the float," Spider said. "We'll switch places in a minute." He climbed out.

The others were right behind him, leaving me to keep the canoe in place. I kept my paddle pressed down against the gray decking.

No sooner had they spread out on the float than it started to rock back and forth.

"Cut it out, Spider!" Gracie said sharply.

"Yeah," Ben said, backing her up. "We don't want to fall over with our clothes on."

"I'm not doing anything," Spider protested.

All five of them staggered as they tried to keep their balance. The movement forced them to drop onto their hands and knees near the float's center. I noticed the water all around us was calm. All the rippling waves were coming *from* the float not toward it. If

Spider wasn't making it rock and waves weren't making it rock, what was doing it?

I glanced down where the canoe was rubbing against the float. The others looked there at the same time.

"Look!" Ben shrieked, pointing.

Gripping the edge of the float was a pair of thick, pale hands—gigantic, swollen, blanched-white hands. Strands of brown seaweed and stringy green spaghetti grass clung to them dripping seawater.

Spider stood up and swung his paddle, smashing its blade down on one of the hands. It had no effect. He swung it again then another time, but no blood appeared on the back of the hand and it didn't let go. It didn't seem to feel the pain. The hands kept pulling down and pushing up, pulling down and pushing up, either intending to rock the five of them off the float or raise itself from the depths and climb on.

I swung my paddle at the other hand, but when I did the gap between the float and the canoe opened up. I was no longer holding the boat to the float.

As I drifted back I tossed two paddles across to Luca and Jake. They caught them and joined the battle with Spider, the three of them smashing the paddles against the thick hands. But the hands refused to let go their grip and kept rocking and lifting and pulling down on the float.

"Go to the other side and pick us up," Spider yelled. "We'll hold that thing here." He whacked at the hand with his paddle, at the same time trying to stay low and maintain his balance. It was awkward getting in a solid downward swing.

I struggled to turn the big canoe and move it around to the opposite side of the float. I was about to say something when Spider stood up above the others. With the towel-cape around his shoulders he was General Washington again leading the charge—

and he was Tinker. That was it. *The thing was after him, not me or the others.*

"Spider," I screamed. "Get rid of the towel, the sunglasses and the hat! It thinks you're Tinker."

Jake and Luca swung their paddles like samurai swords or machetes—*whack, whack, whack, whack, whack.*

"Dump the beach outfit and get ready to jump aboard!" I yelled. "Hold onto your paddles. We'll need them."

Spider stripped off the sunglasses, cap, and towel and threw them into the water close to the bloated hands. They immediately let go and slipped beneath the surface allowing the float to stabilize.

"Let's go!" Spider yelled. "Now, now, now! Jump in!"

They did—Luca and Jake behind me, Ben and Gracie in front of me.

I heard the waters churn where the hat, towel, sunglasses, and pair of hands had gone down. The thing had surfaced.

"Paddle!" Spider screamed at us as he leaped into the canoe. "Paddle!" He landed on my lap and lost his own paddle over the side.

We stroked for all we were worth, whimpering in terror as we strove to gain speed and make it to the beach. There was more splashing and churning close behind us and I heard wood cracking—Spider's paddle snapping like a toothpick. We all looked back.

There barely 20 feet behind us was something trying to catch up. On the surface of the water we saw what looked at first like a huge jellyfish, a swirl of drifting tendrils emanating out from a round center. But when it caught the moonlight we realized the tendrils weren't jellyfish tentacles—they were strands of blond hair. This wasn't a jellyfish, it was the top of a grayish bloated head inching its way above the surface. It showed itself the way an alligator does, partly exposed, eyes glowing in the moonlight. But this was no alligator. Whatever this was, its eye sockets were empty.

As the water grew shallower the thing rose higher out of the water, enough that we could see fabric below the blond hair—a blue jacket with white on it: a team emblem, New York Yankees! It was Croaker! We were sure of it. We turned and put our backs into the paddles, a minute later grounding the bow of the boat on the camp beach. We leaped out and raced uphill toward the safety of the camp buildings. I took one last look behind us and watched the thing that had once been Croaker slide back into the waters and disappear.

Outside our cabin we tried to make sense of it. Had something happened when Croaker was anchoring the float? This wasn't just a drowned body, a floater popping to the surface after being freed from under the float by our movements. It had gripped the float, rocked it, and snapped the lost paddle. It had followed us most of the way to shore. We all drew the same conclusion. *Croaker hadn't walked off the job. He was dead. But not fully dead.*

What had happened to us—to Spider on the float—had been a case of mistaken identity. It had been about revenge.

We woke our counselor Darren and spilled our story. He was skeptical but nevertheless followed us to the waterfront. The war canoe was exactly where we had beached it. The float was empty. No person or thing stood or sat or lay on it or held on beside it.

"Look," Luca said, pointed at the war canoe.

The broken paddle was there with the other five. So was the blue ball cap and the yellow beach towel. No sunglasses. They were probably on the sea bottom near the float.

Darren began to laugh. We stood stone-faced, unwilling to join in. "Good one!" he said. "Great, great story." We protested that it was true, not a prank on him, but he just laughed some more. "Okay, party's over. Let's put the canoe and paddles back on the rack so Tinker doesn't find out. Then it's back to bed. I know you were bored without waterfront this week so I won't tell your parents about this."

We couldn't let it go, though. We had figured out the truth. Croaker hadn't quit and left. He was dead, perhaps from an accident or possibly murdered. We six knew we had a bunch of pieces to the puzzle but didn't know how to fit them together. One thing was sure: we couldn't go to Tinker.

So Friday morning we went to Mrs. Wesley, the nurse we had pulled the stones-on-the-roof prank on. Besides being the nurse she produced the camp newspaper each week so campers would have a keepsake detailing the week's activities. She was the only investigative type we knew. She listened intently and seemed to be supportive.

But then while we were at lunch she ratted us out to Tinker who called us on the carpet. He insisted we tell it all again. We told him, at times no doubt sounding accusing. Oddly he seemed more worried than angry and let us go without scolding or punishing us. That was Friday.

On Saturday morning we woke to a light drizzle. After breakfast all of us campers packed our gear, cleaned up our cabins, and piled into the meeting hall for the goodbye ceremony. Mr. Tinker had always led it but gave each counselor a chance to speak.

But Mr. Tinker didn't show. After a half hour the counselors took over and finished up the formalities. Another hour passed. The buses failed to show up. Mrs. Wesley sent people out to search for Tinker. She also phoned the North Ferry to see what the holdup was. Kids began calling home to say they'd be late and something was wrong.

"The North Ferry isn't operating," Mrs. Wesley announced. "They've been shut down due to an emergency. Your buses have been rerouted to the South Ferry and will arrive from the other side of the island. Everything will be four to five hours later than originally planned."

It was suppertime before we got home. The North Ferry never did run that night so our buses had to use the South Ferry and drive an extra 75 extra miles.

The next day *Newsday* ran a front page story saying the North Ferry had been shut down from Friday night through Sunday morning. Not one of the three ferry boats that alternated trips was allowed to the ferry slip on the Shelter Island side. A photo showed the terminal, the wooden pilings, the bulkheads all roped off with Crime Scene tape.

The *Newsday* reporter had persuaded the ferry's ticket-taker to make the same statement he'd made to police, which is what the newspaper ran.

"On the 5:30 p.m. boat out of Shelter Island we loaded eight cars. The fellow in the very front got out of his car—a lemon yellow Volkswagen beetle that matched his jacket—and leaned on the front gate. I told him not to do that, it was dangerous and there were signs in red. I remember him because he wore his hair in a hippy ponytail that stuck out through the back of his ball cap. I joked about what it said: *Supreme Commander*. But he wasn't in a joking mood. He was the nervous type and tried to light a cigarette, so I reminded him it was no smoking. Then he leaned on the front gate again—he seemed distracted—and I warned him again not to lean on the gate. I turned away for a second to collect from another driver and then decided to tell him it was okay to smoke *inside* his car. Just as I turned I saw somebody or some*thing* dripping wet and covered in seaweed climb over the railing—from the water side onto the car deck. It wrapped its arms around the ponytail guy, pinning his arms to his sides. Then this big thing picked him right up off the deck and they tumbled over the side together—splash! By the time I got to the spot, they were both gone. We hadn't even left the dock yet."

The article said divers had spent all night and some of the next morning searching for the missing persons. The ferry boat had to be shut down because its prop wash made the search difficult for the divers. Even after the bodies were located they would have to search for weapons and other evidence.

Although no names were released pending notification of kin, it was thought that the first victim found wearing a New York Yankees jacket was Camp Quinipet's caretaker. The condition of his body suggested it had been submerged for months. The second victim was presumed to be the Camp Executive Director, last seen at work on Friday when he questioned us. It was his driverless yellow VW that was left aboard the ferry.

Divers had to raise both bodies at the same time because they were inseparable, entangled in seaweed. The arms and legs of the bloated caretaker were wrapped around the man in the lemon yellow windbreaker. The blue *Supreme Commander* cap was found jammed in Tinker's mouth.

All the caretaker's finger bones were found to be broken in numerous places.

The Tattooist

Even though Chuck, Ramon, and I are adults now—big strapping men all over six-feet-four—none of us will go into corner grocery stores or convenience stores late at night, only into large supermarkets with bright lights and plenty of people. And we won't enter a tattoo parlor for love or money.

It was 1963 and we had run away from home, hitchhiked our way through a series of rides from Eastern Long Island to Elizabeth, New Jersey. I was thirteen, my cousin Chuck and our sidekick Ramon were twelve, and it started because we broke into an old house in our hometown and discovered a wine cellar. We popped the corks on a few dusty bottles and, even though we wouldn't have known if a bottle had gone bad, we did some tasting. The port and Chablis and chardonnay, however, didn't satisfy us the way Snickers bars always did. But it seemed silly to let that wine sit there in a deserted house that was about to be torn down. So we absconded with three mixed cases that we hid in our Uncle Edgar's barn two miles away, in a secret attic above the calf pens.

Two days later, on a Saturday morning when we went to check on our stash, we rounded the corner by the calf pens and saw Uncle Edgar's legs on a stepladder, his torso and head up in the secret attic. He'd found us out! And we knew he'd squeal to our parents. We backed out of the calf pen area, ran out of the barn, and lit out for the woods.

It was mid-February, very cold, and several inches of crusted snow covered the ground. Right then and there, at ten o'clock in the morning, we decided the only way out was to run away from home. We convinced ourselves Florida was the place to go. It was warm, we could grab jobs as orange pickers, and we could live on the beach in the warm open air, even at night, until we could find a place to rent. So, without packing so much as a pair of clean underwear, with $6.84 amongst us, we three set out to escape our parents' wrath by thumbing our way to Florida.

Nine hours later, after shivering beside many roads with our thumbs out, and after a hair-raising, high-speed ride down Sunrise Highway with three intoxicated men, we caught our fifth ride, this time with a fiftyish man with a ponytail in an old Volvo. He took us through New York City to Elizabeth, New Jersey—120 miles from our starting point.

He was the first one to whom we spilled our story. A big mistake. Shortly after we did that, he yawned, stretched, and pulled off on a dirty side street and parked across from a sleazy diner, saying he needed a cup of coffee if he was going to stay awake.

"Be right back," he said. "Stay in the car. It's not a good part of town to be on foot." Then he crossed the street and disappeared into the diner.

"He's going to call the cops, isn't he?" Chuck asked.

"Bet your butt he is," I said.

"We never should have told him," Ramon said. "Now what do we do?" It was seven o'clock, dark, and colder than the afternoon had been.

"Well, either we sit here and wait for the cops to surround the car—which, by the way, means eventually having our parents beat the crap out of us, or," Chuck said, "we make a break for it right now." He put a hand on the door handle, awaiting Ramon's and my decision.

"What the heck," Ramon said. "We've been in a warm car long enough. Florida or bust."

With that, Chuck opened the passenger door and the three of us slipped out, one after the other, and hid behind the car. We checked the diner window to make sure the coast was clear, then fled down the sidewalk and around a corner, running three more blocks before slowing. We walked another ten or fifteen blocks with our collars up and our hands jammed into our pockets.

"Man, it's cold," Chuck said. "We gotta get inside. Maybe there's a Laundromat still open."

"I'm not sure anyone washes their clothes around here," Ramon said.

Many of the buildings were boarded up, while others had broken windows. Only a few had lights. It was how parts of London must have looked during the Blitz.

"Toto, we're not in Kansas anymore," I said, trying to lighten the mood.

Ramon looked at me stupidly.

"You know," I said. "The Wizard of Oz? Dorothy? She says it to her dog, Toto, after they land in Oz. The flying house? The ruby slippers?"

"Oh," Ramon said, rolling his eyes. "Another literary reference, eh? I get it." But he wasn't smiling. None of us was smiling. We were cold and tired and really, really hungry.

"It's time to spend some of our cash," Chuck said. "We've got to eat something. And that'll get us indoors for a while, too. We can warm up. You know, take our time looking for a package of Twinkies." Nobody argued.

On the next corner, just below a burned-out streetlight, we could see what looked like a local neighborhood grocery store. A sign for Coca Cola and another proclaiming Boar's Head Meats hung in the front window.

A strange, hand-printed sign in the lower corner said: *Tattoos by Bando.*

"Looks like as good a place as any to get Twinkies," Ramon said, so we stepped inside.

"Ah, that heat feels great," Chuck said, and for a moment we just stood soaking it up inside the door. All around us the shelves and the coolers were stocked with the basics—bread, milk, eggs, butter, cream, soda, macaroni, spaghetti, cakes and cupcakes, candy, popcorn and potato chips. I saw a deli case near the back wall, and at one end of it was a counter with a cash register. Behind the counter was an open door that appeared to lead into a back room.

"I don't see anybody," Ramon said. "We could just scoop up a bunch of stuff and run."

That's when a deep ugly voice from the room behind the register said, "Go lock that door before somebody comes in, moron. I told you to do it before."

"Somebody is working," Chuck said.

But something felt wrong. I wanted to grab the door handle and flee, but before I could, a man appeared in the doorway by the counter. He was short and dark-skinned, Cuban or Mexican, possibly an Indian from Central America. His mouth dropped when he saw us, as if we had caught him doing something naughty. The look quickly became a forced smile.

"Well, hello, boys. Didn't hear you there. Come in, come in. We're still open." As he spoke, he edged around the corner of the counter and strode down the aisle. "What can I help you with?"

"Uh, nothing," I said, but Ramon cut me off.

"Twinkies," he said.

"Sure," the man said. "No problem." He reached for the door with his left hand, not letting us see his right hand and arm. "Shop around. I've just got to lock up. Closing time, you know? You'll be my last customers."

"Great," Ramon said. "That'll give us a minute to warm up, too. It's getting really cold out there." Ramon didn't seem to sense that something was amiss.

"Okay, but not too long," the man said, not leaving the door. He yelled toward the back room, "It's okay, Dad, just three boys come in to get some Twinkies." Then he nodded, trying to appear pleasant. "Go ahead, one pack of Twinkies each. There's no charge tonight. I've already emptied the cash register." Something told me he had, too.

"Wow! Free Twinkies," Ramon said, his eyebrows arching in surprise and delight. "Somebody's watching over us tonight." I sure hoped so.

Another man nearly six feet tall with a black mustache and an acne-scarred face appeared in the back doorway. He was too close in age to the first man to be the father. And his coloring was different, he was paler, so he couldn't be a brother. Something wasn't right.

"We hate to hurry you, boys," the man with the mustache said without smiling, "but we have to close." His face looked tense, his words rang hollow.

Ramon grabbed three packs of Twinkies from a shelf and walked toward the register. What was he thinking? The first man had said we could take them for free.

"The man by the front door told us we could have the Twinkies free," Ramon said. "Could we also get some water?"

The man's eyes narrowed as he glared at his companion by the front door.

Suddenly a moan arose from the back room, then "Police. Call the police."

Ramon's eyes flicked toward the back room, then back to the scar-faced man. I sneaked a sideways glance at Chuck. His eyes had grown wide, his mouth making an O. The two of us turned for the front door and saw the short man's fingers on the latch.

Click! He had locked us in.

"Sorry, boys," he said. "I tried to give you an out. But it's a case of wrong time, wrong place."

A wicked grin came over his face then and I felt a chill run down my spine. He raised his right hand from behind his body and light glinted off something. Polished steel! A machete!

"Back room, boys!" he ordered. "Pronto."

The back room was square, about twenty by twenty, with no back door or window, only a heavy door with a huge handle on it built into the wall. I was pretty sure it was a walk-in cooler like Uncle Edgar had in the milk house at the farm. No escape except the way we'd come in. A small plank table sat in the middle of the room with a single three-bulb light fixture above it. It looked like it was set up for a card game, except there were only three chairs. An old man lay slumped in a corner to our right. Blood trickled from the corner of his mouth and from his forehead.

"Get 'em into the cooler, Chico," the man with the mustache said, nodding toward the heavy door. "No sound in there."

The short, dark man raised his machete menacingly and we moved toward the door, Chuck in the lead.

"Can't," Chuck said, placing a hand on the heavy door handle. "It's locked." A heavy-duty padlock secured it.

"Watch 'em," the man with the mustache said, then reached down and grabbed the old man by the front of his shirt. He lifted him to his feet and slammed him against the wall. "All right, old man. Where's the key?" he snarled.

The old man's head hung down, his chin on his chest. His tormentor shook him and then slapped his face.

"Wake up, old man," he hissed. "Where's the key to the cooler?"

The old man raised his head a little, shook out the cobwebs. "I don't have it. The owner locks it at night before he goes home."

"The owner? Then who are you?" the man snarled, lifting the old man off the ground even higher by his shirtfront.

The old man wore his gray-black hair in a ponytail, and in the dim light I thought he looked Middle Eastern, possibly even Italian or Greek. But then again, he could have been from the Philippines. It was hard to pin down. He was like the actor, Anthony Quinn, who played a Mexican, an Indian, a Greek, an Italian, and many other parts.

"I'm Bando, the tattooist. The neighborhood kids call me Uncle Bando. The grocer lets me use this room to practice my art when someone comes seeking a fine tattoo. Instead of rent, I tend the store the last hour of each night so the owner can spend time with his family. You gentlemen chanced to come in the last hour before closing. I don't have the key to the cooler, it's on the grocer's key ring."

Apparently satisfied, the bully relaxed his grip and let Bando stand on his own.

"What now?" the man with the machete said. "They've seen our faces."

The scar-faced man didn't seem to know what to do.

"You have the money from the cash register," Bando said. "You can also take whatever groceries you can carry. So you've got what you came for, right? There's nothing else here of interest to the two of you, is there? Unless, of course, you've come for a tattoo."

Wham! The short man buried his machete blade in the tabletop the way an ax bites into a stump. "Idiot!" he spat. "You stupid old man, do we look like we came in for a tattoo?"

I could see the old man's eyes from across the room. No fear, no emotion. Crazy as it may sound, his face appeared relaxed, as if he'd expected this. And for a moment, just for a moment, his eyes seemed to show pity for the man grasping the machete handle.

"Truthfully? Yes," Bando said in a calm, measured voice. "You do look like you came in for a tattoo. And if you release these boys, the tattoo is on the house."

The short man glared at him, then looked up at the other man. "Is he stupid, or what?"

The man with the mustache shrugged and half smiled at Bando's audacity. "He's got guts, I'll say that for him."

"Sit down, gentlemen," the tattooist said, motioning them to the plank table. "You on this side, you on the other side. I have a very unusual pattern to show you, shared artwork, one especially designed for brothers-in-arms."

The machete blade remained buried in the tabletop.

"There are hundreds of examples of my work pictured here," Bando continued, gesturing toward a thick loose-leaf binder on the table. "But I think you'll want to check the last page." He flipped the binder open. "This one."

The two hoods gasped.

"That's incredible," the short one said.

"Awesome," the other added.

Chuck, Ramon, and I leaned in for a closer look. A full-page color photograph showed an incredibly detailed tattoo of a skull with two snakes entwined around each other, their slithering bodies twisted through the eye sockets, nose and mouth holes, and ears. But upon closer examination I could see that the grinning death's head was actually two tattoos, a pair of practically seamless images making up a whole. The men in the picture were using their right hands to clasp each other's biceps above the elbow, so that their right forearms were side-by-side except facing in opposite directions. When fitted together, the individually tattooed forearms made up a single larger image. It was like a pirate movie in which the two ripped halves of a treasure map were pieced together to reveal the secret hiding place. In the tattoo, the snakes' brilliant swirling colors reminded me of gas and oil slicks on the water by the docks, and the grinning skull looked like it might speak at any moment.

"That is my famous Brothers-in-Arms Tattoo," Bando said. "I've done it only once, and that was in Vietnam for the two mercenaries you see in the photo."

"Incredible," uttered the man with the mustache, mesmerized. He glanced across the table at his partner. "Whaddya think, Chico? Should we go for it?"

"Nobody else in Jersey will have anything like it. I'm game if you are. But what about them?" The short man nodded toward us. "And the old man?" His eyes narrowed as he and his partner each sneaked a sideways look at the machete.

"I said I'd do the tattoo if you let the boys go," Bando said. "You must promise."

The hoods looked at each other coldly.

"Oh, all right, we promise," said the scar-faced one, his voice condescending. "And you, too. But only if you four promise not to turn us in." He smiled, and I noticed that one of his eyeteeth was missing.

Bando quietly said, "Last month a storekeeper was killed on the East Side. He was hacked to death during a robbery gone sour. Nothing to do with you two, right?"

Was this old man crazy? These two had said they'd let us all go if we promised not to turn them in to the cops for the robbery. Now he'd made it clear he knew they were also murderers. How could they let us go after that?

"Couldn't have been us," the short man said. "We both had alibis. I was with him, and he was with me." He grinned broadly.

The scar-faced man nodded. "It's the God's-honest truth. We were together."

Bando's mouth curled into a cryptic smile. "Very well, gentlemen," he said. "Then let's proceed. First we must wash down your arms with alcohol to reduce the risk of infection."

The men rolled up their sleeves.

"Boys," the tattooist said, "grab my leather bag and the bottle of alcohol next to it, right there on the shelf."

Ramon reached for the bottle and I pulled down the bag. The bag was heavy, as if it contained a couple of sacks of nails.

"Just a minute!" the scar-faced man said. He reached behind him and slammed the door that led out to the store, then placed his right hand on the left side of his belt and pulled out his own machete. "Just in case," he said. "No tricks!" He swung the glinting blade above his head and buried it in the tabletop.

With both men having quick access to machetes, we had little hope of escape. And I knew, once they had their tattoo, they wouldn't keep their promise.

"May I have my bag now?" the old man said. "And the alcohol?"

"Here, Mr. Bando," Ramon said as we placed the alcohol and the bag on the table.

"You boys can call me Uncle Bando. As I said, all the kids around here do."

We nodded and said weakly, "Uncle Bando."

Uncle Bando opened the leather bag and withdrew what looked to be a large, heavy bib, the kind they put over your chest when they X-ray you, except this had a square cut out of the center. It reminded me of something surgeons might use in an operating room, so only the opened-up area would be exposed.

"Gentlemen, you'll need to join your forearms as in the photograph—a Roman centurion's salute, a very manly greeting. Grip your friend's lower biceps muscle. Once you lock arms, though, you mustn't move. I'll scrub your arms with alcohol and then we'll lay this leaded mat over your arms. There's less chance you'll tremble that way. Are you ready?"

"Don't you have to shave our arm hairs?" the short man asked.

"Not necessary."The tattooist waited.

The short man gave a what-the-heck shake of his head and placed his right forearm on the table. The man with the mustache did the same and they looked as if they were about to grip hands and arm wrestle. Instead they locked arms in the Centurion's salute.

"You don't have to squeeze," Uncle Bando said. "If you do, your muscles will tire and your arms will be shaking soon."

He took a cloth from the bag, poured alcohol on it, and swabbed the men's arms. Then he draped the leaded bib over them from elbow to elbow. The bib was the perfect length, as if it had been custom made for the length of the two men's arms. The tattooist used Velcro straps to secure it around each man's elbow. It resembled a sling for a broken arm, except this one was double-ended.

The men leaned toward the center of the table to peer inside the open square, but their heads blocked the overhead light and cast shadows over the opening so they couldn't see anything.

"Sit up straight and relax, gentlemen. There will be a little pain. But you're tough, you two, you're street-hardened, and you can take it. And no need to worry, you can easily reach your machetes."

For a moment I considered snatching up the machetes, but I wasn't sure we had the strength to pull the blades free. And I knew we didn't have what it took to use them on the men.

Uncle Bando withdrew another cloth from his bag, this one brown and only slightly larger than a washcloth. It looked soft, like a chamois cloth for polishing a bowling ball. He placed it over the square opening. Then—and this I didn't anticipate at all—he bowed his head, closed his eyes, and began rubbing his hands together as if washing them. But he had no alcohol on them. I guess he was creating energy.

"Where's the needles, doc?" the short man asked with a nervous laugh.

"And the ink?" the scar-faced man asked.

"That's not the way I work," Uncle Bando said. He placed his hands on the soft cloth and began kneading it and the tissue beneath it, like a masseuse, his fingers opening and closing the way a cat flexes its claws.

Both men grimaced. It didn't look like Uncle Bando was massaging their flesh, it appeared he was simply working the soft cloth. Why were they wincing?

"The pain's not too much for you, is it, gentlemen?" he asked, smiling slyly, his eyes still closed as he worked.

"No," the man with the mustache said through gritted teeth.

"How long does this take?" the short man said. "And once it's softened up, when do you start with the needles?"

"About another minute, that's all. And no needles. Just another minute."

Perhaps I imagined it, but I thought I heard the faint sounds of cracking and grinding, like a tree branch rubbing against another limb in the wind.

And then it was over. Uncle Bando pulled his hands away, made them into a steeple in front of his face, thumbs touching his chin, fingers touching his nose as if in prayer, and he stood up from the chair.

"Finished, gentlemen," he said. He plucked the cloth from the square hole, folded it and placed it in his bag. "Ready to see the magic?" He grasped two corners of the leaded bib like a magician about to whisk a handkerchief off a top hat.

The men nodded, their faces relaxed now that the pain was over.

Uncle Bando lifted off the leaded bib.

"What the—" both men gasped, and Chuck, Ramon, and I gasped, too.

There before us was the Brothers-in-Arms Tattoo.

But it was different from the one in the photograph. The one in the loose-leaf binder had shown two arms. What lay before us on the table—*shared by the men*—was a single tattooed forearm. The hands and wrists had disappeared, and from one man's elbow to the other's elbow, there was nothing but a solitary arm covered by the skull-and-snakes tattoo.

“Time for us to go, boys,” Uncle Bando said, calmly buckling the clasp on his bag as he motioned us toward the door.

We opened the door and stepped out into the store, leaving the stunned hoods staring down at their arm. Uncle Bando hustled us toward the front door.

“Boys,” he called, walking toward us with the three packs of Twinkies. “Don’t forget these. Eat them on the way to the precinct house, four blocks that way. Call your parents from there. They’ll be relieved.”

Later, on the ride home, we would recall that Uncle Bando didn’t know we were runaways.

"What should we tell the cops about those guys in the store? What should we say happened?” Chuck asked.

“I wouldn’t even mention them,” Uncle Bando said. “They’ve got their machetes with them and they have a very tough choice to make. Sad to say, but they have a history of making poor choices.”

Uncle Bando stepped back inside the store for a moment, reached into the front window, grabbed his handmade *Tattoos by Bando* sign, and closed the door again as he left. We waved goodbye to him and started through the frigid night for the police station.

Uncle Bando was right about the men making bad decisions. Before we got a block from the store, we heard two horrible screams pierce the air. We took off running.

THE END

If you enjoyed ***New England: seaside, roadside, graveside, darkside***, you may want to check out Steve's award-winning FreeKs novels—***FreeK Camp, FreeK Show***, and ***FreeK Week***—which feature a 10 pychic New England teens who use their paranormal powers while working together to solve bizarre mysteries. Then, took, there's Steve's Maine gargoyle thriller, ***The Bookseller's Daughter***, which won the New York Book Festival grand prize. Or for something lighter, enjoy his Dumb Jokes for Kids series: ***First Worst Joke Book, Second Worst, Third Worst, and Fourth Worst Joke Book***.

Here's a chance to sample the opening chapter of FreeK Camp, the opening novel in the FreeKs psychic teen detectives series (FreeK Camp, FreeK Show, and FreeK Week). The series features Bando, the mysterious character you just met in the last story, "The Tattooist." He runs FreeK Camp, where he and two other former circus sideshow performers are the mentors for the psychic teens who arrive for a week of training. The FreeKs trilogy now available in paperback, ebook, and audio book.

Chapter 1

No one suspected there was a camp for kids with paranormal powers in the backwoods of Maine—or that its past would put their lives at risk.

The five "different" 13- and 14-year-olds took their seats in the battered pale blue van marked Free Camp #2 which—thanks to someone wielding a red Magic Marker two years earlier—had become FreeK Camp #2. Not only had no one felt the need to erase or paint over the added K, but whenever it faded, it was magically freshened up by someone under cover of darkness. Beneath the camp name someone had added a Smiley face with a third eye—like the CBS eye—in the center of its forehead. It was what Free Camp kids called the mind's eye.

Once they were in, the driver, a tiny man with curly red hair, reached up and closed the side doors, reassuring the parents and siblings in the parking lot, "Don't worry. Never lost a summer camper yet. I'll get them there in one piece." Then, with the families trying not to stare, he opened the driver's door and climbed up onto a child's booster seat. With the door still open so they could see, he strapped a pair of leg-extenders onto his calves. "Got to reach the pedals, you know!" He flashed them an impish grin. "Seatbelts, everybody," he called back to the kids behind him, and buckled his own. He slammed the door once, twice, and finally a third time. "Some days it doesn't want to latch," he said to the families. "But everything else works fine. See you back here in a week."

The odd little man eased the van out of the parking lot into the flow of traffic, encouraging his passengers to show genuine enthusiasm in waving goodbye to their families. They were off, though to where, the kids weren't exactly sure. Free Camp's mailing address had been a post office box in rural Bridgton, Maine, in the state's western lakes region. But the actual camp, according to the brochure, was pretty far from town, more than a long hike. Still, even if it was a few miles away from civilization, a free week at summer camp in July would be a welcome change from their hometowns.

The front passenger seat was empty. It wasn't that they felt uncomfortable sitting next to the midget, as they'd begun referring to him in their parking lot whispers—he seemed nice enough—but he'd neither invited nor instructed anyone to sit there. Once they'd stowed their backpacks, suitcases, and sleeping bags in the way-back cargo area, he'd motioned them through the double side door.

The Hispanic-looking brother and sister had grabbed the comfortable captain's chairs, leaving the third-row bench seat for the other three. The first in was a slight boy with long blond hair and wire-rimmed glasses. Wedged between himself and his armrest was a book, the spine imprinted with the title, *Encyclopaedia of Psychic Science*, and the author's name, Nandor Fodor. In the middle sat another boy—pudgy, pale-skinned, and freckle-faced, a raised brown Mohawk tuft spanning his shaved scalp front-to-back like the Great Wall of China. The last in was a frizzy-haired brunette in wrap-around sunglasses, dangly turquoise pierced earrings, and carved-wood peace-symbol necklace. She held a Free Camp brochure on her lap, an index finger resting on the words "those unique, special, and unusual children who, because their gifts are so very different, may feel strange or alienated from other kids."

The five weren't yet a group, a team. But they'd become one soon, and not in the usual summer-camp way. No, for this group it would happen differently. Fate—and the biggest challenge of their young lives—would draw them closer, soon. At the moment, as they rode peacefully along on a sunny July morning, they had no way of knowing just how lucky they were—for in an hour they would arrive at Free Camp safe and sound. Safe.

The other van, Free Camp #1, which had picked up another five "different" kids two hours earlier, would not. That van had been carjacked by a madman.

About the Author

STEVE BURT's book table has been a fixture at New England craft shows for decades. The generation of teenagers who gobbled down his ghost stories and weird tales has grown up and now bring their own kids to Steve's table to meet him and to buy autographed copies.

Dr. Burt's **Even Odder** collection was a surprise nominee for the 2003 Bram Stoker Award, the horror genre's top prize, in the Young Readers category sometimes dubbed "horror lite." The book made the Final Five but lost to winner **Harry Potter and the Order of the Phoenix**. But the very next year his sequel **Oddest Yet** made it into a Final Four that included Dean Koontz and Clive Barker—AND IT WON the 2004 Bram Stoker trophy!

The original four collections—Odd Lot, Even Odder, Oddest Yet, and Wicked Odd—are now out-of-print, but demand for the stories has resulted in 20 of the series 39 stories being reprinted here and re-released under a new title: **New England Seaside, Roadside, Graveside, Darkside** (2021).

Steve is also the author of a trilogy of novels--**Freek Camp, FreeK Show,** and **FreeK Week**—which feature a dozen "uniquely gifted" teens (levitation, out-of-body travel, telekinesis) who meet a camp in Bridgton, Maine near Sebago Lake. The series won 24 awards including 4 Mom's Choice golds, 3 New England Book Festival Awards, and the grand prize at the Florida Book Festival.

His Maine thriller, **The Bookseller's Daughter**, is set in modern-day Wells, Kennebunk, and York, and centers around a 17 year-old girl and her bookseller mother who are drawn into helping a mysterious stranger locate a Civil War era grave that holds a secret. The book won the 2019 New York Book Festival grand prize. The sequel, **Protect the Queen**, hit bookstands July 1, 2023.

The author and his wife Jolyn split their writing year between The Villages, Florida and Wells, Maine.

www.SteveBurtBooks.com

Made in the USA
Columbia, SC
02 October 2024

43178583R10171